I0659885

# STRONGBOW,

## The Boy Chief of the Delawares.

---

### COMPLETE IN ONE VOLUME.

---

## BEAUTIFULLY ILLUSTRATED.

Office: Harkaway House, West Harding Street, Fetter Lane,
London, E.C.

# STRONGBOW,

## THE BOY CHIEF OF THE DELAWARES.

"THE FIRST GLIMPSE OF DANGER."

# STRONGBOW,

## THE BOY CHIEF OF THE DELAWARES.

## CHAPTER I.

### WHICH OUGHT TO BE A PROLOGUE.

THE fierce burning rays of the noon-day sun pierced through the thick branches of a dense American forest.

Not a breath of air stirred the leaves, no bird rushed through the foliage on hasty wing, the chattering squirrel had sought refuge in the shady depths of the hollow trunk; the fierce orb of day seemed to make all things, both animate and inanimate, bow beneath his power-ful influence.

All, save the little brook, which rattled merrily along its pebbly course, laughing at the sun which added a double lustre to its shining bosom.

The scene was one of perfect peace.

But hush!

A stealthy tread was heard in the mangled copse; some living being was making its way through the forest.

It might be a prowling wolf, or a bear, or a catamount, the fierce tiger of America.

But the wolf seeks his lair during the light of day; the bear loves best the early dawn and the twilight; while the catamount seeks its prey during the hours of darkness.

It was an animal far more savage and ferocious than wolf, bear, or panther.

It was a man from whose breast every feeling of humanity had been driven, leaving nothing behind but fiendish passions.

It was *not* a pale, dark-complexioned man with scowling brows, and mous-taches pointed up to his eyes.

The man, who, on that hot summer day came cautiously through the forest, was not your ordinary evil-looking villain of romance.

On the contrary he was rather good-looking at a casual glance, though when you came to gaze critically into his glassy grey eyes, and study the lines about his thin lips and aliquine nose, it became evident that there stood a man who would suffer no man to come between him and the object he desired to attain.

He reached the little glade, and stood before the brook, a tall, stalwart, good-looking man, of fair complexion, and thirty years of age, or thereabouts, armed with rifle and hunting-knife

On the third finger of his right hand sparkled a costly diamond ring.

The man was dressed in a buckskin hunting-shirt, richly ornamented mo-cassins, and a cap made of the skin of a racoon, the tail of the animal having been left so as to dangle down the wearer's back.

He dashed the stock of his rifle to the ground, rested his arm upon the muzzle of the piece, and looked around him.

"The redskin has judged well," he said, in low tones. "The spot is well chosen. Here shall mine enemy pitch his tent, and here shall they perish by the hands of my trusty allies, if they es-cape the fangs of the rattlesnake and the jaws of the panther. But Black Hand promised to meet me. Will he fail to keep his appointment?"

"The warrior of the Black Hand is here; ugh!"

The white man turned, and saw standing at his elbow, a tall Indian; his scalp-lock decorated with a single feather from the wing of the American eagle, his high cheek-bones stained with a circle of dark blue, and his right hand the colour of ebony.

The warrior was gaily dressed in mocassins, ornamented with stained porcupine quills, and a red and white blanket.

Over his shoulder were slung a quiver full of arrows and a round buffalo hide shield, bearing on it a rude painting of a black hand.

A bow of hickory wood, to which sinews of the deer had been glued, was borne in his hand; a tomahawk and hunting knife, of English manufacture, completed his equipment.

"Come here, Black Hand, seat yourself upon the fallen pine tree with me. I want to talk with you," said the white man.

"The words of my white brother are good," replied the Indian, as he seated himself on the fallen tree indicated.

An hour passed and still they sat talking, or rather the white man talked while the Indian occasionally ejaculated a guttural "Ugh!" or bowed his eagle head in token of assent.

The subject of their conversation was an Englishman!

Time passed on its rapid wings, but it was not till the sun began to decline rapidly towards the western horizon that the Indian and the white man ceased their conversation.

Then the red warrior rose, drew his blanket round his shoulders, and glided off into the gloomy forest.

The white man strolled about a hundred yards farther into the forest, then made a fire, and laid himself down to rest.

*    *    *    *

About fifteen days after the scene just described, a man entered the state land office in the little town of Oakville, in the State of Kentucky.

Some forty years ago that state was very different in appearance to what it now is.

The tracks of land cleared and culti-vated were few in number; towns now wealthy and populous, were then in their infancy; some of them, in fact, were wild plains or uncultivated meadows.

The man who entered the land office did not seem very much enraptured with the appearance of the town of Oakville consisting as it did of about fifty houses—many of them mere log huts.

His eye wandered wonderingly round the little office in which the public business of the town was transacted, until it rested upon a map, at the bottom of which was inscribed—

"GOVERNMENT LANDS FOR SALE."

"I will buy government lands, then, with the small remains of my fortune, and found a home in which I will forget England, and the troubles which there beset me on every side."

A thorough type of the Englishman was the speaker, about five feet nine inches in height, with broad face, curly brown whiskers, and a frame which Hercules might envy; his dress was of English material and make, different in many respects from the habiliments of the long-limbed Kentuckians of the little town of Oakville.

"I reckon, mister, you can't do better than lay out yer cash on some o' them locaytions," said a man of the real Yankee type, stepping from an inner room. "The land air well watered, and the timber fixins is *stoopendous!*"

"I don't want any *stoopendous fixins*," replied Edmund Armstrong, as the Englishman was called: "but I want a quiet spot, removed from the usual haunts of man, where I can be free."

"Sir-r, you *air* in Americy, the land ov the free, whar the everlastin' eagle sits a top of a pine-tree, watchin' over its native land. Sir-r, buy this location, marked Number 267 on the map, and which bears the name of Catamount Creek. Plenty o' water, no end o' timber, deer meat in plenty, and no varmints allowed to come within twenty miles."

"How large is this estate, and what its value?"

"Five hundred acres; one dollar an acre for a valuable settlement not to be matched in the United States. No neighbours within eighteen miles; but then, that's but a step, stranger."

"The farther off my neighbours are, the better for me. Draw up all the necessary documents, and, as soon as they are ready, you shall have the money."

"To-morrow, stranger, at eleven o'clock, conclude you has the deeds in yer pocket."

"And you may conclude you have the money in yours," replied Armstrong.

He then slowly walked out of the office, little heeding a fair-complexioned man, who looked after him, and who, as he wiped his mouth with a cambric handkerchief, displayed a costly diamond ring on his right hand, and made his way towards a rather large boarded house, which bore over its door the ambitious sign, "Union Hotel and Universal Restaurant."

In this *hotel*, if we may so call it, sat a woman of middle age, a boy of twelve years, strong, upright, and like Edmund Armstrong in features.

## CHAPTER II.

### A PAIR OF VILLAINS.

THE next morning, punctually at eleven o'clock, Edmund Armstrong returned to the land office.

His night's rest had more than ever impressed him with the desirability of seeking out a home away from the usual haunts of his fellow beings, where no one could wound those proud susceptibilities with which his frame was replete.

So his heart was filled with joy as he received from the man in authority at the land office the papers which made him sole lord and owner of the track of land, known as Catamount Creek. N.B.—No one knew the name of the aforesaid location except the land agent, an old hunter, who had killed a large number of panthers in the district, and the stranger.

The money was duly paid, and a receipt given.

"Now tell me how far have I to travel before I find myself at Catamount Creek?" asked Armstrong.

"It's about five and thirty miles, stranger."

"And the road?"

"The road's good enough for a dozen miles beyond Oakville; then you'll have to take the blazin's for it."

"But could I not get a guide?"

"Waal, I'm doubtful."

At that moment a low hiss, like the sound produced by an angry gander, was heard in the little back room before mentioned.

The land agent started slightly, and then continued—

"When I say doubtful, I mean it air't impossible. You come round to-morrow, and I'll tell you if there's a guide. I'm better known among these coons about Oakville than you."

"Well, I'll come again, then, in the morning; but if you have not found a guide then, I shall start by myself."

"I guess not, stranger, you'd lose your way. Now I think of it, I shouldn't wonder if some of the hunters don't come in to-day or to-morrow morning."

"I must be off to-morrow."

"Now, how *air* you goin' to tote your traps down; have you got a horse?"

"No."

"Then you'll want one?"

"And I suppose it can't be procured at present."

"I'll get you a horse, and bring it down to your diggin's to-night."

"Thanks."

"And you'll want a waggon too, to hold your fixin's."

"True; and to hold my wife."

"Oh-h! you have a wife then, mister?"

"I have—and a son."

"Good! that boy will be useful; how about rifles and powder?"

"I have a good rifle, a pair of pistols, and a good supply of ammunition. You deal in everything, it seems?"

"Pretty nigh, mister."

"Will there be any use for the weapons?"

"Well, in the way of killing deer and bears, they'll be useful enough."

"*And how about Indians?*"

The land agent hesitated a moment ere he made reply.

"Well, there *air* a few scattered about in the woods; but they're peaceful enough, mister.

Edward Armstrong was a strong man and a brave one; but at first he hesitated, as any brave man would do, to expose his wife and child to dangers which their less robust frames were unfitted to cope with.

But the words of the land agent re-assured him.

After a few more words relative to the purchase of a horse and waggon, as well as procuring a guide, Edmund Armstrong once more left the office of the state land agent.

Again, as he passed through the door-way, that fair-complexioned man with the diamond ring upon his finger watched him.

When Armstrong was out of sight, the unknown came out into the office, and sitting himself upon a chair observed to the agent—

"Well done, Dan; so far you have acted well, and forwarded all my plans."

"That's all right, squire; but I should like to know what those plans might be."

"In good time you shall know."

"I should like to know now."

"I shall not tell you just yet."

"Supposing I don't help you any more unless you tell."

"Dan, you would act very foolishly, for if you refuse to do according to my wishes I shall be compelled to tell the good people of Oakville the whole history of a certain person who was obliged to leave the stage of the Boston theatre very suddenly—a case of forgery, it was reported—and afterwards was manager and treasurer of a certain scheme known as the Indiana Land Society."

"Hold hard, squire, that's quite enough," said Dan.

"Not so; the history may be instructive as well as amusing. The manager of this Land Society recieved large sums of money from emigrants and others, for the purchase of plots of land which were not to be found on any map; and then, when he became too well known, fled away to New Orleans with the money thus gained from his unfortunate dupes, squandered his ill-gotten gains in a gambling house, shot a man in a drunken quarrel, and then going north, once more

assumed the guise of honesty as state Land Agent."

"And if I have done all this, Mr. Wylde, what is it to you?" demanded Dan Jackson the agent.

"Nothing. It might be something for Judge Lynch, though, especially as there is a man in Oakville who invested money in the Indiana Land Society."

The unfortunate agent turned white with fear, and pressed his hands over his face to shut out the vision which arose before his eyes of the stern unrelenting justice which presides at the backwoods tribunals.

Jackson had, in his eventful career, witnessed one or two cases of lynching, and the remembrance of what he had seen left him with a strong aversion to such a fate.

A few moments passed in silence, while Wylde regarded with a look of contempt the unfortunate man whose past career he had just been relating.

"What am I to do squire?" asked the wretched agent.

"Obey all my instructions without grumbling, or asking questions, and you will find me a very easy person to deal with."

"I will."

"That's right. Now, in the first place, all our conversations as well as our actions must be kept perfectly secret. You understand?"

"I do."

"Secondly you promised this man, Armstrong, to endeavour to procure a guide to conduct him to Catamount Creek."

"Yes, certainly; but I don't know where to find a guide."

"You must be that guide."

"I? Why, I don't know where the place is, if there is such a place."

"Ah! at your old tricks again! Well, it is not necessary that you should know anything about Catamount Creek; but it is the spot where we met Black Hand and his band last week?"

"There?"

"Aye; there."

"But, squire, I—I—can't!"

"Pooh! such squeamishness is useless. You *must* be the guide for this simple reason—I can trust no one else."

"You forget he knows me, squire."

"Dan, I know you are a good actor, and as such you can easily change your appearance, voice, and manners. The dress of a hunter is easily procured."

"I suppose I must, then?"

"You must. And listen, Dan, if you breathe a suspicious word, I shall spin a coin in the air, and according to the side which falls upwards shall decide whether to put a bullet through your brains, or hand you over to the tender mercies of Judge Lynch."

"And how am I to explain my absence, Mr. Wylde, when I return?"

"I've been thinking, Dan, that as there is a man in Oakville who invested money in the Indiana Land Society, perhaps it would be as well if you did not show your face here again; you might get yourself in trouble."

"I don't know what I shall gain by leaving."

"Your life, the dollars you received from this Armstrong, and five hundred dollars I shall give you; you may also sell your horse and waggon. Good bye, Dan; I shall see you again to-night."

With these words Wylde left the office, and Dan Jackson sat himself down in the vacant chair.

"I must do it, I suppose. He is hard on a poor fellow though." muttered the man.

It was very lucky that Dan had no more estate purchasers that day, for he was most decidedly in an unfit state for business.

In the evening he walked down to the Union Hotel, and informed Armstrong that he had found a guide, a relation of his own, who would show the way to their destination.

The price of the horse and waggon was also agreed upon, the vehicle and animal being handed over to their new possessor.

"You must be ready betimes, stranger," observed Dan; "the guide will be here an hour after sunrise."

"I shall be ready," replied Armstrong. "I am anxious to get away."

When Jackson returned to his own home he found the fair-haired, black-hearted Wylde waiting for him.

"Well, Dan, have you made your arrangements?" said he.

"I have."

"And what time do you start?"

"About an hour after sunrise."

"Good. Now, Dan, listen to me; in your stable is a good horse to replace the old brute you have sold; here is a rifle with powder and bullets, and here the dollars I promised. Farewell, Dan; take good care of yourself, and be at Washington this day month. I shall see you there."

## CHAPTER III.

### WESTWARD HO.

THE morning after the above described business transactions, before the sun had made half an hour's journey up into the heavens, a man, dressed in untanned deer-skin garments, bearing a rifle in his hand, dismounted from his horse at the door of the Union Hotel, Oakville.

This man was Dan Jackson, the late land agent for that town.

Dan was altered in personal appearance as well as in costume.

Instead of a straggling moustache and a seedy tuft upon his chin, he wore bushy whiskers and beard; the sallow skin had changed to a dark walnut hue.

But the glassy glare of his eyes was the same, so was the sardonic expression of his mouth.

As he dismounted, Armstrong issued from the hotel to meet him.

"You are the guide, I presume, sent by the gentleman at the Land Office?" he asked.

"Yes."

"We shall be ready in a few minutes. My little property is all packed in the waggon; I am only waiting for my wife and son."

The supposed guide nodded, and arranged his saddle.

"Do you think there is any danger from Indians?" continued Armstrong.

"I don't *think* so."

"And you are certain as to the road?"

"I know my way."

At first Armstrong fancied that the

man to whose care he was thus committing himself was a sulky fellow; but on reflection he recollected that hunters and others who reside long in the woods and prairies, acquire a silent, reserved manner.

Before he could enter into any further conversation, his wife and boy made their appearance.

The horse was harnessed to the waggon, the boy and the woman seated themselves in the vehicle, the guide mounted his horse, and the little party moved off down the street.

"Good-bye—good luck to you!" cried a few loungers who had gathered round the hotel to watch the departure of the emigrants.

"Thanks, kind friends," replied Armstrong.

Just as they passed the last house in the city, a man on horseback rapidly approached from the westward.

As he passed them he raised his cap with a hand on which sparkled a diamond ring, and called out—

"May you reach your destination in safety, my friends."

Armstrong lifted his hat, and the stranger, who was none other than Wylde, passed swiftly up into the city.

Richard Armstrong, the son of our emigrant, was, as before said, a strong, stout, healthy boy of twelve years of age, or thereabouts, with features very strongly resembling those of his father.

As soon as the last house was passed, he stepped from the waggon, and joined his father, who walked by the side of the horse.

"Where are we going, father?" he asked.

"Home, my son."

"What, to our old home in Cumberland?"

"No, no."

"Then how can it be home? Our home is across the sea."

"We have no home across the sea now, my son. We must make a home for ourselves in this forest."

"And I may fish and shoot and hunt?"

"You may, when you have nothing else to do. But times are altered, Dick; we must work with our own hands now, for we have no servants to wait upon us."

"I can work, father—I am strong.

Dear mamma shall have a comfortable home to live in. What sort of a house is it?"

"Hush! boy. There is no house till we build one! but don't tell your mother."

"Oh, father, how jolly! We shall be like two Crusoes—build our own house, make our own garden, and do everything."

Before Armstrong could make any reply to his son, the guide turned back and said—

"You'd better get up in the waggon; there's a brook just beyond here."

The father and son did as they were desired, and, in a few minutes, the horse splashed into a stream, of no great depth, but broad enough to make wading a tiresome task.

On the other side of the brook was a level, open pasture, a prairie in fact, clothed with long grass, and bounded on its extreme verge by a cluster of tall, stately pine trees.

But, much to the surprise of Armstrong, the road ceased with the brook.

He looked to the guide for explanation.

"There are three tracks now," replied Jackson. "One leads down to Cedar Swamp, the middle one to your place, and the other to Hickory Falls."

Without any more words the man set spurs to his horse, and trotted away along the middle track, if track it could be called, where only a dozen hoofprints marked the route.

He looked back occasionally, and beckoned Armstrong on.

They reached the pine grove, and passed it.

The whole land, in fact, seemed a succession of open pastures dotted with clusters of pine and oak trees.

There was very little underwood in any of these *timber islands*, as men of the backwoods call them; the scene more resembled an English gentleman's park than any thing else.

Noonday came, and the taciturn guide gave the word to halt in the shelter of one of the groves.

"Stay here; light a fire. I'll bring some deer meat," said he.*

---

* Travellers report that the American hunters seldom use the word venison; but call it deer meat. They also call the flesh of the bear "bear meat;" that of the buffalo is "buffalo meat," and so on.

"Where are the deer?" asked young Armstrong.

"Away beyond the trees."

"Oh! father, lend me your gun. I'll go with this gentleman, and shoot the deer."

"Better stay here. You'll frighten them," observed the guide.

"Stay beneath the trees, and watch how it is done," said Armstrong.

The guide then shouldered his rifle, and walked to the edge of the timber.

The grass was long, and as soon as the trees no longer concealed him, he threw himself at full length upon the turf.

Then, like a snake, he crawled stealthily on till he was within a hundred yards of where a dozen deer peacefully browsed, unconscious of the presence of destroying man.

A puff of white smoke, and a sharp crack greeted the eye and the ear at almost the same moment.

One of the graceful animals fell dead, and the successful hunter, rising to his feet, calmly walked towards it.

Ten minutes after he was in the grove, bearing the two haunches, which are the only portions your true hunter will eat, unless when "meat" is scarce.

A splendid dinner was the result of this shot.

Then the journey was continued through forest and over prairie.

At length it became evident that the sun was about to set.

"Where are we to rest?" asked Armstrong.

"I'll tell you when we get to the wood," replied Jackson.

They soon reached the edge of a much larger wood than any through which they had yet passed.

The guide then halted.

"There are axe marks on the trees, mister, and if you keep by them, you will come to a little open ground by the side of a brook; that's your spot, and you can't do better than build your hut there. It's only about a mile on; you can't miss the way. Good night."

Ere Armstrong could utter a word, he was riding off at full speed across the prairie.

The emigrants were alone.

Alone! Miles away from the nearest haunt of civilized man, with only the wild beasts of the forest, and the still wilder red men who roam the mighty forests, for companions.

For a minute, Armstrong's heart felt a feeling of despondency; but as his eye rested upon his wife and son, his courage revived.

"We must go forward by ourselves, then, boy, since our guide has left us. It is lucky he condescended to show us the way."

"But, Edmund, are you not afraid to venture into this gloomy wood?" asked the wife.

"Afraid, my dear? Did you ever hear of an Armstrong feeling fear? Come along, old horse; let us have time to make things comfortable before the darkness comes."

With these words he urged on the tired animal along a path in the woods, which had never before seen a wheeled vehicle.

The path was in some places scarcely wide enough to give the vehicle passage.

In its best and smoothest parts it was but a rough track, the hoofprints of a solitary horse, and axe marks on the trees, being the only guiding marks.

However, Armstrong held on his course, and, after half-an-hour's journey, had the pleasure of reaching the open spot the guide had described.

"Here we are at last, Dick," said he. "Jump down, my lad."

The boy did so.

His father then turned to assist the wife and mother from the waggon.

The boy gazed round wonderingly; but his wonder changed to alarm as his eyes fell upon a strange object on the other side of the little brook.

That object was a tall Indian warrior, painted in fantastic style, who, from the covert of a tree, surveyed the little party.

"Oh! father, look there!" exclaimed Richard Armstrong, pointing to the stream.

"What is it?"

"An Indian, father, with his face painted."

Armstrong seized his rifle, and rushed to the spot.

No sign of any living being could be seen beyond the brook, and, after a careful search, he returned to the waggon.

"You must have been mistaken, my boy," said he. "Don't give any more false alarms."

"I don't think I could be mistaken, father."

Armstrong was busily engaged in releasing his horse from its harness, and arranging for the night. He made no reply.

A fire was lighted, some pieces of meat cooked, and the three made a hearty meal, despite the slight alarm.

Suddenly the mournful hoot of an owl was heard, and then, from two other parts of the forest, the sound seemed answered.

As Armstrong endeavoured to look through the dark forest, the cry was repeated in longer and more melancholy notes than before.

And it seemed to Armstrong that black figures were moving to and fro beneath the sable shades of the pine-trees.

Half an hour afterwards, when the fire had burned down, and the little glade was enveloped in nearly total darkness, a black figure, which in the gloom looked like a bear, was seen creeping slowly towards the camp.

Our young hero, Richard Armstrong, saw it, and, without moving, laid his hand upon a large axe which lay close at hand.

## CHAPTER IV.

### HIRAM SWIFT

ON came the dark-looking object, slowly creeping along, till it was within four feet of the spot where Richard Armstrong lay.

Then the gallant boy started to his feet, and aimed a heavy blow at it with his axe.

But the weapon missed its mark, for the animal jumped up nimbly, and, *on two legs*, ran back to the wood. Richard Armstrong at once crept to his father's side and roused him.

The stalwart Englishman listened to his son's tale, and then, rifle in hand, walked quietly around the open space in the midst of which his camp was situated.

Nothing could he see save the brook and the waving trees; nothing could he hear save the night wind whispering softly through the green leaves.

He returned to his grassy couch, and laid himself down, but not to sleep; neither father nor son closed their eyes that night.

The morning sun rose, the birds began to sing their hymn of rejoicing, but there was little joy in the heart of the emigrant as he thought of the manifold dangers to which his wife was exposed.

But it was too late to retreat; he had chosen his situation and felt that he must make the best of it.

When Edmund Armstrong and his son led their horses to water, it was evident, even to their unpractised eyes, that not only one, but several Indians had been lurking around the camp. At least a dozen mocassin prints were visible on the soft brink of the stream.

"We must keep our eyes wide open, Dick," said the father, "and if these savages should attack us, we must teach them that Britons are not cowards."

"Cowards, father? The name of Armstrong was never yet branded with cowardice, and I will not be the first to disgrace the good name so long and honourably borne by our ancestors!"

"I believe you, Dick; but these are no school-yard bullies you have to deal with—they are men with strong, active bodies, subtle brains, and cruel hearts."

"Am not I strong and active, father? Is not my brain keen? Though, indeed, my heart delights not in cruelty."

"True; I know you are brave and strong, Dick, but you must be cautious as well."

"That I will, father, I promise."

Father and son then returned to the waggon, where Mrs. Armstrong had prepared a breakfast of that kind only seen in the woods, where game forms the staple food of the hunter and the emigrant.

"Now, Dick," said the father, when

the meal was concluded, "we must build a house."

"But we have no bricks, father."

"We must build it of logs; so come, take up your axe, and prepare for a hard day's labour."

After looking around carefully they decided upon a spot where the river made an abrupt curve, and in the angle thus formed they determined to erect their dwelling.

Armstrong had served a short time in the army, and chose this position on account of its defensive capabilities.

The stream, where it made the curve, was deep, and could only be crossed in a boat or by swimming. Three sides of the house would thus be protected by nature, the back of the log building being faced towards the extreme angle of the triangular piece of land. The fourth side, being towards the open ground, would be defended by the rifles of the inmates.

Such was Armstrong's plan, and having thus come to a decision, he set about his task with vigorous promptitude.

The first act was to cross the river at a spot some distance below the deep portion, and then, keeping along the other bank, look out some suitable trees for building purposes.

It so happened that several tall pine trees grew on the edge of the stream exactly opposite the spot where the back wall of the house was to be raised.

Armstrong selected two of them that grew, and, with a few sturdy blows of his axe, laid them, side by side, across the stream. It then became Dick's task, with his lighter weapon, to trim off the branches.

A bridge was thus formed, and then the sound of the axe became more regular, as father and son laid prostrate tree after tree.

These trunks were piled up side by side as soon as they had been stripped of their branches and rolled across the two tall masts which served as a bridge.

By evening Armstrong calculated that he had felled quite sufficient timber for the construction of his house, and, tired with labour, retired to rest—if rest it could be called, when his sleep was broken, and his mind filled with alarms for the safety of his beloved ones.

That night, however, passed without alarm, and the next day the work of building advanced rapidly.

Two days afterwards Armstrong and his wife were seated within a log cabin, rudely built, it is true, but impervious to wind and storm.

Armstrong was sole owner of that hut, and a feeling of joy came upon his soul as he contemplated it. He had a home at last; one from which his foes could never drive him, as they had from the place of his birth in Merry England.

But where was the son in this moment of triumph?

Our young hero was in the woods practising with bow and arrows at the numerous birds and squirrels that enlivened the tall trees.

His bow was formed of a stout branch of hickory, strung with a silken fish-line doubled and twisted. His arrows were reeds pulled from the banks of the stream, tipped with bones chipped up to a point with his knife.

With these weapons he hoped to do much execution amongst the feathered and furred denizens of that wood, although his success on the first day was not very great.

He was just picking up a pigeon he had hit on the head with one of his shafts when a hand was laid upon his shoulder.

Starting with surprise, he lifted his head, expecting to see at least a dozen painted Indians.

But no such sight met his eye.

By his side stood a tall man dressed in a mixture of Indian and civilised costume, mocassins on his feet, a fur cap upon his head, and a green baize hunting shirt over his body.

This last garment was confined by a leather belt at the waist, where a long-bladed, strong hunting-knife, a powder flask, and a light axe were slung in convenient, but secure positions.

In the stranger's hand was a long rifle, and a clumsy weapon it was *to look at*, the wood-work of the stock being prolonged almost to the muzzle of the piece. But it was a weapon with which such a man as the one now before us could hit a nail upon the head at a hundred paces. It was a trusty weapon, though its stock was rough and unvarnished, and its barrel had a cloudy, semi-rusty appearance.

The stranger was a hunter; on his shoulders he bore a wallet or bag of untanned skin; the hunter's *possible sack*, containing reserves of powder and bullets, flint, steel and, tinder, a small supply of tobacco, leather thongs, and sundry other small things which the owner deemed essential to his ease and comfort.

Such were the dress and accoutrements; now for the man himself.

As before said, he was tall—at least six feet in height; he seemed to have not an atom of superfluous flesh upon his bones, though his muscles, as shown by the open sleeve of his shirt, were firm and hard as strong cords. His age might have been about forty, but his face was so bronzed by constant exposure to sun and wind that it would have been impossible to make a correct guess; his hair was slightly grizzled, but his eye was bright and clear.

"What are you doin' here, boy?" he asked.

"Shooting pigeons," was the reply.

"Whar do ye live?"

"Out there by the side of the stream," said young Armstrong, pointing in the direction he supposed his home to be situated.

"You'll have to travel many a mile afore you find a stream thar. You've lost yourself, younker, and don't know your road home."

"Lost!" exclaimed the boy.

"Aye; but never mind, I'll show ye the track."

"Thank you, sir; but I'm afraid I shall be taking you away from your home."

"No, you won't, lad. Ha, ha, ha! My home lies away beyond your diggin's."

"I did not see it as we came here."

"Likely not, lad; likely not."

"It's in the wood then, I suppose, sir, and that's the reason we did not se it."

"Sometimes in the wood, sometimes on the prairie. It ain't often as Hiram Swift camps two nights in the same locaytion, 'specially when thar's redskins prowling round."

While they were talking, the hunter had led the boy into a part of the wood which the lad had not passed through on his way to the place where he killed the pigeon.

"Are you sure you are leading me homewards?" he asked.

"Sartin. Though I han't seen yer log, I kin guess pretty well whar it's fixed."

Dick Armstrong had recovered from the slight alarm which the stranger's sudden appearance had at first produced, and was now examining his dress and weapons with great curiosity.

"I wish I had a rifle like you," he said.

"It's a good weapon," replied the hunter—for such was Hiram Swift's profession—as he gazed with a complacent smile upon the brown stock and barrel of his trusty gun. "But you have a bow, lad, and a *strong* one, too, I guess."

It was a *strong bow*, as the hunter remarked, and one which few unpractised hands could have managed.

But Dick Armstrong had, in his own English home, been renowned for his skill in archery contests.

"But I want a rifle," said the boy.

"The bow is a good weapon, makes no noise, and arrows are easier to make than powder and lead. Let's see, now, if you can send one through the squirrel on the top of this pine tree."

The hunter pointed as he spoke to a gay little animal which chattered blithely on the very summit of the tall pine.

Young Armstrong fitted an arrow to the string of his bow, and sent the shaft whistling upwards.

A large tuft of fur was seen to fly from the squirrel's side, and the poor little thing, after making one or two frantic bounds among the branches, fell heavily to the earth.

"A good shot," said the hunter, "though you should have made more allowance for the wind. With a little more practice you will be a match even for the Delaware chief, Onotassa. But come along; I see your dad is at the door looking for you."

Again the boy felt surprised.

To all appearance he was in the midst of a thick grove; but the hunter's keen eye could see through a slight opening in the bushes to the open spot where the log hut was situated.

Armstrong, the elder, was, as Swift had said, gazing from the door, alarmed at the prolonged absence of his son.

"THE FIGHT IN THE FOREST."

Ere another minute had passed, the boy and the hunter had forded the stream and were crossing the clearing.

"Where have you been, Dick, and who is this with you?" asked the father.

"I have been shooting, father; and this gentleman brought me home as he said I had lost myself in the wood."

"*Said* you had lost yourself? Thank you, sir; but may I ask how you knew that my son had lost himself when the boy himself knew nothing of that fact?"

"By his trail. He was going round and round in nearly the same track."

"Come in, sir, come in, and partake of our frugal meal. You are doubly welcome after saving the life of my son."

The hunter entered the hut, and, with a simple bow to Mrs. Armstrong, seated himself at the table.

During the progress of the meal, Armstrong asked his guest many questions about the forest, the game it contained, and lastly about the tribes of Indians who roved through the woods.

"Well, thar are a good few redskins about, that's a fact; but most of 'em is friendly; all you have to fear is Black Hand and his gang of plundering Crows. Keep your eyes open, for that redskin means mischief, he does."

"Thanks for your advice. But do you know how many men this Black Hand has under his command?"

"Forty, at least, the scum of this earth, and outcasts from their own tribe: but I must now be off, stranger; good morning; keep a good look-out, and don't go too far into the woods."

With these words, the hunter departed, and in a few minutes had disappeared beneath the gloomy vistas of the forest.

## CHAPTER V.

### THE ATTACK.

WHEN Armstrong retired to rest that night, he paid more than usual attention to the fastenings of his window and door.

His rifle also claimed a fair amount of care: its priming was carefully looked to, its lock tried to see that it was in working order.

With rifle, axe, and pistols beside his couch, the emigrant laid himself down, half-dressed and ready to spring up at the slightest alarm.

The boy, too, was prepared. His bow and arrows were close at hand, so was the light axe he usually carried.

It was a long time before Armstrong closed his eyes, but at length he fell into a restless, troubled sleep—a sleep in which most horrid visions presented themselves to his mind.

The grey light of morning was just beginning to tinge the eastern sky, when a slight noise attracted the emigrant's attention.

It sounded as though someone had gently attempted to open the door.

Armstrong at once leaped from his couch, and peered through a slight opening between the logs of the building.

His worst fears were realized.

Half-a-dozen, at least, of painted warriors were standing upon the clearing, while numerous other dusky figures could be seen flitting about amongst the trees.

"Rouse yourself, Dick! The Indians are upon us!" exclaimed the man, as he seized his arms.

In another minute Dick was ready for action—his bow and arrows in hand, and his axe in his girdle.

Another sound then fell upon the ear of the emigrant, and he at once became aware that an Indian with a knife was endeavouring to cut through the window-shutter.

Dick saw it at once, and without saying a word, discharged an arrow against the only part of the redskin's body visible, which was his throat.

As the string twanged, a loud yell told that the shot had taken effect.

The cry of the wounded man was echoed by at least a score of mouths, and, gathering themselves in a body, the Indians charged against the door.

But they met with a warm reception.

A shot from Armstrong's rifle, and one from each pistol, delivered through crevices in the log wall, left three warriors upon the turf, while a fourth slowly crawled away, with one of Dick's arrows in his side.

This determined resistance drove them back to the forest, from which they began to shower a perfect storm of arrows upon the block-house.

Armstrong fired after them once or twice, and then, to economise his ammunition, ceased, keeping, however, a wary eye on all their movements.

Two or three of their arrows had come through the crevices in the walls, and were fixed in the inside of the hut.

After a short time, finding that their fire was not returned, the Indians ventured to assemble again, with the evident intention of making another charge upon the log hut and its inhabitants.

Armstrong thought he had never seen a more fiendish lot of men than these savages, with their faces painted vermilion and black, and their leggings decorated with scalps, torn from the heads of their victims.

They shook their weapons, and yelled a kind of challenge, which, however, Armstrong was wise enough not to accept.

Still they hesitated to charge, and it became evident that a discussion was going on, and that, too, of a stormy nature.

Suddenly one warrior advanced from the midst, with a green branch in his hand, which he waved to and fro, in token of his desire to hold a parley with the inhabitants of the log hut.

"Ah! they want peace!" cried Dick.

"Accept their terms, for Heaven's sake, dear husband," said Mrs. Armstrong, whose feelings at being thus in the midst of deadly combat, may well be imagined.

"I will, wife, if I can with honour and safety," replied he.

He then opened the door.

"Hillo, there!" shouted the Indian, who held the green branch. "Come here—have big talk—no shoot with fire-bow."

"What do you want?" demanded Armstrong.

"Want fire-bow, powder, tomahawk, everything pale-faces got. Want no house here. Burn house; you go."

"If we go shall we be molested?"

"Indian no touch pale-face scalp, if pale-face go."

"Injin, you lie!" exclaimed a loud voice, coming seemingly from the tops of the forest trees.

The Indian changed colour, then, drawing himself up proudly, exclaimed—

"The Grey Wolf has no forked tongue, his mouth utters words of truth; but Grey Wolf is a great warrior, and will take the scalps of his enemies."

"Take mine to begin with," replied the voice, and, at the same time, the report of a rifle was heard.

Grey Wolf gave a jump upwards, and fell back upon the turf, dead.

The other Indians gave a furious howl, and made a desperate rush forward; but the door was closed and bolted before they could reach it.

Armstrong again used his rifle and pistols with effect, speculating all the while on the causes which had enlisted some unknown, unseen ally in his cause.

The Indians were now growing furious.

With their knives and tomahawks they hacked at the logs in the vain hope of forcing a way in, while the emigrant and his son kept firing upon them as fast as possible.

Presently a peculiar sound was heard, and the redskins darted back to the forest.

But they had no intention of relinquishing the attack; on the contrary, it soon became very evident that they intended to carry on the siege in a different manner.

Smoke was seen arising from the forest bushes, and shortly afterwards the Indians put their plan in practice.

Flaming firebrands were attached to arrows and shot against the house in order to ignite it.

Then huge bundles of grass and branches of trees were seen rolling along the ground, propelled by unseen Indians behind them.

Against these the father and son directed their bullets and arrows, for they well knew the danger they would be in should the foe succeed in placing these bundles of combustible materials against the house.

They were partly successful.

One of the moving masses was seen to stop suddenly, and another evidently progressed with great difficulty; but in the last attack, Armstrong himself had received an arrow in his shoulder, the pain from which made the process of loading and firing very difficult.

"There is a white man among them, father," exclaimed the boy, suddenly. "He is telling the Indians what to do."

"Oh! a base traitor who would thus fight against one of his own colour!" said Armstrong. "What white man can I have offended during the short time I have been in this land? Who can it be?"

"He will be in sight in a minute, and then I will send an arrow at him," said Dick, and, as he spoke, the white man appeared behind a tree, seeming to direct another charge against the hut.

Dick partly opened the door, and, in spite of the showers of arrows, took a careful aim at the man.

The sudden report of his father's rifle as it was discharged from the window caused him to start slightly, otherwise his shaft would have pierced the breast of the renegade. As it was, the barb made a deep wound in his neck, from which the blood flowed in a stream.

Dick watched the shot, and gave a shout of exultation as he saw his white adversary reel and fall to the ground.

"He's down, father! Cheer up, father! the victory will be ours," shouted the lad.

But while thus exulting, neither Armstrong nor his son noticed that one of the firebrands had fulfilled its infernal mission. The roof and one of the side walls were in flames.

"Oh, save me, Edmund, save me!" cried the wife and mother. "Oh, just Heaven, look down in pity upon us."

"We must now make a bold dash for it," said the hapless emigrant. "Let us give them one more volley, and then attempt to cut our way through."

No sooner said than acted upon.

All weapons were discharged, and then all three mounted upon the same horse, they galloped out to meet their foes.

The Indians were not the men to give way before this sudden attack.

On the contrary, they all pressed round the animal, and, in spite of the axes of Armstrong and his son, succeeded in throwing the whole party to the earth.

Dick received such a blow upon the back of his head that he became unconscious, nor did he recover his senses for some time.

## CHAPTER VI.

### IN CAPTIVITY.

WHEN Dick Armstrong awoke from his swoon, he found himself in the midst of the Indians.

He tried to rise, but the effort was useless, for his hands and legs were bound with thongs of deer or buffalo hide.

He managed to raise himself enough to see that he was upon the brink of the little stream, and that of the hut, built with so much toil and trouble, nothing remained but a few charred, half-burnt logs.

Father and mother—where were they?

Again he raised himself, and gazed round and round in hopes of discovering some trace of his beloved parents.

But they were not to be seen.

His head ached fearfully from the effects of the blow, his nerves were unstrung, and his mind confused.

He fixed his eyes listlessly upon a small party of Indians, who were busily engaged in fixing a post in the ground.

The sight amused him, though he was too weak to speculate upon the probable use of that upright post which the Indians were denuding of its bark, and painting in black circles so carefully.

Then the white man he had wounded made his appearance, and curiosity was to a certain extent aroused in his bosom.

He wondered who that white man could be, and he wondered whether his wound pained him very much, as he had a handkerchief tied around his throat.

But doubt was soon at an end.

The unknown came straight towards the boy, and our young hero noticed that his hands were white, and that he wore a costly diamond ring.

"Rouse yourself, you young imp!" said he, in hoarse accents, at the same time kicking the lad with his foot.

The young captive looked up.

"What is your name?"

"Richard Armstrong."

"Then, Richard Armstrong, look at the post the Indians are putting up."

"I see it."

"Do you know its use?"

"No."

"To that post you will be tied, while the fire devours your body."

A cold shudder passed through our young hero as he heard the words—

"*While the fire devours your body.*"

Death was before him at last—death, in one of the most horrible forms the king of terrors could assume.

To be thus cut off in his boyhood—to die, the victim and the sport of a horde of savages! The thought was most fearful.

Many thoughts swept through his brain—thoughts of that home in England where he had spent so many happy hours —thoughts of the school-room and its play-field, full of happy faces—thoughts of those parents whose love was so thoroughly imprinted on his heart, whose love had smoothed down all his childish difficulties and guided his youthful steps.

Then came thoughts of the fiery torture, the scorching flames, the death agony, and of that mysterious unknown after-life.

The Indians worked away stolidly at their self-imposed task of setting up and painting the stout post. When that was finished, they began to pile faggots of brushwood and boughs of trees around it.

The stranger stood, and smiled a satanic smile, while the eyes of his young captive were watching these preparations.

"You see, the Indians are making everything ready; their great amusement is to roast a pale-face."

The boy turned round, and with a calmness which surprised his captor, said—

"You have a great deal of influence with them, I suppose?"

"I have," replied Wylde, for he it was who had instigated the attack upon the hut, and who now stood before the boy.

"Then you can save me?"

"Save you? Ha, ha!"

"Yes, save me. Surely you can have no cause to hate me—or, even if you have, you would not gratify it for the amusement of these Indian fiends?"

"Save you?—hate you? But I do hate you though, Dick Armstrong, and not for a thousand pounds good English money would I save you from the slightest one of those many tortures the Indians will inflict upon you! But see, the Indian squaws are preparing themselves in line, to make you run the gauntlet."

He pointed to an open spot, where the women were indeed ranging themselves in double line, through which Dick was expected to run. The warriors had left this pleasure to the women, fearing lest their own weighty blows should kill the prisoner, and so spoil their sport.

One young man led him to the end of the avenue of squaws, all of whom were armed with switches, and gave the signal to start.

For a few seconds Dick ran between the two rows, but when the blows began to sting his back he turned suddenly, and dashing one old woman to the ground, darted into the wood at full speed.

But in a moment all the warriors were upon his track, uttering loud yells.

Dick's limbs were so cramped from having been so long bound, that he was unable to run so fast as usual. Ere he had gone fifty yards into the wood he became conscious that two tall warriors were only a few paces behind.

He exerted himself to the utmost, but in vain.

The Indians seized him, and, after a short struggle, bore him back to the place from which he started. But they did not trust him between the two ranks of squaws any more.

They led him to the stake, and bound him fast to it with thongs of green hide.

"So you thought to escape, young man, did you?" said Wylde, coming up and dealing his victim a cowardly blow upon the face. "But there are good runners in this tribe, and to get away from them you would need a good horse. You shall not have another chance, though."

Our hero answered not a word, and, Black Hand coming forward, gave intimation to his tribe that the ceremony of roasting the prisoner was to be proceeded with at once.

## CHAPTER VIL

### ONOTASSA, THE DELAWARE CHIEF.

AT the words of the white renegade, Black Hand spoke to his warriors in their own tongue.

The whole band, men, women, and children, formed themselves in a ring round the young prisoner, and began to sing in a harsh, monotonous tone.

Then they moved round and round in a circle, increasing the pace till it became a frenzied galop.

"Oh, great Manitou, thou art good," their song may be thus translated; "thou hast given us our enemies that their scalps may wave upon the tent-pole of our chief, and their blood be poured out that we may drink.

"Black Hand is a great chief; his warriors are very terrible. The pale-faces tremble when they hear the war-whoop of Black Hand. Oh, great Manitou, give us our enemies, that we may return to our wigwams with many scalps."

During the time that this fearful chorus was kept up, Wylde the renegade said nothing, though he kept his eye firmly fixed upon his prisoner's face to see if the boy gave any signs of flinching.

The young face was pale, as well it might be, but no look of fear was there.

Young Armstrong looked anxious, but like a true British boy, he looked brave, as indeed he was.

The song and dance ceased.

An Indian came forward to the pile.

"The pale-face is young," said he, in tolerable English; "the pale-face has no wish to die?"

"I have no wish to die, Indian, but if it be the will of Heaven, I shall not repine."

"Ugh! the pale-face is a coward and fears to die. Why comes the pale-face with fire-bow and axe to drive the Indian from his hunting ground? The young pale-face is a coward, and trembles when the Indian's tomahawk comes near his scalp!"

As he spoke, the Indian made a trial of the prisoner's nerves by aiming a blow at the upper part of his head, severing several curls, and burying the weapon deep in the death post.

But the heroic lad flinched not.

His eyes were raised to Heaven as though supplicating there for that mercy the world seemed unable or unwilling to bestow.

The Indians gave one of their usual grunts at this symptom of courage.

A brave warrior always gives them better sport than a coward, and so they looked forward to some rare fun in torturing young Armstrong.

"How do you like it, youngster?" asked Wylde, with a sneering smile "A pleasant prospect, is it not—to be first maimed, then scalped, and lastly burnt?"

"May your deathbed be as peaceful as mine."

"Silence, you young brute, or I'll blow your brains out," shouted the ruffian, and he raised his rifle as though about to execute his threat.

Armstrong looked him calmly in the face.

The bitterness of death was, in a great measure, passed; the king of terrors had been before his eyes so constantly that half his hideousness had gone.

Black Hand caught Wylde by the arm, and diverted his aim, otherwise that would have been the last moment of Armstrong's life.

"My white brother will not rob the young men of their sport?"

"No, if they will make haste and put an end to the sport."

Again the Indian chief spoke to his followers, and the torch-bearer applied the light to the fire.

Black Hand then came forward to try the victim's strength of mind.

He drew his long, sharp-pointed knife from its sheath, and, after a few flourishes, held its point before young Armstrong's eyes.

Then, drawing back his arm, he aimed a terrific stroke at the boy's throat.

The point of the weapon touched bare neck; he could feel the cold upon his flesh; but, so nicely regulated was the blow that, beyond a slight scratch, from which a few drops of blood rolled, no injury was done.

But still the brave lad murmured not.

The Indian resolved to try another plan.

Taking hold of the hair on the top of the youth's head, he laid the cold blade of his weapon along Armstrong's forehead.

The boy shuddered slightly; but that more from the coldness of the steel than from any fear of death.

"Dog of a pale-face, your scalp shall hang at my girdle!" said the chief, and he grasped his knife firmly to perform the brutal operation.

The point of the weapon pierced the skin just above the ear, and a drop or two of blood trickled down among his fair curls.

The savage was slow and deliberate in his movements, no doubt to prolong the torture of the victim, but ere his knife had scarce penetrated the skin, a rifle was heard, and the weapon fell from the nerveless grasp of the Indian.

Two of his fingers were shattered by that well-directed shot.

"Brayvo, ole rusty stock! Yer ken shoot when this chile's one end o' yer!"

The youth looked towards the spot from whence the sound proceeded, and beheld a man whose origin was most decidedly American, running towards the pile, all the while brandishing the weapon from which came the opportune shot.

There was no difficulty in recognising Hiram Swift, the hunter.

But who were those Indians, who with swift steps ran towards Black Hand and his band?

Wylde saw the sudden attack, he saw the hostile Indians, headed by the old hunter, as they brandished their tomahawks, shot their arrows, and uttered their terrible war-whoop.

The white Indian caught up his rifle, and prepared to blow out the brains of his young prisoner.

But a thought struck him, and, turning suddenly, he discharged the weapon against Hiram Swift.

The hunter, however, kept on his way uninjured, for the piece was dis-

charged without aim, and the ball flew wide of its intended billet.

Black Hand and his warriors prepared to make a running fight of it through the woods.

The attacking party numbered too many warriors to be resisted successfully, and an Indian seldom fights when he knows that the odds are against him.

Wylde accompanied the Crows in their flight, though he longed to take the life of his prisoner; but he feared lest he himself should fall into the hands of the enemy.

The first act of Hiram Swift was to run to the fire, which was just beginning to spread through the pile of brushwood and logs upon which young Armstrong was bound, to cut the thongs and restore the young prisoner to liberty.

"You ain't hurt, boy?" he inquired, in an anxious manner.

"No, sir; though the fire was beginning to be uncomfortable."

"Then take a drop of this, an' just come along with me while we walks right slick into them redskins."

The boy put aside the proffered brandy flask, but showed no unwillingness to take part in the fight.

His own bow and arrows were lying close at hand, and, catching them up, he rushed forward into the wood.

Hiram Swift kept close by his side.

"How is it these Indians don't hurt me?" asked Armstrong. "They look as savage as the others."

"These are Delawares, and it's their notion to be friendly just now," answered the hunter.

The Crows, under Black Hand, were just in the act of making a desperate stand against their foes, in order to give the women and children an opportunity to escape.

"Thar's the Delaware chief," said Swift, pointing to a tall Indian, whose tomahawk had been doing great execution; "that's the chap can teach you how to shoot."

Young Armstrong's eyes being thus drawn towards the celebrated warrior, his feet naturally wandered in the same direction.

The Delaware chief was three or yards from his warriors, and was en single handed with two of Black men.

But these were a cypher to the sachem of the Delawares, who had tomahawked one and buried his knife in the bosom of the second, when a third Crow coming up, sent an arrow through Onotassa's back.

The chief shouted his war cry, and then fell dead.

His killer gave a joyful whoop, and, leaping forward, seized the long scalp-lock of the Delaware, anxious to attach the trophy to his girdle.

That scalp would have given him great power and renown among his tribe.

But fate and our young hero willed it otherwise, for, drawing his arrow up to the head, Dick Armstrong sent the shaft whizzing to the Indian.

It crashed through the man's brain and buried itself in the bark of a tree beside which the Delaware had fallen.

The Crow warrior had not even time to give his death whoop, so suddenly did life depart.

As death found him so it left him, kneeling beside the body of his victim, the Delaware scalp lock twisted round his hand, the shaft of the arrow through his head, the iron barb buried in the bark of the tree.

In another part of the forest could be heard the Delaware shouts of victory; those few, however, who had seen their chief fall, and how the young pale-face had avenged him, were very sorry.

The whole tribe loved Onotassa, who was a sagacious ruler as well as valiant warrior.

The pursuers began to return, and, directed by the sounds of mourning, approached the spot where three warriors were lamenting over the body of their chief.

All their weapons were red, and most of them carried bleeding scalps fresh torn from the heads of their victims, at their belts.

The sight was so repulsive that the youth turned his head away and walked to the spot where Hiram Swift stood, very busily engaged in fitting a new flint to the lock of his rifle.

## CHAPTER VIII.

### A NEW NAME.

"I GUESS we've gi'n 'em somethin' pretty nice and hot," said the hunter, as Dick approached. "Them Delawares is showin' off their scalps, that's for certain. But what's the muss about yonder?"

"They have found the body of their chief."

"What!" exclaimed Swift, leaping to his feet; "Onotassa dead!—scalped!"

"Dead, but not scalped."

"Come along now; let's have a last look at the bravest Delaware that ever drew bow. Come right slick away."

The pair of whites approached the Indians, and every eye was turned towards the boy.

The warriors were holding a consultation among themselves, and their language was of course unintelligible to Armstrong, although Swift had no difficulty in comprehending the substance of their discussion.

Hiram Swift too stared at Dick as the words of the Indian speakers fell upon his ear, and the boy felt convinced that he was the theme of their orations.

The warriors formed themselves in a circle round the dead body of their chief, and courteously beckoned Dick to stand in their midst.

He did so, without fear or hesitation, knowing perfectly well that no harm could be intended to him, as he had never done any injury to the tribe.

He therefore entered the circle, and took up his station at the head of the corpse.

One of the Delawares—an aged warrior, whose face, neck, and arms bore the marks of many wounds—then came forward and spoke in English:—

"STRONGBOW is a great chief, though his face is smooth. His arrows are very terrible; they pierce through the enemies of the Delawares. Onotassa was a great warrior; the Crows and Pequots feared the sound of his footsteps; the scalps of many Crows hang in his wigwam; but he has gone to the happy hunting ground. The Delawares have no chief, though their warriors are many, and plenty of scalps hang on their mocassins. He who slew the slayer of our chief shall lead us on the war-path—STRONGBOW shall be our chief! I have said."

" Ugh ! it is good," said the warriors.

" But I don't know you——"

" The Delawares will obey the voice of Strongbow; many young men shall wait upon his steps. The quiver of Onotassa shall hang upon the shoulder of our pale-face chief."

With these words the warrior slung the deer-skin quiver of the dead chief over our hero's neck, a panther skin was placed over his shoulders, and the Delawares, one and all, hailed him as their chief.

The blood rushed to the boy's head as he thought of the sudden change.

One hour the sport of cruel barbarians ; the next, lord of a brave, noble, and numerous tribe.

The hunter shouted and cheered with all his might, so delighted was he with the glory his young friend had gained.

The warrior who had before spoken then again stepped forward.

" The weapons of the dead warrior belong to the chief who rules in his stead. Strongbow will bear the bow, the lance, and the war hatchet of Onotassa. They are the weapons of a warrior. Strongbow will also replace in his quiver the medicine arrow with which he slew the Crow."

Strongbow—for by this name must our hero in future be known—took the weapons.

" I thank you, brave Delawares, for the honour you do me, though I know myself to be unworthy of the task of leading you on the war path or the hunting ground. There is another and a great reason why I cannot be your chief—my father and mother were either killed or carried away by Black Hand and his band. I must discover their fate."

" I guess these Delawares air jest the chaps to help yer," said Hiram.

The objection on the part of their newly elected chief to assume his authority was duly translated for the benefit of those warriors who could not understand him.

With one accord they signified their intention to accompany Strongbow and aid him in his search.

The youth was well aware of the advantage this would give him, and accepted the offer.

By so doing he had at his back a strong body guard to defend him from his adversaries ; a band of keen hunters who would supply him with meat in the woods, and, moreover, men with keen eyes who would not fail to note every sign and interpret it correctly.

The heart of our young hero was full of sadness as in the midst of his warriors he retraced his steps to the spot where the log hut had been.

All that remained of it was a heap of blackened ashes, which the light wind was gradually scattering.

The happy home was gone.

But there were numerous traces of the murderous conflict.

Arrows with their shafts half buried in the earth, here and there a tomahawk dropped by its owner, a knife, a broken bow, lances, and dark stains of blood upon the grass.

And there, just before the spot where the hut once stood, lay four human beings, or at least all that remained of them.

A flock of vultures arose from their sickening repast, and two grey wolves sneaked away as Strongbow and his Delawares came upon the ground.

Strongbow felt a faintness at heart as he thought how possible it was that his beloved parents might be thus entombed in the stomachs of these foul birds and beasts.

A fearful sight those four skeletons presented, for skeletons they were, every feature being destroyed.

The Indians examined them with attention, and at once affirmed that they were four of the Crow Indians, who had fallen in the assault on the log hut.

" They must have been carried away," said Strongbow ; " perhaps to be subjected to even worse tortures than those I was threatened with."

" Can't be. Them Crows we fit in the wood hadn't got no prisoners; nor did I see anyone in the camp."

" Then what has become of them, do tell me, sir ?"

" Why, that's jist it—it's queer, sartinly. When did ye see 'em last ?"

Strongbow told the hunter how they had all mounted on the horse, how he had been stunned by a blow, and then lost sight of his father and mother.

"There's the hoss—that's somethin' to go upon. The creetur's got hoofs, I guess: and if them hoofs don't leave a trail, then water du, an' that's agin natur."

The hunter lost no time in giving this information to the Indians, and they at once commenced beating backwards and forwards like well-trained hounds in search of a trail. Every blade of grass was carefully scanned by their sharp eyes.

At length, after a quarter of an hour's search, a whoop from one of them called the others around him.

There was the print of the horse's hoof, and, after a careful examination of it, the hunter and the Indians came to the same conclusion, that the animal was going in a south-westerly direction at a good pace.

## CHAPTER IX.

### AFLOAT.

NO doubt our readers have by this time asked themselves the question— What became of Armstrong and his wife after their son was taken prisoner by Black Hand?

When Edmund Armstrong saw his son knocked senseless from the horse, he fought like a lion to rescue him.

His heavy axe descended on every side, and with such vigour that the Indians drew back.

He then saw his son dragged away by the Indians—apparently dead.

Armstrong would have charged upon them single handed, but for his wife.

He was afraid to leave her, nor did he wish to expose her to the dangers of a hand-to-hand combat.

The boy was, to all appearance, dead; and with a sorrowful heart he turned his horse into the forest, and galloped away at full speed, to preserve the life of the one most dear to him.

What direction he took he knew not.

His great anxiety was to obtain for his wife safety from the Indians.

No sooner did the Crows perceive his flight, than, with a loud yell, a dozen of their swiftest runners started in pursuit, urged on by the voice of Wylde, who had his own reasons for not wishing the man to escape.

His vicious heart chuckled with joy, as he mentally saw the attainment of his wishes accomplished.

Away sped Armstrong on the horse, holding his fainting wife with one arm, and urging on his steed with the other.

His right hand grasped the axe, ready to strike down any foe who should venture too near.

The Indians seemed resolved to capture him at any hazards, and pressed onwards, yelling loudly and brandishing their weapons.

Their object seemed rather to take him alive than kill him, therefore no arrows were discharged at the fugitive.

One of the foremost Indians had, after a chase of upwards of a mile, arrived within about twenty paces of Armstrong.

The emigrant saw his danger, and suddenly wheeling his horse round, sent a bullet from his revolver through the Indian's brain.

The warrior, with a most fearful cry, fell upon the ground to rise no more.

On sped Armstrong; but his horse was beginning to show signs of fatigue.

The country through which they were now passing was full of brushwood, and therefore, difficult to be traversed by a horse.

The other Indians were still in pursuit, and gaining upon him.

A second bullet was discharged with fatal effect, for a second Indian fell.

The number of his adversaries was now decreased to ten.

A gleam of hope, too, appeared.

Before him lay a fine open country, sparsely dotted with trees, and flowing across this was a broad river, at least a hundred yards in width.

"Can I succeed in crossing this, I shall gain an advantage over my followers," thought the fugitive, and he shaped course towards the stream.

On arriving at the bank, however, he found that it would be no easy task to swim over on his tired horse, for the stream was swollen by recent rain, and was, moreover, full of trees and branches rent from some mountain forest by the tempest.

These huge trunks and branches were floating downwards, whirling and twisting about with the eddying tide.

He halted, and the Indians seemed to guess what was passing in his mind, for they gave another exulting cry, and came on with all their speed.

"It must be attempted," thought Armstrong, and he urged his horse to the brink.

But when there the frightened animal refused to proceed. Snorting and shivering with fear, it endeavoured to turn away.

Armstrong, however, was determined to drive him into the water, and had just succeeded in doing so when an Indian arrow, striking the poor animal on the shoulder, glanced into its heart.

In a moment all was over; the waters were reddened with blood, and, with a convulsive sob, the horse turned over on its side, and was swept away by the current.

Down went Armstrong, still holding his wife close to his breast—down some feet below the surface of the water, which roared and bubbled in his ears.

He struck out manfully and rose once more.

A large pine tree was close at hand; its thick green branches offered a screen from the eyes of the enemy.

He grasped a branch with one hand, and, after a moment's exertion, gained a support for himself and his wife.

The Indians came crowding up to the bank of the river to see what had become of the pale-faces.

They saw the body of the horse floating along, but the pine tree concealed from hem those they sought.

One warrior was bold enough to swim few yards out into the stream, but the current was too powerful for him, and it was only by making the most desperate exertions that he managed to regain the shore.

The others scattered themselves along the bank and made a strict search, but nothing could be seen by them.

The fugitives had escaped from their hands; the Indians imagined they had perished in the water.

For nearly a quarter of an hour they ran up and down the banks, occasionally shooting an arrow at some substance they saw floating past.

At length, to his great delight, Armstrong saw them retrace their steps, and after a short consultation, retire towards the scene of the combat.

One danger was, for the time, past.

But what new difficulty threatened him?

Whither would the stream carry him, and how should he provide himself and his delicate wife food during that voyage?

How long might that voyage last, too?

A dreadful thought took possession of his soul—thought of hunger, of faintness and dying by slow degrees—thought of seeing his beloved wife pine away, without having the power to aid her or alleviate her sufferings.

Tho tree floated on, occasionally meeting others with a rude concussion.

The waters grew more rapid—they roared and boiled and foamed.

"Oh! Edmund dearest," said Mrs. Armstrong, "what new danger have we to meet now?"

"We have passed the great danger of falling into the hands of the Indians, dear wife. I have no doubt our tree will run aground shortly, and then we shall be saved."

He knew he was deceiving his wife; but under such circumstances he thought the deceit justifiable.

The noise of the waters increased. From a harsh rattle it became a deep, sullen, and constant roar.

Born as he was amongst the hills of the north, he well knew the meaning of that sound. He knew that a waterfall was near at hand.

He raised himself as high out the water as possible and looked ahead.

Right before him, not more than a quarter of a mile distant, he could see a cloud of spray, which told where the stream hurled itself over into the abyss beyond.

Death was again staring them full in the face.

He laid his hand gently upon his wife's shoulder.

"Dearest, hope is passed. We must prepare for death and eternity."

"'SILENCE, YOU YOUNG BRUTE, OR I'LL BLOW YOUR BRAINS OUT,' SHOUTED THE RUFFIAN."

"Is it, then, so near, dear husband?"

"It is"

They bowed their heads meekly and prepared for death, asking forgiveness of the Merciful One, and in their hearts forgiving those who had at any time, or in any way, injured them.

Both Armstrong and his wife were Christians, and, though death was before them, they feared not.

The tree to which they still clung no longer waved or twisted about, but, impelled by the powerful current, shot forward like an arrow.

The spray was flying about them; the roar of the waters deafened them as they rushed on right into the jaws of death.

There was a sudden shock.

Armstrong and his wife were nearly thrown from their raft; but, when the momentary confusion was over, they found to their great delight that the tree had stopped.

Stopped right at the head of the falls!

Like a giant barrier it lay across, from a large rock which divided the cataract in two, to the steep bank of the river.

Armstrong could scarcely believe that it was so for a moment or two, the excitement consequent upon his sudden deliverance was so great.

But becoming convinced that he was really saved, the emigrant lost no time in conveying himself and his almost senseless wife to the shore.

This was no easy task, but at length they reached the bank, and, to their great delight, found themselves once more on dry land.

Both were wet to the skin, both were tired and hungry.

Armstrong had lost his rifle in the fight at the log hut, but he still retained his revolvers and his broad axe. But the fire-arms were useless, for the water had thoroughly soaked the charges in the barrels.

A place must be found in which to rest and dry their dripping clothing. Armstrong searched for such a place, and found, about a hundred yards from the spot where they landed, a sort of cave or hollow in the side of a rock.

He entered.

It was evidently a human habitation, for there was a couch of skins on the earth, and bows and arrows upon the wall.

"This is no place for us," he sighed; "we must search for another spot in which to rest."

With these words he drew his wife to the doorway, when suddenly they found themselves face to face with four stalwart Indians.

---

## CHAPTER X.

### ON THE TRAIL.

AS soon as Strongbow discovered the track of the horse, he was for instant pursuit, but Hiram Swift and the Delawares detained him.

"Whar's yer hoss, boy?" asked the hunter. "How d'ye think to catch up this creetur, and you on foot?"

"I don't know, but I must go."

"So ye shall, and ye'll get them all the quicker by waiting a bit."

"How?"

"You shall go on horseback."

"On horseback! But I have no horse."

"You've got a couple o' very nice hosses."

"You are certainly dreaming, my good friend."

"Not a bit; you just wait till these Indians have finished their feed, and you'll see."

Feed! Was it possible that the Indians were going to waste time in eating and drinking when their young chief was so impatient? Strongbow felt very much inclined to exert his newly-acquired authority and *order* them to proceed at once.

He spoke to Hiram Swift on the subject, but to his surprise that worthy seemed to coincide entirely with the Indians.

So our young hero was obliged to curb the impatience he felt, and wait until the Delawares had finished their meal.

It was some time before this was done, but at length they seemed to have satisfied their hunger.

Just as they rose to their feet and began to look after their arms, a troop of horses were seen coming through the trees, conducted by some Indian boys who had been sent to the village to fetch them.

Hitherto Strongbow had been ignorant of the very existence of this village, which the old hunter now assured him was within eight miles of the spot where the emigrant had built his log hut.

If the Delawares had known that their Crow enemies, under Black Hand, were haunting the neighbourhood at the time when Armstrong first took up his quarters in the wood, they would certainly have protected the emigrant, and driven the enemy far away.

The horses were brought up—fourteen in all—handsome, strong-looking animals, though not very large.

These horses had been captured far away to the south-west, on the great, open, grassy prairies, where timber is an unknown article—where the traveller must carry with him both fuel and water, should he feel desirous of drinking or cooking his food.

A dozen Indians then mounted; the other horses were brought by an Indian lad to Strongbow.

"I said you had two hosses," laughed the white hunter. "Jest you mount one and lend me t'other. My beast is too far away to go and fetch."

"But whose are they?" asked the boy.

"Yours. They belonged to the dead chief, but as you've taken his place, you take all his property, even to his three squaws."

"Thank you!" said Strongbow, as he leaped to the back of his horse. "I'll lend you a horse, and as for the wives, I'll give them to you entirely."

"Don't want 'em, lad," replied the hunter, sternly, and his eye, before so bright and merry, became cold and gloomy.

Strongbow resolved to say no more on that subject at present, but to question the hunter when he was in a more genial humour, for Strongbow judged rightly that he had touched some hidden sorrow.

In less than five minutes the whole party were in the saddle, and proceeding at a brisk trot towards the south-west.

First of all rode Hiram Swift, and the senior warrior of the band, then the Boy Chief of the Delawares, after whom came the remaining eleven warriors in single file.

The remainder of the Indians then returned to their wigwams.

The old hunter had no difficulty in "lifting the trail," that is, in discovering and following the course taken by the elder Armstrong.

The prints of the horse's hoofs were perfectly legible, and, besides, they had the marks made by the Crow Indians in their pursuit.

It took no long time to bring Strongbow to the place where his father had shot the first Indian.

The warrior was lying on the grass with a bullet-hole through his forehead, just as he had fallen.

His companions had been unable, or were unwilling, to risk their own lives by carrying him away.

Here was proof positive that his father was still alive, a fact which greatly rejoiced the heart of the young chief.

On again, till they reached another spot, where the blood-stained and crushed-down grass proclaimed that a human being had fallen.

But that human being was not to be seen.

The fact for a moment surprised the hunter, but by riding his horse for a hundred yards round the place he soon discovered the reason.

The pursuing Indians had returned from the chase of the fugitive, and had borne off their dead companion.

The trail told all this plainly enough to the practised eyes of Hiram Swift and the Indians, though to Strongbow nothing was visible but a dark stain of blood on the grass, and a number of footsteps around.

But the hunter saw that the Crow Indians had followed the trail of the horse, and that the pursuers had also returned from their pursuit, having either lost or killed the emigrant

That Armstrong, senior, was not a prisoner was a moral certainty, for his track was not among the footsteps of the returning party.

"But they may have made him take off his boots and put on mocassins," suggested Strongbow, when the hunter told him the result of his examination of the trail.

"I guess not. I'll have another look, though."

Swift made a very careful examination of the back trail, as did also one of the Delawares.

They both came to the same conclusion, namely, that no white man was with the party on its return.

Nor was this opinion without basis, for it is a well-known fact that the Indians of North America always turn the toes inward while walking, whereas white men invariably turn theirs outward.

This being the fact, what have our drill-sergeants to say for themselves?

These Indians are staunch and graceful walkers ; they can keep up a good pace for a great length of time, and can run with great swiftness.

Strongbow's father was not with his enemies when they returned.

The question then presented itself to his mind—

Was he dead, or had he escaped?

"Escaped, no doubt," said the hunter, and so also said the Delawares.

"Why do you think so?"

The answer afforded another insight into the manners of the children of the wilderness.

If they had killed him and his wife, they would have stopped to feast and rejoice over their scalps.

The Crow Indians, evidently, had not had sufficient time for any such festivities.

"These tracks are not an hour old," said the old hunter, pointing to the spot where the Crows had diverged from their first track and had gone towards the woody country.

"Then we must keep on."

"No. The sun will go down in less than half an hour, and we must not go farther than the grove of trees yonder, where we shall be able to find wood for our fire and water to drink. In the night we shall not be able to see the trail, and very likely should go astray."

The hunter then spoke a few words to the Delawares, who answered them in their own tongue.

"They are of the same opinion. We should lose time by going on before morning."

Knowing nothing of the mysteries of life in the backwoods and on the prairies, our young hero was obliged to abide by the opinions of those whose home was in the wilderness.

The Indian who rode in front then asked in broken English whether it was agreeable to their chief that they should encamp in the grove which Swift had pointed out.

Strongbow answered in the affirmative, and towards it the party took their way.

All except two.

These two were Hiram Swift, the white hunter, and the Indian who rode next behind Strongbow.

They were seen to leave the party suddenly, and ride off in different directions, one to the right and the other to the left.

The young chief wondered at this sudden and unexpected desertion, and would have asked what it meant, had not his old Indian counsellor and guide, the "Big Elk," furnished an explanation.

"They go hunt—find meat."

Then, after all, it was not a desertion, but a foraging party.

Strongbow, however, resolved to make one himself in the next foraging expedition.

The "Big Elk" very carefully looked around the little grove, which was hardly a hundred yards in circumference, before he entered.

It was quite possible that enemies might be lurking there.

No signs of any foe were perceptible, and the band then entered one after another.

As soon as they were fairly inside the circle of bushes, they dismounted and tethered their steeds around the outside, choosing not large trunks or branches of trees, but flexible saplings.

They always tie their horses thus for this reason:—

If the animals were to take fright, the resistance offered by the large trunk would snap the cord, or else, by suddenly checking the horse, do it some injury.

The slighter resistance of a young

sapling does neither, though, should the horse start, the action of the lithesome stem, as it endeavours to regain its natural position, gradually checks the frisky or frightened steed.

Having thus secured the animals and placed three sentinels among the bushes, the remainder proceeded to the centre of the grove, where the tallest trees grew, and where the ground was clear from underwood and long grass.

Here Big Elk proposed to form the camp, and for that purpose directed one of the warriors to gather dry wood.

The Indian, who in his village would have been disgraced by performing such an act, set about it with alacrity.

The place where the fire was to be built was a slight hollow, and Big Elk at once set two of the young men to hollow out the place still more.

They dug a kind of round hole, a yard in diameter and two feet in depth, piling up the earth they loosened with their tomahawks round the edge of the excavation.

Big Elk was an experienced warrior, and explained that, as there was reason to believe the Crows were not far distant, it would be well to guard against surprise.

By putting the fire in a deep hollow, its glare and light would be thrown upwards, where it would be concealed by the thick, leafy branches of the trees.

When the fire was made, the Indians sat round it in solemn silence.

They were hungry—they had no food to eat; but they did not complain.

They smoked their pipes, filled with a mixture of tobacco and the stringy bark of a species of willow, looking as stolid and contented as though they had fared sumptuously, and were merely indulging in a smoke to promote digestion.

Strongbow was not accustomed to such stoicism; though he bore his hunger without any verbal complaint, he could not help at times pressing his hand upon his stomach.

The maxim, that "nature abhors a vacuum," proved itself unmistakably to him.

Just as the sun went down the rifle of the hunter was heard.

It was nearly half an hour before he returned to the camp, bearing upon his shoulder the carcase of a fawn about half grown.

That was indeed a welcome sight.

Knives were drawn, and in a very few minutes all the party had pieces of the flesh roasting on wooden spits before the fire.

Then in came the Indian hunter with a second fawn about the same size, and which the hunter affirmed to be the brother of that he had shot.

Such a roasting and eating the Boy Chief had never seen before.

The Indians scarcely cooked their food, but, as soon as the outside of the meat was just scorched by the fire, dragged it off the spit and devoured it.

The sentinels, who sat among the bushes, keeping watch over the horses, had their share, and then once more returned to their posts, where, though invisible to the eye, they kept vigilant guard over the camp.

Indian sentinels always sit when watching at night.

The eye being nearer the ground has a greater range; besides, they themselves are not so likely to be noticed.

When the supper was at an end all prepared for sleep, except one warrior, who remained to keep up the fire and otherwise look after the sleepers.

## CHAPTER XI.

### A BUFFALO HUNT.

THE situation was an extremely novel one for our young hero.

Not that it was the first time he had lain by a camp fire in the forest, but on this occasion he was chief of the party, little less than absolute monarch over all he surveyed

The fire cast its glare upwards, shedding a ruddy light upon the gnarled branches of the trees overhead.

Around on the horizon all was dark.

Nothing could be seen save here ar there some great trunk looming out ' a giant of the forest.

Far away in the distant wood, which was at least a mile distant from their encampment, might be heard many of the night sounds of the wilderness.

" Whip-poor-will " gave his melancholy notes to the darkness, while the wolf howled beneath, as he chased deer or fawn through the wood.

Then there was the unearthly·sound of the great owl, which flew noiselessly to and fro on the prairie, or pounced down on some hapless rabbit or partridge. Even insects added their various noises to swell the night chorus of nature.

The air seemed close and oppressive, and Strongbow's mind had for some time been in a state of tumult.

When these combined causes are taken into consideration, it is no wonder that he should feel feverish and unable to sleep.

At length, however, he managed to close his eyes, and then became a prey to fearful dreams.

In imagination he was again the prisoner of Black Hand, and had resumed his old position upon the pile which was intended to consume his body to ashes.

An Indian applied fire to the wood, the flames became hotter and hotter—they scorched his flesh—he struggled to escape but could not, while all the time the Indians kept growling at him with deep, hoarse voices.

At length came his father, who took him by the arm and forcibly dragged him from among the tormentors.

" Hello !  Come, keep quiet, will yer ?"

These were the words which greeted his waking ears, and looking round to see from whence they came, he saw that Hiram Swift was holding him down with a strong hand.

" What is the matter ?" asked the young chief.

" Matter !  Why, you've been kicking about enough to kill—to say nothing of trying to throw yourself into the fire."

" I was dreaming."

" Well, take my advice ; go to sleep, and don't dream any more.  Tuck your buffalo blanket round yourself and your weapons, for we'll have a good shower before long."

As the hunter spoke, the thunder growled far away to the south, and a distant flash of lightning faintly illumined the murky darkness of the night.

It was very evident that a heavy thunderstorm was working up.

Strongbow did not neglect Hiram Swift's advice about wrapping himself up in his rug, so as to keep his body and his weapons dry.

The Delawares all took the same precautions.

Our young chief was sound asleep when the rain actually came, but its force soon dispelled his dreams.

The big drops descended with such force through the openings of the trees that they seemed almost like small shot fired from a gun.

Not only were the human beings disturbed, but the horses, frightened by the thunder and the lightning, began to prance about at such a rate that it was more than the three Indian sentinels could do to manage them.

The pleasure of the night's encampment being thus destroyed, nothing remained but to wait in damp discomfort the return of morning's light, and the cessation of the storm.

They all huddled themselves around the fire, which was almost extinguished, and sheltered themselves as well as they could.

For two or three hours the thunder lasted and the rain fell in drenching torrents.

As the first rays of morning began to lighten the eastern sky, the last heavy drops fell and the last muttered peal of heaven's artillery was heard.

The Indians aroused themselves, and began to replenish the fire to cook their morning meal.

The rain had made them all feel very cold, and the cold, as a matter of course, brought hunger.

An Indian brought forward the remnants of the two fawns, which were soon roasting over the fire in the same manner as the suppers had been cooked the previous night.

Strongbow thought there was not half enough, and could easily have devoured twice as much as came to his share.

The old hunter openly expressed his opinion that he should like to pick another rib.

The Delawares said nothing.

The meal was over at length.

Full of impatience, the Boy Chief ran

to the spot where his horse was tethered, and sprang upon its back.

The hunter and the Indians followed, and when all had taken their horses, the band rode out into the prairie in the same order as the day before.

They had not ridden fifty yards, however, before it was discovered that the heavy rain had entirely obliterated all the trail they had made.

It was, therefore, useless to attempt to follow the track of Armstrong's horse, whose hoof-marks would also be washed out by the storm.

Here again was gloomy sorrow for our young hero.

The trail was lost, and no man now could say whether the fugitives had fled to north, south, or west.

Strongbow placed his hands before his face, which grew ashy white, to hide the workings of his countenance, nor did the Delawares take any notice of this slight exhibition of feeling, for they knew he had endured the torments inflicted by Black Hand's band without a murmur.

In their eyes he was a brave young pale-face.

But what was to be done?

This question was the identical one which Hiram Swift and four of the warriors were endeavouring to solve.

It was rather a knotty question, too, for to follow a trail which had been washed over by such a storm, would require more than double the usual amount of backwoods skill.

At length the deliberations came to a close, and the hunter came to announce the result.

"We've made up our minds to go ahead, younker; thar's more chance o' finding the trail if he's gone, as seems to me, towards the river."

"Do as you like; you know best, only don't think of giving up the search till my father is found."

"We'll find him if we can, and may I be stuck naked in the middle of a dog briar if thar's any men in this part o' the world better able to do it than we. So, keep yer pluck up."

Then off they went again, no longer in file, but spread out like the skirmishers in front of a regiment, sometimes closing up and then extending again.

In this manner a wide tract of country was thoroughly examined as they made their way onwards.

But, when Armstrong passed that way the prairie was dry, and the hoofs of his horse left but a slight impression.

The Indians were unable to discover the slightest trace of him.

"We must hold on to the river," repeated Swift. "The ground is heavy there, and it'll take a power of rain to wash out them tracks."

So on they went.

The river was reached, and, after searching up and down the bank for some distance, deep hoof-marks were discovered in the soft, marshy soil.

They were filled with water, and had, therefore, been made before the storm took place.

Here, then, the horse had plunged into the flood, and half-a-dozen Indians, without hesitation, prepared to swim across.

The stream had subsided a little, the huge trees had been swept down some distance, leaving the current free; but it was still swift and deep.

But the warriors managed to pass over.

For at least three miles down the opposite bank did they search; but, although that bank was also soft and marshy, no hoof-tracks were discovered.

A gloom again settled on Strongbow's brow.

"We must keep on down the bank," said the old hunter. "The hoss couldn't swim up stream."

On they went, every eye on the alert.

The day passed, finding them still on their weary search.

Sunset was at hand, and thoughts of food and rest began to occupy the minds of the hunter and the Delawares.

"See there—buffalo!" ejaculated Big Elk, pointing with his right hand to a part of the open prairie where several black spots were seen. "Plenty buffalo meat to-night."

At the word "buffalo" every warrior began to look to his bow and arrows, and a consultation was held as to the best way to surround them.

The men were proceeding in a westerly direction, the big beasts were right before them, and Strongbow urged an immediate advance.

But the hunter overruled this hasty proposal.

"They'd smell ye afore you'd get within half-a-mile; it ain't to be done that way. We must go pretty nigh up to the timber yonder, and then come down with the wind in our faces."

"Ugh!" exclaimed the Indians, "it is good."

The horses seemed to be alive to the game, and, raising their heads, trotted off briskly.

"Now, all you've got to do is to keep alongside me till we make a rush at 'em; then put your horse after one, ride right up, and let your arrow go well home just behind the shoulder. Pull up, and wheel to the right as soon as your bowstring twangs."

The Indians needed no instruction in buffalo hunting.

They reached the wood, and, from its outskirts, took another survey of the gigantic game.

Big Elk was of opinion that they could be best approached by riding about half-a-mile farther, and then turning up the side of a rising ground on the opposite side of which the beasts were feeding.

This manœuvre was put in execution, and, by the time they reached the crest of the hill, they had the satisfaction of perceiving that the buffaloes were not a hundred yards distant.

Hiram Swift gave the word to charge them, and the whole party urged their horses forward.

The buffaloes looked up from their pasture, and, with loud bellowings, set off at an awkward gallop, in a compact herd, as soon as they perceived the danger.

Our Delawares knew how to act, and in a few minutes Big Elk and another had scattered them by urging their horses into the very midst.

There were about twenty of the great beasts in all, under the command of a gigantic old bull, who was by far the fiercest-looking animal that Strongbow had ever seen.

Our young hero resolved to slay this monster if possible; so, as soon as he saw the herd scattered, he gave his horse the rein and, after calling out to Hiram Swift, started in chase.

The old bull, however, had the advantage of at least a hundred yards' start, and the Boy Chief soon found that, al-though the buffalo is an awkward, shambling-looking animal, he can gallop at a very swift pace, especially when urged on by the shouts and whoops of a dozen Indian hunters.

Strongbow's horse, too, was fatigued with the day's journey, and although the gallant animal understood the fun of buffalo-hunting, it was unable to gain upon the chase so swiftly as the rider wished.

The report of Hiram Swift's rifle was heard, and glancing round, Strongbow saw that the bullet had no been wasted.

One of the huge beasts was motionless on the plain, and the hunter a few yards off was reloading his fatal rifle as he sat on his panting horse.

In another moment Big Elk's bow twanged, and a second buffalo fell to the ground, and, after a vain attempt to rise, expired with a groan.

"I must not be outdone," thought the young chief; "I must kill my bull to keep up my reputation."

The bull was twenty or thirty yards ahead, and, in the hope of crippling him, the boy directed an arrow at his hind quarters.

The shaft fled, truly, but, beyond inflicting a stinging wound, did no serious injury.

With a deep roar, the savage brute turned on his pursuer.

Strongbow had just time to check his horse, and wheel out of the way as the bull bounded past, throwing up the earth with his sharp-pointed horns, and roaring loudly.

As soon as he saw that he had missed his intended toss, he turned again, and made a second charge in a still more vicious manner.

Again Strongbow wheeled round.

But an accident then befel him which nearly put an end to his buffalo-hunting.

The horse stumbled, and the young chief, having his hands occupied with his bow and arrow, was thrown to the ground.

Unlike the Indians, he had no long rope trailing from the saddle bow, and was, therefore, unable to stop his steed, which galloped away.

Half stunned, and confused by the force with which he had fallen, the young hunter rose to his feet.

His bow was lying upon the ground

beside him, and his first act was to stoop down and recover this useful weapon.

It was well he did so, for the next moment the well-known bellow of his huge adversary met his ear, and turning, he beheld the bull charging at him.

Death again seemed to be stretching out his bony hands to grasp our young hero by the throat.

Nor did he present a more pleasing aspect on this than on other occasions.

It was no pleasant prospect to be gored, crushed and trampled under foot by the furious leader of the wild herd, and the prospect seemed doubly unwelcome now that he was engaged in a search for his parents.

It is strange, but when men are on the brink of some great misfortune, the events of their past lives will force themselves upon the mind, which sees with rapidity and clearness acts and persons of long past days. And so, through Strongbow's brain darted a mental picture of his past life, upon which the eyes of his mind were fixed, until a loud snort recalled him to a sense of his peril.

The gigantic beast's shaggy mane seemed to erect itself with anger; the two glaring eyes seemed like balls of fire, and the whole aspect of the animal was terrible in the extreme.

He was within six paces of Strongbow before the latter perceived the whole extent of his danger.

The boy could scarcely repress a cry of alarm as he leaped aside, and discharged his arrow at random.

Then for a few moments he seemed unconscious of what happened.

## CHAPTER XII.

### THE LAND AGENT AND HIS LETTER.

SOME seven or eight days after Strongbow had received his Indian title, a man might have been seen slowly sauntering along the street that led towards the post office of Washington.

This individual was evidently a stranger in the town, for he stopped several times to make inquiries as to the route.

He seemed to be in a hurry, and yet ever and again he would pause in his slouching walk, thrust his hands in his pockets, and whistle a bar or two of "Hail Columbia," in a manner exceedingly indicative of indecision.

Yet he kept on towards the post office, seeming all the while to be doubtful as to the utility of his journey.

It was our old friend Jackson, the land agent, the man who, after acting as Wylde's decoy, and luring Armstrong and his family into the wilderness, had disappeared.

At length he reached the post office, and, after an attentive survey of its outside, entered the building.

"Any letter for Daniel Jackson, Esquire, of Boston?" he asked, addressing an official-looking person.

"That window," replied the person addressed.

"Darn their winders!" muttered Mr Jackson, in an undertone, as he sauntered to the spot indicated by the official-looking finger.

He repeated the question.

"Daniel — Jackson — Esquire — of — Boston," said the clerk, dealing out a packet of letters with as much dexterity as a gambler deals cards.

"No; stop! Yes, here it is—the last."

"What's to pay, mister?"

"Nothing. Pass on."

"Won't ye liquor?"

"Can't come. Send in a cocktail."

Jackson nodded, and after putting the letter very carefully into a breast-pocket, walked out.

Not far off was a splendidly-furnished bar-room, gaily decorated with crystal goblets, bottles full of beautifully-coloured transparent fluids, plate glass, and so forth.

It was so suggestive of something nice to drink that the sight added tenfold to the thirst which the intense heat of an American summer sun had already engendered in Jackson's throat.

It was not many minutes before the ex-land agent was very comfortably seated inside with a "brandy smash," or a "cocktail." or something of that nature before him.

Having taken what he himself would term a "big drink," he took the letter from his pocket and opened it, utterly forgetful of the refreshment he had offered the clerk at the post office.

The handwriting was evidently familiar, for Jackson coloured up as red as his original sallow complexion would permit, and then turned as pale as possible.

Well he might, for the document was in the writing of the man who held and exercised such a fearful influence over him. It was from Wylde.

"Cuss him! I hoped some of the redskins would have raised his hair," muttered Jackson.

He twisted the letter about uneasily, half afraid to read it.

At length he summoned up courage, and perused the contents.

It ran thus:—

"Failed altogether! I must have another try though, for I am determined these people shall not escape me. I owe Armstrong a grudge I would willingly pay, *and which I shall never forget while I wear this diamond ring* upon my finger."

"I thought there was something in that ring," muttered Jackson, taking another drink.

Then continuing the letter, he read:—

"Look me out three good men who know how to live in the woods, how to use their rifles, and how to follow a trail. I don't want any chicken-hearted fools, but men who will stick at nothing, or, as it should be expressed, will stick anything, or anybody. Men who have *particular reasons* for emigrating are the ones; you know how and where to pick them up, so have them ready for me within a week after you get this. Tell them there's plenty of money in the scheme, and that so long as they do what I want, they may do anything else they please. But don't mention names.

"Yours,
"C. WYLDE.

"P. S.—You had better fix them at the State Hotel, where, I suppose, you are staying. You had better keep them and yourself pretty much out of sight during the daytime *for fear of accidents.*
"C. W."

"Here's some scheme on," muttered Jackson; "he can't be satisfied without dragging one into trouble. I won't have anything to do with it."

He thrust the letter into his pocket, called for another drink, and began to reflect.

But unhappily his reflections took a wrong turn, and destroyed whatever calm there may have been in his mind, by thrusting upon him the most alarming visions of the probable consequences of disobedience.

D. Jackson, Esquire, of Boston, well remembered the threats Wylde had before held out, and doubted not that he would fulfil them.

Nothing then remained but to obey orders, and look out for three men.

Full of sorrow, Jackson slowly wended his way homewards; but so occupied was he by his thoughts that he neglected where he was going, nor did he perceive the mistake he had made till he found himself in a part of the town he knew nothing whatever about.

It seemed the least respectable part of that respectable city from which American edicts issue. There was an air of the very shabbiest gentility pervading the place, giving it somewhat of the social aspect of our own sweet regions adjacent to Leicester Square.

The men and women, if not badly dressed, seemed ill at ease in their garments; the negroes in the streets and the few shops looked downcast and woe-begone—more like well-thrashed runaways than the sleek well-fed "ebony property" seen in more *straightforward* parts of the city.

Such the place was, and as soon as Jackson saw it, he resolved that it was the exact spot where the three men required by his friend Wylde might be found.

He entered a small house, devoted to the sale of liquor, and sat down, after ordering some drink.

There were about half-a-dozen men lounging about, all of them apparently inhabitants of the locality.

They were talking to one another in low tones, laughing and making rude jests.

One of them was narrating an anecdote of his experiences at a frontier trading post, and the others seemed mightily to enjoy the tale.

"What made you leave them diggin's, old hoss?" asked one of the audience.

"Climate didn't suit."

"Ha, ha, ha!" laughed another. "I'll tell ye. Bill plugged a chap in the dark one night, and so had to make tracks."

"Is that a fact?" asked another.

Bill nodded.

"There were some tallish talk about Judge Lynch, so while they were hunting for a good rope, this child sloped, he did."

"That's one," thought Jackson, as, while pretending to be busy with a newspaper, he carefully noted every feature of the child who sloped so cleverly after killing or seriously wounding a fellow creature in the dark.

The rest of the gang seemed very much of a similar stamp, and all that now remained was to make their acquaintance, and open negotiations with them to join Mr. Wylde's new scheme for cutting throats.

An opportunity was not long in presenting itself.

One of the party made some observation about its being time to go, and this serving as a signal to the others, they all departed excepting the gentleman who had such a narrow escape from the hands of Judge Lynch.

This gentleman observed that the hot sun so affected his constitution that he did not care to venture out during the day, an observation which made his companions laugh again.

"Fine day, stranger," said he, addressing Jackson, as soon as they were alone.

"Yes," replied Jackson.

"Will ye liquor?"

"Don't care if do."

Orders were given and glasses were refilled, both parties drawing their chairs nearer together.

"A stranger here?" asked he of plugging celebrity.

"Yes; I wish I were somewhere else."

"Ho, then, you're *stuck up*, mister?"

Jackson nodded an intimation that he was stuck up, or, in other words, that his description was in the hands of those whose duty it was to hunt out criminals and bring them to justice.

"Ye needn't fear, stranger; you are right as shootin' here. What do ye say to a game of uker or brag, just by way of passing time?"

"With all my heart," replied Jackson, "and while we are playing I can speak to you about a little matter of business which will put a few dollars in your pocket."

## CHAPTER XIII.

### AN EXPLORING EXPEDITION.

STRONGBOW was not killed or even injured by the charge of the ferocious buffalo. In his backward leap he had not been quite nimble enough, and, although he managed to escape the beast's horns, received a blow from its shoulder which hurled him to the ground.

For a few seconds he lay stunned and bewildered.

But very soon his faculties returned, and he rose to his feet to look round for his savage adversary.

To his infinite astonishment he saw the bull lying upon the green sward, not four yards from him, perfectly dead.

The last arrow had done its work with a vengeance.

It had smashed through skin, ribs, and heart, till its barb was seen protruding from the opposite side of the beast's body to that which it entered.

The Delawares and old Swift were still chasing the remainder of the herd.

It seemed as though they had not noticed the danger he had been in; nor had they, indeed.

Not till Strongbow's horse galloped past one of the Indians did they know that their young chief's life had nearly been lost.

Then, when they saw him standing by the side of the big father of the herd, they set up a loud shout of triumph. Hiram Swift was the first to return, after killing another beast, and then, in obedience to the call of Big Elk, the other warriors left the chase to hold a solemn council.

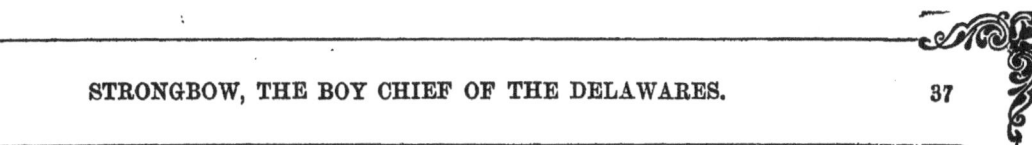

"WITH A DEEP ROAR THE SAVAGE BRUTE TURNED ON HIS PURSUER."

The warriors all gathered round the young hunter, and expressed their gratification at his success.

As they made no mention of his mishap, Strongbow judged it best to say nothing about it.

"But how did ye manage to lose yer hoss, lad?" asked Swift.

"He stumbled and threw me."

"Why didn't ye have that larriat trailing?"

'What do you mean?"

"Why, look at these hunters; they all has their larriats trailing."

Strongbow looked as directed, and saw that each warrior had a strong rope of plaited leather, nearly fifty feet in length, dangling from his horse's neck.

These, the hunter explained, were to enable them to stop their steeds, should they by any unforeseen accident happen to be dismounted.

The warriors then commenced cutting up the slaughtered beasts, cutting away only the prime parts, the tongues, humps, etc.

Strongbow was rather surprised at this proceeding.

"Why," said he, "one of these animals would be sufficient to give them a week's food."

"Aye, but then it's their nature to kill as much as they can. They think almost as much of a good hunter as they do of a brave warrior; and we mustn't let them take the shine out of us."

"I thought the bull would have killed me," said Strongbow, after a pause.

"How so?"

"He charged at me when I was off my horse."

"Ah!"

Strongbow then told the whole history of his hunt.

The old backwoodsman uttered a low chuckling laugh as he heard the story.

"You must be careful, lad. Many's the good hunter that has been killed by a buffalo bull; never touch one unless you're certain of your aim."

"I shall take your advice."

By this time the hunters had collected all the meat they required.

It was attached to their saddles, and then they moved off towards their old trail, intending to pass the night near the river banks.

The bodies of the buffaloes were left just where they had fallen. The wolves and the vultures—the prairie scavengers—would clear away all remnants of the slain.

Even as they mounted their steeds a few of the unclean birds were seen wheeling high in the air, waiting their opportunity, while others far distant, were hastening towards the spot.

Having once more got into their old route, they hastened onwards, intending to get over as much ground as possible, as there was no good camping ground to be seen for some distance.

Grass for their horses, and water, were plentiful, but the warriors themselves wanted wood, both to cook their food and also to serve as a defence in case of an attack being made upon them by a superior force.

The Delawares were leaving their own territory, and two days' travelling had brought them into a neutral ground where many tribes hunted and fought.

Some of these would be friendly, but others were known to be at enmity with the great Delaware nation.

The camping ground was at last fixed upon.

A wood of considerable extent was found on the banks of the stream.

In this, that is about a hundred yards from the open prairie, and not more than twenty from the stream, they made their fire, tethered their horses, and prepared to pass the night.

If Strongbow had been astonished the preceding night at the way the Indians attacked the bodies of the two fawns, he was still more surprised at the furious manner in which they devoured the buffalo meat.

So far as he could judge, each warrior swallowed at least ten pounds' weight of solid flesh before any signs of loss of appetite were perceptible.

Hiram Swift was not far behind them in voracity, and the boy himself began to find a wonderful increase in the capacity of his stomach.

There is nothing like a life of constant exercise in the open air to do away with all the ills of human nature, "barrin' the ager," as Swift expressed himself.

There is no indigestion on the prairies; gout, which, in civilized lands, follows close upon good feeding, cannot travel upon his swollen feet out into these wilds.

The white hunter was, however, more of an epicure than the Indians; he was a sort of a prairie Soyer, and prepared his food in a scientific manner.

When he cut up his buffalo, he brought with the meat large pieces of the hide, also portions of the fat of the kidneys, and the shin bones.

Having put one good steak upon the fire for himself and Strongbow—whose old bull proved too tough for eating—he busily prepared himself for a second course.

A large square piece of buffalo-hide was placed upon the ground, and on it the hunter placed portions of the flesh chopped up fine; some of the liver he treated in the same manner.

He then broke open the bones and extracted the marrow, which he added to the mess.

The buffalo-hide was then tied up, and the pudding thus made was deposited amongst the hot ashes.

While this was being done, one of the Indians, who had been down to the stream to drink, returned with the information that someone had established a camp on the opposite side of the river, about half-a-mile down.

It was proposed by Swift and Big Elk that a party should cross over to see who their neighbours might be.

Eight Indians were selected for this task.

"They will make their bowstrings wet," remarked Strongbow.

"Not they; you'll see," replied the hunter.

"They have no boat."

"They'll make one big enough to hold their bows and arrows, I guess."

"How will they manage it?"

"Come down and see."

So the youth accompanied his preceptor in woodcraft to the water's edge, where the Indians were making their preparations.

They had collected a large quantity of dead wood, which they twisted and tied together with long grass and weeds from the water; it was nine or ten feet in length, and when placed in the water rose a foot at least above its surface.

In this they thrust their weapons, and then waded out as far as possible.

When no longer able to walk, they began to swim very gently, allowing the brushwood to proceed about the same pace as the stream, only making just sufficient exertion to give it a tendency to cross over.

"There's a boat, and a good 'un," said old Swift. "It carries their bows and hides their bodies."

The Indians had designed it for both purposes, which it answered admirably.

Down it floated one end first, the warriors carefully keeping it between them and the opposite bank.

It sailed past the spot where a light blue smoke announced that a fire was burning, and, as Strongbow continued to watch, he saw that it drifted ashore nearly a quarter of a mile below, directly under a group of overhanging trees.

They then returned to their own camp, where Big Elk was awaiting them.

That circumspect warrior had taken the precaution to post the three other men as scouts about their camp, and was now calmly smoking as though he had not the slightest idea of any stranger being in the neighbourhood.

"When will they be back?" asked the Boy Chief of the Delawares.

"I don't know; perhaps to-night, maybe not afore mornin'. I'm going to sleep; you'd better do your eyes over a bit."

So saying, he stretched himself at full length; Big Elk, after finishing his pipe, did the same, and Strongbow, seeing that his experienced companions considered themselves in perfect safety, followed their example.

The boy was heartily tired, for he had travelled a great distance since the morning.

If people eat heartily in the backwoods, they also sleep heartily, though with a certain amount of watchfulness.

So slept Strongbow and his companions.

They had slept three hours at least when a huge owl perched himself on a tree close at hand, and commenced its melancholy complaint to the moon.

The noise awoke Strongbow, though Swift and Big Elk slept still.

The boy opened his eyes.

He could see the owl spread her wings and glide noiselessly away over the treetops, and then another sound fell upon his ear—it was a deep groan. He rose, took up his axe and bow, and walked into the forest. The night was dark; all seemed safe and secure. He turned about to return to the camp. As his eye rested once more upon the fire, a sight presented itself which filled him with horror.

Hiram Swift and Big Elk were sleeping, unconscious of the fact that half-a-dozen Indians were standing over them with knives and tomahawks in their hands about to strike.

Instinctively he fitted an arrow to the string, and sent it to the heart of the foremost Indian. ·

## CHAPTER XIV.

### THE COMBAT.

THE sudden fall of the dead Indian, together with the whoop he gave, caused his companions to start and turn suddenly.

Hiram Swift and Big Elk were also aroused, and jumped up with equal celerity.

A single glance showed them how matters stood, and grasping their weapons, they furiously defended themselves.

A second arrow from the bow of the Boy Chief came whistling through the air, and a second Indian fell dead.

Then with a loud shout, Strongbow bounded forward into the midst of the group with axe in hand.

A hand-to-hand fight ensued.

The enemy were superior in point of numbers, but the others were fighting for life and liberty.

They were self-possessed, too, while the attacking party had not recovered from the confusion caused by the sudden death of two of their party, and the consequent defeat of their plans.

"I guess you got it, old hoss!" exclaimed Hiram Swift, as he plunged his knife to the hilt in the throat of his adversary.

At the same moment Big Elk's hatchet crashed through the brain of a second warrior.

The Delaware uttered his war-cry, then stooping down, swiftly passed the point of his knife round the crown of his adversary's head, and with a second shout, brandished the blood-dripping scalp high in the air.

The Boy Chief was combating with a tall, powerful warrior, armed with knife and war club, to which weapons Strongbow could only oppose his axe.

The Indian aimed a fearful blow at his head, which would certainly have killed him had not young Armstrong parried it with his axe.

The ponderous wooden weapon snapped in two beneath the weight of the blow.

In returning the blow Strongbow's axe was caught by the haft in the Indian's hand, and, after a brief struggle, wrested from his grasp.

Victory seemed to be with the Indian, who still retained his knife.

He leaped forward to plunge it into the boy's heart, but the nimble lad jumped aside, and, with a sudden motion of his foot, well known to all north-country wrestlers, laid the Indian on his face.

Strongbow then threw himself upon the body of his enemy and endeavoured to disarm him.

The Indian resisted, and struggled violently, while the brave young Briton as gallantly maintained his grasp.

For fully five minutes they wrestled thus, then fickle fortune once more seemed to favour the red-skin warrior; he was uppermost, and he still retained his knife.

His knee was upon Strongbow's breast, but the lad gamely clutched the warrior's right wrist, while with the other hand he exerted a fierce pressure on the red-skin's throat.

For at least three minutes, which, to Strongbow, seemed as many hours, they kept these positions, the Indian trying to free his armed hand, and Strongbow as resolutely trying to prevent him from so doing.

Each felt his strength gradually relaxing; so intense was the strain on the muscles, as, with glaring eyeballs, they gazed in each other's face.

Hiram Swift and Big Elk cast approving glances at the young chief, as they stoutly fought with the three remaining enemies.

They hoped and prayed that he might conquer, but the result was doubtful.

At length, by a sudden jerk, the Indian freed his right hand.

The long, keen, glittering knife was brandished high in air, then the Indian drew his hand across his eyes to clear his sight for the fatal blow.

"Ugh!" he cried, and the blade descended.

With a fearful blow from his tomahawk, Big Elk dashed two of his foes to the ground, and, without waiting for their scalps, rushed to the side of the young chief.

But, to the intense surprise of the Delaware, he saw Strongbow roll the body of the Indian aside and rise to his feet.

The brave boy had literally choked his red-skin adversary, and the Indian's knife was seen buried to the haft in the turf, not six inches from the spot where the Boy Chief of the Delawares had lain.

"Hurrah; we've licked 'em! I say, Big Elk, this has been a tallish fight, and a pretty considerable caution to slow dogs. Wagh! how our young chief fought!" cried Swift.

"Strongbow is a brave warrior; he will take many scalps," replied the Delaware warrior, gravely, as he returned to the bodies of those he had slain, to remove from their heads the trophies of victory.

"Well, scalpin' may be all right accordin' to your notions, but this child don't convene to it in any shape."

In this respect Hiram Swift differed from many hunters, who are quite as fond of scalps as Indians themselves; and when we are told that the American authorities on the Indian frontiers have offered rewards for scalps, we can hardly wonder that it should be so.

Again sounds were heard in the wood.

First was heard the howl of a wolf, then the hoot of an owl.

Big Elk put his hands to his mouth, and imitated the sounds.

"It's the party we sent across the river," said Hiram Swift, in explanation; "they are coming back."

He was right; in a few minutes the eight Delawares walked up to the scene as silently as so many copper-coloured ghosts.

"Ugh!" they exclaimed, in guttural tones, as they looked upon the traces of the combat, but no other symptom of surprise escaped them.

The leader of the band then explained the result of their exploring expedition, which Hiram Swift translated for the benefit of the Boy Chief.

As is already known, they swam across the river, and landed some distance beyond the spot where the strange fire was burning.

With all the silence and caution of their race, they crawled towards the spot which they designed to explore, moving like snakes or tigers through the trees and brushwood.

At length they were within twenty yards of the spot, and were surprised to find no one near the fire.

This convinced them that a trap had been set for them, and their care was redoubled.

They resolved to make the circuit of the fire, and had gone nearly round when they came upon the bodies of two dead Indians, who had apparently been guarding some prisoners, for close by they discovered some thongs of hide and green withes, which had evidently been used to fetter human limbs.

But it was too dark to see whither the fugitives had fled.

Farther on they came upon an opening amongst the trees where there was more light, and across this opening was a very legible trail made by a party of Indians. It was a very recent trail, as was evident by the evening dew being brushed from the grass, and the spies determined to follow it.

It led down to the river.

The Delawares then swam back to their own side, landing half a mile below their own camp.

They resolved to keep by the bank of the stream on their return, but still observed every caution.

They had not made more than a hundred yards' progress when they again struck the trail they had seen the other side, and at the same time heard the sounds of combat. Not knowing how many their enemies might be, they were compelled to continue their cautious movements, nor did they arrive at their own camp until the conclusion of the combat.

While they were away, the party that they were sent to reconnoitre had made an attack upon their own camp.

"But what has become of the three scouts?" asked Strongbow.

A search was made, and the three Delawares were found at their respective stations, killed and scalped.

It was evident that the camp had been carefully surrounded, and the sentinels killed before the attack took place.

"These are Shawnees," said Swift, addressing the Indians. "What tribe were their prisoners?"

"The night was dark, the trail was nearly hidden from Little Eagle's eyes; but he believes *that the prisoners of the Shawnee dogs were pale-faces!*"

## CHAPTER XV.

### AN INDIAN PARLIAMENT.

IT is now high time that we followed the footsteps of the father and mother of our hero in their perilous flight after their escape from Black Hand and his murderous band.

The four Indians, whose home was apparently in the cave where the emigrant and his wife had taken refuge, halted as soon as they perceived the pale-faces.

Arrows were instantly fitted to their bowstrings, and directed towards Armstrong and his wife.

On perceiving these hostile demonstrations, the brave Briton drew his revolver, and prepared to make the best resistance he could.

The Indians continued to advance in a threatening manner, with bows bent and tomahawks slung to their wrists.

Armstrong raised his pistol and drew the trigger.

But, alas! he had forgotten that the charge had been thoroughly soaked in the river.

The weapon was useless!

He drew the trigger, but there was no explosion, and, with a half-muttered imprecation, he hurled the useless pistol away amongst the brushwood.

The Indians also saw their advantage, and, ere he could release the axe from the fastenings of his belt, were upon him.

Their object seemed to make prisoners of the pale-faces, rather than to take scalps.

The emigrant resisted, and that most violently.

He had seen too much of Indian cruelty to wish to fall into the hands of any of the race. He freed himself from the grasp of the one only to find himself in the clutches of the others, who held, or endeavoured to hold, his limbs.

The poor, faithful, loving wife was so overcome with the fatigue of her long and dangerous journey, that she could do nothing to aid her husband beyond supplicating the powers of Heaven for assistance.

But Providence seemed to frown on them, as ofttimes is the case with those intended for ultimate favours.

They had again to feel all the hardships of bitter disappointment.

Their trials had already been great—they were to be still greater.

They were to learn that hope is ofttimes dashed to pieces when danger is least expected.

The Indians were slowly, but surely, gaining the upper hand.

Armstrong was on the ground, his enemies on him.

Very quickly they secured his limbs, and bound him with the hide thongs which serve the dwellers in the woods and on the prairies instead of hempen ropes.

Mrs. Armstrong was then secured.

She made no attempt to escape when she saw her husband a captive.

In life or death she had no wish to be parted from him.

The Indians removed their captives to the interior of the cavern, and placing them at the extreme end of it, began to make preparations for a meal.

It was evident that they had been hunting and were returning with their meat, when they saw the pale-faced intruders in their cave.

They now returned to the spot where they had thrown down their venison, and brought it into the cavern.

A fire was made in a corner, which prevented its light from being seen outside, and the feast commenced.

Armstrong could not help envying them as he saw huge slices of meat disappear down the throats of his captors.

In spite of his position and uncertain fate he felt the pangs of hunger; and above all, he knew that his gentle wife must be faint from want of food.

He resolved to make an effort to gain some.

"Have you no meat for us?" he asked.

The Indians looked at him inquiringly.

Not one of the party understood a word of the English language.

Armstrong noted their silence, and at once attributed it to the right cause.

He resolved to make them understand though.

He began to move his jaws, as though in the act of mastication, nodding towards his wife occasionally, to show that he intended her to share with him.

"Ugh!" ejaculated the Indians, as they leisurely continued their meal.

"They intend to starve us," said Mrs. Armstrong. "What a fearful fate!"

"Not so, dearest. That would bring them no glory."

"How so; what do you mean, Edmund?"

"Our scalps, the much coveted trophies, would then be wasted, for no Indian would dare show a scalp unless he struck down the victim with his own hand."

And this is so.

The untutored Indian delights in keeping memorials of his successful actions; but then he cannot write, neither can he cast medals with which to decorate his breast.

So to prove that he has fought like a man, he takes from the head of each enemy slain by his own hand, the hair from the top of the head, and with these does he decorate his neck, his waist, and his legs.

The scalps are his medals, and the more medals he can show, the more honour is shown to him.

Some food was brought ere Armstrong and his wife could say much more.

The Indians could hear them talking, and feared lest some scheme for escaping should be arranged.

The two captives devoured it thankfully.

Mrs. Armstrong, whose hands were unbound, fed her husband.

The captives had scarcely finished their meal, when five or six other Indians stalked in, bringing with them a plentiful supply of deer-meat.

Few words passed between those who had captured Armstrong and the new-comers, who seemed to understand at a glance what had taken place.

Another supper was the consequence, those who had already eaten sufficient taking another steak, we presume, "for company's sake."

Even the second supper, however, had an end at length; then the fire was replenished, and the Indians seated themselves in a circle around it.

Tomahawk pipes were filled and lighted, and the warriors, evidently in a humour for speech-making, began to look at each other.

"They will soon decide our fate," whispered Armstrong. "Would to Heaven I knew a little of their language."

"We shall know soon enough, dear husband. Let us prepare."

Silently they prayed, while a tall warrior rose, laid down his pipe, and thus spoke—

"I am Great Eagle, of the Shawnees. I am a great chief; my enemies cannot breathe when they hear my name; my eye entrances them even as the eye of the snake which carries music in its tail. Great Eagle is brave, and can slay hosts of his enemies, but he cannot count the scalps which blacken in his wigwam, by the side of the lake with the reedy banks. He is chief of the Shawnees, whose hunting-grounds reach from the rising to the setting sun, and whose young men are swifter than the forked arrows of the Manitou, and more in number than stars. They are more subtle than the snake which glides through the grass, and stronger than the oak which will not bow before the great wind. They are like the great fire which runs over the prairie; they destroy everything in their path."

"Ugh! it is good!" said his auditors, puffing great clouds of smoke from their lips.

The modest speaker prepared to continue his oration—

"The pale-faces came to the land of the Shawnees, and they brought with them the cowardly Crows and the Delaware squaws, whose scalps shall, ere long, hang in the wigwam of Great Eagle. The pale-faces kill the game, take the hunting-grounds, destroy the Shawnee warriors with their fire-bows, and speak lies. They say they bring the pipe of peace, but the hatchet is in their hands; it is painted with the blood of my young men."

"Ugh!" exclaimed the dusky listeners.

"But Great Eagle is a brave; his young men are braves. They will sweep away the pale-faces, and the Crows, and the Delawares, as the great streams sweep away the beaver lodges, or as the storm roots up the trees of the forest. The pale-faces shall be forgotten, and their scalps shall wither to dust in the lodges of the Shawnees!"

With these words the speaker sat down, and another warrior arose.

This was a shorter, stouter Indian, with less of forest dignity about him than the other.

He had a watery eye, and a swollen, copper-coloured nose.

The reason will, perhaps be shown in his oration.

"The Shawnee nation is great," said he, "and so are their hunting-grounds. They have much land, and can afford to give unto the pale-faces, who will give in return firebows, powder, lead, knives, and much fire-water. Face of Fire has been amongst the lodges of the pale-faces, and he knows that the rum and whiskyla of the white men is good.

"Let the Shawnees, then, be friendly with the pale-faces, that we may have powder, lead, knives, and much fire-water to comfort our hearts. I have spoken."

The usual response, "Ugh!" followed.

Two or three other warriors expressed their opinions, and then the chief prepared to take the votes of the company.

He took a long, flat piece of wood, on one edge of which he cut a notch.

Those who wished the pale-faces to die were to cut notches the same side, while those who preferred fire-water were to cut notches on the other edge.

When the stick had been round the circle there were only three notches on the side of mercy.

The captives, of course, were not able to understand the speeches that had been made; but when Armstrong saw the stick going round the circle, and the notches cut in its side, he shrewdly guessed the meaning of the ceremony.

He knew that the president was taking the votes of the company.

He could also guess, from the voice and gestures of Great Eagle, that *he* wished for bloodshed, and when he saw the number of notches on that chief's side of the stick, hope died within his heart.

Armstrong, however, little knew what a staunch friend the pale-faces had in the person of the weak-eyed warrior, who loved the white man's rum and whisky.

Fiery Face was not disposed to give up his dreams of fire-water without another effort.

He rose once more.

"I have seen that my brothers desire the scalps of the pale-face; but do they act wisely? Why do not my brothers take these to their people that they may have instead many fire-bows and much powder, with which to destroy *all* the pale-faces?"

These words produced a visible sensation; each warrior was anxious to possess one of those marvellous fire-bows, of which they had all heard, and the dire effects of which some of them had witnessed.

Fiery Face saw the advantage he had gained, and at once followed it up.

"Let the lives of the pale-faces be in their bodies to-night; to-morrow's sun will bring wisdom to my brothers, and we shall have many fire-bows."

After a short discussion this was agreed to.

## CHAPTER XVI.

### THE DESERTED CAMP.

WHEN Strongbow heard the Delaware give his opinion that the prisoners who had escaped from their enemies were pale-faces, he was all impatience to start at once after them.

He hoped they might be his lost parents; but. at all events, if they were white, that would be sufficient reason for helping them.

But in this he was overruled by Hiram Swift and Big Elk, both of whom asserted that there was not sufficient light, and that, as they were all in need of rest, the trail would be more easily followed in the morning.

In Strongbow's opinion it was a loss of time, but he was obliged to acquiesce.

He resolved, however, that if they were not up early in the morning it should not be for want of rousing.

The Boy Chief felt too excited to sleep, and, when he did close his eyes, it was only to wake again in a few minutes with an ardent wish that the sun would rise.

At length, to his great delight, the first token of returning light was seen.

A grey tinge in the eastern sky and a freshness in the morning air, proclaimed that nature was beginning to rouse herself after rest and darkness.

Lighter and lighter grew the grey streak, broader and broader its expanse.

Strongbow shook the old hunter by the shoulder.

" What, in the name o' thunder, is the matter?" asked Swift, suddenly sitting up.

" It is getting light ; let us be off."

" You are right, lad.  I'll call up the Ingins."

In a very few moments all the band were aroused.

There was no time for eating; they wished to visit the camp on the other side of the river before it should get thoroughly light, so as to surprise any enemies who might remain.

Without a moment's loss of time they proceeded to the river bank, constructed a kind of raft, as before, for their weapons, and commenced their way across.

The water felt very cold as Strongbow stepped in, but now that he was an Indian chief he scorned to betray the discomfort he felt.

Hiram Swift and Big Elk, both of whom were splendid swimmers, kept close to our young hero to render him assistance if necessary.

But it was not necessary.

As a schoolboy our young chief had been an adept in all sports; he could swim almost as well as any one of the party.

He found no difficulty in keeping up with the Indians, and had it been a race, he could have distanced many of them.

The opposite shore was reached.

All dripping wet they took their arms; the hunter carefully examining his rifle and powder-flask to see that no damage had been done.

Then right into the wood they walked, slowly, noiselessly, as so many ghosts stalking back to their tombs in the grey light of early morning.

The spot was reached ; but it was evident that the camp had not been revisited, for the fire had died out, and the bodies of the two dead Indians were found close by the tree where the prisoners had been bound.

But the corpses had been disturbed, and, as Strongbow came in sight, he saw who were the disturbers.

Two large brown wolves were growling and snarling over their human repast, apparently so busy that they did not notice the approach of human beings.

The sight was sickening; but in a moment the young chief sent an arrow at them which transfixed the pair.

In their death agonies each wolf seemed to accuse the other of treachery, and, while shaking each other's throats, they died.

The young chief would have had the mangled bodies of the Indians interred, but his warriors felt no inclination to perform such an act, which they considered folly.

" Come along, lad, afore the trail gets cold, or wiped out; thar's no knowin' what mout happen," said Hiram Swift.

The spot was then carefully examined by both Indians and pale-faced hunters, all of whom came to the same conclusion, namely, that the Shawnees had left their prisoners, bound, in charge of sentinels; that the sentinels must have fallen asleep; that the prisoners must have had a knife, with which to cut their bonds, and then to kill their guards.

Finally, it was decided that two prisoners had been there—a man and a woman.

All this was decided from the various marks and tracks upon the ground, to the great astonishment of Strongbow, who was beginning to form a better opinion of the Delawares than at first.

The trail of the escaped prisoners led them direct to the camp-fire, and then ceased.

At least so the Indians thought, and so at first did Hiram Swift.

But the old hunter, who had followed so many different trails in his lifetime, was not going to allow himself to be beaten.

"The feller hev hid his trail, I guess; but if this child don't find it, I expect I may be sent back on a rail to Boston city. Hiram Swift is the boy, I guess."

He walked in a circle round the fire, looking for the least sign.

When he came again to the tracks he halted, and examined them narrowly.

"Now lookee hyar; you've got eyes in your head. D'ye see them tracks?"

"Yes," replied Strongbow.

"Now. what d'ye notice about 'em?"

"Nothing."

"Don't ye think he must hev been a tarnation heavy man to sink his tracks in that depth?"

"Yes."

"Well, the ground warn't very wet last night, a fact which makes me suggestionate that they must ha' walked up to the fire, and then back again in the same tracks. This track is deeper here at the toe than at any other part."

Back they all went to the tree where the captives had been bound.

There the trail apparently commenced and ended, but on looking behind the trunk Hiram Swift discovered a second though lighter trail, leading in a directly opposite direction. This was evidently the true trail of the fugitives, and Strongbow at once prepared to follow it.

"Wait for yer hoss, lad," exclaimed the hunter, in tones of reproof.

"But while we are waiting they are going on."

"And we, when on horseback, can follow twice as quick as on foot. Here they come; you won't have to wait five minutes."

The old hunter spoke truly.

The shrill screaming magpie which Strongbow had heard was the signal made by Big Elk to the Indians who had remained with the horses to bring those useful animals across the river.

It was a fine sight to see the half wild steeds plunge one after another into the river, guided by the voices and long lances of their guards.

At length they all stood neighing and shaking themselves upon the opposite bank, and were quickly claimed by their respective owners.

## CHAPTER XVII.

### A PECULIAR SITUATION.

AGAIN there was hope in the heart of our young hero.

A hero is one who possesses natural nobility of character, who is at the same time brave before enemies, and gentle in the presence of distress.

A true hero will always love his country and his parents far above all other earthly objects; therefore, when we call Strongbow our hero, we do so with good reason.

For if ever son loved his parents with a fervent, devoted love, the son of Edmund Armstrong did.

When first he was struck down by Black Hand's ruthless murderers in the attack upon the hut, his chief thought was for their safety.

When he himself was a prisoner, he lamented for those parents whom he already fancied dead; when he was rescued, his first thought was to ascertain their fate; when he found they had escaped, he instantly started to their help; and now when he found himself so near them as he must be, should the trail prove theirs (and of this he had no doubt), his heart seemed filled with joy at the thought that the darling wish of his soul must be so nearly accomplished.

He had been early taught to obey that precept, "Honour thy father and thy mother."

If any of our readers have a soldier or a sailor brother whose long silence has caused the household to mourn for the absent one as dead, and there came a letter announcing the return of the lost one, they can imagine from the joy they experienced, the blissful sensations which filled the heart of Strongbow.

If ever youth loved sweet maiden, and fondly waited for the hour when he could make her his bride, and there came to his ear false reports of a successful rival who had basely won the love he deemed all his own, that youth must have felt the deepest, blackest of despair.

But, oh! the almost painful bliss of the sudden transition from grief to joy, when he finds rumour a liar, and once more presses the fair one's hand in his.

Strongbow so loved his father and mother; felt such sorrow when he was parted from them; experienced such blissful joy when he deemed their reunion certain.

Along the trail they rode, as swiftly as they could through the trees and brushwood of the forest.

Sometimes it was very difficult to detect the track of the fugitives, and then the best woodcraft was exhibited by Hiram Swift and the Indians.

By attending to them, he soon learnt to tell when a twig had been crushed beneath human foot, or a pebble or a dried leaf displaced. Nor was this all.

He was taught how to distinguish between the track of a deer and that of the wild hog, and to know the footprint of the wild turkey in the wood from that of the crane by the river bank.

As they travelled on, the ground became more rugged, and consequently rather more difficult to trace the fugitives upon.

At length Hiram Swift, who led, came to a halt.

"We must just beat along each side little; the trail ends here, though they must ha' gone on unless the airth swallered 'em."

The Indians accordingly spread themselves out on each side, and, after a short search, again discovered the trail, which had been retraced in the manner before described.

Once more they continued their journey, though very slowly indeed, so uneven and thickly wooded was the ground.

They could have proceeded faster on foot, but Swift would on no account abandon the horses.

Steeds were not so easily procured in the wood as on the great prairies southward, and should they once more meet open ground, the animals would be invaluable.

About two hours before sunset, the trail was once more obliterated.

"We had better camp hyar, and go on in the morning," said Swift.

Strongbow had by this time learned to place implicit confidence in Hiram Swift.

So, when the hunter said, "We had better camp here," Strongbow at once agreed to do so.

The camp was soon formed, the fire lighted, and the usual supper of meat cooked.

Our prairie men are great eaters of meat; they cannot always procure bread.

The meat they eat makes them strong and hearty, and our hero began to find the difference between life in England and life in the woods of America.

A hearty supper, succeeded by a sound sleep, refreshed them all most amazingly.

Yet, so strong was the excitement in the heart of our young hero, that he was awake in the morning long before any of his red-skin friends.

He arose when they were all sleeping.

The gobble of the wild turkey was heard in the woods, and, taking his bow and arrows in his hand, the young chief of the Delawares started forth, having in view the double object of finding the trail, and shooting one of the wild "gobblers," whose notes resounded all around.

He proceeded towards the spot where one of the noisy birds was sounding its call.

He little dreamed that the loud noise denoted treachery.

"INSTINCTIVELY HE SENT AN ARROW TO THE HEART OF THE FOREMOST INDIAN."

Our young chief had learnt sufficient to know that the utmost caution was requisite, so he proceeded as quietly as possible.

After creeping along for some distance, he came upon an open ground, where he could see the noble bird strutting about.

But in a moment the gobble ceased, and with a loud noise the turkey winged its flight away into the woods.

Strongbow watched the direction it took, and resolved to follow, the more so that its note was again heard.

He pushed forward, and soon came to a small brook, on the opposite side of which was the turkey.

The stream looked deep and cold, so that Strongbow felt very little inclination to wet his body again.

He resolved to walk a little way up the brook, to find a place where it was fordable.

A fallen tree which lay right across the brook offered a method of crossing.

Sure and swift of foot, Strongbow darted over, hoping to find his game on the other side.

In this he was disappointed; but instead thereof he found in the soft ground on the further side of the brook several footsteps, evidently made by Indians wearing mocassins.

The tracks looked fresh enough, and there could be no doubt that they had been made recently.

Strongbow resolved to discover if possible where these Indians were hidden, and to discover any other particulars he could.

The tracks all bore in the same direction, and in that direction no doubt was the camp of strangers.

He followed the track, and, at length, came to a thick grove of cane, from the midst of which arose a thin column of blue smoke.

There was a trail which led into the midst of the cane-brake.

"I will not follow this trail," thought Strongbow; "no doubt they have a scout posted to give the alarm if anyone should approach."

So to work he set to force his way through the reeds and canes by another path.

This was no easy task, as the gigantic canes were, in some places, thirty-five or forty feet in height, and as big as his arm.

Many a black snake did he send hissing away; more than one lynx or wild cat ran off hissing and setting up its back like an angry cat.

With the greatest caution and silence he worked his way through the thicket, until he could hear the sounds of voices.

Then he halted and listened.

The language in which the voices spoke was to him unknown, nor could he see the speakers.

He resolved to move forward.

As he was doing so he came suddenly upon the body of a great black bear, which was curled up in its lair.

Strongbow started back, and the bear started up.

The young chief would have sent an arrow at the beast, but the canes grew around him so closely that he could scarcely move his limbs.

The bear, however, showed no disposition to attack him, nor do they often so unless very much pressed.

But the noise he made in crashing through the canes, aroused the Indians, who at once rushed into the thicket in pursuit of the beast.

By accident, however, they hit upon the trail of Strongbow instead of that of the bear, and comprehending at once that a white man had been there, they abandoned the bear for the human being.

Strongbow had a good start, however, and being less in size than his pursuers, made his way through the canes with more ease than his adversaries.

Adversaries he knew they must be, or they would not pursue him with weapons in hand.

He thought of sending an arrow back at them, but on preparing to do so, he found, to his great disgust, that the string was broken.

It had been cut by a sharp, broken cane, or something of that sort.

He had no weapon except his knife.

He had therefore to trust to his legs, for it was useless to attempt to cope with four or five well-armed savages.

He kept on till he came to the tree over which he had passed.

As he reached it he looked back.

Two Indians, armed with long spears, were close behind, and on he rushed.

Ere he had got one third part of the way across, a huge panther appeared at the opposite side, and prepared to contest the passage with him.

Strongbow quickly raised his knife, and the Indians behind raised their lances. There was a short, sharp growl, and then, with a loud splash, the youth and the panther fell into the stream together.

## CHAPTER XVIII.

### FUN AND FIGHTING, IN AMERICAN STYLE.

WITH a little difficulty, and a great deal of diplomacy, our old acquaintance, D. Jackson, Esq., procured the services of the *good men* required by the master villain, Wylde.

Those he had met in the hotel where we last left him proved to be rascals one and all, so that, having opened negotiations with one of the party, it was very easy to gain over the others.

At the appointed place, on the appointed day, came Wylde, anxious and careworn.

The double disappointments— the escape of both Armstrong and his son—had considerably soured his temper, and the long dangerous journey he had made alone through the forests had not, by any means, tended to restore him to his usual mood.

His first proceeding, on arriving at the hotel, was to rate Jackson in a furious manner for not keeping the men separate.

"You fool! Having entrusted the secret to each one of these men, how can you hope for secrecy?"

"What secret?" demanded the land agent.

"The secret of our expedition."

"Well, as you didn't tell me much about it, I couldn't tell them. D'ye see?"

"Hum! Well, how much did you tell them?"

"Only that they are going west to a place where their rifles and knives are wanted."

"Good. I have failed, as I told you."

"I know."

"A second failure would render me a marked man in the south-west."

"I guess we won't fail, cap."

"Then have the men ready to start to-morrow morning, and meet me here in half-an-hour's time. Go at once, and tell them to be ready."

Jackson departed.

During his absence, Wylde walked up and down the room with hurried, irregular strides.

His cheeks were flushed, his eye had an angry look—in fact, his appearance was that of a man prepared to run any risks to attain the object he had in view.

"My usual ill-luck has followed me hither," he murmured. "Why did Providence—if there be any Providence—place me in this position? Here am I, an outcast from English society, merely because my mother was the daughter—the eldest child—of Thomas Armstrong. My mother was the first-born. The property should have been mine, for did he not surrender his birthright when I won this ring from the finger of the legal heir of the house of Armstrong? Mine is the power—mine should have been the wealth; but, fool-like, *he* has ruined himself, and now nothing remains for me but revenge!"

Revenge — that great lever which moves with irresistible strength the human character—was working in his mind.

At length Jackson returned.

A single glance revealed to him the fact that his employer and patron was in no very easy state of mind.

But Jackson was well used to Wylde's strange moods, and said nothing, beyond a mere intimation that his band of desperadoes would be ready an hour after sunrise in the morning.

Wylde was silent for a few minutes.

At length he said, in a low tone—

"Jackson, we must raise some money."

"Whew!" whistled the agent.

" It must be done; I have very little."

" You might turn me up and shake me a good time before you could shake a hundred dollars out of me," said the agent.

" What have you done with the cash I gave you?" asked Wylde.

Jackson made a pantomimic representation of shuffling and dealing a pack of cards.

" Been sporting?"

" Yes," replied Jackson.

" So have I, and confoundedly unfortunate I have been."

Then there was another long pause.

Wylde was the first to break the silence by saying, in his usual low, distinct tones—

" We must seek the money where we lost it !"

" Ah !"

" There is no other way.  Come."

The two men rose from their seats, and walked from the hotel.

The sun had set, and far away from the noisy city twilight was rapidly deepening into night.

But there the brilliant lamps in the shops and streets seemed to outvie the brightness of the sun, and set sable darkness at defiance.

The two men walked along arm-in-arm down three or four quiet streets, till they came to one in which were a couple of large houses brilliantly illuminated. From each issued a stream of light; from each proceeded strains of wild melody.

Passengers hesitated, as though doubtful as to which house possessed the greater charm.

Jackson and Wylde hesitated, though not for any length of time.

Their doubts were soon overcome; their feet had soon crossed the threshold of the largest building; and the next moment they found themselves in the midst of a hall, which would have astonished anyone not used to such scenes.

There was a vast saloon, the ceiling of which was supported by two rows of lacquered columns, and lighted up by a profusion of lamps, which rendered it as light as day.

The walls were adorned with voluptuous pictures, designed, together with the music, to attract loungers, who were pretty sure to yield to the seductions of the gaming-table eventually.

These tables were scattered about the room, with ample space between them to allow a number of men to sit or stand round them without inconvenience to those who wished to walk up and down.

One side of the room was furnished with a long counter, at which a beautiful, splendidly-dressed girl, retailed tea, coffee, or chocolate, to those who liked such beverages; while, at the opposite side, was a similar counter for wines and spirits, presided over by a smart youth of about twenty years of age.

The general company comprised members of Congress and of the detective force, rogues escaped from northern prisons, students from colleges, pickpockets, professors of divinity, English tourists, American trappers from the backwoods; professional gamblers, whose lives were passed in shuffling; merchants, who should have been dealing other wares, and rich young greenhorns from Southern plantations, who expected, or rather calculated to win everything upon the table.

Wylde made his way to one of the tables, followed by Jackson.

The seats were all full, and the worthy pair were compelled to stand by and look on.

There was a youth there—a mere boy of sixteen—who appeared to have lost heavily.  A tall, slender youth was he, with features that would have been beautifully child-like, had it not been for the glittering, sunken eye, and the sternly compressed lip.

The banker of the gambling establishment was raking up some packets of dollars the foolish boy had staked.

" Do you play again?" asked the man.

" Yes, fifty dollars on the queen, and fifty on the deuce."

As he spoke the lad drew two packets of money from his coat-pocket, and placed them upon the table before him, covering his eyes with his hands for a moment, while the cards were being dealt, to conceal his agitation.

Jackson saw his inattention, and made a slight movement.

When the youth looked up to see if he had won, the money was gone, and, at the same time, the voice of the professional gambler was heard, proclaiming that he had lost.

"Robbed! lost!" muttered the youth. "My money was on the table."

"I have not received it," replied the gambler.

"Who has done this?" asked the youth, fiercely, and turning round, he fixed his deep eyes full on Wylde's face.

"Come, sir," said the latter, "if you do not play any more, make room for others."

"I shall stay here just as long as I please," was the reply.

"Pray make room, sir," echoed the gambler, "our table is crowded, you see. If you don't play, be kind enough to pay and go."

"I have been robbed—shamefully and meanly robbed!" continued the youth, fixing his angry glance on Wylde.

"Well, don't stare at me in that way, if you please," replied the other, coolly.

"I stare at whom I like. If you don't like it, you may look the other way."

"Insolence! Come, make room, you young scoundrel, will you?"

And seizing the boy in his grasp, Wylde lifted him from the chair, and threw him behind him on the floor.

"Take care! take care!" shouted several; and at the same time a dozen hands were outstretched to strike up the revolver which the insulted youth pointed at his assailant.

A bullet shattered the large mirror on the wall, and sent the fragments flying upon the heads of those beneath; while a second, aimed more truly, passed through Wylde's shoulder.

Instantly the latter drew his pistol, sent a bullet through the throat of his youthful adversary, and then fell upon the floor bathed in his own blood.

"Let me see him! let me see him!" cried Jackson, pushing towards Wylde. "He is my cousin!"

He pushed his way to the side of his companion, and knelt down by his side under pretence of staunching his wound, carefully keeping everyone else back.

The commotion was at its height when the police entered.

"What means this?" asked the head of that body.

"This lad drew upon the stranger here when his back was turned; but I guess he's been fairly wiped out," replied a bystander.

The police put several questions to the spectators, and being satisfied in their own minds that the *wiping out* had been done fairly, threw a handkerchief over the face of the dead boy preparatory to carrying him off to his home.

Wylde was then carefully borne home to his hotel, under the direction of Jackson and a surgeon.

His wounds were dressed, he was laid in bed, and a sleeping draught administered.

When he awoke in the morning his first thought was to ask for Jackson.

To his great surprise, he was informed that the worthy land agent had left the hotel shortly after midnight, and had not since been seen.

He raised his hand to push back the hair from his forehead, but almost started from his bed with surprise as he missed the diamond ring which usually adorned his finger.

*It was gone!*

But who could have taken it?

There was only one man who could have done so, he thought; that man was Jackson.

"He has the ring," he muttered. "What an ass I was to tell him that the ring had any value beyond its intrinsic worth as a gem. But I will have it back, and I will have revenge; revenge on Armstrong, revenge on Jackson."

## CHAPTER XIX.

### UNDER THE STREAM.

DOWN, down beneath the deep waters of the narrow creek went Strongbow and his adversary, the fierce panther of the American woods.

Our hero felt the teeth and claws of the savage beast as they struggled together under the surface of the stream, and with all the ferocity of one fighting for life, he struck his knife repeatedly beneath the animal's ribs.

At length the blows began to take effect—the huge creature loosed its hold, and, belly upwards, floated up to the top of the blood-stained water.

Four minutes, at least, had Strongbow been under with his antagonist, and his first thought was to rise to breathe.

Up like a cork—for he was a splendid swimmer—till his head shot above the surface of the water and he found himself in almost total darkness.

What little light remained showed him that there was solid rock around him on every side, and above him. The only light which penetrated that gloomy spot came from the entrance, which was beneath the surface of the deep, sluggish brook.

The crystal points of the moist stone wall glistened like diamonds all over the arch, which was almost as regular as if formed by man's hands. In some places festoons of long aquatic plants dangled from the ceiling, draping those parts which were blessed with more light and more earth than the others.

Opposite the entrance there was a sloping shelf of rock, forming a kind of seat. Two strokes brought him to this, and seating himself, he proceeded to examine as well as possible the wounds made by the teeth and claws of the panther.

They were deep, and might possibly be dangerous; but by tearing up his garments, he managed to bandage them in a rude way so as to stay the flow of blood.

Then he began to think of departing.

A thought struck him.

The hostile Indians had seen him fall into the stream with the panther. Seeing, as they must, the dead body of the beast, they would naturally suppose that he had escaped, and would therefore search and watch along the bank of the stream. Such a search would not be readily given up. He must stop there for a time, and take his departure when they had given up the search.

Accordingly, he sat down again, shivering with cold, in his dripping clothes, and endeavoured to pass the time as well as he could.

His cave was about twenty feet long by ten broad, the top of the vault being about six feet high. Half of what should have been the floor was covered with water, the other half was hard rock covered with a light dust.

"If this should be the den of some beast of prey, an alligator, for instance, how should I fare then?" thought the brave boy, as he glanced round; and brave as he was, he silently hoped that it might not be as he thought.

There could be no way to escape except by a fight. If attacked there he must kill his foe or be killed, and as he sometimes saw the reflections of dark objects as they floated over the subaqueous mouth of the cavern, he clutched his knife firmly, resolved to fight, and die, if necessary, like a true Briton.

Occasionally, too, he heard noises overhead, as if people were walking to and fro over the roof of the cave. These he imagined to be the Indians searching for him, and he was right.

He could hardly help laughing though, at the intense astonishment the red-skins must feel at his sudden and mysterious disappearance.

They were astonished, too, for the two foremost had seen him struggling with the panther, and had seen the body of that animal rise to the surface of the water. Of course they expected him to follow, and were intensely surprised when, after searching and watching along both banks of the river, they could find not the slightest trace of any spot where the pale-face youth had landed.

Various opinions were given, but at length they all came to the same conclusion, namely, that our hero was a *devil*, an evil spirit, and once impressed with this belief, they lost no time in hastening back to their own encampment.

Strongbow remained nearly two hours in the cave before he dared to venture forth.

Then, when all was quiet, he stepped into the water, dived down through the mouth of the cavern, and rose in the centre of the stream.

He crossed over to the side from which the pursuing Indians had come, and managed to decipher from the tracks that they had returned to their own camp.

But he himself began to grow faint, and he felt that no time should be lost in returning to Hiram Swift and the Delawares.

His wounds were growing stiff and painful.

His body was cold, while his brow seemed burning.

Strongbow was a youth of robust constitution, but even he was unable to bear every hardship.

As he rolled, rather than walked along the track which led to the camp of his friends, he wished himself, for the time, at home in England, with a kind mother to nurse him and soothe his pillow.

It was but a momentary weakness, caused by illness of body and constant anxiety.

How he managed to perform that long walk through the forest was a wonder to him; but at length he arrived in sight of the fire, which was guarded by three Indians.

Then his strength failed.

He reeled and fell insensible to the ground.

Luckily he was observed by the Delawares, who, in a few seconds, conveyed him to the camp, and placed him upon a couch of blankets and buffalo robes.

All the others, Swift included, had gone in search of the young chief, but were soon recalled by a succession of shouts.

They grouped themselves round their young chief, who remained senseless, and began to consult as to the restoratives to be used.

One of the party, who pretended to be a "medicine-man"—that is, a sort of magician—proposed to operate by means of charms, and for that purpose, drew from a bag a number of toys, such as snakes' heads and tails, owls' feathers, bats' wings, bears' claws, &c., as well as paints with which to decorate the patient's face.

He was about to proceed in his magical or surgical operation, when, luckily for Strongbow, his friend Swift appeared, and with him Big Elk, the Delaware.

This timely arrival, no doubt, saved the youth's life.

"He'll be right in a couple of weeks; what say you, Big Elk? What shall we do with him?"

"The young chief must return to the wigwams of the Delawares, and the pale-faced hunter must go with him to take care of him.

"Big Elk will choose four warriors to follow the trail with him, and will bring back tidings of those the young chief seeks."

"That's good. You know I ain't a coward, Big Elk; I guess you and I have seen a leetle tall fighting together; but somehow I don't much cotton to leaving this youngster."

And so it was arranged.

A litter was carefully prepared and covered with blankets.

Upon this conveyance, which was slung between two quiet horses, was placed the wounded young chief; but not until Hiram Swift had applied to the injuries certain herbs, with the healing properties of which he was very well acquainted.[*]

Then the procession set out on its return, headed by Hiram Swift, who kept a sharp look-out ahead, as well as to the comforts of his patient.

Big Elk and his remaining men watched until the litter was out of sight, and then without a word prepared to follow still farther the trail which had led them thus deep into the wilderness.

---

[*] The *pita* plant, a species of Bromelia, is celebrated in the forests of the South-West States for its medical properties.

# CHAPTER XX.

## FIRST LOVE.

HIRAM SWIFT was so careful of his charge that he proceeded very slowly, consequently it was several days after his fight with the panther before Strongbow arrived at the village of the Delawares.

All the inhabitants, old men, women, and children, turned out to look at the approaching procession, and all showed signs of sorrow when they were informed of the news.

The young chief was carried into the wigwam of Onotassa, Swift having informed the people of the village by means of a messenger, so that the hut was ready when they reached it for the reception of the wounded one.

A nurse was the next thing to be provided.

It was not to be expected that a great warrior and hunter like Hiram Swift would watch day and night by the bedside of his sick friend. Someone must be found to cook food, and perform other menial work.

A nurse was soon found, in the person of Water Lily, eldest daughter of Big Elk.

Water Lily was the most beautiful maiden of her tribe, and the pride of the village.

Her age was about the same as our hero, but she appeared older.

Constantly living in the forest and on the prairie had slightly tanned her cheek, yet she was not so dark as the other members of the tribe.

In person, Water Lily was tall, her shape graceful. The expression of her small mouth, dimpled chin, oval cheeks, and dark eyes, was pleasing in the extreme.

Water Lily had a mind to match her body.

Big Elk, in the course of his wanderings in early life, met a half-caste woman of great beauty, and of more than average education. But love managed to get the better of reason, and the untutored savage became the husband of the white man's daughter.

This was the mother of Water Lily.

At the time when Strongbow became chief of the Delawares, Big Elk had been a widower for about eighteen months; he had taken no second squaw to his wigwam, but devoted himself entirely to the guardianship of his daughter.

This was the beautiful girl who entered the wigwam with Hiram Swift, and after casting a shy glance at the handsome wounded white chief, on his couch of skins, began to prepare a meal for him with all the gravity of an old squaw, and perhaps with quite as much skill.

At all events, Strongbow fancied the food prepared by her taper fingers would have a better taste than if cooked by any of the wizened, wrinkled old hags with whom the camp abounded.

He enjoyed the meal, and he thanked his pretty cook for it—in English, of course, for he did not know sufficient of the Delaware language.

To his intense surprise she answered him in much more intelligible English than he had heard from the lips of any of the warriors.

"Water Lily is glad to see the young chief eat."

The boy stared with all his power, and with such intensity that the maiden was compelled to turn her head to hide her blushes.

"You speak English?" he said.

"Water Lily speaks with the tongue of the pale-faces."

"But how? Surely you have not been amongst the pale-faces?"

"The mother of Water Lily was the daughter of a pale-face."

"And she——"

"Is gone to the blessed hunting grounds."

At that moment Swift entered.

"Come, no yarning here. I'm doctor, and I won't have it."

"But I must talk," answered Strongbow.

"Not a word; keep quiet."

The old hunter was a keen observer of men as well as things.

He had noticed the glances of admiration his young friend and pupil cast upon the Indian maiden, and was resolved to put a stop to any youthful love-making that might arise from their being in each other's society.

Swift was a stoic in his way; he professed to despise the fair sex altogether; they were made, he said, for the express purpose of getting men into trouble.

But, if you asked the old hunter the reason why he professed these opinions, his eye would assume a glistening watery appearance, and his brow would contract

A philosopher would infer from such symptoms that Hiram Swift had at one time known the meaning of love, and had felt the sting of the blind god's arrows.

A boyish folly he would have called it. But, can it be folly to love well and truly, or to feel heartrending pangs of grief when hope has spread her wings, and departed for ever, when the loved one is no more?

For more than a week Strongbow was kept close in the hut, carefully attended by Swift and Water Lily in their capacities of physician and nurse.

Then he was allowed to rise and to stroll through the encampment.

But in some strange way it always happened that his feet strayed towards the hut where Water Lily resided, under the care of an old squaw whose husband had been killed in a skirmish a few months previous.

Or he would wander towards a spring, at which Water Lily was accustomed to fill the gourds which served for drinking vessels.

Many a fine opportunity did he thus have of conversing with her; though why he should seek her company was a mystery which his boyish heart could not fathom.

As yet he hardly understood the meaning of love.

One day, while strolling towards the favourite spring, he caught sight of a light robe and a fairy form glancing through the bushes before him.

He felt certain that it was Water Lily, and quickened his step.

Before he could overtake her he was startled at hearing a piercing shriek.

Forgetful of his wounds and his weakness, he rushed forward at full speed.

A sight met his eye which filled him with alarm.

There stood the fair Water Lily of the Delawares, and before her on the ground was a huge rattlesnake, with head erect, and forked tongue extended in a threatening attitude. The reptile seemed to have completely fascinated the fair girl.

Its rattle was sounding continuously, its head and neck waved backwards and forwards with unceasing motion.

The poor girl had dropped her gourd among the bushes, and seemed too much alarmed to be able to stir.

Forgetful of the fact that he himself was unarmed, the Boy Chief hurried on to the rescue.

Luckily he had his knife in his hand, but that was his only weapon.

As the snake saw him approach, its anger seemed to redouble, though its attention was drawn from the girl to the new comer.

Giving a furious rattle with its tail it sprang forward.

Strongbow leaped aside, and dealt the serpent a blow with his knife on the neck, which severed the head from the body.

A few convulsive writhes, and the enormous length of body was still.

Water Lily was saved.

She had fainted, however, from fright, and was lying senseless upon the ground.

Strongbow hastened to her, and raised her up.

"Dear Water Lily," he said, "the snake is killed; the danger is over."

"Killed?" she said, opening her eyes.

"Yes; my aim was true; it is dead."

"The Water Lily will thank the brave pale-face."

"Thank him."

"Yes. What more can Water Lily do?"

For a moment Strongbow was silent.

"Water Lily can do more," he said.

"What more?"

"She can love."

The fair girl opened her eyes wide, then blushed, and said—

"Water Lily does love the Boy Chief of the Delawares."

Strongbow passed his arm round her waist, and kissed her ruby mouth.

"Ugh!" said a deep voice.

Turning round, the young lovers beheld a Delaware warrior scowling at them in a most ferocious manner.

## CHAPTER XXI.

### ARMSTRONG'S ESCAPE.

A FORTNIGHT had elapsed since Strongbow fought the panther, and a little uneasiness was beginning to be manifested by some of the Indian women as to the fate of Big Elk and his detachment.

Water Lily, who was devotedly fond of her father, shared in these vague alarms.

As for the warriors and the hunter, they felt no alarm, nor would they if the Delawares had been absent two months instead of two weeks.

However, on the fifteenth day, the absent ones walked quietly into the camp.

Big Elk had followed the trail till it led him right into a new settlement many miles away south.

Then the Indian, who could follow with the truth of a bloodhound through the mazy forest and pathless prairie, was at fault.

The child of Nature was stopped by man's art.

He even made some inquiries at the white settlement; but the pale-faces refused to impart any information beyond that a man and woman had stayed one night in the place, and had journeyed on to a little frontier town, where they had determined to join a whole caravan of emigrants going westward.

These two wandering pale-faces were, as our hero suspected, his father and mother.

They had, as our readers have seen, escaped from Black Hand to fall into the clutches of other savages; they had been made slaves, and when their captors designed to make an onslaught upon the Delaware camp, they had been bound up to two trees under the care of two guards, to prevent them from escaping.

But when the Indians deemed them most secure they escaped.

One of the guards was of a drowsy disposition, and sat nodding with his back against the tree to which Armstrong was bound.

His knife was within reach of the white man's hand, and to seize it was the first thought which entered Armstrong's head.

He grasped it.

A moment, and he silently severed his own bonds; another second, and his wife was at liberty.

"Hide in the bushes yonder," he whispered, "I will be with you in a moment."

No thought of bloodshed had then entered his head.

The two Indians slept—he wished to despoil them of their weapons.

He removed the bow and tomahawk from the relaxed grasp of the one whose knife he had obtained, and was about to do the same with the other.

"Ugh!" exclaimed the redskin, half starting to his feet.

There was no time for hesitation; unless he acted with promptitude all would be lost.

His knife entered the red man's heart, who, with a deep groan, fell back dead.

The sound of the dying groan roused the other, who at once threw himself upon the self-liberated captive.

Armstrong was a powerful man, and at once closed with his adversary.

Over and over they rolled in a deadly embrace, each seeking to free the hand which held his knife—each seeking some vulnerable part where the other's life might be assailed.

At length Armstrong's right hand was free.

The deadly blade, ensanguined with blood, gleamed terribly as it waved a moment in the moonlight air, and then descended.

Bones and cartilage gave way beneath the force of that terrible blow, and, sheathed with the very haft in the Indian's body, the white man was compelled to exert all his strength to withdraw the blade from the wound.

Both Indians lay motionless—dead!

With the quickness of thought Armstrong collected the weapons.

One bow was snapped in two, one tomahawk hurled yards away into the midst of a dense jungle.

The other bow, with a good store of shafts from both quivers, and the best of the two tomahawks, he kept for himself.

Then he hastened to the thicket where his patient wife was hiding, holding her hands before her eyes to shut out the horrid scene which had just been enacted.

Few words passed between them—time was too precious to be wasted in long talks.

"What has happened, dearest?" asked Mrs. Armstrong.

"The Indians are dead," replied her husband. "Come away while we have time."

Tired as they were, they dashed into the forest maze, keeping before them a bright star, whose twinkling eye seemed to assure them of hope.

Oftentimes they paused, and listened to hear, if they could, any signs of their being followed.

They could hear the shouts and oaths of two conflicting parties as they battled together, and hastened on again.

All that night they walked until the sun began to shoot his rays above the tops of the forest trees, then they sought the welcome shelter of a hollow beech, in the cavity of which they sat down to rest themselves and sleep for a short time if they could.

It was a short rest though, for they were both too much excited, and too fearful of falling into the hands of enemies to remain long in their retreat.

On again, with weary feet, plodding through the forest, sitting down upon the rich turf at times to gain breath, feeding on some maize they had with them, and the raw flesh of such birds and animals as Armstrong could kill with a shot from his bow.

At night they halted, though not until darkness had completely enveloped the forest, and lay down in a sheltered nook to snatch a few hours' rest and sleep.

Up again before the stars had grown pale, or the first glimpse of dawn had shown in the sky, and on the path once more, a path that led they knew not whither.

They had crossed a piece of open land, and were just plunging into the forest once more, when on looking back they saw Indians again in pursuit of them.

The fear of being captured again, and tortured to death, lent wings to their feet, and they darted through the glades and dells of the wood with the swiftness of frightened deer.

Had they but known that their son was at the head of that band of red-skin warriors, how gladly would they have retraced their steps.

A two hours' walk through the wood took them out of sight of the Indians, who found some difficulty in following the trail — they saw nothing more of them.

Nevertheless, Armstrong and his wife kept on—the patient woman endeavouring to conceal from her husband the pain her tired, bleeding feet gave her; and he only anxious to support her, lest she should faint by the way.

They saw no more Indians, though their journey lasted some days more.

At length—oh! welcome sight, reminding them of home—they saw in the distance a low-roofed log hut, from the chimney of which ascended a thin column of blue smoke.

Towards it they directed their tottering footsteps; and never did the way seem more long and wearisome, than as they toiled across the open prairie, on which it was situated, by the side of a wide-spreading oak.

As they approached a huge dog came at them fiercely; then a woman appeared, with a rifle in her hand.

"Help us," exclaimed Armstrong. "I fear my wife is dying."

The woman called off the dog, but still kept her rifle in readiness.

"A DOUBLE DANGER."

# CHAPTER XXII.

### FRESH PLANS.

"SHELTER for my wife, I besee: you!" said Armstrong, as he bore his fainting spouse up to the door.

"Welcome as if the hut was your own," replied the woman, lowering her gun when she saw the condition of Mrs. Armstrong. "Put her on that couch, while I get her some drink."

The good soul bustled about, and in a short time had ready a cup of that delightful beverage for which we owe the Chinese so many thanks.

The tea seemed to revive Mrs. Armstrong, and she feebly thanked the good angel into whose hands she had fallen.

"Not a word—not a word. Eat some of this new bread and fresh butter, if you can, and then sleep, while I get your husband a good meal. *My* husband, I expect, will be back shortly."

Mrs. Armstrong obeyed, swallowed a small quantity of food, and then fell fast asleep, happy in the consciousness that her husband and herself were in security.

In a very short time the owner of the hut appeared; a tall, jolly-looking man, with broad, red face, and big whiskers.

"Welcome, stranger," he said, as he deposited his spade in one corner, and rifle in the other. "Hope the ole 'ooman has treated you well!"

"Very kindly, indeed, thank you; though I must ask pardon for our intrusion."

"What's the matter? Who's intrusion?"

"Why, we came to your house without invitation, and demanded shelter."

"Well?"

"It was very rude; but we were hardly able to travel any farther, and I hope you will accept my apology."

"Polly G. be blowed—lookee hyar, stranger, you are a green Britisher, I guess."

"I have not been in America long."

"Then I'll just put you up to a dodge. When you sees a log, jest walk right slick up to it, open the door, walk in and sit down. Visitors ain't so noomerous in these hyar parts that we has to give em invitations to keep 'em away. Now, then, ole 'ooman, how about the pork and hominy? Stranger's peckish, I calculate?"

"Your kindness is——"

"Jest you shut up yer head till you gets somethin' to put in yer mouth."

With these words the jovial settler placed a huge dish of boiled pork, hominy, and vegetables before Armstrong, and with the exhortation to "dig away," commenced his own meal.

It was the first cooked food Armstrong had tasted for some days, and as he enjoyed it, he cast frequent glances towards his sleeping wife, thinking how pleased she would be to partake of such a feast.

The settler's wife noticed his looks.

"Don't wake her yet, she shall be well looked after presently," she said.

Armstrong's heart was full. Such sudden relief from their hardships, such unexpected kindness, almost overpowered him.

He almost feared to speak, lest his feelings should betray him into the womanish weakness of tears.

When they had all eaten enough the remains of the meal were removed.

The settler placed a bottle of whisky, a mug of hot water, and a couple of tin cups upon the table, inviting his guest to mix himself some grog.

The wife, however, busied hersel. with some mysterious cookery, the dainty smell of which proclaimed that it was intended for the sleeper.

Then, while pipes were smoked and grog sipped, Armstrong related his adventures.

"Cuss them red-skins!" said the settler, bringing his fist down upon the table with great force. "I'm a man of peaceable natur', but if I comes across Mr. Blackhand, I guess I'll jest plug the varmint. Lost yer son, yer weapons, yer hoss, yer house and everything?"

"Everything excepting our lives and

a trifle of money still remaining in the bank."

" And what air you goin' to do in this fix, mister ?—sail back to England ?"

" No ; I must seek a new home."

" Where Ingins ain't quite so plentiful ?"

" Yes."

" Then you can't do better than go with the next caravan to Pine Valley."

" Where may that be ?"

" It's a new settlement down west, beautiful land and no reds. Why, there's six settlers there already, and there's sure to be a dozen at least in the next lot."

" Is land cheap ?"

The settler put his finger to his nose and smiled significantly.

" Land is cheap, I guess. You just takes what you likes by agreement amongst yourselves, and builds your log upon it. Why, the government surveyor knows no more about Pine Valley than he du about this hyar blessed spot, which are called Prairie-Star Town."

" A rather small town, certainly."

" Yes, but then it will be large in a year or two ; right on the road, you know."

" I didn't see any road."

" Oh, this is about ten miles away from the town ; that's over the hill there."

" But do you think I should be doing right in taking possession of land without paying for it ?"

" Don't you trouble. Uncle Sam likes to get a few good chaps right away to the front, to make the way smooth for parsons, lawyers, congressmen, and all them smooth, city-going fellers."

" I think I'll take your advice."

" You can't do better. So, now, as soon as your wife has had her supper, you can jest turn into that back room. The sheets ain't of the finest linen, but you don't look for that, I guess."

Half-an-hour afterwards, all the inmates of that little hut were sound asleep.

When Armstrong and his wife arose in the morning, they found that their worthy host had gone out into the forest, but had left a message with his wife, requesting them to await his return.

Two hours before mid-day, the settler reappeared, and then, after a hearty meal, they said farewell.

Armstrong had determined to join the caravan, which was to pass through Prairie Star Town that evening, and the settler had made arrangements with a friend to supply them with a light cart, a horse, a rifle, an axe, and a few other necessaries.

These were all ready for him at a certain place.

The good-hearted settler wished them farewell, and retired to his field.

Armstrong took possession of the goods thus provided for him, and joined the train of waggons which at that moment came rolling into the town.

They did not stop long in the little city—it is a big one now, and under another name numbers thousands of inhabitants—the emigrants were all anxious to reach their destination, and added at least a dozen miles to the distance they had already travelled before they formed their camp for the night.

# CHAPTER XXIII.

### BLACK SNAKE.

THE lovers—Strongbow and Water Lily—were much surprised at the sudden interruption.

Before the Boy Chief could say or do anything, the Delaware had glided into the bushes, leaving behind him a most disagreeable, uncomfortable feeling on the minds of the youthful pair.

Water Lily looked very much inclined to shed tears, while Strongbow seemed disposed to rush after the intruder and punish him.

His pretty companion trembled so that he could not leave her, so his arm gradually found its way round her waist and there remained.

" Does Water Lily know the name of the warrior who spoke ?"

" It is Black Snake."

" And why is Black Snake angry ?"

"Black Snake wishes to take Water Lily to his wigwam."

"But surely so brave a warrior has a squaw to cook his meat?"

"Black Snake has a black heart. The Water Lily hates him, and would die rather than live in his wigwam."

The Indian girl stamped with her foot, and it was very evident, from her manner, that she spoke the plain truth when she said she hated him.

Just like the sex! It is so difficult to obtain from a woman the slightest admission that she loves; but mention the name of the man she hates, and her tongue is loosened.

"Water Lily need not fear the anger of the Black Snake while Strongbow is by her side."

"Black Snake creeps in the grass and kills when least expected."

"Then we must find some means of disarming him. Come, Water Lily, let us return to the village."

They were, perhaps, rather longer than they need have been upon the road, but then a dispute arose between them—a lover's quarrel.

Strongbow would insist upon carrying the gourd full of water, which proceeding caused Water Lily to enter a serious protest against his doing anything so undignified.

A chief carrying water through the village!

Such a sight had never been seen!

In the midst of her arguments, she endeavoured to recover the property Strongbow had taken possession of; the water was spilt in the struggle, and they had to return to the spring for a fresh supply.

At length they found their way back to the camp, and, having seen Water Lily to her own wigwam, Strongbow looked about for the old hunter.

He wished to know Swift's opinion of the Black Snake.

Hiram was seated on the ground beneath a tree, oiling the lock of his rifle and whistling a low tune.

"Hi, lad! can't ye see?" said the hunter, as Strongbow nearly fell over him.

"I didn't see you," replied the Boy Chief.

"What! then it's a case."

"What is a case?"

"I've been afeard on it a long time.

"Afraid of what?"

"Why, you've been fool enough to fall in love with that Injin gal."

Strongbow made no reply, but his flushed cheek told the hunter that he had guessed the truth.

"Now, what is the use of my sayin' anythin'? Do you think you'll ever be a hunter, if you goes flirtin' and dancin' after every copper-coloured jade you catches sight of?"

"Copper-coloured jade! Why, you must be blind, Mr. Swift, if you cannot see that she is very beautiful."

"Certin she is good-lookin'."

"And good as well."

"Thar's no denyin' it."

"Then why should I not love her?"

"I don't say as how you oughten, but it would be better if you didn't."

"Why?"

"Because Black Snake means to put her in his wigwam."

"Ah! then it is true?"

"It is. So if you love the gal, jest you look out for Black Snake; that's my caution."

Strongbow was silent again.

Young love, first love, with all its ardent hopes and impulses, had taken possession of his heart. He thought first of rushing away into the wild woods, with the beloved of his heart; then he remembered how frail and weak her slight figure appeared, and how ill-fitted for a life in the wilderness.

"What shall I do?" he asked.

"Wait till Big Elk sits with the warriors round the fire; then ask him for his daughter."

"Your advice is good. I will take it."

He had not long to wait.

Big Elk had been home two days, when he intimated his desire to have a talk with the warriors of his tribe around the council fire.

So the Delaware braves assembled together, and discussed the affairs of their nation.

Hiram Swift stood by, leaning upon his rifle, watching, listening, but saying nothing.

Strongbow and Water Lily appeared, hand in hand.

"What would the young chief of the Delawares?" asked Big Elk, rather surprised, though he took care to conceal it.

"Strongbow loves the Water Lily," was the reply.

"Ugh!"

"Strongbow would take the Water Lily as his bride, and the light of his wigwam."

"Ugh! the Boy Chief of the Delawares has spoken well. Big Elk will bestow his daughter, the Water Lily, upon Strongbow. Do the warriors of the Delawares give consent?"

"Ugh! it is good, it is good," said all the braves, with one exception.

This was Black Snake, who had not been seated in the circle, but stood outside.

"It is not good," cried he. "Black Snake has room for the Water Lily in his wigwam. He loves the Water Lily; he is a renowned hunter; there is no lack of meat in his cabin. Why, then, should Big Elk give the Water Lily to this pale-face boy who cannot hunt?"

"Big Elk has spoken; he will give his daughter to the Boy Chief."

"Black Snake will not be robbed of his bride! He will be revenged!" shouted Black Snake.

With these words he laid his hand upon his knife, and advanced in a threatening manner towards the young pair.

"Back," said Hiram Swift. "Keep back, Black Snake, or you will rue the day."

The old hunter lifted his rifle half up to his shoulder.

The Delaware well knew the meaning of the gesture, and at once dropped his weapon.

With a low moan, and a threatening movement of his hand towards Strongbow and Water Lily, he walked slowly back towards the wigwam he usually occupied.

---

## CHAPTER XXIV.

### LOVE AND SUPERSTITION.

AFTER some little palaver among the Delawares, it was agreed that Strongbow and Water Lily should be united.

But not for some time to come.

Your Indian is superstitious; he believes in the signs shown by the sun, moon and stars, and has great faith in omens as well as in the prophecies of the medicine-man.

Big Elk consulted his medicine-man, and the result of the consultation was that Strongbow was doomed to wait a year ere he could claim the lovely Water Lily as his bride.

But his heart was full of hope.

He was young, and after the first burst of bitter grief at the supposed death of his parents, he applied himself diligently to the task of making the best of his peculiar situation, and becoming a thorough denizen of the wilderness in character.

So he hunted with the Delaware braves, and with them trod the war path.

His fame soon became known throughout the land.

The arrows sent from the bow of the Boy Chief were winged by death, so sure and so swift was their flight.

A week had passed since the scene by the council fire.

Strongbow had sufficiently recovered from his wounds to be able to take part in a hunt, and as a trophy of the chase, he brought a splendid bearskin, to be made into a rug for his beloved.

She thanked him, smiled graciously, and allowed her small hand to remain clasped in his while he detailed all the history of the chase.

How he had roused the bear from a hollow tree; how he had sent two arrows through its body, and then with his knife ended the life of the shaggy brute.

"Water Lily is glad that Strongbow has slain the monster bear, but will he bring Water Lily a branch from the cedar tree, which grows in the midst of the great swamp?"

"I will; but what do you want with the cedar branch, dear Lily?"

"To prove by it whether I shall be yours or not. It is the custom of my tribe. But the way is long; the swamp is dangerous. Water Lily will not demand the cedar branch."

With these words, the brave girl renounced her right to a talisman, without which neither she nor the man of her choice could have any luck.

For it was a superstition of her tribe that the maid who married without a branch of that mystic cedar hanging to her dress should have naught but ill-luck through life.

Strongbow, who knew the superstition, saw at once the depth of her love and self-devotion.

Rather than expose her lover to the dangerous journey into the midst of that haunted swamp, she would willingly suffer all the bodily troubles consequent upon the neglect of such an important ceremony. But the lover would not allow her to have any cause for uneasiness.

He resolved to seek out the dismal swamp, to pluck from the mystic cedar tree a goodly branch, and to return home in triumph ere anyone could know that he was gone.

He left Water Lily at the door of her home, and proceeded to his own tent.

His weapons were all there—the bow he had inherited from the last chief, his arrows, his knife, and tomahawk.

He waited patiently till it was nearly sundown, and then sought Swift.

"Where is the Haunted Swamp?" he asked, when at length he found himself in the hunter's presence.

"A good thirty miles from here."

"Which way?"

"Due south."

"There is a mysterious cedar tree in it, is there not, where the Indians go and gather branches for the young women before they marry?"

"There is."

"Did you ever go there?"

"Yes."

"What, right up to the tree?"

"Yes, and pulled a branch."

"Did it bring you good luck when you married?"

"I was never married."

"Then why did you pluck it?"

"Don't ask questions, boy," replied the hunter, almost rudely.

He turned uneasily away.

Strongbow was surprised for a moment, but soon recovered himself.

"I didn't mean to say anything to annoy you," he said.

"I know it, boy; never mind."

"I want to know the way to the swamp, that is all I have to ask."

"Go right south as you can for about thirty miles; you will come to a sort of dry ditch. Keep along this ditch, to the right, and you will see seven pine trees planted in the form of a cross. Walk from the head of the cross to the foot, and keep on in a straight line till you come to the cedar tree."

"I am going."

"I guessed as much. When do you start?"

"To-night, when the moon rises."

"Then take a good quiver full of arrows, for thar's b'ars in that swamp and look out whar' you puts yer feet, for the snakes down that diggin's air a caution."

"I'll take care."

"And there's a Black Snake you must look out for."

"I know. If I don't return in two days, you can conclude I am lost."

By this time the sun had gone down.

Strongbow and Swift returned to their wigwam, and, by the light of the fire, made a hearty supper.

"How came the pine trees to be planted in the form of a cross?" asked Strongbow, his head full of his intended expedition.

"That I'll tell yer another time. Don't ask me now."

They finished the meal in silence, and then sat at the opening of the tent.

Hiram Swift appeared to be full of melancholy.

Well he might be, for the mention of the Cedar of the Haunted Swamp brought to his mind a tale of woe.

Strongbow, on the other hand, was full of the anticipation of the pleasure his Water Lily would feel when he returned in safety with the cedar branch.

At length the moon rose.

"I must be off," said Strongbow, rising.

"I guess I'll go with you a piece," said Hiram Swift, jumping up, and seizing his rifle.

No more was said.

In silence they commenced their perilous journey.

## CHAPTER XXV.

### THE JOURNEY.

HIRAM SWIFT led the way, and Strongbow followed close in his footsteps.

"Don't arouse the camp," said the Boy Chief; "I don't wish anyone to know where we are gone."

The hunter gave a nod to signify that he would be cautious, and then motioned his young companion to throw himself on his face.

Like snakes or lizards they crawled noiselessly past the confines of the Indian settlement, and disappeared in the forest from the sight of any straggler.

"Now we must blind our trail, I guess," said Swift, "or we shall have the red-skins on our track."

"I am doing no wrong by fulfilling one of their own ceremonies."

"You don't want them to know it?"

'Not until I have done it. When I return with the cedar branch in my hand, I care not who knows it."

"This way; water leaves no trail."

So saying, Hiram Swift led the way to a small brook, over which either of them could have easily leaped.

The stream ran on with a merry rattling noise, dancing over its pebbly bed in haste to join a larger torrent.

Hiram Swift stepped out into the middle of it, and then, turning to the right, began to ascend its course.

In this he was followed by Strongbow.

For nearly a mile they waded along the river course, the water at no place rising above mid-leg, and in some parts being scarcely six inches in depth.

Then they landed, and plunged into a dense wood.

The forest was composed principally of gloomy pine trees, with here and there a still more gloomy-looking cypress.

It was not a place where much under-wood grew, and so they were enabled to proceed at a pretty good pace. Here and there they saw bunches of long, coarse grass, which the old hunter avoided care-fully, on account of the snakes which usually infest such places.

Outside the forest, the moon was brightly, but under the pine t

was scarcely enough light to enable them to avoid the dangerous spots.

"How can you find the way? Are you certain we are going right?"

So questioned Strongbow, feeling very anxious to know by what means his friend and guide steered his course through the trackless forest.

The reply was one which convinced him of the great amount of practical wisdom which may be learnt from the backwood professors of natural philosophy.

"I kin tell by these pine-trees."

"I wish you would show me how."

"Well, look at them when we comes to another opening."

Strongbow at once paid the greatest attention to the trees, trunks, roots, and branches.

They appeared to possess no peculiarity, so he gave up the enigma.

"I guess the north wind blew smartish when these trees were young. See, they all has more branches on the south side than where the frost nipped 'em."

A rapid glance convinced Strongbow that Hiram Swift was correct in his reasoning; the trees all had a more luxuriant appearance one side than the other.

So with a thank for the information thus given, they passed on.

Daybreak at length began to make the bright moon look pale, and the two wan-derers began to think of taking a little rest.

Not that old Swift needed it.

He could have continued his walk for another such distance, but he knew that his young pupil had scarcely recovered from the severe wounds inflicted by the panther, and was, therefore, not in a fit state to make a long journey without halting.

So they sat down upon a little rising ground, and made a simple meal of the dried venison they had brought with them.

"We've done half our journey, I expect," said Swift. "We'll get to the swamp afore sundown."

"But why?"

"The tarnation bad part o' the road is to come. This wood's nought to what we'll have to go through when we gets a piece ahead."

"In Heaven's name, then, let us get on."

"Don't be in such a hurry; rest an hour."

The Boy Chief was impatient, but he had such confidence in his guide that he curbed his own inclinations in deference to the opinions of his guide.

So they rested an hour, Swift quietly smoking his pipe, while Strongbow thought.

Thought, first of home and parents, lost for ever, he feared, then of more recent scenes—of the Delaware village, and of the fairest flower in its wigwams—the Water Lily.

In his mind's eye he could see her, just at that moment, arising, flushed and rosy from her night's rest, and from the door of her tent casting stolen glances towards the wigwam where he was supposed to be sleeping.

Then he thought of the strange doubts which would agitate her mind when hour after hour rolled past, and she saw him not; for he knew that she loved him, and, blessed with that knowledge, felt in his own heart something of the sorrow that would wound her gentle bosom.

He almost repented his hasty journey, but it was too late to retreat.

To give variety to his thoughts he endeavoured to draw Swift into conversation; but the hunter had one of his taciturn fits, and answered in such a manner that our hero soon became silent.

They sat in silence till the sun's beams began to show over the tops of the tall trees, and things animate in nature resumed their activity.

Hiram Swift then rose, and with the simple words, "Come along, lad," pushed forward on his journey.

The hunter occasionally glanced up at the sun and then at the tree tops to see that he was going in a proper direction, keeping in a southerly direction, without bend or hesitation.

He trod lightly, avoiding all such places as might leave a marked and easy trail.

Strongbow followed closely, his anxiety to reach the swamp giving him strength enough to keep up with the hunter's long strides.

The forest began to grow more tangled, and at times the undergrowth of bushes and weeds so detained them that they could make but slow progress.

Travelling by a beaten path, even with many bends and curves by the way, is a very different thing to forcing one's road through a pathless forest across thickly wooded bottoms, where knife and axe are both needed at times.

At least, so Swift and Strongbow found it, for on more than one occasion they had literally to cut their way through the jungles and brakes which barred their progress.

By the time the sun showed that it was high noon, they were not much more than seven miles from their last resting-place. They were again compelled to halt and take a brief rest.

The spot where they stopped, under the shelter of a gloomy-looking forest tree, was the bottom of a deep dell, beyond which was a dense mass of waving canes and reeds.

Had food been plentiful, matters would perhaps have been more pleasant; but their stock of meat was nearly exhausted, and not a sign could be seen of any kind of game.

So they were compelled to eat what they had, and dream of future feasts.

Again they proceeded, forcing their way through the canes, which were in many places so interlaced with vines and creepers, as to be impenetrable.

However, they kept on, scaring up wild cats and other beasts of prey, and ever and anon waiting till it pleased some leisurely snake to glide out of their path.

At length they once more came to open ground, and after a sharp walk found themselves at the edge of a deep sluggish stream.

It appeared too wide to leap over, so there was nothing to be done but swim.

At least, so old Swift thought, and in he plunged, holding his rifle and powder horn above water with one hand, and swimming with the other.

Strongbow, however, was not disposed to wet his clothes; about fifty paces away he observed what he imagined to be a huge log stranded in the midst of the stream. This would enable him to cross, for he could easily leap to the log, and from thence to the opposite bank.

He was just about to leap when the old hunter perceived him, and at once guessed his intention.

"Hold!" he shouted. "Hold! It is an alligator!"

His warning came too late.

The adventurous youth had already launched himself into the air in his leap.

## CHAPTER XXVI.

### THE ABDUCTION OF WATER LILY.

SOME little surprise was expressed in the Delaware camp when Swift and the young chief were missed.

But the excitement soon passed away.

They had gone on a hunting excursion, it was supposed, and as these excursions sometimes last several days, nothing more was said when noon arrived without any tidings of the missing ones.

Black Snake, indeed, endeavoured to improve his position by hinting that the pale-faces feared him, and had fled in order to avoid the marriage which had been arranged between Strongbow and Water Lily, and also to escape his, Black Snake's, consequent vengeance.

Few, however, listened to him, nor did the Delaware girl for a moment believe that her lover had played the truant without some good reason.

In fact, she almost guessed the reason of his absence.

Black Snake, however, would not let her remain at peace.

If she sat within her wigwam the warrior would lounge about the doorway and annoy her with his hateful glances; if she walked through the camp his noiseless feet would follow her steps, and his odious voice would be heard telling her that he had not yet given up all hope of making her his.

At length she managed to elude him, as she thought, and stole off into the forest, there to meditate upon her absent lover, and pray to her manitou to speed his return.

As she walked along slowly, with eyes fixed upon the ground, a foot-print arrested her attention.

She stooped down to examine it.

Her keen eyes and Indian breeding soon told her that two pale-faces had been that way. Pale-faces, she knew, though the prints were those of mocassined feet, for the toes were turned outward contrary to the Indian custom.

Who could the pale-faces be?

One foot was longer, broader, and made a deeper impression in the soil than the other. One foot was that of a man, the other of a youth.

The youth must be Strongbow, the man the pale-face hunter, Swift.

So reasoned her young heart, and correctly, too, for she had fallen upon the trail made by them the previous night.

Water Lily resolved to follow the trail, a feat which, to her, was no more difficult than waltzing to a French lady, or singing to an Italian.

When she came to the little stream up which the hunters had waded, the trail of course ended.

She searched up and down the stream on both sides, but was unable to discover the place where they had landed.

Water Lily knew then that they did not wish to be followed, and gave up the search.

Her loving heart was full of conflicting emotions—a strong faith in the constancy of her pale-face lover, and a fearful suspicion lest the menaces of Black Snake should have driven him from the Delaware village.

She halted by the river side on a small, lawn-like piece of ground, one side of which was fringed with the flags and rushes of the stream, while on the other side it was skirted by bushes, which grew almost down to the water's edge.

Close to the bushes was the trunk of a tree, which had been felled by some wandering white man's axe.

From its moss-covered appearance, it might have lain there for ages.

Upon this Water Lily seated herself in

silence, with her eyes fixed pensively upon the stream.

As before said, Water Lily was superior in character, intellect, education, and feelings to the other Delaware girls.

So sensitive was her mind, that she felt the silence and solitude of the forest a great relief from the bustle of the camp, where her female companions were always laughing and making sly remarks respecting her love for the young chief.

She was glad, too, to escape from the hateful attentions of Black Snake, and to be free for a short time from the sight of his repulsive figure.

"Oh, why is Strongbow absent?" she said aloud. "The Water Lily pines for his return; he is to her as the sun to the flower; without his light it pines and droops."

Then tears dropped from her eyes, as she thought of the dangers of that terrible journey he had, most probably, undertaken, and in her heart she accused herself of his murder.

A slight sound in the bushes behind her attracted her attention, and with the characteristic caution of an Indian girl, she glanced around.

Nothing was to be seen—nothing more to be heard save the wind sighing as it played among the reeds and sedges by the side of the stream.

She gazed down upon the transparent stream, where her own form was distinctly mirrored.

A new source of dread filled her soul.

"He loves me not because my skin is dark. He has fled."

A low moan escaped her lips as the thought took possession of her breast.

Again the sound which had alarmed her was heard; but before she had time to rise or to guard against any danger, a lasso, thrown by Black Snake's skilful hand, dropped round her nook, and in a moment she was jerked backwards, noosed and helpless.

Then the revengeful Delaware came from his place of concealment, bound the fair girl's hands behind her, thrust a gag into her mouth, lifted her insensible form in his arms, and stepped into the stream.

The Indian followed the same course as that taken by Swift, though he kept to the water for a considerable distance above the spot where the pale-faces landed.

The stream began to narrow rapidly, the current became more swift, the banks were rocky and overhung with every kind of forest tree to be found in that region.

As Water Lily was insensible from the force with which she had been thrown backwards, the Indian had a much easier task than would have been the case had she been able to struggle.

So he kept on at a pace which would have tired anyone but an Indian or a regular backwoodsman.

The water began to assume another aspect.

It no longer flowed smoothly over its bed, but seethed and foamed, while a hoarse noise proclaimed that a waterfall was near at hand.

Presently the stream widened out suddenly, forming a pool, and on the farther side was a ledge of rock, over which a narrow compact body of water fell, to descend step by step in clouds of spray to the little lake.

All around was a forest of pine trees, which seemed to rear their gloomy, majestic heads in grandeur, to shut out this lovely spot from every eye save that of Heaven.

By the side of the fall was a narrow pathway leading up among the rocks over which the streamlet fell.

Pathway, I have called it, but it was such a path as that used by the mountain goat, and the equally active hunters who pursue the daring chase.

But it was no hunter of goats who disturbed its solitude that lovely evening. It was Black Snake who hastened upwards, still bearing the Water Lily in his arms.

The loose stones and shingle gave way beneath his feet, but he hastened on and stopped not till he reached a kind of cavern.

Into this he plunged without hesitation, and, when he had penetrated to its deepest depths beneath the fall, he set down his lovely burden, and with his flint and steel struck a light.

The bright beams of a pine torch soon gave him light enough to discover a pile of skins.

These he arranged close to a large post which was driven firmly into a crevice.

He then placed Water Lily upon them, fastened her to the stake, and removed the gag from her mouth.

The Delaware girl began to show signs of returning consciousness.

Black Snake noticed it, and, after setting some food by her side, hastened away.

When he reached the open air once more he placed a flat stone before the mouth of the cave and hurried back to the stream.

## CHAPTER XXVII.

### THE CEDAR SWAMP.

TOO late for Strongbow to save himself, for he was in the act of leaping when Swift called to him.

He heard the warning cry, and determined to make an effort to save himself.

His feet touched the hard scaly back of the alligator, but rested there scarcely an instant of time as he made a second leap and gained the shore.

The alligator gave a fearful roar, snapped its jaws together, and lashed its tail till the waters boiled and foamed.

Strongbow, however, was safe.

On land he had nothing to fear from the hideous brute.

Hiram Swift approached rapidly and raised his rifle.

"Hold!" cried Strongbow; "let me settle with him."

"Bless the lad! Why, them sticks o' yourn would be no more use agin his scaly hide than a thirty-two pound gun agin the Rocky Mount'ins. Thar's only one place where you kin do any hurt—that's the eye."

"Well, you take the left eye, I'll aim at the right."

All this time the ugly brute sat half in and half out of the water.

His head, shoulders, and fore paws rested on the bank, while his hind quarters were submerged in the stream.

With fierce eyes it watched the two human beings, half afraid to make an attack upon land, and yet not inclined to pass without revenge for the insult of being mistaken for a log.

Swift took careful aim with his rifle, and the Boy Chief levelled an arrow.

Both discharged their missiles together, and after a few convulsive contortions the alligator was dead.

On examining the body it was seen that both marksmen had aimed truly.

Hiram Swift's bullet had pierced one eye, while Strongbow's arrow was buried at least six inches deep in the other.

"That's good tall shootin', I guess," remarked the hunter.

"It would puzzle anyone to beat it," replied Strongbow, with a glow of pardonable pride.

"However, as the critter's no use to eat, we had better make tracks an' git into this hyar blessed swamp afore sundown. Come away."

With these words the hunter led the way again across a tolerably open country till they came to a deep dry ditch or gully.

It had evidently been the bed of a stream, but some convulsion of nature had diverted the waters from their channel and left a gully with a dry pebbly bottom. Strongbow speculated as to the causes which had produced this remarkable change, but could find no satisfactory solution to the question.

"Look out for b'ars, boy," said the hunter, as he glanced at the priming of his rifle. "Them varmint is found in tallish quantities down along here."

"Are they very fierce?"

"The black b'ar runs away, but if you meets a grizzly, you've got to fight."

"Couldn't I do as the black bear does, run away?"

"It's no manner o' use making tracks when old Ephraim is arter ye. The critter goes at a powerful long trot. Why, the Injins reckons a fight wi' grizzly equal to a stand-up rough an' tumble wi' two men. So if you see the critter, slope, unless he sees you; and if he du set his eyes on you—why, fight."

"Do you think we shall see a grizzly bear along this ravine?"

"Very likely; I did once shoot one somewhar here about. But they keeps more away to the west."

After this lecture on bears Strongbow kept his weapon ready for instant use, and his eyes carefully scanned the steep banks of the ditch.

"THE RESCUE OF THE 'WATER LILY.'"

For he already knew that the grizzly bear loves not the forest, but prefers a rugged, hilly country where there are just sufficient bushes to give him an occasional meal of berries and to shelter him from sun and rain.

They saw no grizzly bear, however, though one or two black ones were roused from their lairs. Once Swift fancied he saw the footprint of " Old Ephraim," as the trappers call the grizzly, but, on stooping down to examine it, the old man found he was mistaken.

So onward they plodded till at length a branch crevice ran off from the gully, as though a tributary brooklet had shared the fate of the larger stream.

"Now we finds land ag'in," said the hunter, as he stepped out of the ravine and stood once more on prairie soil.

The aspect of the country was desolate and wild in the extreme.

The soil was clothed with a long, coarse-looking grass which grew sparsely on the sandy soil.

A few stunted trees were seen here and there, lifting their tattered heads, as though to invoke pity from the pitiless heavens.

Some little distance from the spot where they emerged from the ravine was a little group of pines, which seemed much more vigorous and healthy than any other vegetation they could see.

Strongbow made a remark on the subject, to which Hiram Swift returned the following answer:—

"They ought to be green, for they were planted on a grave, and watered with blood !"

"What can this mystery be?" thought the Boy Chief; but as his companion was evidently unwilling to give any solution to the mystery, he forbore to ask.

The hunter led the way to the group of pines, and when they reached them, Strongbow perceived that they were arranged in the form of a cross.

These, then, were the trees that Swift had spoken of before they started on their dangerous journey.

At length they stood under the shade of the pines.

Beneath the largest was a mound of earth.

A grave !

Evidently a grave, from its shape.

And at the foot of the grave was a rude wooden cross, formed of two slabs of timber, roughly fastened together.

Rank weeds, of coarse and vigorous growth, grew all over the lone prairie grave, and almost concealed the cross from view.

But with his keen hunting knife, the man of the prairies cleared all these away, and then addressed himself to the task of banking up the mound afresh, and putting the grave in trim order.

Then he began to scrape away the lichens from the wooden cross, carefully keeping his face away from our young hero lest the latter should detect the tear which trickled down his weather-beaten cheek.

As Strongbow watched him at his work he saw a simple name cut deeply into the wood—

KATE!

'Twas done at last!

The hunter's task was finished when, with the barrel of his rifle, he had removed the weeds and rubbish far beyond the shadow of the trees.

He looked towards the distant horizon, then once more at the grave.

For one minute he knelt beside the cross, then rising, and drawing the back of his hand across his eyes, he recommenced his journey across the prairie at such a rapid rate that Strongbow could hardly keep up with him.

As they walked on the character of the soil changed.

There was less sand, the ground becoming black and boggy, while here and there were patches of bright green verdure, telling the wanderers by their very brightness of the treacherous nature of the soil beneath.

Sometimes, too, they passed pools of dark-looking water, the borders of which were fringed with tall flags.

Farther on was the dark outline of the swamp forest, in the midst of which grew the mysterious cedar, whose branches were supposed by the simple Indians to possess the power of conferring matrimonial happiness.

But the sun was going down rapidly in the far west, and they still had a good distance to travel.

" We must hurry, lad," said Swift,

STRONGBOW, THE BOY CHIEF OF THE DELAWARES.

speaking for the first time since leaving the grave.

They did hurry, and at length entered the forest.

Then their way began to be more difficult.

Big vines and creepers hung from bush to bush, spiky thorns projected from every branch, tearing their clothes and lacerating their flesh.

"We are handy to it now," muttered the hunter; "we'd better camp thar, I guess."

"Is it a good place?"

"As good as any, if you ain't afraid of sperrits."

"I'm not afraid of anything."

The hunter then moved off to the right, and presently the forest became more open.

The trees were larger, and the soil firmer.

At length they emerged into an open space, in the midst of which grew a large cedar tree, the branches drooping upon the ground.

The two pale-faces walked straight to it, and at length were in the gloom of its drooping boughs.

Strongbow reached his hand up and plucked a branch, but as he did so, he fancied he saw an Indian peering at him from the other side of the huge trunk.

"Hist!" said he, "look there."

"What is it?" asked Swift.

"I fancy I saw an Indian behind the tree."

"Fancy it must be; thar's no Injin hyar."

Nevertheless, Strongbow was not satisfied, but dropping on the ground, crawled carefully round the trunk of the cedar.

No Indian was there, nor did the soft yielding soil show any signs of the presence of a third person.

"I feel certain I saw one," muttered the Boy Chief, as he rose again to his feet.

"We'll look round about, at all events," said Swift, and, with rifle ready for instant service, he carefully examined the swamp for a circuit of at least a hundred yards round the tree.

The same result followed.

There was nothing to show that the swamp had ever been visited by any human being save themselves.

"'Twas fancy," repeated Swift. "Let's see about campin'."

To this Strongbow at once agreed, as there only remained a few minutes of twilight.

Dead branches were plentiful under the cedar tree; a pile of these was quickly collected, and a fire made.

Just as they were about to seat themselves a pair of full round eyes appeared in the gloom of the adjacent bushes.

"Don't move," said Swift, as he lifted his rifle.

Strongbow remained motionless till the hunter had levelled his rifle and fired.

"There, I said it was an Indian!" exclaimed Strongbow.

"I guess we'll eat him, then," replied Swift.

He moved off to the spot where the eyes appeared, and, in a few moments, returned with the carcase of a fine young buck upon his shoulder.

Of this they made a hearty supper, and then lay down to sleep.

Strongbow was the first to awake at early dawn, and, as he opened his eyes, he saw to his great surprise two Indian arrows fixed in the trunk of the cedar tree within a foot of his head.

---

## CHAPTER XXVIII.

### GHOSTS AND BEARS.

"HYAR'S Injin devilry with a vengeance," exclaimed Swift, when Strongbow had aroused him, and made him sensible that hostile arrows had been aimed at them during the night.

"They must have been bad shots, or they would have killed us," observed Strongbow.

"And perhaps they didn't want to."

"Then why shoot at us?"

"It's plain enough, boy, they didn't want to kill us, or they'd ha' done the job."

"Perhaps they thought we were dead."

"Perhaps they'd ha' raised our hair for us if they'd thought so. No, boy, it's a warnin'."

" Of what ?"

" That's jist the thing as puzzles me."

" Suppose we look round."

The hunter nodded, and looked to his rifle preparatory to beginning the search.

" Now, it's plain as a pine tree that the arrows must ha' come from the cane brake yonder, so we'll look round thar."

The Boy Chief strung his bow, and took an arrow in his hand as he walked by Swift's side towards the thicket, from which it was evident the deadly messengers had come.

Their eyes glanced into the dense cover before them, and if they felt a slight sense of fear, it was not because they knew not how soon they might be struck down, but because they could not tell what unseen hand held their fates.

But no arrow hissed from the cane brake, no painted Indian showed his face, or howled his war whoop.

All was silent save the echoes which came ringing from some distant part of the swamp, where the wild turkeys could be heard loudly calling each other, or noisy ducks kept up a continual commotion on the waters of some sluggish stream or pond.

They reached the edge of the cane thicket, which was perhaps seventy or eighty feet long, where it faced the cedar tree.

How thick it was they could not tell, for the canes grew so close together that the eye could not possibly see more than a foot into the jungle.

Hiram Swift kept his eye constantly upon the canes, to see if they had been pushed aside by the person who shot the arrows; while Strongbow carefully examined the soft soil before the jungle, to detect, if possible, the print of a hostile footstep.

But both were at fault.

There was no sign that the canes had ever been disturbed save by the elements, and though Strongbow's own feet made impressions half an inch deep, he could not see so much as a blade of grass which had been crushed by other steps.

In this manner they completely circled the brake, and then were no wiser than when they first saw the mysterious arrows quivering in the tree over their heads.

Hiram Swift was evidently nettled at the idea of being baffled by an " Injin,"

and stood for some time with his head resting upon the muzzle of his rifle, studying to find out the key to the enigma.

But the mystery was not thus to be solved.

Though the hunter carefully inspected each bush, each bunch of reeds that grew in sight of the cedar, he was unable to discover the slightest sign which might give his acute mind an idea whether friendly or hostile hand had directed those arrows.

" I'm boun' to believe in ghostes arter this," exclaimed Swift. " Come away out o' these diggins, lad, afore wus happens."

" What have ghosts to do with this matter, and why should ghosts carry about such arrows? Spirits, you know, need not food nor weapons for procuring food, and, as you said, they didn't want to kill us, or they would have done. Besides, what object can ghosts have in haunting this lonely swamp where man seldom ventures ?"

" You ax the Delawares. They'll tell yer thar's a sperret haunts this hyar swamp, and kills all the Iroquois and Crows as comes nigh. And thar's no doubt I've seen a few o' them red-skins lyin' dead and scalped nigh about the spot whar we camped."

" Then the spirit is friendly to the Delawares ?"

" Yes."

" Then I don't believe in such a spirit. It is most likely some Delaware warrior who takes advantage of superstition to gain an easy victory over any warrior of another tribe who may venture near this mystic tree."

" Them as has seen it says it is like a squaw, and a pale-face one, too. They says her face is as white as a lump o' chalk, and her long hair golden colour."

" Our ghost has been seen, then ?"

" Sartain. A Delaware brave see the critter when he camped down hyar. He shot, too, did that Delaware, but the critter only laughed when his arrow whistled through her. *He* war the fust man killed, though, when the Chickassees dug up the hatchet."

" I still refuse to believe in ghosts or any spiritual apparitions. My old tutor's logic settled the question in my mind."

" What did he say ?"

" That if there are good and evil spirits, the former are too happy to pass their time in haunting lonely places; while the bad ones are under the rule of the arch-fiend, who enjoys their torments too much to allow them to revisit the earth."

This argument silenced the old hunter, but did not convince him.

Though not naturally of a very superstitious mind, the events of the past night had made a deep impression on him.

How could it be otherwise when two arrows had been shot and the shooter had departed without leaving any other trace of his unwelcome presence?

While talking they had left the mystic cedar tree far behind.

Once beyond the sight of it the old hunter's spirit and courage began to revive.

He walked more briskly, and his eye assumed a less troubled expression.

They returned by their own trail, and found themselves at the gully in much less time than it had taken to make the first journey.

Then nature began to assert its force, and the old hunter halted his companion while he went to look for a toothful of fresh meat.

So Strongbow remained in the ravine while his companion strolled into the forest.

For a long time nothing was heard of the hunter, who appeared to be unsuccessful in his search for game.

At all events his rifle was not heard.

After waiting half-an-hour, Strongbow crawled out of the ravine, and looked around for a sight of his friend.

Swift was not to be seen; but after listening for a few moments, Strongbow heard the well-known report of the long rifle.

There could be no doubt then that they would have some fresh meat, for Swift was never known to miss his aim.

So our hero hurried back to his place in the ravine, and began to build a fire.

He had a good one when the hunter reappeared, staggering beneath the weight of a huge shaggy burden he carried on his shoulders.

" What have you killed?" asked Strongbow.

" A b'ar."

" It's not a very large one."

" No, a cub; but it's heavy, though."

" Down with it."

" Easy, boy. The b'ar will bust, I guess, if he's chucked down among them rocks."

" Come along, then. I'm hungry."

" So am I."

It was a difficult matter for the hunter to scramble down to the bottom of the gully, but at last he succeeded in doing so, and laid his prize by the fireside.

It was a cub, but so fat, that, as Swift had said, there would have been danger of its " busting," if he had thrown it down.

To remove the skin was the work of but a few moments, and then the most delicate portions of it were laid upon the hot coals to cook.

" If this ain't a heap better than jerked deer meat, I'm a sinner," said Swift, as he turned the savoury steaks.

" It smells good; but look! We have visitors."

" Whar?"

" Up there. Look?"

" Jer-rusalam! It's the old b'ar."

" How did she find us?"

" Smelt my tracks. She's come after the cub, I reckon."

The old bear, a big black brute, was peeping over the edge of the cliff, looking down upon the scene, and very evidently inclined to be angry with those who had stolen her cub.

Strongbow snatched up his bow.

" Send your shaft through her eye. If you miss, I guess my gun don't."

Strongbow took careful aim, and let fly a shaft, which struck the animal between the two eyes, causing her to give a roar of pain.

Then she swayed her body to and fro, meditating the best place to descend upon the hunters.

But whatever her meditations may have been, her designs were frustrated, for Swift's rifle was heard, and then the huge black mass was seen rolling from rock to rock, till with a dull thud it reached the bottom of the gully.

The hunter quietly reloaded his trusty gun, and proceeded with his cookery.

## CHAPTER XXIX.

### A MYSTERIOUS BEING.

THE meal over and the hunter's pipe duly smoked, Swift and his young friend were about to proceed, when another black head was seen peering over the edge of the ravine and a loud snorting noise was heard.

"It's the he b'ar come to look after his ole 'ooman," observed Swift.

The he *b'ar* was evidently in no very amiable frame of mind; the death of his spouse and offspring had inflamed his heart with a wish for vengeance; he only gave one look, and then commenced scrambling down.

"Don't shoot, boy," said Swift, laying his hand upon Strongbow's arm.

"What! will you let him come down?"

"Yes."

"Will he not attack us?"

"No."

"He looks fierce enough."

"That's like enough. But I'll tame the consumed critter."

The hunter took up his rifle, and stood watching the descent of the clumsy animal, while Strongbow waited patiently.

At length the bear, who descended tail first, planted his hind feet upon the firm ground.

Swift raised his rifle, glanced along the barrel, and fired.

His aim was unerring.

The ball struck the bear fairly on the brain, and tumbled him backward, lifeless.

"Three b'ars in one day. That's good work. I guess I'll skin the brutes; their hides is worth ten dollars."

The hunter served the two large bears as he had served the small one.

When he had stripped off their shaggy skins and rolled them up into a bundle, Strongbow asked the following question:—

"What do you do with the money you get for these skins?"

"Buy powder, lead, 'bacca."

"Of whom? There are no shops."

"Thar's traders, though, brings sich traps round. But, don't say anything about powder when we gets back, or else them red-skins 'ull want rifles. They thinks my powder-horn is medicine, and can't be empty."

"But don't they see you buy of the traders?"

"No. They hides the powder—I hides the skins."

With this explanation Strongbow was forced to satisfy himself; but he resolved that when the traders came he would, by some means or other, procure a rifle.

When Swift had finished packing the skins, he placed them for safety in a crevice of the rock, in such a position that wolves could not interfere with them.

Some of the best portions of the carcases were then cut off and packed up for future consumption; and the little party then moved off.

They travelled as fast as they could; but night overtook them long before they could reach their own encampment.

They could not well travel by night, as the moon was hidden behind dense masses of cloud.

So there was no help for it but to build a fire and bivouac in the forest.

This was no hardship to either of the two.

So their camp was prepared, and, after a hearty supper, they lay down to sleep, but not until Strongbow had looked at and kissed the little cedar branch he had carefully stowed away in his wallet.

The tired hunters kept no watch that night.

Swift had given his opinion that it would not be necessary, as they were then in the Delaware district, and therefore among friends.

So both slept soundly when a huge fire had been made to blaze up to scare away wolves and other beasts of prey.

They slept, and the wolves kept at a good distance; but there were other beasts of prey who prowled about that forest, creatures who cared not for the ruddy glow of the fire, which served to reveal the forms of the sleepers, while the watchers were hidden in the deep shadows of the woods.

There were Indians prowling about,

and waiting for an opportunity to kill and scalp.

Swift knew it not, Strongbow dreamed it not, but such was the case.

Our young hero was awakened from a sound sleep, and from a dream of the Water Lily, by a half-uttered exclamation of surprise,

He dashed to his feet and seized his bow just in time to see that Swift was a prisoner in the hands of three Indians, who had contrived to pass cords round his feet and hands while he slept.

It would be useless to attack the captors, so reasoned the boy.

Swift must be freed by stratagem.

Two bounds, and he was lost to view in the depths of the wood.

But that brief time had enabled him to gain some information as to the men who had captured his friend.

One was Black Snake, of the Delawares; another was Black Hand, chief of the Crow Indians. The third appeared to belong to neither tribe.

When he had gained a place of safety, Strongbow's heart began to reproach him for deserting his friend.

There were three Indians.

Surely two Englishmen could overcome such odds, even supposing that one of them had the misfortune to be a prisoner.

He turned back, and walking stealthily, approached the camp.

Swift was a prisoner, and bound with his back to a tree.

His life was evidently about to be sacrificed.

Black Snake, the Delaware lover of Water Lily, had the hunter's rifle in his hand, the muzzle of it pointed towards its lawful owner.

After a few moments' conversation with Black Hand and the other Indian, he raised the weapon to his shoulder and took careful aim.

Strongbow hastily fitted an arrow to his bowstring, and was about to launch it at the traitor, when to his great surprise, he saw Black Snake suddenly fall to the ground.

Swift's rifle was discharged in falling, but the ball hissed harmlessly over the tree tops without injuring anyone.

"What can this mean?" thought Strongbow.

He looked about for an explanation and soon found what he sought.

He saw Black Hand stoop down a. draw from his companion's body an arrow, the shaft and feather of which were of a bright blue colour.

Then the Crow chieftain vanished amongst the brushwood, leaving the third Indian standing by the dead body of Black Snake.

But he stood not long. A sense of mysterious danger urged him to fly.

Before he could take six steps, however, he, too, fell upon the ground, pierced by one of those strange blue shafts.

Then Strongbow recovered from his astonishment sufficiently to see that his friend was still bound to the tree.

"I must release him, even though I fall pierced through with one of these mysterious arrows," thought Strongbow, and he began to make his way round towards the tree to which Swift was bound.

He kept pretty well under cover, for he cared not to risk himself unnecessarily.

Love had made him selfish; he was not master of his own life now, it belonged to Water Lily.

The youth had nearly reached his friend when, to his intense surprise, he saw a female figure before him.

The stranger was dressed in the Indian style, with many fantastic ornaments on her deerskin clothing; but it was evident that she was not one of the red-skin race.

Her hair was floating over her shoulders like a tangled web of golden thread, and the skin of her arms and neck was white as alabaster.

Strongbow's thoughts instantly wandered to the description Swift had given him of the mystic being who haunted the cedar swamp.

The female before him tallied exactly with the one whose shade guarded the talismanic tree.

Those arrows too.

He could see the quiver which hung at the back of this fair-haired woman; the arrows in it were dyed blue, the arrows which had slain the two Indians were of the same colour, and so also were those which some mysterious hand had planted in the trunk of the cedar tree.

Then there was truth in the Indian superstitions; this was the guardian of swamp.

But no spirit though.

For as Strongbow followed close behind her, he saw the bushes bend before her as she passed along.

She carried in her left hand the fatal bow, and in her right glittered a long knife.

She glided along silently, approached the old hunter from behind, severed his bonds, and then, ere Swift could turn to see who had restored him to liberty, darted behind a thick bush.

Hiram Swift stared round, but could see no one.

"Jerusalem!" he ejaculated, as the cords fell to the earth.

He took them up and examined the places where the knife had passed through them.

"Cut, that's sartin, though how a rope could cut itself, this child can't opine. But whar's that boy, I'd like to know?"

"Here."

Strongbow stepped forward as he spoke.

"Then it was you?"

"What do you mean?"

"You took me out o' these buffler hide fixins."

"No, I didn't."

"Then who on airth were it?"

"A woman."

"What, a reg'lar squaw?"

"A strange woman in a dress of deer-skin. She had a white skin and hair like threads of gold."

The hunter's cheek grew pale.

"You're jokin', lad."

"No, I saw her cut the thongs."

"Then we're in luck. Anybody who gets help from the sperret o' the swamp ain't gwine to die in a hurry. But which way did she go?"

"Here, behind this bush."

The hunter rushed to the spot, and kneeling down, examined the ground minutely.

"Je-rusalem!" he again exclaimed. "May I be chawed up by grizzly b'ars if there ain't the print of her foot; a small foot with a mocassin."

"Of course, she went this way."

"We'll foller if we can. But I say, lad, you made two good shots; why did ye let that durned skunk, Black Hand, carry his carcase off?"

"I did not shoot."

"Who then?"

"She it was who sent the arrows."

"Then, I say ag'in, we're in luck. Thar's nothing like bein' backed up by golden hair; she always does the right thing with her friends."

---

## CHAPTER XXX.

### ARMSTRONG IN HIS NEW HOME.

To follow the thread of a story closely it is necessary to turn aside sometimes out of the fair, well-beaten paths pursued by honest men, and dive into dens of villany.

Therefore, in order that our readers may understand our motives, we leave the forests, the Indians, and the hero of the tale, to take a walk into the most crowded part of an American city in search of our villain.

Our villain, as everyone knows, is Wylde.

The precious scoundrel, after shooting a man, and being himself shot in a gambling house, was, as our readers know, carried to his room in an hotel of doubtful reputation.

That he was robbed by his principal agent, Mr. Jackson, we have already informed our readers.

But though thus robbed, the sick ruffian was neither penniless nor friendless.

He had friends—if friends they can be called—who were bound to him only by ties of bloodshed.

A hasty note addressed, as soon as he recovered his faculties, to the chief of a society of which he was second officer, brought money and medical attendance.

The great king of terrors—death—who is supposed to execute justice in mundane affairs, seemed to have been trifled with.

He would stretch out his bony hand as though determined to grasp his prey—then he would retreat as though mercy had entered his heart and determined him to let the sinner live; then again he would put all his terrors on his grisly brow and beckon the howling rascal to come and meet his doom.

But the proverb, "Those whom the gods love die young," seemed in this case to be reversed, for it certainly seemed as though the wretch whose name was most in detestation in heaven, would live to see the successful accomplishment of all his villany.

Wylde began to grow strong.

But not at once.

The rascal was not to escape without some bodily pangs, and it cost him a month of anguish, of weary tossing upon a feverish couch, of restless days, and nights of horrid dreams, ere he could once more put his feet to the ground, and stand erect in the natural posture of a man.

Then, with returning strength, came returning villany.

He knew that his victims, Armstrong and his boy, had escaped.

He also knew that no hand but Jackson's could have abstracted the money he won at the gaming house where he met his almost mortal wound.

He resolved to be revenged on him, and to carry out his original plan of causing the destruction of both father and son.

While thus lying in his room no other amusement was allowed him but the perusal of the daily and weekly papers.

He always was a keen devourer of news, and not the smallest paragraph escaped him.

When he was just able to rise and walk about for an hour each day outside the house, his eye fell one day on a paragraph in the "Washington Globe," which ran as follows :—

"EXTRAORDINARY ADVENTURES.— A month or two back a 'Britisher' who had cut the old country, purchased a tract of land up west, and erected his hut upon it. The man had with him a wife and a son. They had not been upon their settlement many days before they were attacked by a party of Crow Indians, led on, as the man avers, by a white renegade; their log was burnt, their son killed, while the man and his wife only escaped with great difficulty.

"While travelling through the forest, hoping to find some settlement, Armstrong (such is the man's name) and his wife had the misfortune to fall into an ambush of Red-skins—of what tribe he could not say —and both were made slaves by them.

"One night, however, Armstrong managed to escape, after killing two Indians left in charge of him, and reached Prairie Star Town, where he joined a caravan. The man is, we believe, doing well on a new settlement."

So ran the newspaper paragraph, and of course Wylde knew at once that it referred to the man he so hated.

"Curse him! his good luck is always in the ascendant. He is doing well in a new settlement, while I lie here, helpless, robbed of all I had, and deserted by those in whom I had trusted."

The villain turned his face to the wall, and groaned in bitterness of spirit.

"I must and will end this affair. May I be given but one month's strength, and then, if I do not wipe off all old scores, let the name of Wylde be struck off the list of the living!"

The prayer was granted.

He grew well, he grew strong, and he grew rich, by means of a constant attendance at the gaming-table.

Then, when he grew strong enough to be in the saddle once more, he longed to be off.

A horse, a rifle, and a knife, were his necessaries, and with these he started on his journey.

A good week of riding brought him to Prairie Star Town, where he began to make inquiries in a cautious manner.

"Armstrong? Yes, I guess I've heard the name afore."

"A big man, with bushy, big whiskers."

"That's him, sirr. Air you his brother, or any kin?"

"I am not," replied Wylde.

"Then what mout you want with him?"

"That has nothing to do with you."

"Then you can go next door for information."

Had the man been alone those words would have been his last; the fiery-blooded renegade would have shot him down.

As there were two or three other persons present, he contented himself with making the remark—

"I thank you for your want of civility, my friend. I will inquire next door."

To the next house he went, and there, after a certain amount of talk, gained the information he required.

By the time he had learned all he could about Armstrong, it was night.

The sky was wrapped in complete darkness, and a thin, drizzling rain was falling.

Wylde had little inclination to encamp in the forest, or on the prairie, in his weak state of health, and under such an inclement sky.

He asked for shelter, and found it in the house of one of the settlers.

As to a hearty welcome, every backwoods traveller receives that when he enters a house.

Next morning he was up with the dawn, and after a hearty breakfast, the renegade resumed his journey.

He had at least forty miles to go.

The greater part of the journey was across pathless prairies, though here and there a little tract of forest land gave diversity to the scene.

His eye glanced over the fertile soil; he noted its rich appearance, and saw how easily it could be converted into waving corn-fields.

In his bitter, black heart he cursed the rich earth and the fair scene.

Cursed it, and wished that it might become barren, because Armstrong dwelt there, and would draw plenty from the teeming soil.

By the time he had finished his journey it was sunset.

From the edge of a grove of trees the bad-hearted man watched the orb of day as it descended behind a lowly log hut, where he doubted not, the emigrant dwelt.

"This night shall their race be run," he muttered, as he clenched his fist and shook it in a threatening manner towards the hut. "Oh, Edmund Armstrong! you have often thwarted me; but now revenge is at hand! But it is too light yet; I must wait till darkness closes round the scene."

He then tied his horse to a sapling, and carefully loaded his rifle.

"One charge must suffice for him, and if the knife is not enough for the wife, I am no judge of woman's heart."

Having finished these operations, he walked up and down impatiently in the shadow of the trees until the last tinge of red had died out in the west—until the bats, owls, and wolves had commenced their nightly concert, and everything else was silent.

"Now is my time," he muttered, and, taking his horse's bridle from the branch, he walked on towards the hut.

At length he stood within fifty yards of the building, and then he stood still to listen carefully.

Not a sound could he hear.

Encouraged by this circumstance he walked boldly up to the hut, and peeped in through a crevice by the side of the rude window-shutter.

A cheerful fire was burning in the chimney-corner, rendering every object in the hut distinctly visible.

Oh, how the renegade's eyes glared as he fixed them upon the form of Armstrong!

The emigrant was seated at a table reading a book which had been given him at the settlement.

The poor, patient wife was nowhere to be seen.

"She may be in the corner of the room which I cannot see," thought Wylde, and it seemed that he was right, for Armstrong spoke and received an answer.

"I can delay my vengeance no longer," thought Wylde, as he placed his rifle to the crevice.

But ere he could draw the trigger, he received a blow upon the head which stretched him senseless upon the earth.

## CHAPTER XXXI.

### WATER LILY'S ESCAPE.

MAN is born unto trouble as the sparks fly upwards!"

But, then, there are some men so made and constituted that trouble has no effect upon their minds.

They only feel bodily sorrows—hunger, thirst, the pain of wounds, or the griping anguish of disease.

Others there are whose bodies escape scatheless, in order that their minds may be tortured by feelings of doubt and despair.

In this latter class we may place Strongbow.

For, surely, if ever mortal man endured mortal agony of mind, our hero did, when he returned to the Delaware camp, and found that his beloved Water Lily was missing.

To say that he lost no time in following would be to assert a fact not worth hearing.

So eager was he to find her that he waited for no companions, but vaulted on the back of his mustang.

The loiterers about the camp informed him that the girl's footsteps had been traced as far as the fallen log by the brook side, but that, beyond that point, there was no trail.

Heedless of trees, of brushwood, and of overhanging branches, the Boy Chief urged his horse forward at full speed through the tangled mazes of the forest.

He reached the log, and saw the place where she—the loved of his soul—had been seated ere the treacherous noose dropped over her and deprived her of power to resist.

Then, there was the trail of Big Elk, and the warrior who accompanied him in his search for his daughter.

The youth followed for a few yards in the tracks of the Indian.

He crossed over the stream, and speedily perceived that Big Elk had explored the forest on the other side.

Strongbow was about to do the same, when an idea flashed across his brain.

Hiram Swift had waded up the brook, asserting that water left no trail.

Was it not possible that the ruffianly assailants of the Delaware girl might have done the same thing?

He resolved to try the experiment.

The mustang was, therefore, urged once more into the bed of the stream, and began to ascend towards its mountain source.   On! on! on!

Though he urged his good steed forward at its best pace, the Boy Chief's heart was far ahead.

He had passed the spot to which he had waded in Hiram Swift's company.

Then, as the course of the brook became wider and more shallow, Strongbow fancied that he could see where heavy feet had displaced the many-coloured pebbles from their bed in the stream.

This sign filled him with hope.

He knew that these tracks were not made by Big Elk and his companion brave; so to his hopeful young heart there could be no doubt that the sign had been caused by the captors of the fair Water Lily.

So, with renewed courage, he pressed forward, resolved to rescue the fair girl or share her captivity.

Leaving him to make the best of his way in search of his loved one, let us now see how it fared with Water Lily.

Scarcely had Black Snake left the cavern to which he conveyed his prize, when, with a deep drawn sigh, consciousness returned to the fair Indian maiden.

Her first feeling was one of surprise to find herself in such a strange place.

The second thought bore more affinity to truth.

She felt certain that she had not come to that gloomy cavern of her own free will.   Who, then, had brought her?

Water Lily endeavoured to sit up to see if the cavern contained anybody or anything which might enlighten her upon the subject; but, on attempting to rise, she found that her hands were secured.

However, she managed to struggle to a sitting posture, and then glanced round.

The torch left by Black Snake shed a murky light over the scene, enabling Water Lily to perceive that she had been placed on a bundle of skins, and that some food, with a gourd of water, had been placed within her reach.

She stooped down and drank heartily.

The limpid fluid cooled her feverish blood, and enabled her to think with more calmness.

She recollected that she had been sitting upon a fallen tree by the water side, that she had suddenly become conscious of some hidden danger; but, with that circumstance, memory ceased.

The gourd attracted her attention.

It was very similar to other articles of the kind to be found in every Indian lodge.

But it possessed one peculiarity.

It had on its sides some rude carving.

But that in itself would have been a circumstance of no importance, had she not recollected seeing an Indian of her own tribe stealthily carving such an article but a few days before.

"THE PALEFACE BOY SHALL NOT WED THE WATER LILY."

She had seen Black Snake decorating such a gourd with his *totem*, or armorial bearings, the head and extended jaws of a serpent; and this gourd on the ground before her bore a similar ornament.

Then there could be no doubt that Water Lily had been brought to the cave by her rejected suitor.

No sooner was this point settled than she resolved to escape.

She was bound, it is true, and had no knife; but that was no reason for hesitating.

The Indian maiden soon changed her position, so that the sharp edge of a rock came between her wrists.

Then she sawed away—with pain and difficulty it is true—but with untiring perseverance, until at length the thongs snapped asunder, and her hands were free.

To unfasten the other bonds was then an easy task, and in a short time she bounded to her feet with limbs unfettered.

"I am free now!" she exclaimed, proudly; " and let the treacherous Snake beware how he attempts a second time to capture the Water Lily of the Delawares."

She then took the torch in her hand, and surveyed the cavern to find the outlet.

There was a little recess in the wall to her right hand, and towards this the girl took her way.

A temporary disappointment at finding that it was not the mouth of the cave gave way to joy when she discovered a store of weapons.

There was a knife, a bow, and half-a-dozen arrows.

These she hastily took possession of, and then renewed her search for the door of the cavern.

At length her patient investigation was rewarded by discovering a crevice, through which beams of sunlit air danced merrily.

Here, at all events, was a means of communication with the outer world.

But how could she force her way between those huge masses of rock?

She pushed with all the wildness of despair, scarcely daring to hope that success would attend her efforts.

Judge, then, of her surprise, when what appeared to be the largest mass of granite gave way and shook.

Her heart beat so rapidly that for a short time she could scarcely breathe.

Then, with redoubled energy, she renewed her attack upon the cavern door.

Had she been of English birth, she would have given a loud " hurrah !" as the ponderous obstacle rolled slowly back, and fell with a crash upon the rocky ledge in front of her temporary prison.

In poured the fresh air, whispering of liberty, and the glorious sunbeams, which warmed her heart with hope and confidence.

She stepped forth upon the rocky plateau free and unharmed.

But where was she?

Which direction should she take to return to her home?

She had not the slightest recollection of the path by which Black Snake brought her to the cave, and, therefore, had to trust to chance and her own wits to find her way home.

The rocky mountain path left no trail which she could detect; the prospect was wholly strange to her.

She took the downward path, the right one; but it led her into defiles and ravines so dangerous that she fancied no human being could have borne her up them.

So she returned, and, after a few moments' consideration, prepared to descend the other side of the hill.

The high-minded girl had gone about half of the way, when she perceived on a part of the path where a little sand had gathered the print of a mocassin.

It was the print of a man's foot, and that man evidently a red man.

Water Lily was sufficiently well versed in the learning of her people to know all this, and more.

She soon discovered that she was following the man whose foot had left the mark.

So a process of reasoning was at once set at work in her mind, which gave the following result.

The footstep must belong to the man who brought her to the cavern; that man must be Black Snake, and Black Snake, having secured his victim, must be now on his way home, in order that no suspicions might be excited by his absence.

On two points she come to a correct

conclusion; on the third, namely, that Black Snake was on his way home, she was mistaken, for that warrior was much too astute to believe that he could conceal his evil deed for any length of time.

So Water Lily continued descending the hill till at length she found herself in a partly wooded plain, where groves of forest trees were seen plentifully scattered about the verdant, meadow-like prairie.

A stream ran through the open space, and, believing this to be the one which passed so near to her own village, she hurried to its banks, determined to trace its windings till she found her dear home once more.

## CHAPTER XXXII.

### THE REUNION.

STRONGBOW continued his pursuit, keeping a careful look upon the bed and banks of the stream.

But he found nothing to induce him to quit the direction he had chosen.

In due time he came to the open pond or lake beneath the waterfall, and then for a time he was at fault.

"I wish I had brought Swift with me," he muttered; "he would find a trail in a short time."

The youth was not to be daunted.

He rode his horse round the lake, examining its sandy bank with the greatest attention.

At length he found the place where the Black Snake stepped ashore, and at once followed the trail.

It led him into the steep, rugged path, but when once in it he knew that he was right.

The steep cliffs on both sides would prevent anyone from leaving the track.

So on and on he rode until he came to the mouth of the cave.

His good steed was a sure-footed Indian horse, but the hardy animal had no easy task to carry its rider up the precipitous incline.

The cavern was empty.

Our young hero could see at a glance that it had been occupied the previous day, or at all events at no very remote period; there was the cooked deer-meat, still fresh enough for human food, lying upon the floor.

Strongbow gazed around.

Night was coming on, and he had not yet discovered whether he was on the right trail or not.

The leather thongs which had bound Water Lily's wrists were upon the floor; it needed but a glance to tell our young hunter that the small loop of hide he saw could never have encircled the wrist of a stalwart warrior.

Other things induced him to the belief that his beloved had been there, and had managed to escape.

Which way, then, had she gone?

The question required mature deliberation.

Strongbow sat down to rest himself, and to consider as to the next steps to be taken.

At length, as it was growing dusk, he roused himself.

"What a dolt I have been!" he exclaimed. "She has not returned, or I should have seen the trail. I might have been a couple of miles nearer her had I gone right on."

He rose to proceed, when his foot struck against something.

He stooped to see what it was, and found it to be the remnants of a pinewood torch.

A splendid idea suggested itself.

The young Chief of the Delawares resolved that he would follow the Water Lily's track by torch-light.

That he was on her trail the imprint of her soft foot soon convinced him.

Water Lily was, by the time Strongbow had prepared his pine torches, a day's journey ahead.

The Boy Chief knew it, and he also knew her to be so fleet of foot, that the only way by which he could overtake her was by travelling all night, for while lifting the trail he could only proceed at a foot pace.

The sun went down and darkness suddenly covered the scene.

The Boy Chief lighted one of his torches, and by its glare he discovered the prints of Water Lily's feet.

He had prepared a number of these torches, and had packed them on the back of his mustang.

But the progress he made was slow.

\*     \*     \*     \*     \*

Water Lily tripped lightly along after her escape, until she, too, was benighted.

This fact, however, alarmed her but little.

She collected fuel, made a fire, and then lay down by its side to sleep.

It was no hardship for her to pass a night under the canopy of heaven with the soft prairie turf for a couch.

She kept her weapons firmly grasped in her hands, resolved, if surprised, to sell her life dearly.

The brave girl had been reclining by the camp fire half-an-hour when she suddenly became aware of a pair of great shining eyes fixed steadily upon the flickering flame.

"An Indian warrior!" was her first thought, and acting upon the impulse of the moment, she was about to crawl off.

The peculiar hard breathing noise made by animals of the deer tribe convinced her of her mistake.

She knew then that it was a deer, and recollected that the hunters of her tribe were accustomed to shoot them by the light of torches, at which the silly animals would stare while the hunter took careful aim.

Water Lily resolved to kill the deer, and eat, for she had not tasted food since leaving her father's wigwam.

She stealthily fitted an arrow to her bowstring, and then let fly at that part where she judged the animal's shoulder must be.

A loud groan, a scampering sound upon the ground, and a plaintive bleat proclaimed that the shaft had flown true to its mark.

Water Lily rose and proceeded in the direction of the spot.

She found a fine young deer, three parts grown, about twenty yards from her fire; her shaft had passed completely through its shoulder blade, and thus effectually prevented its escape.

As she stooped over it the elegant animal gave its last groan, and the beautiful eyes which had betrayed it were closed in death.

To cut away the choicest portions and bear them back to her fire was the next task, and, that done, the Delaware girl made a capital supper.

Once or twice a thought crossed her mind that wolves might be attracted by the scent of the slaughtered deer, or that Black Snake might see the light of her fire, and so return to recapture her.

But, in spite of these imaginings of fear, nature asserted its sway, and she slept soundly until the first rays of the rising sun glancing upon her eyes awoke her.

Then she continued her weary wanderings once more.

The country was still strange to her; but as she kept very near the course of the stream, she imagined she must reach home after a time, and so, with hope in her heart, kept on.

But as the sun grew high in the heavens when she had walked many weary miles, and still she recognised neither prairie nor forest, she began to feel alarmed.

The river grew wider and deeper, till at last the unwelcome conviction forced itself upon her mind that it was not the stream by the side of which she was sitting when Black Snake attacked her before carrying her away to his cavern.

Water Lily was lost!

She knew it; and, after giving way to a few tears, sat down beneath a steep bank to consider as to the best way to find her home once more.

There was only one plan that she could think of, and that was to retrace her own trail.

But that plan would lead her past the cavern again.

Black Snake would be there, perhaps, or he was perhaps even at that moment following in her footsteps.

A rustling sound in the bushes overhead caused Water Lily to look up.

A pair of glaring eye-balls stared full into hers; a loud roar fell upon her ears.

With the quickness of thought she discharged an arrow, and leaped aside just in time to avoid the spring of a huge catamount which from the bushes had marked her for its prey.

But the daughter of Big Elk knew how

to use the bow almost as well as her father; and she had the satisfaction of seeing the fierce brute roll over and over and then die.

This adventure gave her a new source of alarm.

She had no idea that wild beasts were so numerous and ferocious in that part of the country.

But still no thought of fear entered her brave soul.

She was resolved to encounter any danger and difficulties rather than again fall into the hands of Black Snake.

Nothing should separate her from the youth of her choice.

She began to retrace her steps towards the cave from which she had escaped.

But long ere she could reach it night again came on, and once more she was compelled to encamp in solitude upon the verdant prairie.

Of food she had as yet no lack.

As she sank upon the soft turf, she began to feel the effects of two days' fatigue.

Sleep overcame her.

A sound sleep, from which she did not awake until dawn once more lightened up the scene.

Then Water Lily awoke.

Glancing around she saw at some distance from her a man on horseback.

The face she could not see, as the rider held down his head; but the dress of skin, together with the long flowing mane and tail, convinced her that it was a warrior of her own race.

Most probably Black Snake, or, what would be quite as bad, a warrior of the hostile tribe of Crow Indians.

What could the Indian maiden do to escape?

The prairie was almost level, and only an occasional tree or bush afforded a chance of concealment.

Flight alone could save her, and trusting to the forlorn hope of not being yet observed, Water Lily started off at full speed, at right angles to the course she had been pursuing.

Water Lily was swift of foot—none of the Delaware maidens more so.

She ran for life; fear lent wings to her heels.

She glanced back over her shoulder.

Oh, horror!

The horseman had seen her, and was following at a rapid pace.

On ran Water Lily, and on came the stranger; the horse gained upon the girl rapidly.

Without again looking back, she continued her flight till she could hear the hoofs of the horse thundering upon the turf.

Escape then was impossible.

Nothing remained but resistance.

She turned suddenly, fitted an arrow to her bowstring, and was about to discharge the missile, when a well-known voice came.

"Hold! It is I. It is——"

"Strongbow!" exclaimed Water Lily.

"Yes—thank Heaven I have found you alive and well," said the youth, leaping from his panting steed, and running up to the Indian girl, who trembled with excitement.

"But from whence comes the Boy Chief?" she asked.

"From the Delaware village, where I heard that you were lost, and vowed never to return until I had discovered your fate."

"Water Lily thanks the pale-face chief, whose bow is strong and whose arrows are swift," replied the Delaware girl, blushing and looking down.

"Will you do nothing but thank me?"

There was a pause, and then came the words—

"Water Lily will love Strongbow more."

If we say that our young hero threw his arms round Water Lily's neck, and kissed her half-a-dozen times, we shall not depart very far from the truth.

So while he is kissing, and the Delaware girl is recovering from her astonishment, let us point our pen afresh, and commence a new chapter.

## CHAPTER XXXIII.

### FLIGHT AND PURSUIT.

KISSES, like all other earthly things, must come to an end.

So Strongbow and Water Lily were obliged to leave off for want of breath, and then commenced the cross questioning.

"Strongbow has been long away from the lodges of the Delawares."

"I have, dear; but where ⁓ you think I have been?"

The girl shook her head.

"Water Lily does not know."

"Would you not like to know? I am certain you would, for, like the rest of your sex, you possess a great deal of curiosity."

"I should."

"Then I will tell you. I have been to the haunted swamp, and I have plucked a branch from the cedar tree; see, here it is."

As he spoke the excited youth held aloft the branch he had journeyed so far to obtain.

Water Lily gazed upon it, then upon his face, and then turned her blushing face to the ground.

"The way was long," she said, "and there were many dangers in the path, yet the pale-faced chief encountered all for me. Water Lily will love Strongbow so long as the great Manitou, master of life, gives her breath. She will be obedient, will rear his wigwam, fetch his wood and water, and cook his meat."

"She shall do nothing of the kind! She shall be my wife, not my slave; and if she fetches either wood or water while I am at hand to do it, may——"

"A great warrior must not do the work of a squaw. Listen: I am half English," said she, dropping the style of speech used by all Indians, who speak of themselves in the third person, "and have heard that it is not usual for the pale-face men to perform menial labour more than Indians. It is not the custom for warriors of my tribe to do anything, except hunt and fight; and you, as the chief of my tribe, must not depart from its customs."

"Well we shall settle all this at a future time. Now, tell me what has happened? How came you so far away from home?"

She told him all.

Just as the narration was finished she glanced up, and said, with a look of horror—

"See, our enemies are at hand!"

Strongbow looked in the direction she indicated, and, at about half a mile distance, saw a party of Indians on horseback coming towards them.

They were coming from the direction which the young lovers would take in returning homewards.

"They are our friends, the Delawares," replied Strongbow, thinking that they were warriors of the tribe who had followed his trail.

"Those braves are not Delawares, I know, by the dress. They are Crows or Iroquois; both enemies."

"Then we must make tracks."

"But they are mounted."

"Yes, though I don't believe they have so swift a horse as mine. Come, let me help you to his back."

"And leave you here? No."

"I go with you. Together we don't weigh more than one of those podgy braves."

No more persuasion was necessary, and Water Lily sprang lightly to the back of the brave mustang.

Strongbow mounted, and away they went.

"Eight of them!" he muttered. "We shall be captured certainly if they overtake us. On, on, good horse!"

The good horse comprehended that his master was in danger, and took monstrous strides across the prairie.

Eight whooping, yelling savages, were behind in pursuit.

The prairie appeared to be perfectly level for miles, as far as the eye could reach, but, suddenly, the fugitives found themselves going down hill, and saw before them at the bottom of the declivity a river of some hundreds of yards in width.

" Lost !" exclaimed Water Lily; " you cannot swim with your injured shoulder."

" I will try ; but what can you do ?"

" The daughter of Big Elk has learnt to swim."

So the horse was kept right on towards the stream, across which Strongbow and Water Lily hoped to escape by swimming.

" To the right !" exclaimed the girl, suddenly.

" Why ?"

" There is a canoe behind those trees, with paddles in it."

She pointed to a group of low cottonwood trees, and, sure enough, there in their shade was a canoe, with its sides gaily painted, and ornamented Indian fashion.

" I wonder to whom it belongs ?" said Strongbow.

" To our pursuers, I should think."

" Then it is a lawful prize. Forward, good horse, that we may gain tho middle of the stream before they reach the bank."

But the Indians were gaining on them rapidly, and it seemed doubtful whether they would be able to carry out their plan.

The canoe was reached, the fugitives leaped to the ground, launched the canoe, and entered it.

The horse they could not take with them in their frail craft, and, therefore, it was left upon the bank.

Water Lily, who was skilful in the management of Indian canoes, took up a paddle, and, with a few strokes, sent it from the shore.

An Indian came thundering up upon his reeking steed.

With a yell he jumped from the saddle into the stream, and began swimming after them.

Water Lily exerted her strength; but there was a leak in the bottom of the canoe which allowed sufficient water to enter to retard their progress considerably. The Indian was gaining upon them.

" I must kill him," said Strongbow " Our safety must be secured even at the expense of his life."

Water Lily shuddered.

Though an Indian's daughter, she was averse to bloodshed.

Strongbow noticed her look of horror, and, laying down his tomahawk, took up a spare paddle.

" Keep off !" he shouted, as the Indian drew within a yard of the canoe. " Keep off ! or it will be worse for you !"

The Indian heeded not, but continued his efforts to gain the boat.

He reached out one hand to grasp the stern.

At that moment Strongbow raised the strong ash-wood paddle, and with it dealt the redskin a tremendous blow upon the head.

The dark features disappeared for a minute beneath the waves; then the pursuer was again seen some few yards behind, still making efforts to reach them.

Presently he was seen to be swimming wildly, then the motion of his arms ceased, and, after a convulsive struggle had passed through the frame, a senseless body was seen floating with the current of the broad river.

" We are saved," said Strongbow.

They were saved from the pursuers, but they little anticipated what fearful peril awaited them upon the opposite bank of the stream.

## CHAPTER XXXIV.

### THE JUDGE ON THE WESTERN CIRCUIT.

THE blow which stretched our villain Wylde senseless upon the earth, just as he intended taking the life of Edmund Armstrong, was administered by a woman.

But that woman was a wife—a fond, loving wife—who had shared her husband's prosperity and adversity, and was ready to brave any dangers for his sake.

The peril she saw him in nerved her arm, and directed the blow.

It happened luckily for the emigrant that just as the would-be-murderer raised his rifle to his shoulder, Mrs. Armstrong opened the door of the hut with the intention of bringing in some pieces of fire-wood which lay outside.

She had just taken hold of one of them when she saw a man kneeling upon the ground, and pointing the muzzle of his gun through a crevice in the boards.

One glance was sufficient to show her the dangerous position of her husband.

Delay might cause his death!

With difficulty she repressed her inclination to scream out, and then raising the billet of wood in both hands, brought it down with all her power upon the murderer's head.

Her husband's life was saved!

The man fell with a half-spoken curse on his lips, his rifle exploded harmlessly, and then Mrs. Armstrong herself fainted from terror and excitement.

Out came Armstrong, alarmed beyond measure at the sound of the gun, and the exclamation of his wife.

As he stepped from the door of the hut his foot struck against her body.

"Heaven help me!" moaned the man. "At last the partner of my life is taken from me, and I am alone. Wife! wife! speak to me! look at me once more ere death for ever seals up those loving eyes."

He knelt down by her side, and kissed her cheek.

As he did so her warm breath fanned his face.

"She lives!" he exclaimed, altering his tone, "she lives, and while there is life there is hope."

With these words the husband lifted his wife up, and tenderly bore her into the hut.

A little cold water sprinkled on her face revived her.

She was able to sit up in a few moments, and explain what had occurred.

"You are not hurt, then, dear wife?"

"Not even a scratch."

"Thank Heaven again. But this villain, what became of him?"

"I left him lying upon the ground outside the cabin."

"The rascal; he shall suffer not only for the attempt upon my life, but for the alarm he has caused my wife."

Armstrong arose, and taking a coil of good hempen rope in his hand, went out.

He found Wylde lying just where he had been struck down by Mrs. Armstrong.

The heavy blow had deprived him of his faculties.

Having bound the villain's hands and feet, Armstrong dragged his captive in no very gentle manner into the log hut.

Then he tied him up in such a manner that escape was impossible.

Thus secured, he felt sure that his prisoner could not escape.

Armstrong then seated himself beside his wife, and questioned her.

"Did you see anyone with this ruffian?"

"Not a soul."

"Did you hear him say anything, or make any kind of remark or exclamation?"

"Not the slightest sound before I felled him with the wood."

"I should like to know whether he has any accomplices or not. I shall go and look round."

"Edmund, for my sake as well as your own, be cautious," said the heroic wife.

"I will; fear not."

The emigrant carefully looked to the loading of his gun, and, after placing an axe in his belt, sallied forth.

He was cautious, as he promised his wife he would be, though he did not, in an excess of prudence, neglect to search thoroughly.

Wylde's horse was found a short distance from the hut, and was detained as prisoner as well as its master.

There was nothing to show that the villain had any partners in his attempted crime; and, somewhat satisfied with the result of his search, Armstrong retired to his cabin.

Though he retired to rest, it can hardly be said that he slept.

His eyes, though closed, were directed towards the prisoner, and would have instantly opened had his ears caught the slightest sound.

Wylde recovered his consciousness soon after Armstrong's return to the hut.

He was confused, and astonished to find himself in such a condition; but a few moments were sufficient to give him time to remember what had taken place.

But who could it be who had defeated him in his plans?

He had seen no one—heard no one; he had brought no friend with him, so that treachery was not to be thought of, and he had taken a careful survey of the premises before approaching, to see that no one was abroad.

The blow had come upon him suddenly and mysteriously. Ere he fell he had just caught sight of what seemed to be a gigantic black mass standing beside him, and then all was vacancy.

One circumstance soon forced itself upon his mind.

He was a prisoner, and that, too, in the house of his hated foe.

No doubt retribution was now at hand, and he, the guilty one, was doomed to suffer for all the sufferings he had caused others.

But Wylde did not care to suffer.

He moved himself as far as possible to see how he was bound, and whether there was any chance of escape.

The movement was executed with only the slightest noise, yet, slight as that sound was, Armstrong's eyes at once opened, and his hand clutched the rifle.

So Wylde saw at once that he must give up all hope of escape while in the presence of so watchful a keeper.

"You have caught me; may the capture do you good," he growled.

"It will, I have no doubt."

"What do you intend to do with me, pray?"

"I intend to give you up to the officers of the law."

"Pshaw! there's no law in these wilds."

"Pardon me," replied Armstrong, with mock politeness, "there is a judge in the next town."

"Not a bit, or I should have heard of it."

"I am right. There is a judge in the nearest settlement."

"Pooh!"

"His name is 'Lynch'; you may perhaps have heard of him."

Wylde's face became pale as ashes, and no longer wore a contemptuous expression.

"To his officers I shall give you up. Now go to sleep if you can, and pleasant dreams to you."

Wylde was completely cowed.

He had no answer to make, nor did there appear the slightest chance that he could escape from his relentless foe.

Sleep with pleasant dreams!

The very thought was mockery, for how could he sleep when all around him the air teemed with scenes of his past bad life?

He shut his eyes to keep out the tormenting visions, but they forced their way through his closed eyelids into the deepest recesses of his brain.

Armstrong seemed motionless; but whether he slept or not was best known to himself.

Daylight at length began to pour its first rays of light through the crevices in the log walls of the hut.

One bright beam especially came glittering through the very chink which Wylde knew so well.

Up rose the captor, Armstrong, pale, thoughtful, but evidently determined.

He carefully looked to his prisoner's bonds, and then went out to saddle his horse.

This was soon done, and he re-entered.

A stroke of his knife set Wylde's legs at liberty, though his hands remained bound.

"Now, then, villain, your horse is ready; I shall allow you to ride," said Armstrong.

"Thanks," replied Wylde.

He had recovered, to a certain degree, from the feelings of fear which overcame him when he first found out the dangers of his position, and was prepared to die —not as a brave man, certainly, but without any great show of moral or physical cowardice.

A brief word of parting in his wife's ear, and Armstrong placed his captive upon the horse; then, mounting his own, the strange couple took the track leading to the settlement.

The emigrant had a rope attached to the bridle of Wylde's horse, so as to control it, and another cord tied to his captive's body, so as to secure him, even if he lost the horse.

"Now, remember this," said Armstrong, cautioningly; "if you make the least attempt to call out or give any alarm, I will certainly slit your tongue. So beware, and keep silence."

Wylde nodded, and in silence they continued their journey.

A more unsociable one it would be hard to imagine; but at length they reached the outskirts of the settlement.

A man was seen strolling towards them, rifle in hand.

"Hillo, stranger!" said he, "what kind o' varmint mout that be? Blow me if ever I see a cattymount on hossback afore!"

"A catamount! What do you mean?"

"Wa-al, if thet critter you've got thar ain't a catymount he oughter be. A slicker-lookin' rascal this child never sot his two little eyes upon. Whar did ye pick him up?"

"He was prowling round my hut last night, and so got caught."

"I say, stranger, you're a Britisher, but you've got grit in yer, I guess, or you wouldn't ha' whipped this hyar two-legged cat. Did ye fight long?"

"Not at all. My wife did it all for me, except tying his hands and legs."

"Your wife! Then, huraw for Madam Bull, and may I be cowhided if she ain't a tarnation tall screamer! Oh, yes; this coon will hev to be introdooced to the judge, I guess."

"That's why I brought him here."

"All right, come along, my beauty; I'm the head constable. Come, hop off o' that hoss."

"What authority have you thus to order me?" said Wylde, speaking for the first time.

"Thunder and—— wa-al, it's no use cussin'. Look'ee hyar, boss, this rope hev hung heavier men by a stun or two than you. Thet rope's my legal docyment, and this hyar rifle is to enforce the law. Come down, now."

In the presence of such positive proofs of the stranger's authority, Wylde could no longer resist.

He dismounted as well as he could, his descent being hastened by a sharp jerk of the rope fastened to his waist, which the stranger now had hold of.

"Now, come along, Mr. Britisher, and see me chain up the wild cat. I'll bet thar will be just a tall spree when I has to hang him!"

"Are you executioner, then?"

"Sometimes."

The official functionary then led the way into the midst of the little town.

I think I have before stated that it possessed a gaol.

This gaol being situated in the midst of the score of log huts was, of course, a very prominent object.

So was the prisoner, as he walked towards it, escorted by his probable executioner.

A little crowd soon assembled, composed of all the inhabitants, with the exception of two or three who were away in the woods hunting.

Wylde scanned every face, but read not a single sign of pity.

Yet—stay, there is one face which exhibits emotion, though the emotion is caused by fear.

The face is that of Daniel Jackson, Esq., attorney, actor, swindler, &c.

Daniel had gone out west with the intention of reforming, and, no doubt, he would have been respectable (for a time) had not the fates ordained that he should see his old friend and associate, Wylde, brought in as a captive.

Wylde saw Jackson, and for a moment felt inclined to denounce the traitor.

But, as has often been said, "second thoughts are best."

He kept his eye fixed upon his treacherous friend until he reached the door of the gaol.

Then, when his hands were unbound, he made a rapid signal with his fingers.

Jackson saw it, and although his face grew more pallid than before, he made a corresponding signal.

## CHAPTER XXXV

### PERILS ON THE WATER.

THE canoe which Strongbow and Water Lily had so fortunately obtained, saved them from all further anxiety on account of the Indians who had pursued them.

They kept on their course across the river, after freeing themselves from the attack of the swimming Indian; not in a direct course, but inclining to a point some distance down stream.

"I am sorry I was compelled to kill him," said the young chief, pointing to the body of the Indian.

And he was sorry, too, for, though brave as a lion, Strongbow was not bloodthirsty.

"So am I," replied Water Lily, in a tone of sadness.

She rowed a few strokes with her paddle, and then looked back.

"See!" she cried. "Look at the horse."

"What horse?" asked her lover.

"Your horse. There!"

Strongbow looked, and beheld two of the mounted Indians making vain attempts to lasso the noble steed.

But the high-spirited animal was a match for his pursuers.

He doubled and twisted about in such a manner, that even when it appeared impossible that he could escape, the noose dropped harmlessly to the ground.

A third Indian then took part in the chase.

With a terrific bound, Strongbow's steed leaped clear of all foes, and, at full speed, hastened down to the water's edge.

The Indians were after him, and, without a moment's hesitation, the gallant brute leaped into the water.

Ere an Indian could come within forty yards of him, he was beyond the reach of their ropes.

"He sees us; he is coming after the canoe!" cried Water Lily.

"Bravo, good steed!" shouted Strongbow.

The good horse was indeed swimming after the boat, as Water Lily had said; but it was still some great distance behind.

The current was running strongly, and the fair Delaware maiden had quite as much work as she could do to guide the boat.

At length they neared the shore.

Smooth water appeared before them, and it seemed probable that their troubles would cease as soon as they could touch the point of land towards which they were steering.

A dozen yards more and they will reach land. Ha! what is that?

Is it a concealed rock, or a tree torn from its bed by the fierce tempests?

Which of the two could it be that gave the boat such a shock?

Again, again! It can be no tree or rock; it must be a living being which thus follows the canoe, and causes its slender frame to quiver with violent blows.

"Oh! Heaven! it is an alligator!" cried Water Lily, in great alarm, as she dropped her paddle, and looked over the bows of the boat.

Strongbow followed her frantic looks with his eyes.

There, beneath the surface of the water, appeared the hideous form of the gigantic lizard.

Its whole body, arms, hands and claws, were clearly traceable in the limpid stream, above the surface of which rose his scaly serrated back and shoulders.

The snout and tail of the fearful beast were protruded still higher above the surface of the river.

With the tail he was lashing the clear water into a froth which speckled and disfigured the surface of the river.

The fierce brute was not more than three yards away from the canoe, its long scaly body glistening with a sheen like that of the best ring mail worn by the knights of old.

Strongbow discharged an arrow.

In vain! He might as well waste his shafts upon adamantine rock as upon that invulnerable coat of mail.

The arrow glanced through the water, struck upon the hard covering of the gigantic saurian, and then was lost to sight.

Though not sufficient to draw blood, the wound seemed to be not without its smart.

Master Alligator assumed a more furious aspect than before.

He half raised himself out of the water, then, turning with the swiftness of lightning, dealt the canoe a blow with his tail which divided it into several pieces.

Strongbow and Water Lily were hurled into the rapid stream.

"Oh, mercy! The monster is coming this way. Oh, save me, save me if you love me!"

So shrieked Water Lily as she found herself struggling in the water with an infuriated alligator within a few feet of her.

"A LASSO, THROWN BY BLACK SNAKE'S HAND, DROPPED ROUND HER NECK."

Strongbow too well understood the fearful purport of the summons and of the loud screaming which succeeded it.

"Swim, swim for your life!" he cried. "I will be with you."

The young chief of the Delawares had been thrown some feet beyond Water Lily, but as soon as he heard her voice, he turned back.

The Delaware maiden was a capital swimmer, and was exerting all her powers to escape from the amphibious monster. But it seemed as though all her endeavours would be of no avail.

Strongbow had lost his bow in the river at the moment the canoe was smashed.

Without it his arrows were useless.

But without hesitation he drew his tomahawk from his belt and threw himself between the alligator and the damsel of his heart.

Little cared the alligator for the uplifted arm or the threatening axe.

The fierce beast had felt the tingle caused by the youth's arrow, and was in good earnest.

His huge mouth, armed with horrid rows of teeth, appeared—open wide to swallow up the victim.

Down came the axe. No child's blow was struck by the boy chief's strong arm; but had he hammered the edge of the steel weapon against the breach of a heavy cannon, he would have made almost as much impression upon it as upon the skull of the alligator.

Oh, Strongbow, save yourself; save yourself!" cried Water Lily, as she beheld the perilous position of her lover.

It seemed as though her warning voice had come too late.

The brave youth leaped back, waist deep though he was in the water; but the teeth of the scaly brute had fastened in his robe of skin; another moment was only needed to give his limbs as a prey to the alligator.

"Thank Heaven!"

Such was the fervent exclamation of Water Lily as the sharp ringing report of the well known prairie rifle was heard, and the alligator roaring with pain, turned away.

Blood and froth issued from its hideous head as it lashed the water with its tail in the convulsions of death. But Strongbow was safe.

He had made a second leap back just as the shot was fired, and had gained the bank of the river in safety.

His first thought was, not to see who had saved him, but to carry the half-fainting Water Lily to a place of security from the attacks of such foes as that by which they had just been assailed.

Having done this, he turned round to see whose timely aid it was had saved them both from such deadly peril.

A man was running towards them; in his hand was a rifle, from the muzzle of which smoke was still issuing.

They both recognised him, though they wondered how he came there.

It was Hiram Swift the hunter.

## CHAPTER XXXVI.

### PERILS ON THE LAND.

"HURRAW for you, young fellow!" shouted Hiram Swift, as he came up.

"Why, where on earth did you come from?" asked Strongbow.

"From the group o' wild chiney trees thar."

"I thought you were following me."

So I thought till I found out Big Elk. It war his trail I follered, like a chunk-head. Well, you're one o' the true sort. That beast would ha' chawed you up, thoug, I reckon."

"I expect he would. This is not the first time you have saved my life, and I am grateful."

"You said you had seen the Big Elk, my father?" said Water Lily.

"He's thar, lookin' out for meat."

"Thar," meant, according to the hunter's finger, away across a huge stretch of prairie land, farther than the eye could see.

The great grassy plain seemed flat as a table, reaching right away in the distance, till the green shade of the earth mingled with, and was lost in, the blue vault of heaven.

But though it appeared perfectly level, it was not, as the hunter well knew.

There were many valleys there where whole armies might encamp without being seen by anyone standing upon the river bank.

"It's a long way," said Strongbow.

"No, I guess an hour's ride will do it."

"Then let us make haste," observed Water Lily, "or Black Snake will——"

"I guess he won't."

"He would do anything to get me into his power again."

"Now, don't you be afeard; Black Snake ain't a-goin' to move his bones from whar they're now layin'. His flesh mout travel, sartin, seein' as 'tis in the wolves' bellies."

"I don't understand you, sir."

"What, ain't this young scamp told yer as how Black Snake caved in—shot by a blue arrrow?"

"No."

"It's true. He'll never hurt ye any more."

"I forgot to tell her," said Strongbow. "But it is quite true, dear Lily, that you will never be persecuted by that man again; he is dead! Here comes my horse though; we'll catch him and then be off."

"Whar's yer hoss?"

"There, trying to land just above."

"Woh! good hoss," exclaimed Swift, running to the spot indicated, and assisting the animal to reach the shore.

The mustang was uninjured, and, in fact, rather improved by the bath, which had freshened its limbs.

Swift led it back to the owner, and then pointed the way to the grove of trees where he had left his own steed.

The horses were duly mounted, and then away they went.

The old hunter knew well how to lead them in a straight line across the prairie to any part he wished to visit.

Ten minutes had elapsed, and the river was no longer visible, though a streak of verdure of a deeper hue than the coarse grass and weeds of the prairies told where its silvery current rolled on between the reedy banks.

Hiram Swift looked back occasionally,

and, by taking the bearings of certain objects on the hills the other side of the river, directed their course with as much certainty as a sailor could have done by compass.

It required care though, for the sky was leaden-grey, and not a glimpse of sunshine enabled them to judge of the position of that luminary.

Suddenly, as they journeyed on, a horseman was seen ascending, as it were, up out of the earth.

"It is Big Elk!"

"It is my father!"

Both Water Lily and the hunter recognised the Delaware brave long before the whole of his body was visible.

"What can have brought him here?" asked the Boy Chief. "Where did he come from?"

"Thar's Indians abroad, depend on it," replied Swift.

On came Big Elk, at the utmost speed of which his horse was capable.

As he approached the party, he shouted out a few words in his own dialect.

"I thought so. He's been precious near havin' his hair raised. Hold hard!"

In obedience to Swift's command, Strongbow reined up the bold steed which bore him and his betrothed, to wait for the Delaware.

Another moment and he was with them.

A short but affectionate greeting took place between father and daughter, but Big Elk was too much of a warrior to waste time in words when foes were at hand.

Swift remained silent, waiting for his red-skin friend to explain what new danger was at hand.

"The Iroquois are cowards and squaws; their scalps shall hang in the smoke of the Delaware lodges."

"Iroquois thieves, is it?" muttered Swift.

"The Iroquois and the Crows have banded together to take the scalp of a Delaware brave, but they shall go back howling to their wigwams, and shall make petticoats for the squaws."

"That's all right, old hoss; but how many o' these varmint is on our trail now?"

Big Elk opened and closed his hands

four times, to signify that the enemy numbered forty warriors.

"Then I guess we had better just make tracks, or we'll be in the midst of 'em."

"Come," said Big Elk, pointing to the west; "come, let us leave the Iroquois dogs and Crow thieves."

No more was said, but the horses sped away at their full speed.

The wind roared past them, but it could not drown the sound of the loud whoop uttered by the pursuers.

Turning back in his saddle, Strongbow saw a troop of Indians pursuing them.

It seemed that the Indians had only expected one scalp, that of Big Elk; but the sight of three horses, one of them bearing a double burden, made them still more eager in the chase.

On they went, pursuers and pursued, through a thick growth of tall grass and flowering plants, matted together with wild pea vines, and other creepers.

The flowers had all faded, and the vegetation presented a somewhat parched, dried-up appearance.

At the commencement of the chase the pursued fugitives gained slightly upon their pursuers.

But their horses were tired, and Strongbow noticed with sorrow that the red men were slowly but surely gaining upon them.

The foremost of the party was hardly three quarters of a mile behind.

Whips and thongs were used upon the sides of the jaded beasts, who, however, needed but little inducement to do their best.

So intent were all upon escaping that they did not notice the thick haze gathering upon the horizon before them.

At length a peculiar smell greeted Hiram Swift's nostrils.

Instantly he pulled up his horse, and pointing right in front, exclaimed—

"The prairie is on fire!"

## CHAPTER XXXVII.

### JACKSON AT WORK.

NO sooner did Jackson perceive and respond to Wylde's masonic signal than he began to set to work.

He would have escaped, if he had thought escape possible, and would have sought a refuge in some other hiding place.

But, he knew well enough, to attempt such a thing as flight would arouse suspicion, and then he would soon be overtaken.

For Jackson's horse had fallen ill and finally furnished a meal for the wolves; indeed, he was only staying in the settlement to purchase another animal before continuing his journey.

He knew, moreover, that if he did not obey the signalled command of his late master, Wylde, the latter would denounce him.

Then, without the slightest doubt, Daniel Jackson, Esq., would also become an inmate of the log prison.

So Jackson went to work.

He moved about stealthily from house to house, watching for an opportunity to lay his hands on the articles he wanted,

namely, a saw with a small, thin blade, a file, and a bowie-knife.

With these implements in his possession, he had no doubt that Wylde would be able to break his way out of a much stronger prison than that in which he was then incarcerated.

After paying a short visit to nearly every house in the place he procured what he required.

But he had to procure the articles at the little general store, and pay a good sum for them too.

Now, how to convey them to his friend was the next anxious consideration.

He walked down to the prison with a leisurely step, as though he had only gone to see the villain out of curiosity.

A man was on guard there.

Jackson walked up to him.

"Nice job you've got, stranger?"

"Ye-es; putty tidy."

"Got the darned skunk inside?"

"Ye-es; an' thar' he'll stop, I guess."

"Ain't there a leetle hole where a fellow might peep through at the critter?"

"Not one big enough for a flea to look through, mister. Just walk round the log, now, an' see if you kin diskiver one."

Jackson availed himself of this permission, and walked around the building.

Though roughly built, it was of a very substantial kind, not a crevice of any kind being visible.

So Jackson returned to the front of the building, and once more entered into conversation with the gaoler.

"A nice tight house, mister."

"Ye-es. We takes care o' rogues when we catches 'em."

"Where does the light an' air come from, now?"

"The critters don't want light to see to do nothin', I guess. As for air, why, if they gits smothered, it saves us the trouble of hangin' 'em. They gets air enough through the keyhole."

All this time Jackson's searching eyes were wandering up and down the building. But not a sign of any opening was visible, excepting a crevice about an inch in width, above the top of the door, and another below it.

The people seemed to know that the door was the weak point in their gaol.

This was evident from the fact that the gaoler paid no attention whatever to the backs and sides of the building, but remained steadily posted before door.

The articles—the saw and file—must go through the doorway.

Having made up his mind upon this point, Jackson began to consider how he could pass away the time until dusk, for he was not so foolish as to suppose that he could convey such things into the gaol in open day without being detected.

"Do you stay here on the watch all night, mister?"

The man nodded.

"Ye-es, two on us."

"Two!"

"Ye-es, sure."

"You do take good care of 'em."

"You're right, mister."

"What time does the second man join you?"

"Sundown."

"Ah! Well, I don't know that I ought to stop here, mister. I'll be off and look after some meat."

"I say, mister, could ye bring down a flask o' whisky presently? I likes a drop at nights."

"All right; I'll bring some."

With this reply Jackson moved off, thinking that upon the whole he had opened his proceedings with success.

His mind was busy as he stalked through the forest glades, hatching projects for escaping once more from the power of Wylde.

"I must be away before he can make his way out; I must not be mixed up in any business of his. Who knows?—perhaps he may even kill me when he is at liberty."

So he walked and plotted.

At length he saw the antlers of a deer topping above a clump of bushes right before him.

He at once began to approach the animal, so as to get a shot.

It was some time before he could crawl near enough, but at length he managed to get within range, and fired.

The animal turned out to be in pretty fair condition, and, after packing up the prime parts, Jackson returned home.

It was nearly sunset before he reached the house of the settler who had for two or three days given him hospitality.

He presented his meat to the host, swallowed a hasty supper, and was about to stroll off, when he overheard the man give directions to his son as to the place where his horse was to be tethered.

"Stake out the critter along by the wood across thar. Thar's better grass over yonder."

Following the direction of the settler's finger, Jackson saw that it indicated a portion of the prairie adjacent to the outskirts of the forest.

"I must make free with your horse, my friend," thought he, "even at the expense of being called ungrateful."

He then hurried down to the prison.

The man who had done duty all day was still there, and evidently prepared to remain all night.

He had his rifle and blanket, and his companion was armed also.

Jackson did not forget to bring his rifle with him, as he did not intend to return.

He approached the two worthy watchmen, one of whom was seated with his back to the door of the gaol, while the other was standing close by.

The first move of the wily ex-agent was to seat himself beside the man on the ground, putting his back also to the door of the prison.

"Here's the whisky, my friend; take a good drink," said he, producing his flask.

The invitation was readily accepted; then pipes were filled and lighted, and a conversation took place, the prisoner, of course, being the theme.

The two gaolers evidently considered it a waste of time and trouble to keep Wylde in prison.

They were for hanging him right off, and no doubt would have done so, had their wills been law.

But the head men of the place had decreed that Judge Lynch should preside over Wylde's fate; and therefore the two young men could do nothing but obey.

"Thar's no doubt the critter's guilty, and oughter be hung right slick away. If he ain't guilty, 'tain't much matter," said one.

"Well; I dare say you will have the pleasure of seeing him strung up," replied Jackson.

A hard breathing behind told Jackson that Wylde was listening; so, to convince the prisoner that he was obedient to command, the ex-agent thrust the handle of the knife beneath the door.

A few seconds after he felt it drawn from his hand into the prison.

This action was accomplished with the greatest secrecy, so that neither of the two men on watch had the slightest suspicion of what was going on.

Then he waited a little time, till he could get his saw in such a position that he might push it beneath the door without trouble.

"What are ye fidgetin' about, stranger?" asked one of the men.

"I had a big stone under me, and couldn't sit easy."

"Heave it out then. Hand us your bacca pouch, Bill."

Jackson pretended to move away the stone which had annoyed him, and slipped the saw under the door.

In a few minutes he had supplied Wylde with the file in the same manner, and then, after a short time longer spent in conversation with the two gaolers, he moved off.

"I shall go and turn in," said he. "I want to be off early in the morning."

"What, not stop and see the critter in here hanged?"

"No, good-night."

He proceeded for a short distance in the direction of the houses, until he thought he was beyond the range of the gaolers' eyesight.

But they were men who could see in the dark almost as well as cats; and as they watched his retreating figure they were not a little surprised to see him turn away and make off across the strip of prairie towards the timber.

"That feller's arter no good," said one.

"Hush!" whispered the other.

A slight rasping noise in the prison had attracted his attention.

"Arter the coon and fetch him back," said the first.

"I reckon if he don't come his scalp will," was the reply; and catching up his gun the speaker started off noiselessly in pursuit.

The other man then walked round the prison.

At one of the angles he paused, feeling certain that there the noise was produced.

The sound continued.

Drawing a six-barrelled revolver the man sat himself down upon the grass, and waited to see what could be the meaning of this.

## CHAPTER XXXVIII.

### THE PRAIRIE FIRE.

FIRE! That terrible word! what a fearful meaning it conveys.

Terrible as it may sound in the crowded city—with all the picturesque adjuncts of galloping horses and dashing engines crowded with brass-helmeted firemen, rushing, roaring mobs, pale women and children huddled together upon the house-tops shrieking for help, while the red flames pouring forth from shattered windows almost scorch their naked feet—how much more fearful is the sound when it arises in the midst of a sun-burnt prairie, and the lone wayfarers see the dreadful scourge rushing rapidly towards them and know that flight is useless.

What a thrill of dread passed through Strongbow's heart as he saw the black clouds of smoke arise, and grow higher as the flames rolled up the side of a declivity which was hidden from him!

At length it appeared.

From right to left a long line of flames —two miles in length—towering upwards and rushing onwards, thundering and roaring in the breeze which was sweeping it down towards them.

It was not for himself that the bold British youth feared.

He thought of the gentle being who sat behind him on his steed, and whose arm was clasped more tightly round his waist as she shudderingly looked upon the flames.

It was an agonising thought.

Must her fair, fragile, young body fall a prey to the devouring element while he should be close at hand to hear every heartrending scream, to watch every change of her countenance, and yet be able to give no aid?

"Back! back!" he exclaimed. "It is better to fall into the hands of our enemies than to be burnt alive."

"Don't know about that, lad. Stop whar ye air for a minit till old Swift gets his wits back."

"But the fire is coming this way."

"It 'ull be nigh quarter of an hour afore it comes down here."

"See, young warrior of the pale-face, our pursuers are squaws. They dare not approach the fire-spirit."

So said Big Elk as he pointed back.

The pursuers had halted.

They were evidently in what Swift termed a "p'ison fix."

They were loth to lose the scalps of the pale-faces and the Delaware warrior; but they plainly saw that if they advanced they should come upon their intended victims at about the same time as the fire, and would become involved in a common fate.

Though they loved scalps they loved their own lives more.

They halted, therefore, and, after a short consultation, turned away at full speed.

"We got rid o' them varmints, at all events," said Swift, with a chuckle.

"But how about the fire? We cannot escape that."

"Don't know about that, lad. 'Tain't my notion to be roasted, anyhow."

Strongbow was silent.

The old hunter spoke confidently, and hope began to return.

Strongbow turned to soothe his lovely companion, who trembled violently, and was evidently much alarmed, though she said nothing.

She had been nurtured among the Indians, and had learned their stoicism.

Swift and Big Elk had dismounted from their horses, and were holding a hurried consultation in the Delaware tongue.

"We shall be saved," whispered Water Lily, as she listened.

"How so, dearest?"

"They will make fire extinguish the fire."

Strongbow was puzzled.

He saw the two men tearing away a quantity of grass, which they placed in a heap. Swift then set it on fire.

The flames sparkled, then burst forth, and in a few seconds the heap was in a blaze.

Big Elk in the mean time carefully led the horses to the windward of the fire which had just been kindled.

He wrapped some pieces of skin round the heads of both animals, and stood watching Swift.

When the heap of grass was in a thorough blaze, he kicked it along in a straight line, *across the wind*, for a distance of three or four yards, thus setting quite as much of the prairie on fire.

Then, with his skin blanket, he beat out the flames that burned back towards the windward, leaving them to roll and spread on towards the retreating Indians as fast as they could.

In a few minutes a space of some yards in circumference was burnt clear, and into this smoky, scorched harbour of refuge he led all his companions.

"We air all right now, I guess, and we ain't had too much time neither."

The big fire was within a hundred

yards of them, but, by following in the wake of the flames they themselves had kindled, they were soon beyond the reach of danger.

The smoky, parched ground scorched the feet of the horses. while the thunder of the flames alarmed them to a high degree.

Had not their eyes been blindfolded, they would have been frightened beyond restraint, and most certainly would have carried their riders into the midst of the flames.

"This 'minds me o' the last day as I used to read on in mother's book," said old Swift. "We managed to pull through this by a little device o' mine; but dodgin' won't be no good *there*. I guess we'll have to stand up right slick and straight."

Strongbow thought so, too, and said so in a tone which showed that his mind was deeply impressed with the thought and the awful scene.

At length the flames reached the spot where Swift had kindled *their* fire, and then dwindling down to mere nothingness, suddenly roared away to the right and left, leaving behind a black, smoky plain.

"Pull the blinds off yer hosses and away wi' ye. It ain't onlikely as them Injuns 'ull manage to pull through this 'ayar blaze."

"Would they think of doing as you did?" asked Strongbow.

"Well, they mout; or the varmint perhaps would do as Big Elk did once."

"How was that?"

"Why, the chief war out on a perairie on the scout when he seed fire four sides all at once. The Injuns he war arter had sot it afire. Well, he couldn't get out o' the fix nohow, but warn't agoin to knock under for them varmint o' Crows, so he jist kills his hoss, cuts open the belly, pulls out the entrails, and crawls in. The fire war awful hot, and he war pretty nigh stewed. When the fire had burnt out he puts his head out, and looks for the Injuns; they had scattered over the plain lookin' for him, so Big Elk crawls into the hoss again, and they presently comes up, and kicks up a rare noise, cos he was burnt right up, and there warn't nothin' left. When they was gone Big Elk made tracks home, he did, and laughed at them varmint as thought to trap him."

"Big Elk is a great warrior," said Strongbow.

"Ugh!" was the response, as the Delaware urged his horse onwards.

For many miles ahead of them nothing could be seen but a vast black plain. Behind they could see the smoke rising in huge clouds as the fire swept onwards.

It was a lonesome ride, but at length they reached a stream of water, on the opposite side of which was green grass and some scattered trees.

## CHAPTER XXXIX.

### A GRIZZLY BEAR.

THE feeling caused by seeing the green turf once more was almost the same in the bosoms of Strongbow and Water Lily as that which the mariner experiences when he beholds dry land after a long and stormy voyage.

It seemed as though the poor tired horses were glad to find themselves near greensward once more.

Without word or sign from their riders they plunged into the stream and waded across, drinking as they went.

As soon as they had crossed the party dismounted.

"We must eat, I guess," said Swift.

"But what have we to eat?" asked Strongbow.

"Nothin'."

"Then why tempt us by talking about it?"

"It don't foller that we ain't a-goin' to have nothing because we've got nothing. Thar's timber, and it's a likely place to start a young buck."

"Shall I go with you?" asked Strongbow.

"No."

"I should like to."

"No, boy; look arter yer gal."

"What is the matter with her?"

Strongbow stopped not to hear his answer, but darted off.

Water Lily was lying upon the ground in a swoon.

The excitement caused by her perilous adventures, and the fearful scenes through which she had passed had proved too much for her, and her body had given way.

Strongbow knelt upon the ground by her side, and did everything he could to restore Water Lily to consciousness.

The warrior of the Delawares, too, lost all his dignified mien, when he saw his daughter's pale face and senseless form.

But he did not lose his presence of mind though. All the remedies which Indian surgery boasts were brought into play, and at length Water Lily recovered.

She was exceedingly weak though—unable to stand in fact.

"My daughter will rest here till another day shines," said Big Elk. "The Boy Chief of the Delawares and the hunter with the fire-bow will keep guard over her."

"And what of you, dear father?"

"Big Elk will remain with his daughter, even though the warriors of his tribe should call him 'squaw,' and make him petticoats."

"Thanks, thanks," murmured the poor girl.

"Hush!" whispered the chief, holding up his finger, as he saw that Strongbow was about to speak.

The youth held his tongue, though his eyes spoke volumes in proof of his ardent affection for the poor sick girl.

Hiram Swift returned very soon with a goodly supply of meat.

A fire was kindled, and cooking began in good earnest.

Strongbow, however, had little heart for food when he saw that his betrothed was unable to eat.

When the meal was finished a consultation took place as to what ought to be done under the circumstances.

"She must have rest," said Strongbow.

"You're right, lad, and she shall have a whole day."

"A whole day?"

"Yes. We'll camp right up in the timber to-night and stop thar all day to-morrow. She won't be up to much for a day."

"What says the Big Elk?"

"The pale-faced hunter has spoken the mind of a Delaware warrior."

"All right, then; we'll make tracks."

"But how are we to get her up there?" asked Strongbow; "she cannot walk."

"The arms of Big Elk are strong; he will carry his daughter to the shade of the big trees."

The Indian did so.

He wrapped up his daughter in a robe of buffalo hide, and lifting her up in his strong arms, bore her with the greatest ease to the grove of timber, where they intended to camp for the night.

Swift led the way, and Strongbow followed with the three horses.

The old hunter had noticed a good camping place; it was soon reached, and the invalid was carefully placed on the ground.

Though not professional nurses, the strong, rough men paid her quite as much attention as anyone possibly could have done under the circumstances.

The night passed away.

In the morning, Water Lily was still unable to walk, and Swift expressed a doubt whether she would be able to do so on the following day.

"Say, Delawar', we'll make a canoe for the gal, I guess. You can paddle her along the bank, while I an' the boy take care of the hosses."

"It is good."

"We can do the canoe to-day, and get out o' these diggin's to-morrow."

Big Elk nodded, and in a short time the three males of the party were hard at work.

There were plenty of birch trees in the grove, and a number of these were soon stripped of their bark.

A framework was made of saplings, the pieces of bark were sewn together over it with thin strips of deer hide, and by evening the canoe was nearly complete.

"We'll have to give the gal another day's rest," said Swift, as he wrapped himself in his blanket that night.

The following day the canoe was finished, and, being taken down to the water, was found to balance beautifully.

Water Lily was much better in the afternoon of the second day, and it was arranged that they should start early the following morning.

Big Elk and Swift went away to hunt and get a plentiful supply of meat, so that they might not have to halt by the way, so that Strongbow and Water Lily were left to themselves.

With the girl leaning upon his arm, Strongbow sauntered down to the water to show her the boat he had taken part in the building of.

It was moored to the bank by a stout rope, and looked quite handsome as it sat lightly upon the stream.

"Step in, dear Lily, and see how it will bear you," said the youth.

He tenderly assisted her into the canoe, which proved quite capable of carrying three or four times the weight.

"Remain a moment while I fetch the paddle, and we will go a little way up the stream," said Strongbow, starting off to the camp fire.

"Do not be long," replied Water Lily.

She gazed up the stream and down to see if her father was visible, but as she could not catch a glimpse of him, she turned her eyes to the opposite bank.

As she looked a slight rocking motion of the boat startled her.

Turning, she beheld a huge grizzly bear standing on the bank just where the rope was fastened.

The animal had touched the boat with his paw, and sent it a little way out into the stream, thus causing the rocking motion which alarmed Water Lily.

For a moment her faculties were paralyzed.

She well knew the fierce character of the grizzly bear, so different in its nature from its black congener.

She had seen the best hunters of her father's tribe covered with wounds, received in encounters with the ferocious brute, and she knew that when once an animal of that kind began an attack death alone could terminate it.

No wonder, then, that she felt fear.

A few moments' reflection, however, convinced her that for a time she was safe.

The bear, as soon as he saw that she was beyond his reach, showed no inclination to venture into the water in pursuit of her.

He stooped down, and touched the surface of the water with his paw, then drew back, shaking the member like a cat which has wetted its feet.

He growled horribly, and then moved backwards and forwards up the bank.

Water Lily then began to think of her pale-face lover.

If he should return, and not see the bear, his death would be almost certain.

She thought of screaming; but that, she reflected, would only draw him into the danger from which she wished to preserve him.

Presently, in one of his walks up and down, the bear stumbled over the rope, and fell heavily to the ground.

Still Water Lily was in safety.

Presently, he began to draw the rope towards him with both paws.

He seemed to see that by so doing, he would be able to reach the girl after a time, and gave a loud growl.

This increased his anger, and sent a notion into his thick head that the rope had something to do with keeping the object of his hatred beyond his reach.

He caught it up in one of his paws, and shook it about rudely.

Water Lily could no longer control her feelings, but cried aloud—

"Help—help!"

The sound reached Strongbow's ears, and he comprehended at once that some danger threatened his beloved.

Throwing down the paddle, he seized his bow and arrows, and hastened to the spot.

The sight almost froze his blood.

There was the huge brute seated upon its haunches, clumsily hauling in the rope, while Water Lily's screams filled the air.

She seemed almost distracted with fear.

Only for a moment he hesitated, and then, drawing an arrow to the head, discharged it right at the brute's body.

The missile seemed to bound back from the huge frame, and, with a horrid roar, the bear turned to confront his new assailant.

"Save yourself! Fly from the fierce brute, or he will devour you!" cried Water Lily.

It was too late to fly, however.

Strongbow well knew that the bear would overtake him in a few minutes, and that the only chance he had was to remain and fight for his life.

The bear dropped on all fours as soon as it saw Strongbow, and advanced with clumsy, shuffling, though rapid steps towards him.

The bold youth drew another arrow, and sent it from his bow.

The second missile took more effect, and buried itself right up to the feather in the bear's chest.

For a single moment the grizzly seemed staggered at this rough reception; but, after a momentary halt, he again rushed forward. Strongbow threw down his bow, and firmly clutched his knife.

The huge brute reared itself up on its hind legs; the great paws and sharp nails were in a moment clasped round the body of the bold boy; the huge mouth, with its great white teeth gradually approached his head, the bear's hot breath fell upon his cheek.

He stabbed again and again with his knife, and then a mist floated before his eyes.

## CHAPTER XL.

### FRUSTRATED.

TO say that Jackson ran, after he had supplied Wylde with tools, would be but a common-place mode of describing the way in which he cleared the ground.

He took huge strides with his long legs, stepping over fences, bushes, and other obstacles, with the greatest ease.

Then he turned back.

To his intense disgust he saw, in the clear moonlight, a pursuer following him rapidly yet stealthily.

The pursuer had a rifle in his hand, and seemed to be gaining upon him rapidly.

But the horse was close at hand—the horse he had seen staked out upon the prairie.

Shaping his course towards it, he drew the pin which fastened it, and leaping upon its back, galloped off.

Just in time, for, as the animal moved away, the pursuer fired, and Jackson heard the bullet whistle past his head at no great distance.

No matter, he was safe; for, ere the angry gaoler could reload, Jackson was far beyond the reach of his rifle.

For a long distance Jackson kept upon the open prairie, never going very far from the wood, though, lest circumstances should arise which might make it advisable for him to hide in its depths.

He had not much fear of being followed till daybreak, for there was not sufficient light to enable anyone to follow his trail.

After riding for six or seven miles along the prairie, he turned into the wood, at a part where it seemed tolerably free from undergrowth, and rode on beneath the leafy arches of the forest, at right angles to the path he had been pursuing.

Leaving him upon his journey, let us return and see how it fared with Wylde, in the prison.

As before said, one of the gaolers had seated himself upon the ground before the place where Wylde was endeavouring to make his escape, and with a revolver in his hand, was fully prepared to resist any attempt that might be made at escape.

The scraping noise continued.

Presently the point of the saw protruded, and a long-drawn sigh was heard, expressing the prisoner's satisfaction to the result of his labours.

The watcher kept himself perfectly quiet, and allowed the work to continue, till one of the logs was sawn completely through, about three feet above the ground.

Then for a few minutes all was silent again.

But the prisoner was eager to be gone, and soon set to work to make a second cut through the log.

Just as the saw again appeared through the walls of the prison, the report of the other man's rifle was heard as he fired at Jackson, and at the same time the one on watch spoke up.

" What ur ye doin', critter, eh ?"

Wylde made no reply, but in a noiseless manner withdrew the saw

" Lookee hyar, mister," continued the man, "if you thinks you're gwine to come any o' yer possum tricks on this coon, you've made a little mistake, I guess."

Still no reply.

The man drew his revolver, and prepared to encounter the prisoner.

"HELP FROM AN UNKNOWN HAND."

At that instant the other man returned from his fruitless pursuit.

"Hillo, Billee, did ye lay the varmint in his tracks?" asked the one who had been keeping watch over Wylde, thereby desiring to be informed whether Jackson had been shot or not.

"No!" was the angry response.

"How war that?"

"The skunk made off on old Amos's hoss."

"What d'ye think this hyar critter in hyar ur up tu?"

"Don't know."

"The concarned varmint hev got a saw, and is cutting away like winkin'."

"We had better have him out, and shoot him right off."

"That's right; d'ye hear, critter, come out an' be shot."

"Leave me alone," replied Wylde; "I am doing nothing, so just allow me to sleep while I have the chance."

"Then jist you put out that saw, wherever you got it from."

"I have no saw."

"Billee, boy, jist you get a pine-knot torch. I guess we'll see about this."

Off started Bill to procure the necessary light.

"Let them enter," thought Wylde; "they know not that I am armed, and it will be strange indeed if I cannot overcome one of my enemies with a single blow. Thanks, friend Jackson, for providing me with this excellent bowie."

He then noiselessly took up a position behind the door, ready to strike down the first man who entered.

The man with the pine torch approached; Wylde could see the rays of light glimmering through the crevices in the door of his gloomy cell. With deadly knife upraised he stood in readiness.

The jingling of a bunch of keys was followed by the sharp snap of the bolt as it shot back, and then the whole place seemed filled with light. So powerful was the glare that Wylde's eyes were dazzled.

He struck wildly with his bowie, but the gaolers had no difficulty in evading the blow.

Ere he could repeat the stroke they threw themselves upon him, and although he fought with desperation, the villain's hands were soon secured.

Many of the men of the settlement had by this time assembled, drawn to the gaol by the report that the prisoner had escaped.

"He ain't gwine to 'scape while Bill Smith has got him in charge," said he with the pine torch.

"An' I guess he'll have to throw about a cartload of dust in my eyes afore he slinks off," said the other.

"Let's Lynch the varmint!" cried a bystander.

"Let's Lynch the varmint!" echoed the others.

"Thar's a good tree handy!"

"Wa-al, we'd better *tree* the coon while we has the chance!"

"Hyar's a rope!"

"An' hyar's a ring-tailed roarer as don't mind pullin' t'other end!"

"Off with the tarnation skunk!"

Such shouts as these were heard on all sides; and in spite of all the gaolers could say or do the wretched man was dragged out of his cell.

They hurried him away to the big tree; a rope was fastened round his neck, and the other end thrown over a stout branch.

"Give the critter five minutes' grace and then pull!" cried one, who seemed to act as master of the ceremonies.

There was silence.

The wretched man, who stood so near death, could not speak.

Conflicting emotions rent his soul in pieces, and played havoc with his mind.

Big drops of perspiration stood upon his pallid brow, yet, villain as he was, he trembled not.

He knew that craven fear would not prolong his days, but rather add to the jeers and gibes which would assail his dying moments.

He also knew that a bold, hardy comportment in the presence of death would procure him at least a trifle of respect as a brave man, and one who had "died game."

A man held a watch in his hand, and watched its dial by the lurid light of the flaming torches.

"Time's up, lads; pull away!"

"Hold!" cried a voice, in authoritative tones.

All looked round and saw the head-constable, if we may so call him, of the little settlement—the man who had taken Wylde into custody when he was captured by Armstrong.

"What's the meanin' o' this hyar little bit o' fun, boys?"

The men speedily explained to him that the prisoner had made an attempt to escape, and had also tried to murder his gaolers.

"Wa-al?" was the response.

"We're going to Lynch the scoundrel."

"Now, lookee, boys, don't be fools. Let's keep the critter for a day or two, try him for both crimes, and then if Judge Lynch don't have him tarred and feathered and burnt alive, my name ain't no account in this section of the state."

"Hurraw for Old Rusty," shouted the mob, and then, as they thought of the fun in store for them, they no longer hesitated about relinquishing the prisoner into the hands of the proper gaolers.

Two men extra volunteered their services to see that Wylde did not escape.

The scoundrel was carried back to his prison, the woodwork he had destroyed was repaired, and there on the damp earth he was left lying with his hands bound.

How could he possibly escape?

## CHAPTER XLI.

### ROUND THE CAMP FIRE.

WHEN Strongbow returned to consciousness he found himself lying upon the turf by the river side.

The grizzly bear was stretched out by him, dead, and the whole place seemed saturated with blood.

He tried to raise himself, but could not stir.

"It must be the bear's paw which lies across my chest," he thought. "I will remove it."

He raised his hand, but it fell back upon the grass. He was completely helpless with loss of blood.

"Oh, he is dead—he is dead!" moaned a faint voice by his side; "killed for my sake, and now I am alone."

It was Water Lily who spoke.

"Who is killed? Am I dead, and are these the happy hunting grounds?"

"Hush!"

A soft hand was laid upon his lips, and then brushed back the hair from his pale forehead.

"Am I dead? Are you a spirit?"

"Hush! I am no spirit, but your own Water Lily. But you must be quiet."

"I saw the beautiful Lily floating upon the stream. I tried to rescue it, and --where am I?"

"You are with the Lily."

Strongbow closed his eyes again. Even the exertion of talking was too much for him.

Water Lily bathed his lips, staunched his wounds as well as she could, and then waited patiently for the return of her father and Swift.

What a time it seemed before they came!

"Jerusalem! Thar's been a pretty good lot o' fighten, I guess. What's all this hyar, gal?"

"The bear attacked me, and I fear he has lost his life in saving mine."

The trapper knelt down, and felt Strongbow's heart.

"He ain't lost his life, but it's a touch and go case, that's sartin."

"Big Elk will seek herbs with which to heal the wounds of the young chief," said the Delaware warrior, and without another word he moved off for that purpose.

The old hunter then stripped off Strongbow's hunting shirt, and with a piece of soft skin washed away the clotted blood from the fearful wounds in his breast and back made by the bear's paws.

By the time he had finished Big Elk returned with his herbs and bark of plants, which were then placed upon the wounds, Swift expressing the greatest confidence in the Indian mode of surgery.

This done, the hunting shirt was replaced, the senseless youth conveyed to a soft couch of rushes, and all that remained was to wait with patience for his convalescence.

"He'll be able to travel in a day or two," observed Swift, adding in a moment "we'll name this bit o' water Invalid

Creek, I guess, as two o' the party had to be doctored hyar."

For some hours Strongbow was senseless, but when he awoke his memory had returned.

"Is Water Lily safe?" was the first question he asked in a low voice.

"Yes; but you keep yer mouth shut."

The youth made one more attempt at conversation, and then finding that no one would answer him, was compelled to be silent.

All that night they remained at the old camping ground which they had resolved to abandon.

The next morning Strongbow felt better, and said so.

Swift at once took off the bandages, and after a careful examination of the wounds, gave his opinion that at least another day of rest and quiet was needed.

Fresh poultices were placed on his limbs and body, and he was told to keep himself perfectly quiet.

Another day passed, and in the evening Strongbow found himself well enough to sit with the other members of the party round the camp fire.

A silent party it was too.

The Indian, naturally grave and taciturn, said nothing, except when spoken to.

Water Lily occasionally addressed a low whisper to her lover, who replied in the same tones.

The old hunter was in one of those half melancholy moods which he often indulged in. He seemed, in spite of his fondness for the young people, to wish to be alone, for there are seasons in life when solitude is a luxury preferable to the allurements of human society.

He felt his nature deeply stirred within him by the events of the past few days. The visit to that lonely grave on the prairie, the strange vision he had seen of a face, pale and wan, but strangely familiar to his eyes, together with the mysterious blue arrows which had delivered him from death; all these things made an impression on the old hunter's soul.

He felt as though some great change in his circumstances was near at hand, though whether that change was to be for the better or worse he knew not.

The hunter lighted his pipe, and then throwing himself back upon the luxuriant carpet of grass in such a position that his face was completely hidden from human observation, gave himself up to an unlimited indulgence in the train of reflection that circumstances had called up.

The silver moon shed her soft light upon him through the tops of the trees, and a host of winking stars looked down upon him through azure fields of immeasurable space.

The hunter's thoughts were absorbed so, that he noticed not the things of this earth.

Had he not been so absent-minded, he would have noticed a figure working its way through the tangled grass, or crouching behind bushes; a grim shape, hiding behind rocks, a dark shadow creeping close to the earth; a head first raised, then depressed eyes shining with the fierce cunning of the hungry panther, a strong and vindictive arm, and a hand clutching a knife.

Such a hand and arm too! Black as jet from finger nails to shoulder, while the remainder of the body, the naked chest and neck, exhibited only the tawny, red hue, common to the skins of Indian warriors.

It was the dreaded warrior, Black Hand, who crouched in the grass, who hid behind trees and bushes; he it was whose shadow kept so close to the earth; whose strong arm held the glittering steel on which the moonbeams seemed to love to play.

How persevering is vengeance in the pursuit of its object, and how shrinking and timid virtue sometimes is, even when engaged in the best of causes!

How often, too, do the bad passions burn more deeply, and possess more iron energy of determination, than the good ones!

Vengeful anger is indeed a terrible and fearful passion.

Black Hand's heart beat fast with expectation.

There was a wild, malevolent excitement in his breast, as he crawled serpent-like along the earth, and drew nearer to the objects of his anger.

Behind him came another figure, not quite so stealthy in its motions, though it, too, moved quietly enough.

The second figure wore a coat, a wide-awake hat, striped trousers tucked into knee-boots, and other articles of civilized attire.

What was this white man doing there following the Indian warrior? He was a friend of Black Hand's evidently, but no friend to the little party assembled round the fire.

On they crawled—on hands and knees —now bent like worms and now flat on their faces.

Nearer and nearer, till at length they crouched behind a bush only a yard or two from the unconscious party.

No noise had betrayed their coming, no careless striking of feet against loose stones, no tell-tale crackling of twigs, no rustling of leaves betrayed their presence to either of the four persons by the fire.

Yet what was it caused Big Elk to lay his hand upon his tomahawk, and peer jealously into the darkness on every side? He felt a vague sense of the presence of a foe—a kind of instinctive feeling that some enemy was at hand.

But see! There in the distance where the moon showers a flood of light through an opening in the trees!

What form is that which comes as silently as the two others, not crawling or crouching like the two others, but half stepping, half gliding over the dewy grass?

The dress of deerskin, the embroidered mocassins, the belt of wampum, and the head gear of feathers are those of an Indian squaw, while the weapons—bow, arrows, and knife, are those of a redskin warrior.

But no Indian squaw or even half-caste ever owned so fair a skin or such a shower of golden locks.

Pure European blood, unadulterated, must flow in those veins; if there can be veins beneath that death-like skin.

It is the mysterious lady of the haunted swamp.

But what does she here?

From tree to tree she glides silent and ghost-like till she reaches one not more than half-a-dozen yards from the Indian spy and his pale-face companion.

At first she does not perceive all the party at the fire; her eye rests with a beam of satisfaction upon Strongbow, Water Lily, and Big Elk.

Then Swift raises himself from his recumbent position.

Good Heaven! what a look of mortal agony shoots across the pallid face of the silent woman! See how she bites her lips and presses her hand upon her bosom!

What can all this mean?

## CHAPTER XLII.

### THE TWO SPIES.

JACKSON continued his ride through the forest until nearly daybreak, then he halted to rest his stolen steed for a time.

He had shaped his course as nearly north-east as possible, steering by the stars.

When he dismounted at last by the side of a little brook, and stretched himself upon the grass, he did what he had not done for a long time—gave himself up to thought.

He began to reflect upon the probable consequences of his action.

That his object in visiting the gaolers had been discovered he could not doubt, for one of them had fired at him.

How, then, would it fare with Wylde?

If he was found out in an attempt to escape, his life would, in all probability, be at once sacrificed

"I have sworn to rescue or avenge him," muttered Jackson, "though I hate him. What unlucky chance ordained that I should run against him down here? I thought he was at least a hundred miles off."

He made use of several oaths, and then began to consider what was to be done.

"I must buy up some Indians. A few dollars would buy up a whole tribe of the redskin brutes."

Then he shuddered, for he recollected being once tied up to a tree, and feeling the keen point of a scalping-knife pressed against his forehead.

"I must be cautious, though, or they will rob me first and then scalp me, the redskin thieves. I suppose I shall find Iroquois in this part."

Thus scheming and thinking, he took

about two hours' rest, and then, about the time when he thought his pursuers would be starting on his trail, he continued his journey.

Far away to his left he saw smoke ascending, and towards it he directed the head of his steed.

As he approached it he saw through a long avenue of trees a party of Indians seated around a fire. There were four of them.

Jackson instantly drew rein.

"I wonder what tribe they belong to," he muttered; "Crows, Iroquois, Black Feet, Delawares—ah, it would not do to meet any of the Delawares, as they are not particularly friendly with the captain."

For some moments he remained still watching the Indians.

"I must get nearer and see if I can tell their paint," he muttered.

"Paleface, look this way; see."

Jackson started.

By his side with a hand upon his bridle, was a stalwart Indian warrior.

Jackson laid hands upon his rifle, but ere he could unsling it from his back the Indian had the muzzle of a pistol within two feet of the white man's head.

"White man no shoot—come to fire and see Indian paint."

And with these words he led the horse towards the encampment, keeping the pistol still close to Jackson's head as a warning to him to make no resistance.

As they were within three hundred yards of the fire, Jackson saw that resistance would be unavailing.

When they reached the camp of the four Indians, the one who had hold of the horse motioned Jackson to dismount.

The white man obeyed without a moment's hesitation. He knew that his life was in their power.

"The pale-faced warrior who talks aloud is welcome; my young men will give him some meat to eat."

As the warrior turned to give the necessary instruction, Jackson noted that his right hand and arm were stained black.

A kind of joy filled his heart.

He had often heard Wylde speak of Black Hand as a murderous ruffian, and at the same time a trusted ally.

"You are Black Hand, chief of the Crows?"

"I am Black Hand," replied the warrior, turning proudly; "and the Yengeese tremble when they hear my name."

"Black Hand is a great warrior."

"Black Hand is a great warrior, and has taken the scalps of many pale-faces. The Iroquois and the Delawares fly from the sight of Black Hand, and hide themselves in thick woods."

"I know one pale-face who does not tremble when the name of Black Hand is spoken."

"Ugh!"

"A pale-face who is tall in stature, and strong as the buffalo on the prairie."

"His scalp shall hang at the girdle of Black Hand."

"He has smoked the pipe of peace in the wigwam of the chief whose hand is black."

"Ugh!"

"It is the White Pine."

White Pine was the name given by the Indians to Wylde on account of his great height and fair complexion.

"The White Pine has sent me to Black Hand."

"What needs the pale-face warrior? There are many buffaloes on the prairies and deer in the woods; let him hunt, eat, and be satisfied."

"He has sent me to Black Hand to ask the chief of the Crows to dig up the war hatchet, and deliver the White Pine out of the hands of his enemies, the pale-faces."

"Ugh!"

Jackson waited some time to hear the answer, trying, in the meantime, to draw some conclusion as to the Indian's intentions from his countenance.

But Black Hand's face was as composed as a marble statue. The keenest physiognomist could not have decided from that tawny countenance whether the Indian was thinking of food or foemen. At length he spoke.

"Why should Black Hand dig the hatchet, and send his young men upon the war-path?"

"That the White Pine may escape from his enemies."

Again the Indian became silent for some minutes.

"What shall be given to Black Hand?" he asked, when he again opened his lips.

"The White Pine will give the Crow warriors many blankets and knives, with much tobacco and fire-water."

"Ugh! it is good!"

"The White Pine is very rich, and will load the warriors with presents."

The Indian gave a grim smile.

"And what will the warrior who talks aloud give to prove that his heart is red?"

"I have nothing to give."

"He will give his rifle with plenty of powder and lead!"

The Indian laid his hand upon his pistol in a threatening manner as he spoke, and Jackson at once saw that it would be dangerous to refuse.

"Black Hand is a great warrior, he shall have the fire-bow."

The Indian took the weapon with a pleased expression of countenance, and then announced his attention of proceeding at once to the main body of his tribe.

The journey would take a day and a half, as neither Black Hand nor his attendants had brought their horses with them.

The return journey to the white settlement, however, could be accomplished in about ten hours by Indians on horseback.

A few words from Black Hand, and the party started on their long walk through the woods.

Jackson kept his horse, but Black Hand did not envy him that, for he had the long-coveted rifle.

They kept as much in the woods as possible, as, by so doing, they would be the better able to keep ahead from the white men, by whom Jackson imagined he was followed.

Night came, and with due deliberation a camp was chosen in the midst of one of the many detached clumps of timber which grew near the outskirts of the great forest.

They built a fire in the midst of a thick cluster of bushes and prepared to pass the night there.

But, as it grew more dark, they were surprised to see the light of another fire glowing in the midst of a second grove about half a mile from that in which they were concealed.

The Indians could not rest without knowing who had camped near them, so,

leaving two of the number to guard the fire, Black Hand, followed by Jackson and two of the red men, began to approach the spot in as silent and stealthy a manner as possible.

They reached the edge of the timber in which the fire was still burning so brightly.

"White men are there," said Black Hand, "their scalps shall hang at my belt."

Jackson looked.

Seated around a fire he beheld four persons.

Two were white men, two Indians.

The whites were Hiram Swift and Strongbow, the Indians Big Elk and Water Lily.

"They are enemies to the White Pine," whispered Jackson, as he gazed upon the little bivouac.

Black Hand motioned his two warriors to remain, and then, drawing his knife, with a fierce and bloodthirsty gesture, began to crawl forward, followed by the white traitor.

Crouching in the long grass or beneath bushes they approached like crawling snakes.

At length something seemed to alarm Big Elk, and, as we have already seen, he gave a searching glance all around.

He saw nothing, however.

He was unaware of the presence of the two men whose stealthy approach was described in the last chapter, for Black Hand and Jackson were the men.

Neither did anyone dream that the pale, golden-haired woman in the Indian dress of deer-skin was intently watching everything that took place.

For more than ten minutes the two spies kept in their place of concealment, gazing with earnestness and ill-constrained passion upon the unconscious hunters.

Then Black Hand raised his keen knife high in the air, and made a motion as though gathering up all his energies for a leap upon Hiram Swift.

But Jackson laid his hand upon the red man's arm.

"Not now," he whispered; "go back, bring your men, and fall upon them when they are asleep."

"Black Hand will strike them all. See! the young pale-face is as a sick squaw—he lies upon the grass, he cannot raise himself."

"Bring up your warriors. The White Pine will give many rifles if the two pale-faces are his prisoners."

"Ugh! it is good."

The two spies then crawled away silently as they came, and the mysterious woman, unseen, unthought of by them, glided after them.

## CHAPTER XLIII.

### BEFORE THE COURT.

THE renegade Wylde lay in his log prison carefully guarded.

Strict orders were given that no strangers should be allowed to approach the building.

Settlers in that far-west region knew that many white outlaws infested the forests, prairies and hills, men who, scorning to labour, or even to make a living by simple hunting, spoiled all the unfortunate trappers and settlers they could lure into their ambushes.

Not a man in the little town doubted that this prisoner was one of those pests of backwood society; and many of them took it for granted, from Wylde's manners and conversation, that he was a man of high standing among his lawless associates.

Such records as exist of the settlers who first pushed their way westward of the great river Mississippi, make frequent mention of such white savages, who, either by themselves, or in league with roving bands of red men, rendered themselves a terror to all new settlements, till increased numbers gave increased power, and enabled the honest workers to drive their foes away, or exterminate them entirely.

It was for the speedy execution of justice on such offenders that the terrors of Lynch law were invoked.

In districts where police were entirely unknown and magistrates were only heard of occasionally, the hard-working settlers could not wait for the tardy course of regular justice.

It might be months ere a judge visited their district, and, during that time, the prisoner might escape, be rescued by his companions, or the whole settlement might be swept away by a tribe of hostile Indians.

So these hard-handed, strong-minded sons of the soil fell into the habit of taking the law into their own hands in all cases which required punishment.

Nor did these bold men act without due deliberation.

There was a rude love of justice in their breasts which kept them from flagrant wrong.

A man taken in any act of theft or murder was placed on trial before a judge, and a jury of twelve freemen.

He was allowed to call evidence in defence, though, if his witnesses could not give satisfactory proofs of their own good character, their testimony did not bear much weight.

It may be said that in such a court the case would often go against the prisoner, through prejudice.

Perhaps so.

But, on the whole, less injustice was done than in many more civilized courts, where cunning lawyers, by dint of ingenious sophistries and pleadings, often save rogues from well-merited punishment, and thus defraud honest men of the justice they seek to obtain.

It was decided that Wylde should be tried by a judge and jury of the good citizens of Prairie Star town.

Armstrong had returned to his new settlement in order to bring his wife, whose testimony would be required at the trial, the time for which was fixed for the evening after he returned to the town.

The day came at last.

Evening shades began to settle down over the earth; the settlers left off their labours in the field or forest.

People began to gather beneath a group of trees, in what is now a fashionable square in a smart and populous town; but was then merely a rugged grove at the back of the log shanties of the settlers.

As it was growing dark they had provided themselves with plenty of artificial light in the shape of pine knot torches, which threw a weird, lurid glare over the scene.

A commotion among the younger fry announced that the constables *pro tem.* had gone to fetch the prisoner.

"Make way for the judge and jury," cried a man.

The people opened a way, and a tall man, with grizzled beard and hair, and calm, thoughtful countenance, made his appearance.

He gravely took his seat upon a fallen tree, upon the trunk of which was spread the American flag of stars and stripes.

Holding a paper in his hand, he called aloud the names of twelve men, who, as they answered, seated themselves in a semi-circle on the ground with their backs towards the judge.

The prisoner was then brought forward, and placed facing both judge and jury.

"Let everybody keep silence," shouted the man who officiated as chief constable.

The buzzing sound of conversation at once ceased.

"What is your name, prisoner?" asked the judge.

Wylde made no reply.

"Do you not hear me?"

"I do."

"Then respect the court, and make an answer."

"My name matters little. Since you are determined to try me, I well know what will be the result of that trial."

"Again I ask, what is your name?"

"Call me anything you like, and proceed with this farce."

"Take care that the farce has not a tragical end. Since the prisoner refuses to give a name, the court decides that he shall be known during these proceedings as Henry Jones."

After this speech the judge and the foreman of the jury made notes in their books of the name by which Wylde was to be known.

"Henry Jones, you are brought before this court charged with two crimes; the first is attempting to murder Edmund Armstrong in his own cabin, the second is an attempt to escape from prison, and to stab your gaolers. Do you plead guilty or not guilty of the charges?"

"As you like."

"Again I ask, warning you to pay a little more respect to the court before which you stand."

"And again I say that it is a matter of perfect indifference to me whether you write down guilty or not guilty."

"As the prisoner refuses to plead, the court wills and decides that the trial shall proceed as though he had pleaded 'Not Guilty.'"

Both judge and jury entered "Not guilty" in their books.

"Bring forward the witnesses against this man," said the president of the court.

Armstrong and his wife were then led forward, and an oath to the effect that they would speak the truth was administered.

"What have you to say against him?"

Mrs. Armstrong made reply.

"I was sitting in my husband's cabin on the evening of the —th, when I noticed that the fire was nearly out, and opened the door to procure some wood. I saw the prisoner kneeling upon the ground, with his rifle pointed through a crevice in the wall towards the place where my husband was sitting. I saw that my husband was in danger, and raised up a block of wood, with which I knocked the prisoner senseless."

"What happened then?"

"I fainted, and remembered no more till I found myself inside the hut, where was also the prisoner, who had been secured by my husband."

"You acted well. Do you wish to cross-examine this witness, prisoner?"

"No; I only want revenge!"

"What have you to say?" continued the judge, addressing Armstrong.

"On the evening mentioned by my wife, I was sitting in my cabin. While she went to the door for more wood for the fire, I suddenly heard the report of a rifle, and at the same time my wife screamed. On going out I found both her and the prisoner lying senseless upon the ground. The muzzle of the prisoner's rifle had been thrust through a crevice in the wall, and the bullet had passed through the roof of the cabin. I secured the prisoner, and brought him here for trial."

"Good. Do you wish to ask any question, prisoner?"

"No; but as I said before, I want revenge, and will have it."

The two gaolers were then called upon, and gave evidence as to their being appointed to watch the prisoner; how they had heard the noise of a saw, and on opening the door of the prison, had been assaulted by the prisoner, who was found to have been armed with a bowie knife.

As Wylde refused to cross-examine the witnesses or make any defence, the jurymen were then called upon to consider their verdict and give the same according to their consciences and the evidence which had been given.

"Guilty, guilty, guilty!" they all whispered to each other, till the word came to the foreman.

"Thar ain't no doubt about it, judge."

"Then how do you find the prisoner?"

"He's as guilty a coon as ever war brought afore a court."

"You find the prisoner guilty?"

"Sartinly."

"Of both charges, or only one?"

"Both, judge."

The judge then rose.

"Prisoner, you have had a fair trial," he said, "and the jury finds you guilty of the crimes whereof you are accused. I, for my part, quite agree with them in their verdict. You have been found guilty of two attempts to murder, and that proves you to be a very dangerous man, one not fit to live in civilized society. Thefore, to prevent you from injuring any one in future, it becomes my duty to pass sentence of death upon you. The sentence of this court is that you are to be carried to the nearest tree, strong enough to bear your weight, and there be hanged by the neck until you are dead, after which your body is to be carried out to the prairie that the beasts of the earth and the fowls of the air may devour it. And may Heaven have mercy on your soul!"

"Am I to have any time to prepare for death?" asked Wylde, wiping the perspiration from his brow.

"No, no!" shouted the crowd; "string the varmint up at once."

"Silence, you howling curs!" shouted the condemned man, as he turned round fiercely.

Several revolvers were instantly drawn, and had not the gaolers with some of the jury sheltered the prisoner, he would undoubtedly have had more than one bullet through his body.

"Order, order!" cried the judge.

He was, as before said, an elderly man, and one of better education than the majority of the settlers. Therefore, his voice had more influence.

As soon as he had stilled the outcries, he made a short address to the people, in which he urged that as the prisoner was a convicted and hardened criminal, and, therefore, unfitted for immediate death, time should be given him.

After some murmurs this was assented to by the majority of the bystanders, and the judge then announced that the execution would not take place till the following morning.

So Wylde was led back to his cell, the whole concourse accompanying him, hooting, yelling, and cursing at him in a most energetic manner.

Two men inside the prison and four out, took upon themselves the task of guarding him, and thus he was left.

## CHAPTER XLIV.

### KATE!

BIG ELK was evidently very restless both before and after the departure of the two spies, Jackson and Black Hand.

His Indian instinct seemed to sniff danger in the night breeze, and his keen eyes darted hither and thither into every nook and corner of the surrounding forest.

Hiram Swift caught some of his alarm, and, a few minutes after the two enemies had withdrawn, took up his rifle with the avowed intention of walking round the camp.

He had nearly made a circle at about fifty yards distance from the fire when he came upon a track; following it till it came out into the open moonlight, he made an examination which convinced him that two men had been near the camp fire and had crawled stealthily away.

Who were these two men, and what did they want?

The trail told him plainly enough that one was a white man and the other an Indian, but that was not enough for Hiram Swift's mind.

He followed the trail till it came to the edge of the grove, and then looking over a wide expanse of prairie, saw two figures making their way with all haste to the next timber island.

He fancied too that he caught a glimpse of an Indian squaw, but it vanished suddenly while he was fixing his eyes upon the two spies.

He hastily returned to the camp and announced his intention of following these two men to learn who they were.

"Look well after the camp, Delaware. Thar's no knowing what varmint may be slinking round."

"The eyes of Big Elk are open."

"Are you going, Swift?" asked Strongbow, looking up from his couch on the grass.

"Yes, lad."

"Will you be long?"

"Not very long."

"I wish I could go with you."

"So do I, lad."

The hunter then carefully looked to his weapons and glided away.

He reached the spot from which he had first seen the retreating figures.

Casting his eyes over the prairie, he could still discern the indistinct forms of the two men.

He began to follow the trail which the moonlight showed quite distinctly upon the dewy grass.

But he was obliged to be very cautious, lest they should look round and discover him.

Hiram Swift threw himself upon his hands and knees, and began to crawl away over the grass at a rapid rate.

At a little distance he looked very much like a huge bear prowling round in search of a meal.

The two fugitives entered the "timber island," or grove, towards which they had been travelling.

The old hunter fancied that, as they reached its edge, they turned round to see whether they were pursued.

He was right in his conjecture.

Black Hand had glanced back to see whether the two warriors he had taken with him on his scouting expedition were following him in his retreat.

He could not see them, but a huge dark object which the Indian supposed to be a bear was following after him.

"Ugh! Black Hand will have bear skin. White man go further in wood—go to camp fire."

Jackson made his way towards the spot indicated, Black Hand ensuring him a welcome reception by imitating with his voice the howl of a wolf.

The Indian then took up his station in some bushes near the point for which the supposed bear was evidently making.

The object came on.

Black Hand clutched the rifle he had taken from Jackson, and moved aside some bushes which impeded his aim.

Then he remembered that the report of the weapon would reach the distant camp of the enemy and put them on their guard.

Black Hand laid down the rifle and resolved to strike the bear with his tomahawk.

As he gazed upon the approaching animal the Indian became possessed of an idea that the bear was very strangely shaped. It walked more awkwardly, too, than the majority of the bear family.

His curiosity became excited, and he watched the near approach of the bear with the greatest interest.

Bear!

That was no bear: it was a human being; one of the hated pale-faces too!

Another eager, earnest look.

That cap of skin, that deer-hide hunting shirt, that long rifle, were fresh upon Black Hand's memory.

It was the hated white hunter, the sworn ally of Black Hand's deadly foes, the Delawares.

A thrill of fierce joy throbbed in the heart of the Indian, as, in imagination, he slew the hunter, and triumphantly scalped him.

"'KEEP OFF!' SHOUTED STRONGBOW, RAISING THE PADDLE."

A noble opportunity for glory and revenge was about to present itself. He would strike down the white man, and then return to surprise the camp of his foes.

But what if those foes should be watching the progress of their friend?

Caution must be used. The hunter must be lured into the wood out of the sight of prying eyes.

So when Hiram Swift was within forty yards of the edge of the wood, Black Hand retired a few paces till he reached a position in which he could not be seen by anyone on the prairie.

He stationed himself behind the trunk of a tree, and then waited.

His eyes were fixed upon the track by which his victim must come, and, at last, he saw the head of the white hunter peering through the bushes.

Hiram Swift was evidently suspicious that a trap might have been set for him.

His keen grey eyes peered round the copse, searching out every recess. Yet they failed on this occasion to discover the subtle Indian, who, with his body pressed close to the trunk of a tree, stood motionless as a rock.

At length Swift seemed satisfied that the coast was clear, and again began to move forward.

The fatal moment was at hand, for he approached the ambush of his treacherous foe.

Black Hand grasped his tomahawk with such force that his hand seemed almost to crush the wood. No second blow of that terrible weapon would be needed.

The Indian gloried in the thought that he was about to strike down a foe; the scalp of the well-known white hunter would be a trophy of which he might be proud.

But, to his intense disgust, he saw that Swift was coming towards him in such a manner that he would be unable to get a fair blow at his head.

Black Hand considered in his mind what was to be done.

To make a false blow would never do, for the hunter was active and strong, and the loss of two seconds of time might, perhaps, lose the victory.

His mind was soon made up.

He waited till Hiram Swift was within two yards of the tree; then, rushing out suddenly, with one push of his foot sent the hunter sprawling on his back.

The long rifle dropped from Swift's hand as he fell, and there he was lying on the mossy turf at the mercy of a vindictive and bloodthirsty foe.

"Ugh! white man kill much Indian; now Indian take white scalp."

With these words Black Hand raised his tomahawk, and made a step forward with the intention of dashing out Swift's brains.

But at that moment a pale, ghostly form appeared between him and his foe, and an outstretched arm stayed the descending stroke.

Black Hand started back in amazement, but in an instant, recovering his senses, dashed away into some adjacent bushes.

Hiram Swift hastily rose to his feet, and recovered his weapon.

"'Tis the same face, yet it can't be the same body," he muttered, "for I myself placed that in the lonely grave on the prairie down by the swamp."

Then the pale, mysterious woman spoke—

"Away, white man! haste away to your camp! your friends are in great danger!"

"It's the same voice!—Kate!"

An agonised expression again crossed that pale face, and pressing her hand upon her bosom, the mysterious individual glided behind some trees ere the hunter could intercept her.

Unmindful of Black Hand, and the danger to which he exposed himself, Hiram Swift rushed after her.

But she was not to be seen, and, although he could trace her for a few yards, the slight trail was soon lost.

"Thar's a trail, then; she's alive, that's sartin. My name's not Hiram Swift if I don't find out all about it."

# CHAPTER XLV.

## MORE MYSTERY.

IN vain Hiram Swift searched; he could not discover the slightest trace of the hiding place of the mysterious person whose face, form, and voice reminded him of one he deemed many years dead.

At length he with reluctance gave up the search.

Then he remembered Black Hand; but the Indian seemed to have vanished with the fair-haired woman, and like her to have left no trace behind.

"I'll have a good hunt round this hyar wood, I guess," muttered Swift, as he began again to look for some sign of the presence of the two persons who had so lately stood before him.

Then came to his recollection the warning words—

"Haste away to your camp! your friends are in danger."

"I'll go; I'll do as she says," said the hunter to himself.

It seemed to him that the pale woman of the haunted swamp had taken himself and his friends under her special protection, and had followed them away from her usual haunts for the purpose of watching over them.

The hunter's heart and head were sorely troubled.

The face, the voice, the tall, stately form, the long, golden locks all belonged to one whose mangled body he had placed in a lonely prairie grave. Yet she seemed not to recognise him or to know who he was.

But why did she start, and look so pained when he called her by that name?

These were all mysteries the hunter was unable to solve.

He began his journey back to his own camp, not crawling on hands and knees, as he came, but walking erect.

The hunter was too deeply wrapt in thought to take any precautions for his own safety.

Not that such precautions were needed, for Black Hand had been so frightened by the sudden appearance of one who was deemed supernatural by all his tribe, that he dared not take another step towards the white man or his friends while he knew they were under the protection of the Spirit of the Cedar Swamp.

So Swift passed on unmolested.

He reached the camp where Big Elk, Strongbow, and Water Lily were seated.

"Ugh!" exclaimed the former, when his glowing eyes discerned the form of his white friend.

"What is it?" asked Strongbow.

Big Elk made no verbal reply, but pointed with his hand to the hunter.

"You are back, then, at last," said the Boy Chief of the Delawares.

"Yes."

"Have you seen anyone?"

"Yes."

"Who?"

"The two fellers."

"Who were they?"

"One of 'em is Black Hand."

As this name fell upon his ears, Big Elk's hand grasped his tomahawk.

"That murderous redskin who would have burnt me alive?"

"The same."

"And who is the other?"

"Don't know for sartin."

"But you have an idea?"

"Yes."

"Then in Heaven's name give it us! Why, what is the matter with you to-night, Swift? You are as silent and reserved as can be."

"My idea is that t'other fellar war the white coon you see with Black Hand at that burnin' spree."

"Ha! would to Heaven I had my strength and could meet the villain face to face!"

Swift made no remark.

After a few minutes' silence, Strongbow said—

"What is the matter with you to-night? Tell me, and let me soothe your sorrow."

Heaving a deep sigh, Swift began.

"You remember a place on the prairie down by the swamp, whar a grave was, with a wooden cross?"

"I remember it well, and how you cleared away the weeds from it."

"I've seen to-night the person I laid in that grave nigh a dozen years ago."

"Impossible!"

"It's true."

Strongbow shook his head.

"And what's more, you've seen her too."

"I?"

"Aye, boy."

"Where could I see one who has been in the grave for so long a time?"

"In the swamp under the cedar tree. She is what the Indians call the spirit of the swamp!"

Strongbow was silent for a few minutes, but at last he spoke.

"Why should the sight of this spirit, or whatever it may be, agitate you so? Surely you are not superstitious?"

"Not as a rule."

"Then be a man once more."

"I am not superstitious; but, boy, the person I laid in that lonely grave was a fair girl who, for a few weeks only, had been my loving wife!"

Every eye was turned towards the hunter, who hid his face with his hands.

"Hush!" said Big Elk, holding up his finger to enforce silence.

Everyone listened attentively.

A sound which resembled the groan of a human being in agony was heard.

Big Elk and Swift at once started to their feet, fully determined to discover the cause of such uncanny sounds.

Each took a different path.

Some ten minutes elapsed, and, as yet, nothing had been discovered, when Swift heard the hoot of an owl, a signal that Big Elk required his presence. Proceeding to the spot, he found the Delaware bending over the dead body of a Crow Indian, whose body was transfixed by a blue arrow.

And, while he looked, that deep groan was again heard.

They resumed their search, and, after a little time, succeeded in discovering who it was.

In a little thicket, but a few yards distant from his dead companion, was a second Indian, also transfixed by a blue arrow.

The man was not dead, though mortally wounded, and he it was whose groans had first alarmed the little camp.

Big Elk drew his scalping-knife, and would have at once put an end to the Crow warrior's life, had he not been restrained by Hiram Swift.

"Let him live, Delaware, if he can; harm enough has been done to him."

"Black Hand spares not."

"Never mind, you shall hang Black Hand's scalp at your girdle some day; that will be worth a dozen such locks o' ha'r as this coon's."

Big Elk reluctantly sheathed his knife.

"See what is fastened to the shaft!" said he, directing Hiram Swift's attention to a piece of deer-skin which was fastened to the arrow.

The hunter gave a long, low whistle as he detached the slip of hide.

Well he might whistle, for it bore upon it a sentence written in the English language in characters of blood.

People who could write were not very numerous in that region, and very seldom wasted their talents in writing inscriptions to place upon the bodies of dead Indians.

The inscription ran thus:—

"These Indians were slain by one whom they would call the Spirit of the Cedar Swamp, but who takes the opportunity of stating during a short interval of reason that she is a poor white woman, whose reason was deranged by injuries received from Indians."

Again and again Hiram Swift read the letter by the light of the moon.

Then he folded the document, and placed it in the breast of his hunting-shirt.

"Let us return to the camp."

Big Elk nodded his head in assent.

They reached the camp-fire, seated themselves, and were about to relate their adventures, when another and more fearful sound was borne to their ears upon the night.

## CHAPTER XLVI.

### THE CONDEMNED.

WHEN Wylde was led back to his log prison, sentenced to die the following day, he then gave up all hope.

He deemed that his friend Jackson had done all that he could do, and, therefore, resigned himself to his fate.

No hope of mercy had he.

Those who show no pity cannot expect that others will sympathise with them.

The words of the judge had made some impression on his mind; he remembered that the stern man had said, "Let him have time to prepare for death."

Death was to be his fate.

Appeal from the sentence was useless, for the court by which he had been tried recognised no higher tribunal.

Judge Lynch sat to administer justice according to the supreme will of the people; therefore, if the people condemned him, no power could rescue him.

And so he sat down to prepare for death—that undiscovered country from whose bourne no traveller ere returns.

The school of philosophy with which Wylde was best acquainted taught him to believe that after death all was a blank; but now, when he saw himself so near the verge of that great mystery, his mind refused to believe the very doctrines he had laboured so hard to acquire.

He thought of death, that great disjunction between animation and mere matter.

From whence came that animation? Did *man* breathe into his nostrils the breath of life?—No.

Then could man destroy that spirit, that vital principle which man had not the power to give?—No.

Hereafter! That great mystery, the life and soul of all our faith, all our hope, was vividly brought upon his mind.

Wildly he speculated on the nature of that future state. Were the old pagan poets right?—was the Grecian Hades the place to which his disembodied spirit would be consigned?—or should he believe in the Indian mythology of happy hunting grounds for the good, and arid prairies without food or water for those whose lives had been evil?

In none of these fables could he place the slightest faith, for the still, small voice of conscience was ever present, whispering in his ear remembrances of early days, when, as a child, he sat on a mother's knee, and listened, with infant eagerness, to the rudiments of our Christian faith; of the punishments which await the wicked, and the bliss in store for those whose conduct has been free from wilful evil.

Despite his philosophy, he felt compelled to believe in the old priestly superstitions, as he and his fellow atheists were wont to term those pure doctrines in which we place our trust.

He remembered that, when a child, he had seen a little, fairy-like sister fall into her last sleep, peacefully contented with a firm belief in the truths which had been impressed on her pliant mind.

"And why do I fear to die?"

The answer would force itself upon him, spite of all he could do to drive it from his mind.

He feared to die, because he dreaded the hereafter he had been accustomed to laugh at.

And that mental answer to a mental question shattered the very foundation of his philosophy.

Then came pride.

He had always boasted of his belief—or rather want of belief—and now, when the hour came to prove the truth or falsity of his system of reasoning, he could not bring himself to acknowledge that he had been wrong.

"They will laugh, when they hear in the distant cities that Wylde died in the acknowledgment of what he had spent his life in denying."

Foolish man! If thy spirit confess its error, why should the lips refuse to do the bidding of that spirit?

Why heed laughter when thy ears will be stopped by the cold clay of the grave?

So Wylde reasoned with himself, and

tried to convince his mind that it still ad- hered to the old atheistic doctrines it had so readily believed to deaden the prick- ings of conscience.

But his soul refused to be comforted; there was a deadly, undefinable terror in his heart.

And so the time passed, slowly enough to the gaolers who guarded the prisoner, yet swiftly—oh! too swiftly for the un- happy man who lay in that log prison waiting for *eternity*.

Hark!

A loud-voiced clock which some back- woods missionary had placed in the little chapel noisily proclaimed the hour of midnight.

How much that was hidden would be revealed to him ere another midnight.

Then some night-flying owl came and shrieked hideously at the door of the rude cell.

Why would old superstitions crowd upon his mind?

Why was it that he remembered the old fable that the shriek of the owl fore- told death?

Again that still, small voice whispered in his unwilling ear—

*Because of the hereafter !*

One!

Again the clock struck.

Why would it strike so loudly, and thus proclaim the rapid flight of that time which for him would soon be for ever past?

It must be to tell him that only *one* more rising sun should shine upon his condemned body.

And so the hours fled, each hour bring- ing fresh food for reflection, and drawing him nearer the fatal moment.

In vain he tossed about and tried to banish the hideous thoughts which pre- sented themselves.

He could only think of that one word— *Hereafter !*

The morning light began to shine through the crevices in the cell—coldly it glimmered, bringing neither warmth to the body nor hope to the heart.

At eight Wylde was to die.

So Judge Lynch and fate had willed it, and from their decision what hope was there of escaping?

Birds began to twitter in the trees near about the little prison, but it seemed as though they had lost their usual cheerful voices, and were bewailing the fate of the unhappy man who was condemned to die.

Then people were heard without.

Early-rising settlers came down from their log huts and conversed in low tones with the men who guarded the prisoner.

But there was no hope to be gained from their conversation; they seemed to have made up their minds to execute justice, though with as much decorum and quietness as their rude minds were capable of.

Seven o'clock came.

The door of the prison was opened, and a man made his appearance, bearing a substantial meal of hot cakes, deer-meat, and a small flask of brandy.

"Eat hearty, stranger," said he, setting the provisions down before the prisoner.

"How can I eat with my arms bound in this manner?"

A short consultation took place between the gaolers, resulting in the unbinding of the prisoners' wrists so as to allow him to feed himself.

The first thing Wylde did was to seize the brandy flask and swallow its contents. This done, he swallowed a single mouth- ful of meat, and then resumed his re- clining position.

In a few minutes the door was again opened, and a man dressed in black was led in by the gaoler.

"Hyar, critter, hyar's a minister come to have a chat wi' yer."

"I want no minister."

"Better harken to what he's got to say," replied the man; and, with more delicacy than could have been expected, he drew his companions from the cell, leaving Wylde alone with the preacher.

"Friend, I hear you are to die this morning. Pardon me if I intrude, but if the prayers of an old blind preacher will be of any comfort to you, they shall be freely offered on your behalf."

"Friend," replied Wylde, "I thank you for your courtesy and the kind spirit which prompted you thus to visit me, but I want no prayers; all I ask is to be left alone till my last moment comes."

"But think of *hereafter*. Would you die unprepared?"

Wylde leaped savagely to his feet as the word "hereafter" fell upon his ears, and for a moment could scarcely restrain himself from striking the old man.

"Leave me," he said. "Here, gaoler, take this old man away, before I so far forget myself as to offer him violence."

The old man shook his head sorrowfully as he walked away, saying—

"My prayers shall be offered for you whether kneeling in this cell by your side, or far away on the wild prairie."

## CHAPTER XLVII.

### BENEATH THE TREE.

EIGHT o'clock came.

Wylde's heart beat rapidly as he heard footsteps approaching the door.

The prison was opened.

A large party of men, with the settler who acted as chief constable, made their appearance.

"The time has arrived. Come forth, prisoner," said the man.

"Then you are determined to show no mercy?" replied Wylde.

"We are to execute the sentence passed on you, not to talk of mercy to one who does not understand the word."

It was strange how the settlers in a great measure dropped their uncouth manner of talking when they spoke to the prisoner.

They were his judges and executioners, yet they respected him; and, now that his death appeared inevitable, refrained from insulting the unhappy man.

Wylde rose from the ground and walked towards the men.

Cords were produced, with which they bound his arms tightly.

The face of the unhappy prisoner changed colour, but he made no remark, not thinking that anything he could say would take effect upon his captors.

"Come," said the leader.

Out they led him from his darksome prison into the open air.

The morning sun was shining dimly above the forest trees, and Wylde looked upon it as those only look who never expect to behold the face of that luminary again.

Then away to a group of trees.

Beneath those trees men and women were waiting—a quiet, stern-looking mob of people, who had assembled there to see the execution of the sentence they, by the mouth of their judge, had pronounced.

The company had none of the appearance of a London mob waiting for the execution of some well-known criminal.

There was no shouting, no ribald language, no picking of pockets, or fighting beneath the shadow of the gallows.

Every man's face bore a stern, unyielding expression, as though they had one and all made up their minds to go on with a disagreeable but necessary task.

As Wylde and his conductors approached, they fell back from one tree, leaving the whole space overshadowed by its branches clear.

Wylde was led beneath this tree.

Then there was a deep silence.

At length the man who had officiated as judge stepped forward.

"Prisoner," said he, "I fancy you need not to be reminded of the sentence passed upon you at your trial."

"I well remember it."

"Before you die, have you anything to say — any last message to send to friends or relatives?"

"Not by your hands," replied Wylde, with a sneering smile.

"On the honour of a man who never broke his word, any instructions you may give shall be faithfully carried out."

"I have nothing to say."

"Have you no token of remembrance you would wish to send to anyone for whom you entertain feelings of friendship?"

"No."

"Let him send me back my ring—the *diamond ring* he robbed me of—and wore for so many years on his own finger," said a voice.

Looking up from the earth, on which his eyes had been fixed, Wylde perceived that the speaker was Armstrong, who was standing amongst the foremost of the settlers.

The prisoner's face flushed with anger and intense hatred at the sight.

Bursting out into a satirical laugh, he said—

"Ha! ha! you see that even in death I have the best of you. That diamond ring which you and I so highly prized is lost beyond hopes of recovery."

Armstrong made no reply; he cared not to quarrel with a man at the point of death.

Then the judge spoke again.

"Prisoner, you refused the prayers of the good clergyman who visited you this morning; but let me now advise you to confess your guilt, and to breathe one short prayer to Heaven ere you breathe no more."

"I will confess this much," said the prisoner, with a long breath, drawing up his tall form to its full height.

Again there was the most profound silence; even the birds in the branches overhead ceased their twittering.

"I will confess this much, for, as I have lived as a gentleman, I will not go out of the world with a lie on my lips. I did attempt, and did intend to kill that man, who now asks me for a diamond ring, ha! ha! And I did also try and intend to kill the two men who acted as my gaolers, not that I hated them, but that I might escape, and thus have one more chance of taking the life of that enemy of mine. I make no expression of sorrow or regret for what I have done, but, on the contrary, am annoyed that my plans have failed. And with this confession I resign myself to you. Do your worst; I am ready to die."

At these words the judge beckoned a man, who at once stepped forward.

"Do your duty," said he.

The man nodded, and began to uncoil a long rope he had brought with him.

One end of this was thrown over the branch of a tree, the other remained in the hands of the executioner.

Despite his philosophy and his desire to die game, Wylde's face became paler than before; drops of cold perspiration were visible on his face, his lips quivered, and his whole body gave a convulsive shudder as the man fastened the cord in a running noose round his neck and drew it nearly tight.

"Once more I ask you, have you any last request to make?" said the judge. "Another minute, and it will be too late."

"No."

"Then die according to the sentence pronounced upon you by Judge Lynch!"

The executioner drew the end of the rope, and pulled the prisoner nearly off his feet.

But hark! what a horrid sound!

Why does the executioner slacken the cord and gaze round anxiously towards the forest? What can he expect to see there?

The sight which meets his eye is as fearful as the sounds which appalled his ear. He beholds a crowd of red Indians rushing towards him, brandishing muskets, bows, and tomahawks.

The settlers forgot their prisoner in a moment.

"Back, back to the huts—remember the women and children," said the loud voice of the judge.

Not hurriedly and in disorder, but with faces to their foes, the white men retreated to their houses; those who had been given the custody of the prisoner bringing him with them.

## CHAPTER XLVIII.

### A SCENE INSIDE A CHAPEL.

WHEN the settlers had recovered from the slight alarm into which the first appearance of the Indians threw them, they began to feel more confident in ultimately driving off their foes.

Men so skilled as they were in the knowledge of the woods and prairies could at once determine the tribe of their enemies.

They were Crow Indians, led on by the well-known and merciless Black Hand, whose bright tomahawk was seen gleaming in the rays of the sun.

The Indians were at least fifty ir

number, while the white men counted scarcely a third of that number.

Muskets and arrows were discharged by the Indians as they ran forward, while the settlers, slowly retreating, fired their rifles with precision and effect.

The Indians were evidently in the mood for fighting.

Undeterred by the shots which killed their comrades, they pressed forward, uttering most horrible yells.

Led on by Black Hand, they made a desperate charge upon the little band in the centre of which Wylde was placed.

A short, sharp volley from the rifles, and then the white men, with clubbed guns and firmly-clenched knives, struck and stabbed right manfully in their attempt to drive back the mass of foes.

But their efforts were in vain.

Separated from their comrades, they were all pierced with arrows, cut down with tomahawks, or stabbed.

Black Hand, with his own knife, cut the ropes from Wylde's body, and then placed the weapon in his hand.

"Well done, Black Hand! I shall remember this kindness of yours," said he.

"No talk; shoot, kill, scalp."

"Right! I will kill and scalp. But listen, Indian; that big man there must not be killed with the rest. I want him to be made prisoner."

"What for?"

"To roast him alive! Kill him by inches!" roared the infuriated man, all his thoughts of vengeance returning with tenfold force now that his arms were unbound and his hands held a weapon.

"Ugh! it is good."

And then the fight recommenced.

The white men, seeing that the Indians had rescued their prisoner, retreated to their settlement.

The little log huts had been built in two rows, so as to form a kind of street.

In this street the largest building was the chapel before mentioned as containing the noisy clock whose striking had filled Wylde's mind with such maddening reflections.

More than one settler suggested that, as this building was large enough to hold the entire population of the settlement, they should make it their fortification.

No sooner thought of than acted upon.

The word was passed, and the women, hastily gathering up their children, took refuge in the little chapel, while the men defended the approach to the settlement until all were safe within the log walls.

Having performed this duty, they, too, retreated slowly to the sanctuary, contesting the ground inch by inch.

Foremost among the assailants were Black Hand and Wylde, the latter still wearing about his neck some strands of the noose which the hangman's hands had placed there.

Furious with rage, he rushed forward and attempted to lay hold of Armstrong, who, however, knocked him back with his fist.

Then he turned towards the stern, grave old man who had personated Judge Lynch.

"Ha, judge!" he hissed, making a stab which the other avoided; "it will soon be my turn to try you. No hanging, though; my men cannot afford a rope; but we will drive a nice pole into the earth, and we will tie you to it, and you shall be roasted alive, and perhaps eaten by the redskins."

"I shall eat as toughly as I fight," replied the other, parrying with great difficulty the furious stabs which Wylde aimed at him.

Wylde wished to play with the old man as a cat plays with a mouse before eating it.

But the representative of Judge Lynch was no mouse.

He fought well, and at last gave the renegade a blow on the left shoulder with his good broad axe.

Had not the blade of the weapon been turned aside, the limb would certainly have been lopped off.

As it was, the force of the stroke sent the villain bleeding to the ground.

But at the same moment the old man fell pierced through the throat with an arrow.

With a fiendish yell, Wylde scrambled to his feet, and passing the point of his knife round the judge's head, plucked off the bleeding scalp and held it aloft.

Blows and bullets were aimed at him by the white men; but he seemed to have a charmed life.

Bullets fle·  ·ide of their mark, and

the hard steel seemed to have lost the power of penetrating human flesh.

The settlers were at last compelled to retire within the chapel, the doors of which were then firmly barricaded.

Brave, stout-hearted women were those wives and mothers who had gathered their children together and taken refuge there.

No shrieking, no screams, no appeals for mercy.

They knew that the savage shows no pity, and that their cries would produce no good.

Even the children and babes seemed to have caught some of the heroic fortitude of their parents, and, though the poor little things trembled and looked frightened as they felt, they made no clamorous noise.

The rifles of the men who had fallen without were in the hands of the Indians.

Bullets came crashing and splintering between the heavy slabs of which the walls were composed; but the Indians were indifferently acquainted with the use of fire-arms, and little harm was done.

Not a few of the noble women aided their husbands and relatives; some armed themselves with rifles and pistols, helping to keep up a steady fire, while others loaded spare weapons.

Yet, while thus employed, there was nothing of the Amazon in their appearance; nothing unfeminine in their pale faces, which were all beautified by a lofty expression of female heroism.

Presently the firing of the Indians slackened, and the men posted at the windows reported that they were holding a consultation.

"Well, I think we had better consult as to what is to be done," said Armstrong.

So the white men ceased firing also, and gathered in a circle to discuss their danger and the best method of extricating themselves from it.

"Can we not cut our way through, and so escape?" asked Armstrong.

"Whar 'ull we go tu?" asked a man.

There was a silence.

"I guess that won't du, mister," said the man who did constable's duty, leaning on his smoky rifle.

"What then?"

"Stop hyar, and fight the varmint."

"I am quite agreeable to that, but——"

Armstrong stopped speaking, and his eye filled with tears.

"Why, Britisher, you fout well; you ain't gwine to h'ist the white feather, air you?"

"Not I, but I fear for my wife's safety."

"Whew! that's awkward. Whar is she, mister?"

"At my clearing. I took her back last night, so that she might not see the death of the scoundrel, who is connected with our family."

"That's bad."

"I fear that if these red thieves find her——"

"They'll scalp her to a certainty."

Then again there was silence for some few minutes.

At length a tall young lad, of eighteen years or thereabouts, spoke up.

"Couldn't we hold out agin these hyar coons while somebody goes on to the next settlement and raises the nation? Thar's lots o' hosses out yon; if it war possible to get out o' this log, the thing mout be done."

The men looked from one to another, and acknowledged that it might be done.

"But who is to go?" asked Armstrong.

"I guess I shan't," said one brawny fellow. "It ain't gwine to be said as ever Josh Trueman turned his back agin any tellin' o' redskins. I stops to fight, I du, I guess."

And the man dashed the butt of his rifle upon the ground in a manner suggestive of a wish to engage in a hand-to-hand encounter with any number of Indians.

"I don't know the way," said Armstrong.

"Well, let's draw lots," suggested another.

The idea was at once acted upon.

There were fifteen men present, and for them fifteen slips of paper, of exactly the same size and shape, were prepared.

On one of them Armstrong wrote the word "Go."

The person who drew that slip, was to venture through the midst of the band of hostile Indians, and bring aid if possible.

They had been fighting nearly an hour, consequently it was about nine o'clock.

There was no hope of receiving aid till between four and five in the afternoon.

Just as the clock struck nine, the slip was drawn by the tall youth who had first proposed going.

And, at the same moment, a rifle was heard, and a bullet went crashing through the face of the clock, shattering its machinery, and thus silencing Time's herald.

Wylde had fired the shot, for he hated even the clock, which, during the night, had so loudly and persistently warned him to prepare for death.

Having drawn the slip the gallant young fellow prepared for his dangerous journey.

" Whose hoss is fastest ?" he asked.

" Mine," said the constable.

" Whar's the critter located ?"

" In the patch at the back o' my cabin. The cussed thieves ain't been thar yet."

The youth nodded, slung his rifle at his back, braced up his waist belt, looked to his ammunition, and then, with knife in one hand and revolver in the other, started from the chapel at a quick run.

His friends watched him from the window, and wished him good speed, while the pale-faced women offered up many a prayer for his safety and success.

But ere he had gone twenty yards, a loud whoop proclaimed that he was discovered.

In an instant a dozen redskins were after him.

The gallant youth held on his course— he wished to reach the horse ; when once on the animal's back, he could afford to laugh at his pursuers.

A rifle shot was heard, but the lad had turned an angle which led him to the gate of the field in which the horse was, so that the watchers could not tell the effect of the fire.

Had they seen it their hopes would have fallen.

The shot was fired by Wylde, who was well skilled in the use of the rifle.

The bullet struck the young man between the shoulders.

After running a few yards more he stumbled and fell, faint with loss of blood.

On came the Indians, eager to take the scalp of the pale-faced youth.

But he was not dead, nor in any way disposed to give up the natural covering of his head without making some resistance.

Three Indians outstripped the others and raced onwards for the prize of hair.

As they came up to him, the youth raised himself on his elbow, and shot them down one after the other with his revolver.

This done, he fell back dead by the side of those he had slain.

A fourth Indian ventured near, and as the young hero was dead, had no difficulty in securing the coveted trophy.

He uttered a loud whoop, and placing the scalp upon the point of his knife, walked back in triumph.

Then the Indians began to fire again, keeping up the fusillade with the greatest spirit and vigour.

Some of them were observed to be busily employed amongst the branches of the trees, and at first the settlers were puzzled to know what they could be doing.

A grand charge of the main body under Black Hand and Wylde drew off their attention, however, to nearer and more apparent danger.

On they came, whooping and yelling like demons, right up to the door of the little chapel, against which they hammered and hewed away with their tomahawks.

Every man and woman within who could fire a gun discharged it, and the volley made great havoc amongst the red savages.

They retired beyond the range of the settlers' rifles, and seemed to be waiting for something.

That something soon made its appearance.

A number of the Indians were seen dragging forward a huge branch with which it was evident they intended to batter down the door of the settlers' fortification.

" We must be prepared for the worst," said Armstrong. " Let every rifle and pistol be loaded."

" And when they air empty, we'll have a free fight, I guess," exclaimed his neighbour.

"BUT AT THAT MOMENT A PALE FORM APPEARED BETWEEN HIM AND HIS FOE."

# CHAPTER XLIX.

### THE DESERTED HUT.

GRAND sights are sometimes seen beneath the arching branches of American forests, and grand sounds are sometimes echoed along the leafy aisles.

But at other times the ears and eyes are greeted by sights and sounds, which in themselves are horrible.

Such a sound was it that fell upon the ears of Strongbow and his friends, as they sat by their camp fire.

A long, shrill, yelling chorus, partaking of the nature of the human voice, and yet seeming too fiendish and horrible in its loud tones to proceed from any human throat.

Hiram Swift and Big Elk well knew the meaning of that awful sound, for they had heard it before, and knew that it foretold danger.

"Big Elk, we must make tracks," said Swift.

"Ugh!" replied the Indian, rising, and grasping his weapons.

"What is that sound?" asked Strongbow.

"It is the war-whoop of Black Hand and his tribe. Them varmints mean death, they do, I guess."

"For the love of Heaven, take this poor girl to a place of safety. As for me, I can suffer torture and death, if I know that she is safe."

"You'll go too, I reckon?"

"I can't; I am too weak."

"Then we'll carry you."

"Not so; haste away and save yourselves and her. The savages will be content with my scalp."

"You jest get up," said Swift, stooping down, and lifting Strongbow to his feet. "We ain't goin' to be took by that skunk, yet a time."

Assisted by Big Elk, he hurried the wounded youth along till they reached the river once more.

The canoe was there just as they had left it.

Strongbow and Water Lily were placed in it, with instructions to keep down in the bottom of the craft as much as possible.

Hiram Swift and Big Elk also placed their weapons in the bottom of the boat.

"What are you going to do yourselves?" asked Strongbow.

"You'll see, lad," muttered the hunter.

"But you must not remain behind."

"Just you keep yer mouth shut, or some o' them lop-eared coons may hear us."

Thus rebuked, Strongbow was compelled to be silent.

Hiram Swift then unfastened the rope which held the canoe, and, tying it round his body, waded out into the stream until the water reached nearly to his neck.

Then, striking out for the opposite bank, he began to swim, towing the light boat after him.

Big Elk followed, acting as a sort of rearguard.

In this manner they crossed the stream, but Hiram Swift had no intention of landing so near his enemies.

From the opposite side arose a loud and prolonged whoop, telling that the Indians had already reached the spot where those they sought had been encamped.

"They'll be arter us, I guess. They'll know we had a boat."

"What shall we do then?"

"Keep up stream under the shade of these rushes," suggested Water Lily, for the first time speaking.

"A good idea, sartinly, for a squaw. We'll foller up that like shootin'."

Big Elk nodded, and the canoe was headed upwards.

The water was shallow enough to allow Hiram Swift to walk at times, instead of laboriously dragging the canoe after him while swimming.

They had not proceeded very far thus when, by the light of the moon, they saw their redskin enemies swimming across the river in pursuit.

Black Hand had recovered from the alarm into which he had been thrown, and was now endeavouring to make amends for the short interval of cowardice.

But, as the white men kept well under the shadow of the towering rushes which fringed one bank of the river, he could see nothing of them.

In vain he and his Crow Indians searched up and down the bank; they could not discover a place where the little band of fugitives had landed, for the simple reason that they had not touched the shore.

Black Hand's band scattered up and down the stream, but could meet with no success in their search.

In silence the fugitives pursued their way mile after mile.

At length, just as day was about to dawn, a strange, unlooked-for sight met their eyes.

A log hut was standing partly upon the bank of the river, and partly on some piles fixed into the bed of the stream.

The building had, no doubt, been erected by some enterprising settler, who had thus endeavoured to found a home and a settlement in that lonely neighbourhood.

But it seemed as though his efforts had not met with their deserved success, for the hut itself had the appearance of being deserted, while the little patch of ground which had once been cultivated had been allowed to return to its primitive state.

The door of the hut was ajar, but not a sound of any living being could be heard.

Hiram Swift made the canoe fast to one of the posts which supported the hut, and then clambered up the bank.

Entering the hut, he gazed around, and then started back in amazement.

"Here, come up, quick!" said he, beckoning to Big Elk.

The Indian hastened ashore, and looked down where Swift's finger pointed.

A horrible sight was before the eyes of the two men.

Upon the rude floor of the hut lay three skeletons, partly enshrouded in fragments of clothing.

"What mischief is this?" said Swift.

Big Elk stooped down, and taking up one of the skulls in his hand, pointed to a mark which extended all the way round it.

"The pale-faces have been scalped; warrior, squaw, and child," said the Indian, replacing the skull by the side of the other bones.

This, then, was the mystery of the hut; this explained why ruin and desolation had taken the place of prosperity.

The unfortunate settlers had fallen victims to the ferocity of the Indians.

"We'll stop here, I guess," said Swift, after a long pause.

"And these——?" replied Big Elk, pointing to the bones.

"They shall be buried."

With these words, Hiram Swift gathered up the ghastly remains of humanity into a deer-skin which he had with him, and carried them out of the hut.

He then lifted Strongbow and Water Lily out of the boat, and carried them into the hut.

For nearly two hours they remained in the hut, resting and planning how to escape from their bloodthirsty pursuers.

"By thunder, I guess I can fool them redskins!" exclaimed Hiram Swift, after many plans had been discussed.

Big Elk looked as though he would like an explanation.

"Thar's a branch o' this river runs along t'other side o' them live oaks, and comes into the main stream about six miles up. We can tote the canoe across—it's only a matter o' two mile—blind our trail when we get out on the prairie, and then come down the branch stream into the main river again. Them varmints 'ull think as how we're gone right slick up into them hills thar."

"Ugh! it is good," said Big Elk.

"But how can you carry the canoe?" asked Strongbow.

"On my back, lad; it ain't heavier than a sojer's knapsack. Big Elk will help you."

Despite the insecurity of their position, Strongbow could not help laughing at the idea of comparing the canoe to a soldier's knapsack.

Strongbow was sitting at the side of the hut farthest from the door, Water Lily was by his side, Big Elk and Hiram Swift were standing with their backs to the door.

Their weapons were piled in one corner to be out of the way.

Suddenly, as they thus stood talking and laughing, the Indian and the hunter were seized from behind by a party of Black Hand's warriors.

The Crow Indians had been searching amongst the tall rushes by the river's bank, and had discovered the hut.

The sounds which issued from it told them that the fugitives were inside, and so they took their measures accordingly.

No sooner did Strongbow see his friends thus seized, than something of his old energy returned to his weakened, wounded frame.

He rose to his feet with difficulty, and staggered towards the weapons piled in the corner of the hut.

The assailants perceived this movement, and rushed forward to prevent him from so doing.

Thus freed of part of their enemies, Hiram Swift and Big Elk struggled with renewed vigour to release themselves from those who had pounced upon them.

Big Elk managed at last to slip away from those who held him, and leaping down to the bank of the river, shouted the Delaware war-whoop.

Then, diving into the stream, he was lost to sight.

Inside the hut the struggle continued.

Hiram Swift fought desperately against the Indians; but he was overpowered and forced down.

Water Lily lent her little strength to aid him, but without avail.

In ten minutes after the first appearance of the foe, the three were prisoners, with their hands bound.

One or two of the Indians were bleeding from severe wounds, and one of the six who attacked the hut had lost his life.

## CHAPTER L.

### WAITING FOR BLACK HAND.

THE prisoners were secured, and, although Black Hand's braves looked angry and indignant at having experienced so stout a resistance at the hands of the captives, they made no attempt to kill or scalp.

One man appeared to be the leader, and acting according to his instructions, the wounded youth was placed in the canoe and paddled off down the river.

Once more he was parted from Water Lily and Hiram Swift.

"Farewell, dearest," said he, feebly raising his head to take a last look at her. "In this world or the next we shall meet again."

Then he was carried away down the stream in the light canoe, and the tall, waving rushes concealed her from his sight.

The Indian who had charge of him took the boat down to a point nearly opposite the grove in which they had camped the previous nights.

There they landed.

Strongbow was carried to a spot about twenty yards from the water, and placed on the ground near a fire.

Round this fire were seated two Indians and a white man.

The Indians were warriors of the Crow tribe; the white man was Jackson Wylde's friend and accomplice.

They were very busily employed in roasting and eating some meat.

When they had satisfied their hunger, Jackson condescended to recollect that possibly his prisoner was hungry.

"Here, you little cuss, eat that!" said he, tossing a piece of half-cooked meat towards the lad.

"How can I feed myself when my hands are bound?"

"He not run—no walk," said the Indian who had brought Strongbow from the hut by the river side.

"Then you may unfasten his hands."

The Indian cut the thongs and kindly threw the meat within reach of our young hero, who took it up and tried to eat it.

But his stomach refused the food.

He could not eat while his heart was full of thoughts of Water Lily.

He laid himself down at full length, and covered his face with his hands that the Indians might not witness the emotion which convulsed his countenance.

He had lain thus for nearly half an hour when footsteps were heard near at hand.

Someone was evidently approaching the camp.

Hastily composing himself, Strongbow raised his head to see who the new arrivals might be.

To his astonishment he beheld two well-known forms—those of Water Lily and Hiram Swift.

"Why, boy, you are hyar before us, then," said the old hunter, cheerily.

"Yes, but have you any idea what our fate is to be?"

"No."

"Where is Big Elk?"

"He managed to get right away."

"He will avenge us, then, even if he is unable to save us."

"No doubt o' that, lad; but hush, don't let that white skunk hear what we are sayin'."

The white skunk was Mr. Jackson, whose ears were opened to their widest extent to hear anything that might be said by the prisoners.

But from their low tones, and the caution they used, he was disappointed.

Water Lily crept as close to her lover as she could; to be near him was her chief joy.

They exchanged a few fond whispers of eternal affection, for theirs was a love which not even danger could destroy, or for a single moment divert from its course.

"I wonder what has become of the rascally Black Hand," said Strongbow, after a pause.

"Don't know," replied Swift.

"Is he amongst those fellows?"

"No."

"I wonder what he is up to?"

"The cuss ain't thar, that's sartin. Keep yer ears open; we mout learn a trifle from them chaps' clapper traps."

Strongbow kept his ears open, as desired by his friend.

The Indians and Jackson conversed in a strange medley *patois* of mingled English and Indian dialect.

Black Hand's name was frequently mentioned, but the captives were seated at such a distance from the fire that they could not catch the whole of the conversation.

One of the Indians left the fire, seeing that the prisoners were in conversation, and fearing lest they might be planning an escape, rebound Strongbow's hands.

As the man returned to the fire after the completion of this task, Jackson was heard to exclaim—

"I guess it won't do to let 'em run till Black Hand comes back."

This expression set the prisoners' heads working to know whither the redoubtable and cruel chief could be gone.

Hours passed away, and still that warrior did not appear.

Evening came, and the camp was removed to a group of trees about half a mile from the river.

The prisoners' bonds were carefully examined, a watch was set, and every preparation made for passing the night; but still the bloodthirsty chief of the Crows did not make his appearance.

"I wish we had about half o' them two score warriors Black Hand has got with him. This child don't somehow feel easy; his scalp feels oncomfortable," said Jackson.

"Ugh! Black Hand return in two days with many scalps of pale-faces! Bring back White Pine with him," replied an Indian.

"Ha, ha! I guess he'll laugh, Wylde will, when he sees these coons we've tricked so nicely."

"Black Hand bring back one prisoner."

"I reckon he'll bring back a couple, Ingin. A white man and his wife."

"Black Hand and White Pine take scalp of prisoner, then put on fire, make big burn. Ugh!"

The copper-coloured scoundrel grinned and chuckled with delight, as he thought of the fine fun there would be in roasting the five prisoners.

But Strongbow had other food for reflection.

Jackson had stated that Wylde and Black Hand intended to bring back two prisoners—a white man and his wife.

Who could these prisoners be?

# CHAPTER LI.

### THE MEETING.

RETURN we now to the little settlement where Wylde so nearly met the death he merited, and see how it fared with the settlers who were besieged in their little log chapel.

The Indians, as stated last week, were bringing forward a huge branch of a tree, with which to batter in the door.

During this process Wylde and Black Hand kept at some distance from the place, with a dozen of warriors.

The others cut off leafy boughs with which to screen themselves from the deadly aim of the white men, and thus partly concealed, dragged forward their rude battering ram.

Armstrong and the others in the chapel loaded every fire-arm they had, and placed their knives and axes in such spots as were most convenient.

On came the Indians, screened by their modern Birnam Wood.

Flash, flash! crack, crack! sounded the rifles of the valiant white men, as they poured a destructive fire upon their dusky foes.

At least one-third of the Indians fell in the agonies of death.

But, undaunted by such a fearful lesson, the survivors rushed on, and in a few minutes were banging away at the door.

It crashed, it splintered, and at last gave way.

In bounded the Indians with a terrible yell, brandishing their glittering tomahawks above their heads.

In silence the white men met the savage onslaught; axe clashed against axe, knife struck against knife, and for a few moments there was a deadly confusion of human beings hacking and stabbing in mortal combat.

Then, as the stubborn, furious wave slowly rolls back from the rock on which it has spent its fury, the Indians retreated a little way before the determined resistance of the daring white men.

But only for a short distance.

For in a few seconds another loud yell was heard, and Black Hand, with his reserve warriors, rushed forward to aid his retreating braves.

Once more the conflict raged.

Men dead, men wounded, were thickly strewn upon the ground; but the survivors pressed forward over the bodies of the dead and dying to add to the bleeding mangled mass.

But soon, too soon, it became evident that the settlers were outnumbered.

Gradually, and not without a most desperate resistance, they were driven back to the extreme end of the chapel.

Then the bloody work began.

Knives and tomahawks were plied; ghastly blows were given and received.

But at length the white men were all laid low, and their hapless families were at the mercy of the savages.

The scalping-knife did its bloody work, and horrid trophies of victory were plucked from the heads of strong men, fair women, and helpless children.

All were scalped, save one.

That one was Armstrong.

It seemed, through all the desperate battle, as though the Englishman bore a charmed life.

Only one wound had hurt his body, and even when all his comrades were killed, he still retained the axe which he had wielded with such fearful effect.

But alone, in the midst of such a fiendish band as that ruled by Black Hand, what could he do?

He fought bravely, but at such odds as twenty to one fighting was useless.

Armstrong was dragged down, his axe was wrested from him, and his hands were securely bound.

Then came forward the well-known figure of his relentless enemy, Wylde.

"Ha, ha! my noble Armstrong, so the tables are turned at last. It is my turn now to be judge, and, by virtue of that office, I doom you to death."

"Do your worst; I am not afraid to die, for I can face my Supreme Judge with a clear conscience."

The only answer Wylde made to this speech was to strike his helpless prisoner a heavy blow on the face.

"You are brave now," said Armstrong, tauntingly. "Not long ago I saw you with a pale face, quivering lips, and trembling form. My face does not change its colour, nor do my limbs shake, though I am in your power and cannot expect mercy."

"Every word you utter shall add a pang to your torments!" screamed the infuriated maniac, who was fast becoming perfectly frantic with rage and hatred.

"I can bear them."

"I will torture your mind as well as your body."

"You cannot; my conscience is at ease."

"Ha, we shall see. You shall have rare company in the fire; the skewers these redskins will sharpen shall pierce other flesh besides yours."

Armstrong's brow grew black with fury; he struggled and tried to burst the bonds which held him so securely.

He fancied that Wylde was alluding to his wife.

No wonder, then, that his cheek flushed with anger, and that he longed to strike the villain dead.

"You hear, scoundrel as you are," said Wylde, pricking his prisoner with the point of the knife he held in his hand.

"I do."

"I have a great mind to scalp you alive, Armstrong."

"Do so."

"It would be good fun; but still, on second thoughts, I'll leave your hair on your head. It will be very nice to dip those flowing locks and bushy whiskers in tar or naphtha, and then set them on fire. Ha, ha, ha!"

"The torments you can inflict on me are nothing in comparison with those you will have to undergo *hereafter!*"

"Curses on you!" said Wylde.

Armstrong smiled in a contemptuous manner, and the renegade had great difficulty in restraining the impulse which urged him to thrust his knife up to the hilt in his prisoner's heart.

Nothing but the thought, the hope of inflicting more dire and terrible torments upon his victim restrained him.

But that one word "*hereafter*" had such an influence upon his mind that he moved away, after leaving strict orders that the prisoner was to be guarded most carefully.

He did not care to hear Armstrong's

words, for they pierced his soul like a keen knife.

While this conversation was going on the Indians were busily employed in plundering the log huts of the settlers.

This done, and the bodies of the dead stripped of everything that appeared valuable in their eyes, they completed their work of destruction by setting the cabins on fire.

Even the chapel shared the same fate; flames were applied to it, and dead and dying were soon involved in a mass of flame and smoke.

The shrieks of some unfortunate beings who were not dead sounded as pleasant music in the ears of the savages who had perpetrated the horrid deed.

They paid little more respect to their own dead than to the bodies of the pale-faces.

Such Indians as fell within the chapel were allowed to consume with it, while those who had fallen in the open air were allowed to remain and become the prey of the vultures which wheeled round and round high above the scene of the frightful massacre.

Exertion produces hunger and fatigue.

The Indians were sensible of this, for as soon as they had completed their task of murder, pillage, and arson, they began to gather around their chief and the prisoner, and to eat food which they had brought with them or found in the houses of the white settlers.

But Wylde was impatient.

He kept urging Black Hand to set his men in motion.

He feared lest his villainy should be known elsewhere.

It was just probable that another messenger might have been sent besides the one killed, and he wished to be as far as possible from the place.

After an hour's rest, Black Hand gave the word.

His band diminished to half its original number, moved off in single file, the prisoner, securely bound, being placed in the midst of the rank.

They dived into the depths of the dark, gloomy forest.

"My poor wife," thought Armstrong. "She is to be their next victim, and I cannot move a hand to save her."

But the Indians seemed not to be aware

of the spot where Armstrong's hut stood, and Wylde had forgotten the circumstance in the mad whirlwind of passions which confused his mind.

All that day they continued the march till night came.

Then a camp was formed.

Armstrong was bound to a tree by his arms and feet, the trunk to which he was fastened being within a few yards of the spot where Wylde had established himself.

"Holloa, there! Are you hungry?" shouted the renegade, holding up a large piece of deer meat before the eyes of his prisoner.

Armstrong made no reply.

"I know you are hungry, but you shan't have a mouthful. Hunger shall be added to your other torments."

"*Thirst* will be one of your punishments *hereafter*, and not a drop of water will you have to cool your tongue."

With a muttered oath, Wylde relapsed into silence.

The prisoner's bonds were examined, and then the captors prepared for sleep.

Armstrong could not sleep.

His limbs were so tormented by the tightly drawn thongs.

Darkness came on.

The fires burnt low, and nothing was seen but the sleeping forms of the Indians.

Nothing!

Stay!

A pale, ghostly figure came gliding from the woods, and made its way towards the captive.

The figure was that of a pale woman, with long, golden hair.

Her dress was of deerskins rudely sewn together, and ornamented in Indian fashion.

"Fear nothing; your life is safe," she whispered, as she glided past.

The words brought hope.

But who could she be?

All night long he tried to solve the mystery, and when morning came he had found no clue.

A weary march again, and then the party neared a camp where Jackson and the others were sitting.

Wylde approached the prisoner.

"Look yonder," said he; "do you see those prisoners? I said you should have rare company in the fire."

"Good Heaven, my son!" moaned Armstrong, and then he fell senseless to the ground.

"Lift him up," said Wylde, to the Indians, who stood round about, "and pour some cold water upon his face."

The renegade feared lest excess of emotion should kill at least one of his prisoners, and thus deprive him of part of his contemplated fun.

It was with no feeling of humanity in his breast that he ordered cold water to be dashed upon Armstrong's face.

"My father alive," cried Strongbow, "and a prisoner in the hands of these monsters! Oh, Heaven! What crime has been committed by our family that we are thus sorely punished?"

"That your father?" said Hiram Swift.

"Your father?" echoed Water Lily.

The unhappy youth bowed his head on his breast, and sobbed aloud.

"Cheer up," said Water Lily, in soothing tones. "My father has escaped, and may, perhaps, bring his warriors to our rescue. If not, we shall all share the same fate, and be united in death."

"But my mother!—I know not her fate."

"The Providence you believe in will protect her, if living."

"It's my idea we ain't none on us booked for t'other side o' Jordan this journey," observed Hiram Swift. "I've been in wuss fixes."

"I hope we may escape, but the prospect is certainly gloomy," replied Strongbow.

"Hark, listen to them," said Water Lily.

The redskins were in earnest consultation with Wylde and Jackson on some matter of importance.

They were discussing the best method of torturing their prisoners.

## CHAPTER LII.

### COMBAT THE FIRST.

WHEN Big Elk escaped from the Indians who had captured his daughter and friends, he made the best of his way into the midst of the thick reeds which fringed the river bank to a depth of fifteen or twenty feet.

Partly by swimming, and partly by wading, he managed to get into the thickest part of the dense mass of vegetation, without leaving any continuous trail by which his enemies could track him.

In this hiding-place he remained, up to his neck in mud and water, until certain sounds, which his sharp ears easily detected, informed him that his enemies were retreating with their prisoners.

Then he began to make his way towards the bank.

Big Elk, however, did not move without caution.

He thought it quite probable that a scout or spy had been left on the spot to watch for him.

This, however, was not so very important a matter.

The bold Delaware felt himself quite a match for any adversary, provided he was not taken by surprise.

He knew his own bravery by heart, even if the scars on his body had not been constantly before his eyes to remind him of many deeds of daring performed while on the war-path.

However, to guard against surprise, he exercised all his Indian craft.

A breath of wind blowing over the grove of reeds would have caused less agitation among their waving tops than did his steady movements as he made his way towards the firm brink of the stream.

Having reached the extreme edge of the reed bed, the Delaware cautiously put out his head, and gave a searching glance all around.

The hut was plainly visible at the distance of only about a hundred yards.

Big Elk's eyes flashed fire as he saw standing at the door of it one of his Indian foemen, in full war-paint.

From the stripes upon his face, the eagle's wing in his hair, and the gaily-painted shield which hung over the warrior's shoulder, there could be no doubt that the watcher was a young chief, who had remained behind for the purpose of discovering and following up Big Elk's trail.

It would be something to boast of.

It would be a deed which would place him almost on an equality with the renowned Black Hand, could this young chieftain return home with the scalp of the great Delaware warrior hanging at his girdle.

The youth was tall and well formed, not more than twenty years of age.

His countenance betokened daring resolution, while his limbs showed that he possessed a large amount of physical strength.

He had evidently examined the spot where Big Elk plunged into the midst of the reeds, and, having followed the trail till it led to the water, was meditating what course to pursue.

Slowly, and with great caution, Big Elk retired again into the reeds, and made his way nearer to the hut.

It was a work of time to travel that short distance in the way adopted by the Delaware; however, he at length found himself within ten yards of the hut and the young Crow chieftain.

The latter was still standing as when Big Elk first saw him.

His eyes were alternately fixed upon the ground and then upon the waving reed bed, where he evidently expected to find some trace of the presence of the enemy whose scalp he had promised himself.

Having taken a quiet survey of his foeman for a few seconds, Big Elk began to consider how he should act.

The Delaware had only his scalping-knife with him, while the other was armed with lance, bow, axe and tomahawk.

It was very evident that in an open combat the weapons of the Crow would be more than a match for the simple knife and muscular strength of Big Elk.

Stratagem must be used, then.

But how?

Big Elk set his wits to work, and soon worked out a plan.

There were at least four yards of open ground between the borders of the reed bed and the spot where the watcher stood.

The first thing would evidently be an arrow should the Delaware show himself, for the enemy had his bow in his hand.

So the enemy's head must be turned, and his attention diverted, while Big Elk crosses the intervening space.

Acting upon a thought which suggested itself, the Delaware gathered up several small stones, and then, hiding himself once more, pitched one of them among the flags which grew on the other side of the lonely log hut.

The rustling sound it made in falling caused the Crow to turn his head instantly.

He made one step towards the spot where the reeds were visibly agitated, and then checked himself.

"A bird fluttering among the rushes," thought he, as his eye watched the whole surface of the place where Big Elk was concealed.

But he did not seem quite satisfied though, for his eye wandered from one spot to the other.

A second stone which Big Elk threw without being observed caused him to think more seriously on the subject.

"It must be a large bird, at all events, to cause such a disturbance."

So he himself pitched a stone towards the spot, hoping to drive the feathered creature up into the air, and thus solve his doubts.

But, as no bird appeared, the young warrior at once came to the conclusion that the Delaware had escaped from one reed bed to the other, and that it was indeed Big Elk whose movements had made the rustling noise.

His whole attention was fixed upon the spot.

Profiting by this, Big Elk crawled stealthily from his concealment and glided like a snake towards his enemy.

He then stood upon his feet and laid a hand on the shoulder of the young warrior.

"Ugh!" exclaimed the latter, turning round hastily.

But ere he could raise a weapon the arms of the Delaware were thrown around him.

The Crow struggled violently, and in a few seconds the two combatants were rolling upon the ground together.

Both were strong, hardy men, and both well knew that it was a combat for life and death.

Woe to the vanquished!

Little mercy is shown by Indians or by the hardy men who match themselves with the red children of the American forests and prairies.

Quarter is seldom asked and seldom given.

The Crow managed to drop his bow, which rather inconvenienced him, and clutched his knife.

Big Elk was similarly armed, yet he had the advantage of being above his adversary as they struggled together upon the ground.

So the Delaware dropped his own weapon and trusted in the strength of his muscles to disarm his adversary.

A fierce struggle it was, and many ugly scratches were received on both sides ere the mastery was decided.

But at length the powerful and time-hardened muscles of the Delaware warrior prevailed over the more youthful sinews of his adversary.

The Crow's hand gradually relaxed its grasp and fell to the earth.

Big Elk at once seized it, and with his hand knocked all other weapons out of the reach of his discomfited foe.

"A Delaware warrior will show Hard Head the way to the happy hunting grounds," said Big Elk, as he raised his weapon to strike.

"Ugh! Hard Head can die."

"The young squaw Hard Head took to his wigwam two moons ago will mourn for the loss of her warrior; but there shall be comfort for her in the wigwam of Big Elk the Delaware."

"Big Elk is a dog!" exclaimed the young man, and his countenance exhibited every sign of fury as he heard the mocking words of his successful adversary. "Waving Birch would die rather than become the squaw of Big Elk."

Again the Delaware raised his gleaming knife.

But his better feelings prevailed, and

the arm which held the weapon again dropped by his side.

" Hard Head loves the Indian girl who dwells in his wigwam ?"

The Crow warrior bowed his head.

" Hard Head's scalp belongs to Big Elk, but the Delaware warrior will tell Hard Head to go home to his squaw if he will promise to return with his scalp when the moon rises above the water of the river."

" Hard Head will stand upon this spot alone and unarmed when the moon rises. Hard Head's word has never been broken."

" Then go, and fail not to return," said Big Elk, as he rose and gathered up the weapons he had wrested from his adversary.

The young Crow rose to his feet, much astonished at the clemency which had been unexpectedly shown him.

" Go !" said Big Elk, pointing to the track which the others had taken.

" Hard Head will be here," replied the youth, as he turned to depart.

Big Elk watched him until a hollow in the ground shut the brave young warrior from his sight.

Then he began to prepare for his own departure.

Having selected the best weapons from those left in the hut and those he had won from his adversary, he destroyed all the remainder.

He then planted the shaft of a lance in the earth, and on the top of it fixed a piece of bark, upon which he had rudely drawn several of those symbols which serve the Indians instead of writing.

These symbols signified to those who could understand them, that Big Elk was gone, and that the young Crow's life was therefore spared.

Having given one last glance round to see that no eye watched, the Delaware gathered up his weapons, and left the place at a swift walk.

He had made up his mind to rescue his daughter and her companions in captivity, and to do it he knew it would be necessary to call in the aid of the warriors of his own tribe.

From several things which he had noticed, Big Elk was inclined to believe that he was not so far from his own wigwam as he had at first imagined, and he resolved to find out the Delaware village ere he took any farther steps.

He knew well that important prisoners were tortured with every solemnity, and that, therefore, two or three days must elapse ere Strongbow and the others would be immediate danger.

## CHAPTER LIII.

### THE PALE WOMAN AGAIN.

FOR more than an hour Strongbow and his companions in captivity sat listening to as much as they could hear of the conversation going on amonst their captors.

An animated discussion it was.

Evidently Wylde wished to put them to the torture at once.

But this was a proceeding to which Black Hand and his Indians strongly objected.

Having captured them, Black Hand wished to put them to death with due solemnity; to make them, in fact, a sacrifice to his deity.

The Indian is religious; that is, superstitious, and believes that atonement for misdeeds is best made by offerings.

Black Hand was conscious of having neglected his religion for a long time, and was resolved now to make up for the past neglect.

" The prisoners are mine," said Wylde, rising after the all-important pipe had been passed round the circle.  " The prisoners are mine, and I, therefore, demand that they shall be burnt alive immediately."

Black Hand shook his head, and several dissentient grunts were heard.

" The Manitou has thrown a cloud over the mind of the White Pine," replied Black Hand, rising; " he cannot remember things which he saw. The prisoners were captured by my young men."

"DRAWING AN ARROW TO THE HEAD, HE DIRECTED IT FULL AGAINST THE BODY OF THE BEAR."

"And what of that? Did you not promise to give them up to me?"

Black Hand smiled.

"Where are the fire-bows, the powder, the lead, the blankets and the firewater which White Pine promised my young men?"

"Let me have the prisoners, Black Hand, and in five days each of your warriors shall have a fire-bow, plenty of powder and lead, and you shall have a large keg of fire-water."

"The White Pine has two faces. Black Hand will see the fire-bows in his camp before the white men and the Delaware girl are given up to the White Pine."

"Well, will you let me burn them in the morning?"

Black Hand considered for some short time.

At length he replied—

"White Pine shall do as he pleases with the prisoners in two days. Let White Pine send his friend now for the fire-bows, and himself remain in the camp of Black Hand until he returns."

At this strangely cunning proposition of the Indian, Wylde was considerably taken aback.

He moved a few paces out of the circle and beckoned Jackson to a consultation.

To tell the truth, Jackson was very much afraid; and when he saw Wylde moving away, thought that his chief had come to a resolution *he* had formed some time ago, namely, to quit the very unpleasant society of Black Hand and his gang at the very earliest opportunity.

"Are you going, captain?"

"Not yet."

"I guess we'd better make tracks."

"You are a fool, Jackson."

"How's that?"

"What have I been striving so hard to obtain for these past six years? What did I risk body and soul for, but certain property which is now in the hands of the English Chancery Court, and which will be mine when that man and his son are dead."

"I have heard say, captain, that property which once finds its way into chancery never comes out again."

"That man knows not how to manage things, though I could easily disperse the other claimants to the estate."

"In the same way as you mean to disperse the rightful heir and his son?"

Wylde nodded.

"But about this affair. It is very evident that these redskin rascals will not consent to my leaving the camp until they get some rifles."

"Well?"

"You must go."

"I, captain?"

"Why not?"

"I should be lynched as safe as a bank if I ventured."

"Humph! Don't talk about unpleasant subjects, Jackson. But you must go and purchase rifles."

"Where is the money to come from?"

"I have sufficient. These brutes of settlers had been hoarding up their cash."

"Well, captain, if I must go, I must, but I don't see the force of starting right off at once."

"First thing in the morning, then."

"Right; but, I say, cap, if you want to get rid of them, why don't you slit their throats at once?"

"Don't you see that Black Hand has set eight men to guard them? We should not be allowed to go near them."

The two friends then returned to the circle, and Wylde made a neat speech to the Indians.

He said that his friend would go to fetch the fire-bows and the fire-water in the morning, and that he himself would remain with Black Hand for the purpose of torturing the prisoners, and also as a hostage for the return of his companion.

To this the Indians, after some talk in their own language, assented.

Very little more was done that day except to eat and drink.

As night came on, the watch placed over the prisoners had particular orders given them by Black Hand.

The orders were not to allow White Pine or his friend to approach any or either of the victims destined for torture.

Wylde overheard the instructions, and therefore prudently resolved not to attempt to oppose them.

He knew Black Hand to be a most valuable ally, but one whom it would be a dangerous task to transform into a foe.

So, therefore, he withdrew, with his

friend, Jackson, to the side of the camp, at the greatest distance from the spot where the prisoners were placed.

Night came on, and the fire burnt low.

The Indians were all asleep, save the eight sentinels, who sat silently upon the mossy turf.

So motionless were they, that it would have been difficult to tell whether they were asleep or not.

Everything was silent; even the breeze seemed to slumber, and the leafy tops of the trees stirred not.

Hour after hour passed away.

The prisoners slept but little.

Their limbs were so cramped by the tight bonds round them, that sleep was an impossibility.

Occasionally they dozed, but the fearful pains caused by the non-circulation of the blood soon aroused them.

Suddenly Strongbow fancied he saw a figure moving in the wood.

It came nearer and nearer.

As it drew nigh, the youth was able to distinguish it more plainly.

He then saw that it was the pale, mysterious woman of the cedar swamp; the one whose reappearance had caused so much amazement in the honest, simple heart of the old hunter.

Strongbow watched her movements attentively.

When she arrived within a few yards of the camp, she stopped and carefully surveyed the scene, paying particular attention to the sentinels.

"They must be asleep," said Strongbow to himself, "or they would surely see her."

They were asleep, excepting two, and even they were slowly yielding to the drowsy god.

With eyes fixed upon the ground, the two Indians sat, endeavouring not to yield to the influences which compelled them to slumber.

The strange woman glided forward.

She paused a moment by the side of Strongbow, whose eyes were fixed upon her pale face.

Seldom had he seen a face of such matchless yet peculiar beauty, or hair which so much resembled in colour and texture the product of the silkworm.

Her finger was raised in a warning attitude.

"Hush!"

The word, though gently breathed, reached the ears of Strongbow and his gentle companion Water Lily.

Neither spoke a word.

Bending down over them, the pale woman slit their bonds with a keen knife.

"Don't rise," she whispered, "but crawl gently between those two men who sleep so soundly."

As she spoke, the stranger pointed to a couple of savages, who were most unmistakably in a sound slumber.

Just as the two released captives began to stir to get away from the place of their captivity, one of the sentinels slowly stretched himself and gave a look round.

Strongbow and Water Lily remained perfectly motionless, while the pale woman threw herself flat upon the ground behind them.

In a few seconds the Indian satisfied himself that all was secure, and then closed his eyes again.

Strongbow immediately began to move in the direction indicated, followed by the two females.

As soon as he was fairly among the trees, he rose to his feet.

"Mysterious being," said he, "I thank you for this proof of your kindness. But my father and my best friend are still in the power of those savages. Will you aid them?"

"I will."

"Can I do anything?"

"No. Provide for your own safety. Walk straight forward; let that pale star be your guide. Stay, here is a knife and a rope; they may be useful to you. Stay not here, but haste away."

Full of faith that the stranger would perform her promise, Strongbow led Water Lily off in the direction indicated.

He soon lost sight of his fair liberator, who returned towards the Indian camp.

But ere she could do anything to aid the remaining captives, a noise told her plainly enough that the Indians were astir.

"I must mislead them from the young couple," she murmured. "The others are safe for a time at all events."

Acting upon the thought, she moved off in a different direction to that taken by the young hero and Water Lily.

She seemed careless about attracting attention; in fact, she made as much noise as possible, in order to draw Black Hand and his band after her.

The ruse was perfectly successful.

Guided by the sound, the Indians, who had just discovered the loss of two of their prisoners, darted off through the woods.

But the strange woman fled quite as swiftly as they pursued, and so led them on for nearly half a mile into the timber.

Then she glided behind a clump of thick bushes, and led forth a milk-white horse by the bridle.

Mounting in haste, she galloped away, pursued by nearly the whole tribe of Indians and the two renegades.

Black Hand was not with them, however.

The chief possessed more cunning than many of his tribe, and was not so easily misled.

It may be asked, why, then, did he allow his followers to pursue the strange woman?

The answer is simple.

He had noticed the beauty of Water Lily's form and features; he wished to take her to his wigwam as his squaw.

He followed for a short time, and then returned.

## CHAPTER LIV.

### COMBAT THE SECOND.

STRONGBOW and Water Lily lost no time in making the best of their way to as great a distance as possible from the scene of their captivity.

After a journey of two or three miles, they found the forest become more hilly, and consequently the path was more difficult to travel.

Still they kept on, guided by the star pointed out by their strange liberator, and full of confidence that she would in the end achieve the liberation of the other captives.

Not hearing anything of Black Hand's braves, they naturally imagined that they had escaped safely without observation.

Nevertheless, they did not slacken their speed on that account.

They little thought, however, that Black Hand himself was after them.

Presently they came to the brink of a precipice which barred their way.

From right to left, as far as the eye could reach, there was a wall of perpendicular rock, at least twenty feet in height.

"We must descend here," said Strongbow.

"But how?" asked Water Lily.

"By this rope."

With these words he fastened the cord to the root of a tree.

"Wait here, dearest," said he, "while I try the strength of the cord."

"Do not leave me long, dearest."

"Not I. If you fear to descend, I will soon be up here by your side again."

"I fear some danger."

"There is nothing to fear."

"I hope not; but I have a vague feeling that our perils are not yet at an end."

"Dismiss such foolish fears from your mind, my love. At all events, if dangers come, I will protect you with my life."

"But your wounds are not yet healed."

"My strength has returned, and I feel strong enough to combat with a dozen Indians on your behalf. Now, then, watch me, while I glide down the rope, so that you may know how to manage."

The active youth, whose wounds were rapidly healing, grasped the rope and rapidly descended to the ground beneath the cliff.

"Safe!" he cried, as he alighted. "Now, dear, you may descend without fear; your weight is not more tha mine."

The lovely Indian girl hesitated for few moments.

"Come," said her impatient lover "our enemies may be upon the trail."

The fair girl grasped the rope, and lowering herself gently from the cliff, began to slide down.

The exercise was one to which she

was not accustomed, and the skin was almost chafed from her hands as she lowered herself.

"Hold! have a care!" cried Strongbow, when she was about half-way between the summit of the cliff and the ground.

Water Lily stayed her progress.

"What is the matter?"

"Ha, villain! what would you do?" exclaimed the excited youth.

"Ugh! the Delaware maiden shall reach the ground directly," exclaimed a voice above.

Casting her eyes upwards, Water Lily observed the fiendish features of the Crow chieftain, Black Hand.

"Pretty one, come up again—not go with paleface," said he, and suiting his actions to his words, he exerted all his strength and drew the rope up two or three feet.

But the exertion was too great for him, and he suddenly relaxed his hold.

The jerk as Water Lily again descended was terrific, but the Indian damsel stoutly maintained her grasp upon the cord.

"Ugh!" grunted Black Hand, as he peeped over the cliff and saw her still dangling in mid air. "Hold tight, never mind; soon go to ground."

The hideous scoundrel then drew his knife from his belt and began slowly to saw away at the rope.

"Hold, rascal!" shouted Strongbow. "Villain, what would you do? Oh, for my trusty bow and arrows, that I might send a shaft through his heart!"

Meanwhile the Indian calmly continued his task, chuckling to himself with great self-delight.

"Slide down, dearest, slide down," cried the Boy Chief of the Delawares. "If you fall, I am here to catch you."

Encouraged by his words, Water Lily began to descend the rope more rapidly.

Black Hand, seeing his victim likely to escape his clutches, proceeded to cut through the rope.

But Water Lily was within three feet of the ground when her support gave way, and she dropped safely into the arms of her lover.

"Ugh! the Delaware Water Lily shall yet become the squaw of Black Hand," yelled the infuriated Crow chieftain, as he saw his victim thus escape.

But at that moment an arrow, aimed from behind, pierced his right shoulder, and for a time frustrated all his thoughts of vengeance.

Turning hastily in the direction from which the shaft had come, he beheld Big Elk, the Delaware warrior, rushing towards him, tomahawk in hand.

"Big Elk! Ugh!" exclaimed Black Hand.

"Big Elk, who has taken the scalps of many foes," replied that warrior.

Both warriors stood gazing at each other for a few seconds.

At length Big Elk moved forward.

"A Crow wigwam shall be desolate; the Crow warriors shall return from the war path without their chief," said he, raising his knife.

"Ugh! Big Elk is a dog. His scalp shall hang in the lodge of a Crow warrior," answered Black Hand, bending his bow, and drawing an arrow to the head.

But his hand trembled, so great was the pain caused by his adversary's weapon.

Ere the missile could leave the bowstring, Big Elk had rushed forward, and wrested it from his grasp.

Black Hand stepped back, and released his tomahawk from his belt.

Nothing daunted, Big Elk followed his foe.

The glittering tomahawk flashed in the light, and descended with fearful violence, the blow being aimed at the head of the Delaware warrior.

But the wary Big Elk was fully prepared for it.

Stepping back a pace, he caught his adversary's wrist in his right hand, and held it as in a vice.

The Crow warrior struggled for a moment, but the grasp of the Delaware was too powerful.

In a short space of time the weapon was wrested from Black Hand's hold, and remained in the possession of the conquering Delaware.

"A Crow warrior shall go to the happy hunting grounds without his weapons," said Big Elk, and then the bright axe descended with crushing force on the skull of its original possessor.

Death was instantaneous, and, with a triumphant yell, Big Elk tore off the plumed scalp-lock of his vanquished foe.

## CHAPTER LV.

### THE MEDICINE MAN.

HAVING thus given Big Elk the victory over his enemy, Black Hand, it behoves us to explain what occurred to him between the time when he left the deserted hut by the water side and his opportune appearance to rescue Water Lily from her peril.

Having left young Hard Head, the Crow warrior, Big Elk made the best of his way to the place where the wigwams of his tribe were pitched.

It was more than a day's journey on foot, though our friends, in travelling to the spot where we left them, were some days upon the road.

Big Elk, however, could find his way home by a much nearer route.

The configuration of distant hills, the bark and branches of trees, the direction of a water course, were all so many finger-posts pointing out to him the way he should go; and so at length he reached his wigwam.

The Delaware warriors received him with as marked demonstrations of joy as their stoical, taciturn habits allowed.

He at once assumed the command of the party, and called a meeting for the purpose of impressing on them the necessity of at once rescuing the pale-faced youth who had been elected by them to be their chief.

This every warrior was willing to do; but to rouse them to a proper pitch of frenzy, Big Elk made a speech, inciting them, by all the means in his power, to take a terrible vengeance on the band of Black Hand.

The rash, the thoughtless, the ignorant, were all aroused by his eloquence, as, in his own vehement manner, the Delaware chief explained the dangers he had escaped, and to which their Boy Chief was still exposed.

The effect of this speech, coming as it did from one so well-beloved, and so highly esteemed for wisdom and love of country, was that of a moral earthquake.

Big Elk's heart bounded within his bosom, and his soul triumphed with hope, as he beheld them brandishing their knives and tomahawks, and heard them shouting the war-cry of the tribe.

" It is Black Hand who has sold the pale-face chief to be a slave ! Black Hand shall die !" shouted one, and the last sentence was echoed from fifty dusky throats, as so many glittering axes were waved in the air.

" The Crow warriors are dogs. They shall all die ! Their scalps shall hang in the hunting lodges of the Delawares," said Big Elk.

" Hoo-hoo-hoo ! Pow-hoo-ee !"

The dreadful war-cry echoed back threateningly from the surrounding trees.

Big Elk, however, was determined to add fuel to the fire of hatred already kindled in their hearts.

He determined to appeal to their superstitious feelings.

A black post was therefore planted in the ground, and word was sent to the tent of the great medicine man of the tribe, to the effect that his opinion on the subject was required.

A circle was formed by the Indians, having the post for its centre.

They stood round this post, putting on their war paint in fantastic streaks of black, red, and other colours.

But they soon opened out to admit the great prophet, the medicine man who was to assure them of success.

This being was an Indian of more than middle age, dressed in garments of the most fantastic fashion. Upon his head he wore the skull of a bear, the skin of the back and shoulders hanging down his neck. Round his waist was the skin of a rattlesnake, stuffed with such nicety that it appeared as though the animal was alive.

In his hand the medicine man carried a bag, which contained all his charms, such as teeth of bears, rattles of snakes, feathers, claws of owls, and similar rubbish.

These mystic elements he rattled loudly, as he danced into the midst of the circle.

Two Indians had rude drums, on

which they beat with their hands, chanting a rude song all the time.

After dancing round the circle a few times, the medicine man began to sing as he whirled about.

The faster he moved, the wilder became his song, and the more excited his gestures.

His actions appeared almost frenzied.

The eyes of the assembly followed him, and every bosom thrilled with the wildest throes of superstition.

It became dark, and torches were kindled by those who stood round the circle.

The glare of the lights showed every angry distortion of the medicine man's countenance.

His eyes protruded as if bursting from their sockets; his lips and widely-distended jaws were covered with foam.

At length he fell upon the ground, writhing in the most horrible convulsions.

His last intelligible words were, "Hoo-hoo-hoo! Pow-hoo-ee!"

After lying motionless for several minutes, sense began to return to the fantastic form.

The medicine man again began to move.

First he rose to his knees, then stood erect upon his feet. Grasping his axe and knife in his hands, he shouted—

"Owychee-Manitou has delivered the Crows into our hands. The feathers of our arrows shall be red with their blood. The wolves of the prairie shall fatten on their flesh. Their squaws shall plant corn for the Delaware tribe."

"Death to the Crows!" shouted the listeners.

"Let not the children of the great Delaware nation hang back from the slaughter. Let not their knives cease from drinking the blood of the Crows!"

"We will not cease from the slaughter," was the response.

"Let the children of the great Delaware nation go forth on the war path as the panther glides through the wood; let their steps be noiseless, and let no trail show where their feet have pressed."

"We will leave no trail!"

"Let the children of the great Delaware nation strike their enemies with strong blows; let their tomahawks sink into the skulls of the Crows, even as the axe of Oconestogee sinks into the soft wood of the black-painted war-pole."

As he spoke, the medicine man struck a heavy blow, and buried his axe in the trunk of the painted pine tree.

"We will strike strong blows!" shouted the Delawares with one voice, as they rushed towards the pole, striking at it furiously with their tomahawks.

So eager were they in their onslaught that in a few seconds the war-pole was shivered to pieces.

Each Indian endeavoured to secure a fragment, believing that by so doing he would be certain to win a scalp.

Loud sounded the war whoop as the Delawares danced round and round the spot where the pole had stood.

At length a gesture from Big Elk suddenly stopped them in the midst of their frenzied dance.

The men were fit for action.

Waving his hand, the bold warrior commanded silence.

Briefly he gave his orders—dividing his men into three bands, who were to follow each other at distances of about a mile from each other.

Placing himself at the head of the foremost, he gave the signal to march.

The noise was changed for total silence, as without the slightest sound they filed away into the dark recesses of the adjacent forest.

In half an hour no warrior remained in the village, excepting those who were deemed too old to go forth upon the war path.

They remained to take charge of the women and children, a task they were quite competent to perform, as the little town of wigwams was well defended by natural fortifications, which rendered it difficult for an enemy to assail it on any side.

The bold, hardy warriors, commanded by Big Elk, marched on swiftly.

Their footsteps made no sound, nor did the track appear as though more than one man had passed along the narrow path.

Hour after hour they marched without wearying, till at last Big Elk judged that he was not more than two or three hours' journey from his foes.

Then he halted his men in a thick part of the wood.

In order to ensure the victory, it would be necessary to find out exactly the position in which the enemy was en-camped.

This, as our readers already know, the Delaware chieftain had no means of ascertaining.

A young warrior, who, for the first time in his life had taken the war path, was called forward and dispatched upon this delicate and dangerous mission.

Hope and pride glowed in the youth's eyes as he braced up his belt and started upon his perilous task.

He longed to distinguish himself, and now had a glorious opportunity.

Quickly he disappeared in the forest, and then the remainder of the men sat down in silence among the bushes to rest themselves, and stay the cravings of hunger with such food as they had brought with them.

Not a fire was kindled, for the thinnest vein of smoke might betray them to the watchful eyes of their savage foemen.

Big Elk was confident of success, for he understood the nature of his adversaries.

So he waited in patience for the return of his spy.

The young warrior, however, was a longer time gone than he had anticipated.

Big Elk grew anxious.

He hastily gathered up his own weapons and crept away on an independent scouting excursion.

He had not got more than half a mile when he heard sounds of people conversing in the English tongue.

Big Elk recognised the voices as those of Strongbow and his daughter.

It seemed as though they were in danger, from the excited tones of Strongbow's voice.

The Delaware rushed forward hastily to aid them, and saw what we have already described—Black Hand in the act of severing the rope by which his daughter was descending to the ground beneath the cliff.

How he saved his daughter and defeated his enemy the reader already knows.

## CHAPTER LVI.

### THE ATTACK.

AS soon as Big Elk had fastened the scalp lock of his defeated foe to his girdle, he descended the cliff to see if any harm had befallen his daughter.

She was safe and sound by the side of her lover.

Having given way to one expression of paternal affection, he again became the grave Indian chief.

"The pale-face chief has escaped from the Crow dogs?" he asked.

"I have, thank Heaven. It was lucky you came up in time to kill that rascal though, or poor Water Lily would have had an ugly fall."

"Ugh! Black Hand was a squaw—his braves shall wear petticoats."

"But how about Swift and my father? Cannot we rescue them?"

"The pale-face braves are still in the hands of the dogs of Crows?"

"Yes."

"Strongbow can lead the way to their camp?"

"I fancy so, if we can only climb up these rocks again."

Big Elk scanned the face of the cliff, and, after a few seconds' survey, discovered a method of ascending.

"Look," said he, pointing with his finger.

The object which he indicated was a tall pine tree, which had grown near the foot of the cliff.

It had been partly rooted from the ground by some fearful tempest, and lay with its trunk and branches resting against the foot of the precipice.

It was a natural ladder.

Big Elk ascended first, lopping off such branches as would incommode his daughter; then Water Lily ascended, and last of all Strongbow.

"Come with Big Elk," said that warrior, when all were safely at the top of the cliff.

"Remember our friends."

"Big Elk has not forgotten."

Strongbow and Water Lily followed their guide into the forest.

A short walk brought them to the spot where all the Delaware braves were assembled, and great was the surprise of Strongbow and Water Lily to see them.

The Indians themselves would have shouted their war-cry for joy, had not Big Elk, by a most impressive gesture, commanded silence.

They were, therefore, obliged to content themselves with offering the young chief and his companion the best and daintiest parts of their provisions.

Little time was given them for eating, however.

In a short time the young scout returned and gave his information.

"There were," he said, "but a few men by the Crow camp, the others having evidently gone off in various directions. Two white prisoners were there, and one white man who was not a prisoner. From the preparations which had been made the prisoners were evidently doomed to torture."

"Let us make haste, then, and rescue them," said Strongbow.

Big Elk, however, knew how to wait.

He knew that so important a ceremony would not take place during the absence of three-fourths of the tribe.

His plan was to wait till all the warriors had returned and then destroy the whole band.

Big Elk would be content with no smaller revenge.

So he moved his men still nearer to the camp of the unsuspecting foemen, and then sent out other scouts.

These reported that the Crow warriors were returning, having apparently given up the chase of the fugitives.

"Strongbow will remain here with the Water Lily of the Delawares," said Big Elk, as he prepared to surprise his foes.

"No; I can fight, and I will, too, to rescue my father from their hands."

"The young chief's wounds are not yet healed."

"No matter; they can heal to-morrow as well as to-day."

"Strongbow has no weapons."

"I will procure them."

"The Water Lily will be defenceless."

This last appeal touched Strongbow's heart.

He hesitated for a few moments, and then nodded his head to signify that he would remain with Water Lily.

"You are safer here, dear," said the fond girl, laying her hand on her lover's shoulder.

"But I cannot protect you should any stragglers surprise us. I have no weapons."

"I will ask my father," said she. "He will give you something with which to protect yourself."

This request being made, a knife and a long lance were handed to the youth, together with a bow, quiver of arrows, and an axe.

Then the snorting noise made by a deer was heard, and in obedience to this signal the Delaware warriors rapidly disappeared after their leader in the depths of the wood.

Strongbow gazed after them for a few minutes, till the hindermost had passed from his sight.

Then the love of winning renown overcame all other considerations.

He resolved to follow, and take part in the conflict which he knew must ensue.

"Remain here, dear Lily," he whispered. "I *must* go."

"Why?"

"Because I am the Chief of the Delawares."

"Ah me! You will thrust yourself into danger."

"I must not be called a coward. Now, listen to me: crouch down here in the midst of these thick bushes, keep the bow and arrows, and the lance, to guard yourself in case you should be assailed. The knife and the axe will be sufficient for me."

"If you will go, dearest, take all the weapons; you will need them."

"No, I cannot leave you defenceless."

Stooping down, he kissed her cheek, and then, with hasty strides, followed the Delaware braves.

Water Lily crouched down in the bushes, and fervently implored the Divine Power above to protect her father, her lover and her friends.

The Delaware warriors looked surprised, though they said nothing, when Strongbow joined them.

The youth soon made his way to the head of the band, and made Big Elk aware of his presence.

"The Lily is safe, and I am here as Chief of the Delawares!" he whispered.

"Ugh! it is good," replied Big Elk, looking with pride upon the young hero.

The scouts sent ahead soon brought back word that they were within a hundred yards of the enemy, most of whom had returned to the camp.

Big Elk then gave the word to surround the whole party and, at a given signal, to advance.

The Delawares then dispersed themselves in little bands, and took up positions on all sides of the foemen's bivouac.

It was nearly sunset when a loud hoot seemed to give notice that an owl had flown forth from his hollow tree, to take a noiseless ramble through the dark forest glades.

The sound seemed ominous.

At the sound dusky warriors began to advance on all sides.

The Delawares had hemmed in their foes without the latter being aware of it.

Suddenly the fearful war-cry sounded.

The Crows started to their feet in alarm, and gazed anxiously around, not knowing from which side the noise proceeded.

Again and again it pealed on their ears from every side of the camp.

Then the Delawares were seen issuing from the forest, and rushing down upon their foes.

The small parties united as they advanced, until they became large bodies of angry men, thirsting for conquest.

The Crows, though alarmed, lacked not courage.

Not an opening was left for escape; foes were seen on every side.

They grasped their weapons and resolved to die like braves.

First came a flight of arrows which sent many a dusky warrior to the happy hunting grounds.

Then came Big Elk and his braves, brandishing their tomahawks.

"The Crows are squaws; the Delawares will whip them with rods!" shouted Big Elk, as he made his way towards the place where his foes were huddled up together like sheep attacked by a strange dog.

"Petticoats for the Crows!" cried his braves, as they dashed forward.

Then began the battle.

The war-cry and the defiant shout once sounded, there was no more noise heard except the twang of bow-strings, the clash of steel axes, or the gurgling groans of the dying.

Bravely fought the Crow warriors, and bravely fought Wylde.

He was reckless of death, and everywhere seemed to court destruction.

Big Elk marked the White Pine, and endeavoured to force his way to the spot where the renegade fought in the midst of the Indians.

But ere he could fight his path there the white man had vanished.

Strongbow's first act was to rush to his father and Swift, and to cut their bonds.

"Hurraw for you, younker!" shouted the old hunter, and, after squeezing the lad's hand, he dashed into the thick of the fight, armed with weapons wrested from the hands of the dying.

"God bless you, my boy," said the father; "you are indeed a good son."

"Thank Heaven you are safe, father."

"But how did you escape?"

"That pale, mysterious woman Swift spoke of liberated me."

"Do you know who she is?"

"Not entirely—have a care!"

This exclamation was addressed to his father to warn him against Wylde, who was rushing furiously towards the little group.

But a moment afterwards the renegade was thrown violently to the ground by two wounded Delawares, who, even in their death agonies, were not inclined to let a foe escape.

He wrested himself from their grasp, however, and dashed away into the thick bushes in the neighbourhood.

Wylde was the only one who escaped.

The Crows were shot down, killed and scalped to a man.

A more complete victory was never gained by the great Delaware nation.

Scalps were plentiful—nearly everyone of Big Elk's warriors being possessed of a trophy.

Then they raised their war-whoop once more, in which Hiram Swift and Strongbow joined most heartily.

A short rest to collect the weapons and count the killed was necessary, as well as to attend to their own wounded.

Hiram Swift, to his intense delight, recovered his own favourite and trusty old rifle.

The true old weapon had been discharged once by an Indian, who seemed to have been puzzled to know how to load it again.

It was, however, free from injury.

## CHAPTER LVII.

### THE SPY.

GREAT was the joy of the fair Water Lily, when her father and her lover returned to the spot where she had been left.

Safe and sound, without even a scratch upon him, save those, half healed, inflicted by the claws of the grizzly bear.

Big Elk also was unharmed.

The warriors made their camp in the midst of the forest, and the night was spent in feasting and rejoicing.

A solemn feast it was.

Brave warriors recited, in long speeches, the daring deeds they had done in the late conflict, pointing to the bleeding scalps on their belts, and the wounds on their limbs, in confirmation of the truth of their words.

The pipe was smoked solemnly, and all were satisfied with the events of the past day.

A night of sound repose followed, for all were tired.

No need to keep any watch, for they had no fear of being disturbed by any foe.

The next morning they commenced their triumphant march homewards, which was accomplished without any incident more exciting than the everyday occurrences of a journey through the wilderness.

At length they came in sight of their own wigwams.

The old men, the women, and the children turned out in full force to welcome the victorious warriors to their home.

Some few, alas! had their joy turned into sorrow and mourning, as they missed the faces of warriors—husbands or sons—who had gone forth to battle in the pride of their strength and in the confident hope of victory.

Then another solemn feast of scalps took place, the details of which need not be described.

Strongbow and the other whites left the circle as soon as they possibly could.

They wished to hold a consultation as to their future movements, and so withdrew to a retired spot some distance from the wigwams.

" Wa-al, I guess we give them coons a putty elegant lickin'. But I say, stranger, whar d'ye think o' settlin'?"

" I don't know. The whole place was destroyed by those fiends. But I must go back."

" Why?"

" As I told you, my wife is left in the neighbourhood."

" Humph!"

" I sadly fear something has befallen her during my absence. I should like to be away at once."

" And you, lad?"

" I—I——"

" You would like to go, and stay, eh?" asked the father.

" I should like to go with you, but ——"

" That young lady is a powerful counter-attraction, is she not?"

" She is, father; I love her."

For some few minutes all were silent, in deep thought.

Hiram Swift was first to speak.

" Hyar's a dodge, boys," he exclaimed.

" What's that?"

" Why, just this. You an' I goes to your old squattin' ground, takin' half a dozen o' Big Elk's braves along with us, and brings back yer wife. You has a clearin', an' builds a log in this locality, and then you'll all be safe."

" Very good; and then the boy can remain here while we are gone?"

" Ye-es, a few days'll do his wounds a power o' good."

"THE TWO SPIES."

So that arrangement was entered into, and, very early the following morning Hiram Swift, Armstrong, and four of the best warriors of the Delaware tribe started on their journey towards Armstrong's old clearing, in order to transport Mrs. Armstrong and all his household goods to the new spot selected for her home.

They had the best wishes of every one of the party to cheer them on their journey.

All that day Strongbow amused himself by wandering about the forest with his intended bride, and whispering his boyish love in her ear.

In the evening he sat in Big Elk's wigwam and repeated to her the loving tale.

As they sat together in the door of the tent by moonlight, they little thought that a man was lying on the ground with his ear to a little slit in the buffalo-hide, listening to every word that was uttered.

The man was a white man—a man with fearful passions expressed on his face and working in his heart.

The man was Wylde.

In his hand he held a pistol.

The lovers continued their talk, all unconscious of the presence of the deadly foe.

But the lovers looked upon the calm face of the heavens, and, as they looked, they dreamed not of danger.

The renegade did not intend to kill them just then, though he held a loaded pistol in his hand.

He wished to learn something of their future intentions.

But suddenly his eye caught sight of the figure of the pale, mysterious woman coming towards him.

The sight was too much for him, for his mind was filled with superstitious fears and terrors.

He rose to his feet, and ran with the speed of a hunted deer from the enclosure in which the wigwams of the Delawares were situated.

The strange woman followed him, knife in hand.

The noise made by the flying spy alarmed Water Lily, whose ears were more acute than those of her youthful lover.

She held up her finger in listening attitude.

"What sound was that, dearest?" she asked.

"I heard nothing."

"It sounded to me like footsteps."

"Footsteps! that must be seen to!" exclaimed the youth, hastily starting to his feet, and rushing to the door of the wigwam.

Water Lily followed him.

The sight which met their eyes has already been described.

The strange woman was brandishing her knife in a frantic manner, as she pursued the flying renegade.

"Alarm the camp!" shouted Strongbow.

The noise and bustle soon aroused the Indians, who flocked round the young Chief of the Delawares to know what had disturbed him.

"See; there is the white renegade who would have slain us!" he cried.

"Where?" asked Big Elk.

"There. You may see the white robes of his pursuer glancing among the trees.

"Did the young chief see who followed?"

"Yes. It was the Spirit of the Cedar Swamp."

"Ugh!" exclaimed Big Elk, his whole frame trembling.

He too was superstitious.

The wild legends of his tribe had made a powerful impression on his mind.

"She will not harm us. She is my good friend, and will always aid the brave warriors of the Delaware nation," said Strongbow.

"Ugh! Big Elk will follow."

Suiting the action to the word, he gathered up his weapons, and started off in the direction taken by the fugitive and his pursuer.

After a hasty explanation with Water Lily, Strongbow followed after the old warrior.

The ground was hard and dry; therefore the trail was difficult to follow.

But the keen, experienced eyes of Big Elk caught the track and followed it unerringly.

For nearly a mile they advanced into the wood, Strongbow and Big Elk being followed by half-a-dozen braves.

Then the report of a pistol was heard in front.

The pursuers rushed forward in the direction of the sound, and soon came upon the strange woman, who was lying upon the ground, feebly endeavouring to staunch the blood which flowed from a wound in her neck.

## CHAPTER LVIII.

### THE CLOUDED BRAIN.

BIG ELK gazed with wonder and surprise upon the strange sight.

For a strange sight it certainly was that the eyes of the unsophisticated Indian fell upon.

The pale woman—the Spirit of the Cedar Swamp—was bleeding from a fearful wound caused by a pistol bullet.

As Strongbow and the others who followed came up, she opened her eyes.

"Where am I?" she asked, in feeble tones.

"Among friends," replied the Boy Chief.

"What do I hear? After so many years—how many years is it?—I was English once, and spoke your language——"

"You are English now, and I am English.

"Ah, me! how weak I am."

"You must be quiet, and rest."

"Ugh! Big Elk will dress the wound of the pale-faced squaw," interposed the Indian, and, suiting the action to the word, he drew from his medicine bag some leaves of herbs, gums, and fragments of bark, which he pounded up into a poultice and applied to the wound.

During all this time the pale-faced woman exhibited the greatest patience, while it was evident she felt a strong curiosity to know where she was, and why treated so tenderly.

When the Indian had finished his surgical operation, she again spoke.

"I fear that for a long time past I have been bereft of my senses; but lately I have been under a strong impression that one who was very dear to me has been near me."

Strongbow made a gesture with his hand, and the others fell back, leaving him alone by the side of the wounded woman.

"I can guess to whom you allude," said he.

"You! Ah! I have seen you before, in those strange, wild dreams which come sometimes. You were with him."

"I was. He is my best friend."

"Oh! that I could clear these clouds from my brain! A light breaks through sometimes; then, just as I begin to see, darkness comes and swallows up the light."

"Compose your mind, and be calm. Rest assured that you are with friends."

"Friends indeed you must be, since you treat me thus kindly. For a long, long time I have had no friends save the owl, the bat, the bear, the wolf, and the snake."

"For how long have you lived so?"

"I know not; it was—let me see, I think it was in the year 18— that the Indians killed me."

"Killed you?"

"Yes."

"But you live now."

The pale woman looked curiously in his face for some seconds.

Then she feebly passed her hands over her body, and finally over her face.

"I believe I *do* live. Yet I remember hearing Hiram say that I was dead, and I had not the power to open eyes or mouth to contradict him. I know not. I only remember that one day my senses returned for a short time, and I found myself wandering in the forest. But that must have been some time afterwards, for my wounds seem to be healed."

"And what did you do then?"

"That I cannot remember. My senses went as they came, and I recollected no more until I found myself one day in a place which seemed familiar to me; but there was a grave there, and my name upon it, so my senses went again."

"Ah! I have seen that grave. Your name is KATE!"

"Who told you?"

"I say I have seen the grave, and I have seen Hiram Swift engaged in what he considered a sacred task, clearing away the weeds and rubbish from it."

"He is my husband. Where is he?"

"He will be here in another day."

The pale woman's eyes were fixed upon him as though they would pierce the very soul of her youthful companion, as he made the positive answer.

"You are not deceiving me?"

"I am not."

"Ah, me! My wound is mortal. I fear I cannot live till he returns."

"You must!"

"I will!" she replied, resolutely.

"And now remain as you are, while I make arrangements for your conveyance back to our camp."

With these words, the young chieftain left her to hold a consultation with his friend, Big Elk.

The result of the consultation was that the whole of the band had to set to work at once to cut down branches of trees and long brushwood to weave into a litter.

No very easy work, but the Indians were expert hands at basket weaving, and after a time the task was complete.

Then, with the greatest care and tenderness, the wounded woman was placed upon a couch of deerskin robes which had been spread over the rudely-constructed conveyance.

Had she been an empress surrounded by thousands of slaves, more care or attention could not have been shown her than she received at the hands of the rude, untutored Indians and their youthful white chieftain.

They lifted her up, and bore her home to the camp of the Delawares.

Gentle motions, subdued accents, and kind words attended her couch.

At length they reached the little village of the Delawares, and placed her carefully in a vacant wigwam.

A careful nurse was sent to watch her every movement and to attend to every desire.

And Water Lily would not rest satisfied until she had seen for herself that the poor wounded woman was properly and carefully treated.

There was one wish, however, they could not satisfy.

As she lay on her soft couch, tossing from side to side, she kept murmuring to herself—

"When will he come? when will he come?"

## CHAPTER LIX.

### DEATH.

TWO days afterwards Hiram Swift and Armstrong returned to the Delaware village, bringing with them the mother of our young hero.

As soon as Mrs. Armstrong had been placed in the wigwam prepared for her, Hiram Swift was informed of the presence in the camp of that strange, weird woman.

The hunter's cheek turned pale.

"Where is she?" he asked.

"In yonder wigwam," replied Strongbow.

"How did she come here?"

"We brought her into the camp after that villain shot her."

"Shot!"

"Aye, and a very severe wound she has."

"Not dead, then?" he asked, in an anxious tone.

"No."

"Take me to her."

Strongbow conducted his friend to the door of the wigwam, and pointed out where the poor sufferer lay.

Then, beckoning Water Lily to come away, he strolled a little distance from the spot, in order that the meeting between Hiram Swift and the invalid might not be interrupted by any curious, prying observers.

The hunter entered the wigwam.

His footsteps, though light and gentle,

caused the woman to open her eyes and look up.

"Oh! can this be true?" she said, in faint tones.  "Or am I mad again?"

Too agitated to speak, Hiram Swift knelt down by her side.

He lifted one of the thin, pale hands, and pressed it fervently to his lips.

" 'Tis true, then, Hiram!"

"My wife!" muttered the hunter, bending down to kiss her, while scalding tears dropped from his eyes upon her cheek.

"Thank Heaven you are come at last," said she.  "How long have we been parted?"

"Ten long years, my wife."

"Ten years! and during that time I have been mad."

"But now you are yourself again."

"Aye; my senses return that I may recognise you and converse with you before I die."

"Die!  Kate, you mustn't talk of dying."

"I must speak of it, and think of it, for I know I am dying, Hiram.  It is sad to think that we must part again after so long a separation; but it is the will of the powers above, and we must submit."

The hunter bowed his head, and big, heavy drops fell from his eyes.

Ten years ago he had buried, as he supposed, the mangled, half-burnt remains of the body of his young wife.

The pang was a cruel one, but by summoning up all his fortitude and self-command, he was enabled to survive the blow and even to make himself contented.

Fon ten long years he had lived a lonely life, thinking always of the wife whose grave he periodically cleared from weeds and rubbish.

Then that wife suddenly appears living.

His feelings could scarcely be described when he found that she was alive.

The pleasure and satisfaction he felt at the recovery of his wife was so great as to be almost painful.

And now all his newly-formed hopes and plans were dashed to the ground.

She was dying, and she knew it.

Scarcely able to speak, he sat there by her side, gazing intently upon that pale face, every feature of which he knew so well, and upon those deep blue eyes which fixed themselves on his with an unwavering, steadfast, loving look.

Death was plainly written upon that pale face.

Hour after hour the hunter sat by the side of his long-lost wife, who was in such a feeble state that she was unable to speak save at intervals.

After a long silence, she again spoke.

"Did you not say that you thought me dead, dear Hiram?"

"Yes."

"How was I killed?"

"By a wandering band of Crow Indians, who attacked our waggon and burnt it while I was away looking for meat."

"A waggon?  I don't recollect."

"We were going away to look out a nice place to settle in, and had just camped for the evening not very far from a cedar swamp."

"Now I remember.  We had great difficulty in crossing the swamp."

"Yes."

"I only recollect that a dreadful whooping noise came on suddenly, and then I received a fearful blow on the head."

Hiram Swift then, in his own plain, simple language, told his tale.

He told her how, on his return to his waggon, he had found it reduced to ashes, and amongst those ashes the half-burnt remains of a human body.

That body he had mourned over and buried, believing it to be all the world contained of his wife.

But ere the hunter's tale was finished a change came over the face of the invalid.

Every tinge of colour forsook her face and lips, and the lustre departed from her eyes.

"What is the matter?" asked Swift.  "Do you feel any fresh pain?"

The poor woman feebly shook her head—"I feel no pain."

"Are you comfortable, dear Kate?"

"Raise me up."

The hunter placed his strong arm round his wife and raised her into a sitting posture.

"Dear husband, I know you love me!"

"Heaven knows I do!"

"When I am gone, help those who were so kind to me."

"I will."

"Then I can die contentedly."

Her head drooped upon his shoulder—she gave a long, deep sigh—her last !

She was dead !

That pale figure would never more glide through the cedar swamp at dead of the night, scaring the foolish Indian, or the equally foolish white man.

The guardian spirit of the mysterious tree was gone !

Hiram Swift sat till morning light, holding the lifeless corpse in his arms; but when morning came, he laid her back upon the rude couch and sought out his white friends, to whom he told the melancholy news.

During that day, another grave was made near the Delaware village.

It had at the head a slab of hard wood, with that well-remembered name upon it.

For three days after the hunter sat alone in his wigwam, speaking to no one, eating no food, and, in fact, taking no notice of anything, save two long tresses of bright golden hair.

The fourth day he came out pale and stern in look, and mixed once more with his fellow men.

But he dared not trust himself to look in the direction of that grave.

## CHAPTER LX.

### STRANGE FOOTSTEPS.

THE time passed away on rapid but noiseless wings.

Armstrong and his wife were still inmates of a Delaware wigwam, and would be so for some days.

A log hut, far superior to their old one in dimensions, strength, and convenience, was being built by the united exertions of Strongbow, Hiram Swift, and Armstrong himself, the Indians supplying them with meat while they worked, and occasionally assisting in an indirect manner.

Water Lily was never very far from the spot.

She liked to look on and watch her lover as he worked merrily at his task, and though it seemed strange to her that a chief of the Delaware nation should condescend to perform such labour, she she did not love or respect him the less.

As for Mrs. Armstrong, she began to be passionately attached to the lovely Indian girl.

It was arranged that Strongbow and Water Lily should be married on the next birthday of the former, which would take place the following spring.

During the meantime he was to reside with Hiram Swift, who intended to cast his lot altogether with the Delawares.

They occupied a wigwam about half way between that where Water Lily resided and the log hut of the emigrant.

In due time the log hut was completed, and the bold Englishman took up his abode in it.

Then came winter.

A bitter cold winter it was, too ; the frost and snow seeming doubly cold after the hot, scorching summer which Strongbow and his father had spent in the great wilderness.

Nevertheless they were tolerably comfortable, for fuel was plentiful, and so was food.

If the emigrant missed anything, it was the educated society to which he had been accustomed ; and there was a gain even in that loss.

He knew that he was among friends, and that those friends were not hollow or insincere ones, like many he had met in England in the days of his prosperity—men who deserted and disowned him when trouble and want came.

Strongbow was as happy as he could possibly be.

He hunted with Swift and Big Elk, who taught him to glide over the snow on the great snow shoes used by the Indians and backwoodsmen ; he set traps for small game, and if prowling wolves kept the village awake with their doleful howling, Strongbow was always ready and eager to make a pitfall or a cage in which to trap the hungry, ferocious brutes.

During the winter several rumours

were brought into the village concerning a white man who was supposed to live in the adjacent dense woods.

One Indian had seen the pale-face while hunting, another had found his trail in the snow.

Curiosity was excited to know who this man could be.

It had never been the fortune of Hiram Swift to find any trace of this solitary being, or he would certainly have traced the stranger to his hiding-place.

Nor had Big Elk or any of the more experienced Delawares seen his trail, or they would have solved the mystery.

The stranger had evidently been in the neighbourhood of the village, for his tracks had been seen within half a mile of it.

However, as he did not interfere with the Delawares, they made no special search for him, and the unknown was allowed to dwell undisturbed in the retreat he had discovered.

Spring at length came.

Its approach was heralded by a storm of rain, which continued with unabated violence for two days, and completely washed every vestige of snow from the face of Nature.

Then the sun peeped out through the clouds, and the buds on the trees began to burst open, and show a promise of the green leaves of another summer.

About five days after the great rain, Water Lily set out from her wigwam in the evening to meet her father and Strongbow, who had promised to return from their hunt in the forest by the time the sun reached the horizon.

She wandered slowly on, deep in thought.

Her thoughts were of a peculiar kind, as well they might be, for in a fortnight she was to leave her father and become the bride of Strongbow.

The future was before her, mysterious and vague, but the bright star of love was still beckoning her onward in the path which fate seemed to have marked out for her.

That future!

She knew not what it might be; but she had boundless faith and confidence in the bold, handsome British lad who was to be her companion for life.

As she thought on all this, she wandered on until the gathering gloom warned her that it was time to think of returning.

"Perhaps they came another way," she said, half aloud, as she turned about to retrace her steps.

A low, mocking laugh seemed to answer her words, and ere Water Lily could look round to see the origin of the sound, a thick garment was thrown over her head.

She endeavoured to call out, in the hope that someone would hear her cries; but the thick folds of the blanket cloak effectually prevented her from doing so, and at the same time checked her breath.

In this half-stifled condition she was thrown to the ground by her captor, who forthwith proceeded to bind her hands behind her and tie her ankles together.

Then the cloak was removed from her face, and the captive found herself lifted up in the arms of her strange assailant.

Another and smaller, though fully as effectual a gag, was then thrust into her mouth.

Water Lily struggled as much as she could against this proceeding, but resistance was useless while her limbs were bound.

Then he threw her over his shoulder with the greatest ease, and carried her away into the dark, gloomy forest.

The darkness had come on so rapidly that Water Lily was unable to distinguish the form of her captor.

One thing, however, was very certain.

The man's manner and his dress convinced her that he was a white man.

No doubt, then, this was the solitary being whose footsteps had been seen in the winter's snow.

But what could he want with Water Lily?

She had never injured any pale-face.

This was the second time Water Lily had thus been suddenly taken from her home and her friends, and grave doubts crossed her mind as to whether she would escape from this new trouble so easily as she had from the former.

Water Lily, however, possessed a great deal of her father's courage, and resolved not to be disheartened.

She had perfect confidence in the courage and skill of those who would be certain to follow as soon as she was missed.

So she ceased her attempts to escape, finding them useless, and devoted all her faculties to the task of noting, as well as she could in the night darkness of the forest, the path taken by her captor.

He seemed endowed with great strength and determination of purpose.

For mile after mile he threaded his way through the intricacies of the gloomy wood, yet his foot faltered not, nor did his arm grow weary.

At length he stopped and looked around.

Finding that he was not pursued, he made his way towards an enormous beech tree which raised its smooth trunk and wide-spreading head from the midst of a thick clump of bushes.

Through these he forced his way, still carrying Water Lily in his arms.

Arrived at the foot of the great tree, he placed her upon the ground, and threw his cloak over her.

"Not to-night," he muttered. " The morning will be safer."

Water Lily overheard his words.

What was to happen to her in the morning ?

Some danger she could not comprehend was evidently hanging over head, and she earnestly prayed that she might be preserved from it.

After carefully examining the thongs which secured her hands and feet, the man crept into a hollow in the trunk of the tree.

In a few seconds he reappeared with some food, which he began to devour in a ravenous manner.

He did not offer Water Lily any, nor could she have eaten even had the food been placed before her.

His meal finished, the man wrapped himself in a second cloak, and leaned back against the trunk of the tree.

Water Lily thought at first that he slept, but when she made the slightest movement she found his bright eyes glaring at her through the darkness.

The hours seemed to pass slowly to the weary, heart-sick captive, but at length came that scarcely perceptible change in the sky which betokens the approach of dawn.

The grey streak in the east grew brighter and brighter, until at length Water Lily could plainly see the face of her captor.

Then indeed she felt surprised, for it was Wylde the renegade !

---

## CHAPTER LXI.

### RETRIBUTION.

BIG ELK and his companions returned home from their hunt.

The Delaware threw down his load of meat before the door of his wigwam, and wondered why his daughter did not bound out to meet him as usual.

Strongbow, too, felt surprised that she had not met them in the forest as she had promised.

On inquiry, however, the mystery was soon cleared up.

Water Lily had gone out into the forest, and would, doubtless, be back in a few minutes.

The minutes flew, and yet she did not appear.

Big Elk, despite his Indian nature, could not conceal his anxiety.

He made inquiries in every part of the village as to where she was last seen and in what direction she went.

Total darkness came on.

Father and lover tried in vain to find out her trail, but the blackness of night hid it from their eyes.

They shouted.

The only response which came back from the forest was a mocking echo.

Hiram Swift discharged his rifle several times, in the hope that its report might guide back her wandering feet.

Still she came not.

Then a huge fire was kindled on the highest ground in the village, that its light might serve as a beacon.

But hour after hour passed, and the absent one returned not.

Big Elk, Hiram Swift, and Strongbow

sat by the fire all night, with their arms ready to hand.

They held no council as to what they should do, for each had settled in his own mind that the only thing to be done was to follow the trail and bring her back.

At length the dawn came—the same dawn which showed Water Lily the features of her captor.

Without a word Big Elk rose to his feet and strode off into the forest, Swift, Strongbow, and his father accompanying the Indian.

Then, like well-trained hounds, they began to beat about in search of the print of her small feet.

Strongbow was the first to catch sight of the mark of the tiny mocassins.

With a shout he called his companions.

There could be no doubt about it.

They all knew her footstep, and set about following it.

"Poor lass! she's got lost, I guess," said Swift.

"Water Lily is the daughter of a Delaware, and knows how to find her way through the wood," replied Big Elk.

"By gumbo! you're right. Then thar is somethin' the matter."

Instinctively they quickened their pace.

At length they came to the spot where Water Lily's captor first pounced upon her.

The marks of the struggle were still plainly visible.

Hiram Swift bent down, and carefully examined the trail.

"Carried off," he said, "and by a white man too."

"The white hunter is right," said Big Elk, moodily. "Come."

The trail of the white man was more easily followed than that of the Indian maid.

The man's feet were larger, and bore more weight than hers; consequently they made a deeper track in the earth.

The pursuers were lightly clad, and carried no weight, save their arms.

They were able to "lift the trail" at a rapid pace.

Two hours in the daylight enabled them to travel over the distance which Wylde had been nearly five hours in journeying during the darkness of the night.

At length they came in sight of the beech tree.

Hiram Swift recognised it at once.

He explained to his companions that there was a cavity in its trunk, and that probably the villain had taken shelter there.

It was determined to adopt the greatest precaution in approaching it.

They could not hear a sound as they approached it, and Strongbow began to fear that for once the hunter had erred.

But his hopes were revived when he saw Big Elk, who led the way, hold up his hand in a warning attitude.

The Delaware chieftain, having cautioned his companions, crawled on with stealthy, cat-like motions, followed by the three pale-faces.

Suddenly he rose to his feet and walked forward boldly.

He saw his daughter, but no enemy was visible.

The others followed him as rapidly as they could.

On reaching the foot of the tree they all saw Water Lily lying on the ground in the helpless condition in which Wylde had left her.

But in a moment she was free.

"I knew you would come," she said, looking gratefully upon her rescuers.

"But who brought you here?" asked Strongbow.

"That bad man who gave us so much misery before the winter came."

"Wylde!" exclaimed Armstrong.

"Yes."

"Well, I guess we hev had a pretty considerable quantity o' dust flung in our eyes by that coon," said Swift.

"His hour is come, though," replied Strongbow, sternly. "Where is the villain gone?"

"He went that way not long ago, muttering something about looking out a good place."

"Any place is good enough for him to die in," said Armstrong.

His trail was found in a moment, and with redoubled ardour they started in pursuit.

In a few minutes they were in sight of the scoundrel, who was returning towards the spot where he had left his captive.

He perceived them at the same instant.

Only for a second of time did he hesitate; then, drawing a revolver from his dress, he fired three shots into the midst of the group.

Luckily none of the bullets took effect, and perceiving such to be the case, Wylde turned and fled.

Away through the forest, leaping over bushes, stones, and fallen trees like a hunted wolf pursued by a pack of vengeful hounds.

Strongbow, young and active, was foremost in the chase, and kept the renegade well in view.

Presently Wylde was seen to hesitate, and turn first to the left and then to the right.

The cause of his wavering was soon seen.

Right before him was a precipitous cliff.

He held up his hands, but the gesture was too late.

An arrow from Strongbow's bow struck him full in the throat, and with a fearful yell the wretch staggered back over the cliff.

"I'll bet pretty high he's a dead coon," exclaimed Swift, who, with Big Elk and the others, came up at the moment.

They all advanced to the edge of the rock, and looked over.

There was the crushed body, but it still contained life, for a groan was heard, and a slight movement of the limbs was perceptible.

"We had best go down and see him die before we leave," said Armstrong.

"The cuss has had many narrow squeaks," said Swift. "He may get off now onless we settles him."

With some little difficulty a path was found, by which they descended to the foot of the cliff.

As they approached, the renegade opened his eyes.

He evidently recognised them.

"Ha! Are you here, Armstrong?" said he, in a hoarse whisper.

"I am, villain!"

"Ha, ha, ha! Where is Jackson, *who had your much-prized diamond ring?*"

The rascal attempted to laugh again, but the blood choked him, and, with a fearful rattle in his throat, he expired.

## CHAPTER LXII.

### THE HISTORY OF THE DIAMOND.

THE little party stood round the dead man, gazing on his face.

Wylde was dead!

They could at first scarcely believe it; but there was the grim, ghastly, bleeding fact lying on the ground before them.

That restless, grasping mind, which had caused them all so much trouble, would never trouble them again.

Even in death the features wore a sort of sneering, satirical look, as though the villain died while in the act of saying an ill-natured thing.

However, he *was* dead, and, as Hiram Swift observed, "thar's an end on it."

The little party returned to the camp, Big Elk and Swift rejoicing over the death of their foe, the Armstrongs sorry that the blood of a human being had been spilled, yet well satisfied that justice had been executed.

There was one thing which puzzled Armstrong senior.

That was the diamond ring.

He could not well imagine how Wylde, villain as he was, could have given up so valuable a piece of property.

For valuable it was in Armstrong's eyes, for a double reason.

The ring had been the property of his grandfather, and therefore was highly prized by the grandson for that reason.

It had been stolen from the old gentleman, and for many years was lost sight of.

About five years before the period at which our story commences, Armstrong was staying for a time in London, and, while walking through the streets one day, saw the very identical ring glittering upon the finger of an aged gentleman.

Of course a conversation at once commenced.

The old gentleman had not had the ring very long—only a few years, in fact; at least so he stated, and Armstrong afterwards discovered that his statement was correct.

It had been purchased by the old gentleman at a jeweller's shop for a certain sum, and as the wearer kept it merely for its intrinsic value, he was quite willing to sell it for the sum which he paid the jeweller for it. Armstrong at once decided on purchasing it.

The old gentleman requested that the purchase might be concluded before night, or the morning might, perhaps, change his mind.

Armstrong went home for the money, but, to his intense surprise, found that he had not the amount. He endeavoured to borrow, but without success.

It was impossible, it seemed, to get any money for nearly a week, and, resolved not to lose the ring, he decided upon a step which he afterwards bitterly repented.

He took one of the most important of the deeds relating to his property, and deposited it in the hands of the old gentleman as security that the money should be paid within a week.

The stranger was very well satisfied with the arrangement, and Armstrong went on his way rejoicing in the fact that *he* now wore the precious gem on his finger.

At the end of the week he went to the house of the old gentleman to pay the money and redeem the deed.

The place was in confusion.

" Can I see Mr. —— ?" he asked.

" He is dead, sir."

" Dead! why, I wished to see him about the deed of some property I left with him."

" You had better see the lawyer of the old gentleman."

Armstrong thought so too, and soon found out the man of parchment, who explained to him the following facts :—

The old gentleman had died suddenly, and, still more strange, the night after his death the house was burglariously entered, and all the valuables stolen, including the papers. But the old gentleman had just time before he died to say that a certain deed was to be given up to the gentleman who had purchased the ring on payment of a certain sum. Therefore, if the thieves were apprehended and the deed recovered, the lawyer would be most happy to restore

the deed to Mr. Armstrong upon receipt of the money. So with that Armstrong was obliged to be satisfied for the time.

Some few days after this, as he was returning to his hotel late one evening, he had to pass down a narrow, badly-lighted street.

Suddenly he was attacked by three ruffians, who knocked him down and robbed him of his watch, his pocket-book, and, last of all, his diamond ring.

In spite of all his efforts, he could not overtake his assailants, nor could any of the stolen property be traced.

And so for a year things went on in their usual course, till one day Armstrong saw a paragraph in the London papers announcing the discovery of a den of thieves by the constables, who found a large quantity of plunder, and amongst other things some papers supposed to have been stolen from the house of Mr. —— the night after his death.

Post haste he went to the lawyer, and anxiously inquired if the missing deed was among the recovered papers.

It was; but the lawyer had not the pleasure of remembering Mr. Armstrong.

Had they met before? Armstrong explained the circumstances.

But the diamond ring?

That ring had been particularly mentioned by old Mr. ——, and the lawyer could not, therefore, give up the document without a sight of the ring. The deed should be taken care of, and given up whenever the ring and the money were produced.

Armstrong could not help getting in a passion.

'But the lawyer was cool and collected. Possession was nine points of the law, and he begged to assure Mr. Armstrong that the deed was safe in his possession. As for law, why Mr. Armstrong must of course see that it was useless to go to law with the d—l, while the court sat in the infernal regions.

So Armstrong was obliged to depart without his deed; and then began that series of misfortunes and losses which finally drove him from his native land to seek a home in the wilds of America.

So to America he went, as our readers know, and to America we must return to trace with him the adventures of the diamond ring.

## CHAPTER LXIII.

### THE RING RECOVERED.

WYLDE, the renegade, was left just where he died, and, no doubt, the woives and the vultures made a fine feast on his flesh.

Big Elk and Hiram Swift were, as before said, exultant at the death of their foe.

Armstrong could not help thinking about the ring, which he would have given so much to obtain.

Luckily the dying renegade had given a hint that Jackson had taken it; therefore, there was reason to suppose that Jackson still had it, or knew where it was.

But how to find Jackson was the great thing.

Armstrong knew sufficient of the world and its ways to be well aware that such a slippery customer as Mr. Jackson would be the last one to divulge his address.

Of course the emigrant was not acquainted with the whole history of Mr. Jackson's life, or he would have better known how and in what quarter to make inquiries.

When he retired to rest that night he pondered deeply upon the matter.

"It would be useless," he thought, "to seek Mr. Jackson in the pathless forests."

A man with jewellery in his possession would naturally keep in as civilised a region as possible; either that the precious stones might be admired, or that they might be converted into money.

So Mr. Jackson must be sought in towns and cities.

After much deep thought upon the subject, he determined to go in search of the minor rascal.

His wife and his friends were not much surprised when, in the morning, he communicated his intentions.

Hiram Swift, when he fully understood matters, applauded the resolution, and produced from some secret hiding-place about his dress a sum of about fifty dollars in American gold.

"You'll want these shiners, I guess," he said, "so take 'em and pay me when you gets back yer British property."

Armstrong thanked the hunter for his kindness, and, after bidding farewell to his wife, started on his journey.

To guard against dangers in the forest, Big Elk sent a party of his warriors to conduct the emigrant to the borders of civilisation.

Then the emigrant journeyed along by himself.

Four days after starting he reached the thriving town of *Dover*; not the Dover of Shakespeare, but a neat place, with wide new streets, and not the slightest vestige of any old castle.

He walked into the town, and into the best hotel. His costume certainly was not that which an Englishman would expect to see in a large and fashionable hotel; but in America it excited no comment.

When he had secured a sleeping apartment, he strolled out towards the magistrate's office.

He wished to find a constable in whose hands he could rest the matter.

Having done so, he returned to the hotel, and took his seat with others in front of the public bar.

Of course his ears were open to everything which was said, though for a long time he heard nothing of importance.

At length he heard the name of Jackson mentioned, though of course he could not tell whether it was *the* Jackson or not.

However, under the pretence of ordering some drink, he shifted his seat so as to be nearer the speakers.

"Where did Jackson get all the money?" asked one.

"Sold some jewellery; a very handsome and valuable diamond ring."

"Stolen, of course."

"I dare say."

"Is he coming up to-night?"

"He said he would be here by eight o'clock; it wants half an hour to the time."

Again Armstrong shifted his seat, and

wrote a little note, which he sent off at once to the constable.

In a short time that functionary made his appearance at the hotel.

He was so nicely disguised by the aid of false whiskers, etc., that Armstrong did not at first recognise him.

A short conversation took place, and plans were made for the apprehension of the scoundrel.

At the time mentioned by the bar-room loungers, Jackson made his appearance.

No sooner had he entered the room than the constable tapped him on the shoulder.

"I want you, my man, on a charge of forgery. You had best submit quietly."

Jackson thought so too, and allowed the constable to lead him to a private room, whither Armstrong followed them.

"*I* want my diamond ring," said the emigrant.

"Diamond! What diamond ring?"

"The one you stole from your precious friend Wylde."

"I have not got it."

"You had best say where it is. A second charge against you will only double your punishment."

"If I tell where it is you will promise not to make that a charge against me?"

"I promise," said Armstrong.

"Then all you have to do is to go to Soloman, the jeweller, in Fourth Street. I sold it to him for one hundred and eighty dollars."

"Why, it is worth eight hundred at least," exclaimed Armstrong.

"But then he knew I could not prove where I bought it."

The constable chuckled and said—

"Jist you go, mister, and politely ask Mister Soloman to *give* you that ring. Tell the coon you come from me."

Armstrong did so, and, on reaching the shop, saw his long-lost ring in the window, ticketed at a thousand dollars.

"I want that ring," said he, entering the shop.

"You see the price?"

"I want you to *give* it me."

"You must be mad," said the shop-keeper.

"Not so. Jackson is captured, and constable Johnson sent me to *ask you to give me the ring.*"

The jeweller turned pale.

"Why should I give it up?"

"Because you knew it was stolen. You only gave Jackson one hundred and eighty dollars for it."

The man's face became still more white.

"Here, take the thing," said he. "I'll pay that Jackson out if he says anything more about me."

"Thank you, Mr. Soloman," said Armstrong, taking up the ring, and bowing politely as he left the shop.

He was not long in hastening back to the hotel, where he found Jackson and the constable waiting.

"Got yer ring, mister?"

"Yes."

"Then you kin go, Mr. Jackson. I arn't got any warrant for yer; but if you'll take my advice, you'll jist slope out o' Dover like an express en-*gine.*"

Jackson benefited by the hint, and "sloped" to the town of Wilmington, where, unluckily, he encountered another constable with a warrant in his pocket.

In consequence of this unlucky inter-view, Mister Jackson had, for the long term of ten years, to earn his living in an honest manner.

He had to break stones for the benefit of the state.

---

# CHAPTER LXIV.

### THE WEDDING.

OUR readers may be well assured that Armstrong lost no time in returning to his wife and family when he had re-covered possession of his diamond ring.

The journey was performed with tolerable ease and expedition, the party of Indians being waiting for him at the spot where he left them.

About a week after setting out from the Delaware camp, he once more re-turned to that little assemblage of wig-wams.

In this he was opposed by Hiram Swift.

Swift had no particular motive in advising the Englishman to remain in the New World beyond a firm friendship he felt for the father of our young hero.

However, to gain his end, he used a variety of arguments.

One of them was the splendour of the climate and the soil in the New World.

"Yer may talk about yer British fields and meadows," said he, in a very patronizing manner; "but show me whar yer kin find such fields as these, whar the ground don't want no manure or even ploughin'. Why, all yu've got to du is jist to tickle the ground with a hoe, and if it don't laugh at the heavy crop that comes up, my name ain't Hiram."

The Englishman laughed, and so did the Boy Chief of the Delawares.

"Your soil is very fruitful, I admit," said Armstrong.

"Waal, now there's another argiment; ain't things cheaper hvar than in the old country?"

"Well, the land itself is, and so are some other things I have purchased."

"Now, what mout the price of hosses be amongst you Englishers?"

"What sort of horse?"

"Why, like this crittur o' mine, say."

"Such a horse would cost, perhaps, a hundred dollars."

"And hyar it costs nothin' but a throw of the larriat—ain't that dog cheap?"

"It is, I acknowledge."

"What mout a cow cost, mister?"

"Half as much as the horse."

"Waal, there ain't many cows to be picked up by the lasso, but you kin get 'em in old settlements fur six or seven dollars."

Armstrong nodded.

"And we are free hyar, I guess; thar ain't a man but what's jist as good as any other man, and sometimes a heap better; thar ain't no bribery and corruption at our elections, cos we votes by ballot, and the coon as sticks up can't tell who votes fur him or who don't, and every man in the States has a vote, because he's got to obey the laws, and oughter have some kind o' finger in the makin' on 'em."

"That is all very well, and just as it ought to be," replied Armstrong; "but what has that to do with my going to England?"

"Why, yer oughtin' to leave such blessin's as Providence thus puts afore you, Britisher."

"I can come back again when I have transacted the business I wish to."

"But yer won't. If them coons gets hold of yer they'll hold tight."

"If I promise to come back, I will keep my word."

"Honour?"

"Yes, on the honour of an Englishman."

"Then yer kin go."

For a few moments the conversation flagged, and then turned upon general subjects.

## CHAPTER LXV.

### LAST SCENE OF ALL, WHICH ENDS THIS STRANGE, EVENTFUL HISTORY.

AND so Armstrong returned to England.

He had the diamond ring in his possession, and, knowing that Wylde was dead, had no fear of being robbed of it.

A fair and speedy voyage finished, he landed on the shores of Old England, with a considerable amount of money in his pocket, and, by means of the diamond ring, he knew pretty well how to make more cash.

On reaching London his first visit was, of course, to the office of the lawyer who held the deed.

The man had almost forgotten the circumstance, till Armstrong briefly related the facts of the case; then he at once remembered.

"Ah! well, I still have the deed in my strong box," he said.

"And I have the ring and the money necessary for the redemption of the deed," answered Armstrong.

"I must charge a little interest."

Another white man had been added to the population of the village in the shape of a wandering missionary, who, for many years, had devoted his life to the task of endeavouring to convert to Christianity the heathen inhabitants of the vast wilderness.

When Armstrong set eyes upon his son after his return, Strongbow was then in the act of speaking to the good old man, while close at hand stood Water Lily, who, with her eyes fixed upon the ground, seemed deeply interested in the conversation.

And well she might have such feelings, for the subject of conversation was one on which her whole future life was dependant.

Strongbow was then endeavouring to persuade the old minister to perform the ceremony which would unite them for life.

Some few doubts or scruples passed through the preacher's mind as to whether it would be right to make a heathen girl a participator in a Christian rite.

He spoke to Strongbow about his doubts.

"But Water Lily believes in our God," replied the youth.

"That may be, but still, I should scruple to unite you in matrimony unless she had been baptised into the Christian Church."

"That you can do."

The minister was silent for a time.

Then Big Elk approached.

In his hand he held an open paper, which he extended towards the minister.

"Can the stranger tell the words spoken by the paper?" said the Indian.

"Why, what is this?"

"When the daughter of Big Elk was a child there came a pale-face stranger, who threw medicine water upon her, and gave this medicine paper."

The medicine paper was, in fact, a certificate that Water Lily had been duly baptised.

So no more objections could be made to the union of the young couple, and arrangements were made for the performance of the sacred rite at an early date.

The happy day came.

Strongbow, now a tall, strong youth, was almost beside himself with joy; and Water Lily, although she blushed and hung down her head, did not look at all unhappy.

The church was a wide-spreading oak tree in the dense forest, and there, kneeling side by side, the Boy Chief of the Delawares and the fairest flower of the tribe repeated after the old minister that mystic vow which pledged them to live solely for each other.

Nor were those vows ever broken, forgotten, or repented.

A pure and ardent love glowed in their hearts, making each seek only the other's pleasure and happiness.

If the ceremony was simple, the feast was plentiful.

The Indians, having been informed that a feast was at hand, made a great hunt in the forest to provide food for the banquet.

River, forest, and prairie were alike ransacked to provide the endless varieties of fish, fowl, and flesh which were spread upon the table, or rather upon the ground in the midst of the camp.

Plates and dishes were, of course, unthought of; but each person had a knife, and the food was none the worse for being cut from the spit.

Some of the Indians, indeed, gorged themselves to such an extent that they were unable to take part in the dance which followed the banquet.

The Indians dance in a very spirited though not very graceful manner, when they do indulge in that pleasure; and the Delawares, being on this occasion in a very joyous mood, had a double motive for distinguishing themselves.

They all wished to do honour to their young chief and the daughter of the brave warrior who had so often led them to victory.

Round and round they whirled in a ring, till darkness came and put an end to the wedding festivities.

●    ●    ●    ●    ●

A few days after the wedding the pale-face guests in the Delaware camp were seated in the wigwam which had been assigned to Hiram Swift.

A discussion was going on, and the host was speaking.

The subject under consideration was a wish which the elder Armstrong had expressed relative to returning to England.

" I am fully prepared to pay the current price for the use of the money."

The lawyer, on hearing this, at once produced the deed, and received the money which Armstrong counted out.

As soon as this piece of business was settled, Armstrong would have departed had not the lawyer detained him.

" There's another piece of business to be done, Mr. Armstrong."

" What is that?"

" To put you in possession of a legacy of fifteen thousand pounds, bequeathed you in the will of the late Mrs. Armstrong, of Trefellan House, in Cornwall; she was your aunt on the father's side."

" Is she dead, then?"

" She has been dead six months, and your address has been advertised for in nearly all the newspapers in England."

This news, so sudden and unexpected, almost stunned Armstrong.

The old lady whose death had thus suddenly made Armstrong a rich man had never set her eyes upon the nephew whom she thus befriended; therefore Armstrong could not and did not profess to feel any profound grief at her decease.

However, as soon as he recovered from the temporary suspension of his faculties, he gave the lawyer full instructions as to the manner in which the legacy was to be invested.

" Why, you must mean to go back to America, then, Mr. Armstrong," said the legal adviser, as he listened to the instructions.

" I certainly do intend to do so."

" What, leave Old England?"

" Yes. I like the New World, for though the manners of the people may be strange, they are hospitable, and there is much in their land which might be copied with great advantage in this."

And so to America he returned.

The country seemed so familiar to him as he travelled from city to village, and from village to scattered settlement.

Even the short time he had been absent had made great changes in the face of the forest, though there were landmarks which could not be mistaken.

During the five months Armstrong had been absent more emigrants had found their way down to the neighbourhood of the Delaware camp, and had built their huts and made clearings in the forest.

The Indians did not altogether approve of this, but, their young chief being a pale-face, they made no attempt to interfere with the new-comers.

Armstrong's arrival made a new feature in the course of events.

He was now a rich man, and could, therefore, do more than men of limited means, such as most of the settlers were.

He enclosed a large tract of land, which he purchased of the government, and made a very nice little addition to his wealth by the crops he raised on his plantation.

The business of the place was entirely conducted by him for the first few years, but after a time came one who, in a great measure, assisted him.

This was his son.

The young man had resided with the Indians until the tribe had found it necessary, on account of the scarcity of game, to remove a long distance to the west.

Then Strongbow returned to his father, bringing with him his beautiful wife and a lovely infant.

Water Lily's father was dead, and her husband had resigned his authority in the tribe.

He was no longer BOY CHIEF OF THE DELAWARES.

THE END.

www.ingramcontent.com/pod-product-compliance
Lightning Source LLC
Chambersburg PA
CBHW080828250626
47160CB00008B/2876